Praise for Jane Lindskold

"An engrossing story about a young woman finding her strength and purpose while fighting to survive."

—*The Miami Herald* on *Nine Gates*

"The author has created a gifted and resourceful heroine. Innovative and imaginative."

—*Library Journal* on *Through Wolf's Eyes*

"Thought-provoking."

—*Booklist* on *Nine Gates*

"Exhilarating. Exciting."

—*Publishers Weekly* (starred review) on *Wolf Captured*

"Compelling reading. Intricately plotted and written, Lindskold's latest creates an utterly fascinating world that readers can thoroughly lose themselves in."

—*RT Book Reviews* on *Wolf Captured*

TOR BOOKS BY JANE LINDSKOLD

NINE GATES

GATES

JANE LINDSKOLD

九個門

TOR®
fantasy

A TOM DOHERTY ASSOCIATES BOOK
NEW YORK

NINE GATES

Copyright © 2009 by Jane Lindskold

Excerpt from *Five Odd Honors* copyright © 2010 by Jane Lindskold

A Tor Book
Published by Tom Doherty Associates, LLC
175 Fifth Avenue
New York, NY 10010

www.tor-forge.com

Tor® is a registered trademark of Tom Doherty Associates, LLC.

ISBN 978-0-7653-5622-2

First Edition: August 2009
First Mass Market Edition: April 2010

Printed in the United States of America

0 9 8 7 6 5 4 3 2 1

For Jim, my favorite Dragon

ACKNOWLEDGMENTS

I'd like to thank Jim Moore, my first reader and sounding board.

Melissa Singer, my editor, made some great suggestions, including encouraging me to expand some sections of the book.

Erich Martell helped with various technical details. For help with details about the Bay Area, I'd like to give special thanks to Jude Feldman and Brent Edwards.

Kay McCauley, my agent, kept the faith.

Special thanks to all the readers who have asked both about this book and about the rest of the Breaking the Wall series. I hope you'll bring me your questions and comments via my Web site: www.janelindskold.com.

I

When the attack began, Pearl Bright already held a sword in her hand. Otherwise, the old Tiger might well have died with the very breath at which she knew she was in danger.

Instead, Pearl pivoted and her blade cut flesh. A head flew from a neck, a stranger's hot blood jetted forth to dapple her face and throat. The man stumbled back, sword hilt slipping from nerveless fingers as he fell.

Pearl did not wait to see how her assailant landed. There was no way he was ever picking up that sword again, and too much else demanded her attention.

Around her, what had been a quiet private park had become a battlefield in which Pearl and her associates were outmatched and outnumbered. From a rip in the air, a dozen or more men had run forward. They were clad in the armor and bearing the arms of a bygone day, of a China that might never have existed.

This last did not make those blades any less deadly.

As Pearl swung around to assess the situation, she saw the right arm of Righteous Drum the Dragon removed neatly at the shoulder to drop steaming and smoking onto the grass.

The complex ideograph Righteous Drum had been sketching hung metallic yellow in the air for a long moment, then transformed into an explosion of golden light that caught his attacker full in the face, melting skin to bone, bone to ash.

The ideograph had retained its shape long enough for Pearl to read what Righteous Drum had intended.

Great idea, Pearl thought, *but I'm going to need a little space before I can pull anything that complex off.*

Righteous Drum crumpled to his knees, his eyes glazed as he clapped his remaining hand over the stump of his arm. His pale lips muttered what was hopefully a healing or binding.

Righteous Drum's daughter, Honey Dream, the Snake, had run to protect her father when he had fallen. She stood with the curving snake's-fang dagger that was her chosen weapon in her right hand. With her left she was fishing into the cleavage of her low-cut tee shirt, pulling out slips of red paper already inscribed with elaborate charms.

One of these evidently provided some form of protection that covered both father and daughter, as the man who came racing at them, sword raised, a ferocious battle cry on his lips, learned when his downward cut was halted by some unseen barrier. He reeled back, striving to retain his balance.

Honey Dream did not give him time to recover. Another slip of red paper flew, and when it struck the man in the face the eyelids dissolved beneath a wash of virulent green acid.

Didn't know you'd brought anything that nasty with you, girl, Pearl thought. *Wish I was surprised. Hope you've got a lot more.*

Righteous Drum would be as safe as his daughter could make him. Since Honey Dream had a Snake's regard for a whole skin, Pearl thought they'd do as well as or better than if she gave them her aid. Her own people were much more vulnerable.

It took Pearl a moment to locate Des Lee, for the Rooster formed the center of a small knot of armored men. Then one of these staggered back, blood streaming from where his eyes should have been, the long raking marks across his face showing what a Rooster's Talon could do. The momentary glimpse Pearl caught of Des showed that like Honey Dream he had made enhancing his defense his first priority. Swords torn from their wielder's hands showed that Des had not forgotten the value of disarming one's opponents.

Pearl decided she was being foolish not to enhance her own defense, and while her mind shaped the sequence that would summon mingled winds and dragons to protect her, she looked for the two most vulnerable members of her company.

Like Des, Riprap was surrounded by a small crowd of armored men. One lay on the ground, his head an ugly ruin. Two others were battering at his defenses while a third stood back, muttering something, his fingers sketching patterns in the air.

Pearl would have run to Riprap's aid, but at that moment Flying Claw lived up to his name. The young warrior leapt through the air, screaming like the attacking Tiger he was.

The mutterer was cloven from the top of his shoulder right through his chest. The stroke was so violent, and so efficiently delivered, that it made the near-decapitation that resulted seem almost like an afterthought.

Although battles raged on all sides, still the situation seemed oddly under control—with her own side clearly in the ascendance. Pearl began to think she could turn her attention to completing what Righteous Drum had begun.

Then she caught sight of Brenda Morris. For a moment Pearl's heart went cold in her chest. Then Pearl began to run.

☆

The morning's activity had not gone at all as Brenda could have wished. First, well aware that the session was going to involve the physical combat training she and Riprap had been agitating for, Brenda had dressed practically—even if jeans and a long-sleeved shirt had meant she was going to feel the July heat and humidity. As a compensation for the heat, she had braided her long, dark brown hair, then twisted it into a knot at the back of her head.

If San Jose, California, hadn't been a whole lot more clement than her home state of South Carolina, Brenda probably couldn't have borne the heavier clothing, but she was being practical. When they got to the designated training grounds, there was Honey Dream in all her exotic Oriental beauty. Honey Dream was wearing nothing but shorts and one of those obnoxious tee shirts that showed off why she needed to wear a bra, whereas Brenda could far too easily do without her own.

Something about the sneer that had flickered across Honey Dream's face told Brenda that the other woman knew perfectly well that Brenda had figured she was going to take a fall or two.

Then, to make matters worse, Flying Claw hadn't even looked at Brenda beyond offering a very casual good-morning. He seemed more interested in talking with Riprap about the baseball bat the big black man had brought along to serve as a weapon.

After some warming up and stretching exercises, they'd paired up. Righteous Drum, a square-bodied, slightly overweight man who rather reminded Brenda of Chairman Mao, had chosen Des Lee.

Des's first name was actually "Desperate" and his appearance was as odd as his given name. Taller than average, lean without being gawky, Des wore both his hair and beard in a fashion that emphasized his ethnic Chinese heritage. His shining black hair was worn in a long queue. His forehead was shaved in a fashion common when both the expansion of the railroads and the California gold rush had drawn Chinese to the United States in record numbers. His long chin beard and wispy mustache emphasized his high cheekbones and beautifully sculptured features.

However, Righteous Drum's choice of Des as a sparring partner had little to do with Des's odd appearance. Righteous Drum wanted to see how Des could use the Rooster's Talons, the odd weapons Des had inherited from his grandmother, to parry thrown spells. Des had been more than happy to oblige, although it was pretty clear that Des intended to get Righteous Drum to show him a trick or two in exchange.

Flying Claw and Riprap were sparring even before the

warm-up was formally finished. Waking Lizard, the long-bodied, lean-limbed Monkey, had insisted that Honey Dream begin with him because they could spar spell-to-spell, and Waking Lizard was still stiff from the injuries he had acquired in the course of his narrow escape from the Lands Born from Smoke and Sacrifice.

That left Brenda to practice with Pearl Bright. On the surface, this should not have been a problem. After all, Brenda was nineteen to Pearl's seventy-some years. Brenda had played both volleyball and soccer right up through high school, and although she hadn't joined a team in college, she had remained active. Pearl didn't belong to a gym or even have a treadmill in her house.

But although Pearl's hair was silver and her skin had its share of honestly earned lines and wrinkles, Pearl Bright was far from the classic "little old lady." Her daily routine included tai chi and sword drills that kept her both active and supple. Next to the older woman, Brenda—lean, almost skinny—felt coltish.

Brenda had known Pearl all her life, but only a month and a half had passed since Brenda had learned why "Auntie" Pearl was such a good friend of the Morris family.

This knowledge had made Pearl—already a bit intimidating in her role as exotic former movie star—no less a figure of awe. Moreover, being knocked on her butt by a woman in her late seventies was not something Brenda looked forward to. It was going to finish the humiliation Honey Dream had begun pretty thoroughly.

However, from the moment Pearl said, "When I give the word, cast a Dragon's Tail as fast as you can. I'm coming at you, and if you don't have the spell up . . ." Brenda had lacked attention to worry about anything but Pearl.

Pearl hefted Treaty, her elegant long sword, to emphasize the command. Brenda shivered. She didn't think Pearl would cut her, but Brenda bet the flat of the blade would hurt a lot—even through her clothes.

"Now!" Pearl said. She didn't raise her voice a bit, but such was the force of her personality that the command came across with the force of a shout.

Brenda moved her right hand to her left wrist, slipping off in one swift motion one of the three amulet bracelets there. She didn't pause to check the spell since Des, who was her teacher, had insisted that all "left wrist" castings be defense.

Brenda knew she'd get yelled at if she cast something other than the Dragon's Tail Pearl had specified, but that blade was coming at her way too fast, and nothing mattered but getting something between her and that silvery grey length of steel.

Brenda snapped the amulet against the ground, exploding the bits of polymer clay as much with the force of her will as by any physical act. Treaty was coming at her, but when it landed, the translucent greenish-brown of the Dragon's Tail was between Brenda and the sword's impact.

Pearl grinned, a ferocious rather than joyful expression, and shifted her grip. "Now! Stop me!"

Brenda fumbled for an amulet bracelet from her right wrist. Her left hand was much more clumsy than her right had been—Des had been after her to practice. Then Pearl suddenly wheeled, moving with a speed and grace that spoke of skills honed until the motions were ingrained into muscle memory.

Treaty wheeled with its wielder, the swing intended for Brenda moving, shifting so that the blade hit edge-on. The first Brenda saw of the man who had been coming to attack Pearl was his head sailing off his shoulders and his body stumbling back, the sword with which he had intended to kill Pearl dropping to the ground.

There was screaming all around. A man was running in Brenda's direction, but before he could get close, Flying Claw had intercepted him. Two or three strikes were exchanged, blade-to-blade and—Brenda suspected from the little flashes of light she more sensed than saw—spell-to-spell.

Brenda glanced down at the amulet bracelet in her hand.

Dragon's Fire. Not bad, but she needed to get closer to a target to use it. She looked wildly around, trying to figure out what was going on.

Righteous Drum was on the ground. There seemed to be a lot of blood. Honey Dream was protecting him.

Across the field, Waking Lizard lay on the ground, too, ominously still, but Brenda couldn't see very clearly what was wrong because there was too much activity closer in.

She wouldn't have been able to see at all, but there were several fallen—she suspected dead—bodies where Flying Claw had been standing when he and Riprap had begun their sparring. Flying Claw was aiding Riprap now, and Brenda turned her head away, sickened as Flying Claw—his handsome face ugly now with battle fever—cut a man nearly in two.

Brenda realized that the man would probably have killed Riprap if Flying Claw hadn't been there, but blood was all over and the expression on the man's face as he had fallen had mingled horrible pain and something like innocent surprise.

Brenda felt rather than saw Pearl racing past her, that motion her first realization of her own immediate danger.

A man had detached himself from the group attacking Riprap—probably figuring he had a better chance with the old woman and the young than the unholy terrors the men were proving to be.

His sword cut had been well aimed, sliding through the coils of the Dragon's Tail that still protected Brenda. Had it not been for the odd angle he had been forced to use, he probably would have cut her through the middle. As it was she took a long slice through her tee shirt into the skin of her belly.

Then Brenda's attacker turned to give fuller attention to Pearl. She cut at him, Treaty's blade meeting some resistance. The ferocity of her attack drove him back toward Brenda.

Brenda caught her breath, too startled at the sensation of her own blood running over her skin, soaking her clothing, to feel any real pain. The Dragon's Breath amulet was in her hand. With sudden wrath she smashed it down.

When Brenda extended her palm, a gout of flame, reddish-orange, white-hot around the edges, came forth. Her assailant had been wearing some sort of protective spell, but it must have been weakened by Pearl's assault because some of Brenda's flame eddied through, catching the hair of his eyebrows alight.

The man screamed, and dropped his sword to clap his hands to his eyes. This smothered the flame, but exposed the back of his neck.

Brenda saw Pearl pause in momentary consideration, use a fleeting glance to examine the quieting field, then spin Treaty around in her hand to strike the man hard on the back of his neck with the sword's hilt. He crumpled, but Brenda thought he might be unconscious rather than dead.

Pearl looked at Brenda.

"Serious?" she asked, indicating Brenda's belly.

"I don't think so," Brenda began, but Pearl had nodded and was jogging toward the other side of the field. "Wrap it," she called back. Then, "Des! I need you."

☆

Later, Pearl thought, *I must tell Brenda she did very well, but first to make sure there is a later.*

Des had come in response to her call. His assailants were down, and Pearl thought at least a couple might be alive. The same probably couldn't be said for those whom Flying Claw, Riprap, and Honey Dream had dealt with. Flying Claw and Riprap were still engaged. Honey Dream was kneeling next to her father, working over the stump of his arm.

The arm itself lay to one side, oddly shriveled, and Pearl wondered at the force and malice of the blow that had detached it. She could spare little thought for that, for Des was trotting over in response to her summons.

He moved easily, so it was likely that most of the blood that splattered him belonged to his opponents. It had been very good luck that the attack had come when they had all been not only armed, but wearing at least moderate protective spells.

Or was it merely luck? Pearl wondered. *If Waking Lizard lives . . .*

The old man—he had admitted to being eighty, making him older even than herself—lay contorted on the grass. His eyes were wide and staring, but completely unseeing. His mouth gaped open, and Pearl could see the marks of footprints on his tongue.

"We need to do a sealing," Pearl said to Des. "Righteous Drum realized what was happening almost at once, but our enemies anticipated he would and took precautions to stop him."

"They didn't kill him," Des said. "But then they wouldn't, not until they had a chance to question him. What shall we try?"

"Is Waking Lizard alive?"

Des knelt, checked for a pulse. "He is. Weak, but alive. His ch'i is dangerously diminished."

"Then we can't use any destructive spells in case we kill him as well."

She paused for thought, aware that the sounds of battle from behind were diminishing. They were safe for at least a few minutes.

"Red Coral as a barrier," she suggested. "Confused Gates to distract. That should stop them for a while. After we've talked to Waking Lizard, we'll know better what to do."

"Do you have the ch'i?" Des asked. "I had to use quite a few spells."

"I do," Pearl said. "Treaty did most of my work for me."

"Auntie Pearl?"

Brenda Morris had come up to join them, her dark brown eyes serious and intent. She'd taken off her long-sleeved tee shirt and used it to bind her middle. The black sports bra she'd worn beneath was more than modest enough, but she still looked embarrassed.

"Pearl," Brenda repeated. "I only threw a couple of amulets. My ch'i's intact. Let me help."

There was as much plea as offer in the words, and Pearl knew not to reject her.

"Can you remember Knitting without a crib?"

Brenda nodded. "I've got that one cold—especially if you don't insist on my using the character suit."

She managed a weak grin, and Pearl mentally applauded her. Of the three mah-jong suits that formed the symbolic basis of the Thirteen Orphans' magic, Brenda had the most trouble with characters.

"Actually," Pearl said, "in this case bamboo and dots would be best."

"Bamboo for strength and flexibility," Brenda said, folding herself down so that she could lean against a nearby tree. "And dots?"

"Because you find them easiest," Pearl said. "Thank you. I'll be glad for your help. Does your wound hurt too much?"

"Not right now," Brenda said. "I've got it wrapped so it doesn't pull."

Pearl looked at Des. "Since I have Brenda's help, why don't you go and secure our prisoners? I believe we have a few. See if Honey Dream needs help with her father."

"Flying Claw is with her," Des said. "I'm going to reinforce our security spells. If they hadn't been up to make sure no one noticed our peculiar 'exercise,' we'd already have had representatives of every police force in the city, state, and county here."

"Good," Pearl said. "You're right. We're going to need time to mop up. Thanks."

Des paused long enough to give Brenda a squeeze on one shoulder, then went. Pearl heard him talking to Riprap. Then she tuned him out. Des was far more solid and competent than his rather odd appearance would lead most to think. He'd handle his part. Time for her to do hers.

"Ready?" she said to Brenda.

Brenda nodded. "I've got it set. Give the word."

"Very well," Pearl said. She paused, worked up the sequence of Red Dragons and characters that made up the twisting lines of Red Coral, then nodded. "Knit."

☆

Fading back into reality after assisting Pearl with the two defensive spells, Brenda leaned against her tree feeling very tired. Although she hadn't cast the spells, her ch'i had been used to build them—and quite a lot of that ch'i.

Brenda had understood Pearl's reasoning and agreed wholeheartedly. In an emergency, Pearl could cast a variety of spells, whereas Brenda—who until about six weeks ago hadn't known that magic was as real at the tree bark poking into her back—would need time to prepare and compose.

As she came back into focus, Brenda realized the sword cut on her middle was beginning to hurt. She reached down and pressed her fingers where she'd wrapped her tee shirt. There was a sharp pain followed by an eddying throb.

"How does it feel?" Pearl asked.

"Like a giant paper cut," Brenda said, trying to be honest, but at the same time not willing to make a huge fuss. It was impossible to take her own injury seriously with Righteous Drum lying there on the ground, apparently still unconscious. Honey Dream knelt next to him, her attempt at impassivity not hiding how worried she was. "How is Righteous Drum?"

Des had heard them talking, and now he came to join them, answering Brenda's question as he did.

"Bad," he said. "The arm is off. Even if we'd rushed him to a hospital right away, not even microsurgery could reattach it. The blade that took the arm off was spelled. That's where the only good thing to happen comes in."

"There's good?" Brenda asked, incredulous.

"The same element in the spell that ruined the arm sealed the wound," Des explained. "I doubt that any kindness was intended. Rather whoever did this wanted to make certain that Righteous Drum was put out of action, but not killed. However, he's in no further danger."

Disarmed, Brenda thought, swallowing a hysterical giggle. *Oh, god! They disarmed him . . .*

She must have looked wild around the eyes, because Des squatted next to her.

"Let me take a look at your injury. I'm no doctor, but I have some first aid training."

Brenda obeyed, sitting up a little straighter and letting Des peel back her ruined tee shirt. A couple of times he poured on bottled water to loosen where blood had glued the shirt to her skin.

"Nasty," he said, after careful examination. "But no sign that there was either poison or inimical magic on the blade."

Pearl had been watching, and now Des turned to her. "Brenda must see a doctor. The sword sliced right through her shirt. Foreign matter in the wound could cause scarring or infection. She probably will need stitches."

"I agree," Pearl said. "If Brenda is willing to wait, I can arrange something with a doctor who won't insist on too many explanations. Are you all right with that, Brenda?"

Brenda, who had already been wondering how she'd explain this injury to her mother—and considering whether she had to mention it at all—nodded in relief.

"As long as a real doctor checks it," she said, "I'm perfectly fine with not going to a hospital or something."

"A real doctor," Pearl promised. "I'll make some calls. Before I do . . . Des, what's the situation?"

"We were attacked," Des said, "by sixteen armed and armored men. At least five were capable of spellcasting, but certainly not all of them. That's probably what saved our lives. Of the sixteen, we have four left alive: the one you hit on the back of the neck, two of mine, and one of Riprap's."

Brenda shivered and reached for her bloody shirt. That meant twelve people had died here in just a few minutes. She felt suddenly cold.

"And us?" Pearl said.

"All alive. Righteous Drum's injury is worst. Brenda's

next. The rest of us have various nicks, cuts, and bruises, but nothing too severe."

"Waking Lizard?"

"Knocked out. Woozy. He's tried to tell us something several times, but he can't seem to form coherent sentences. I think he's suffering severe ch'i depletion. Riprap has taken a car and gone for some yogurt for both Waking Lizard and Righteous Drum."

"Righteous Drum is alert enough to eat then? Good. How are the wards?"

"Strong ones up, now, but it's probable someone will have caught the eddies from our opponents' arrival. Our earlier wards were meant to keep any casual passerby from noticing anything odd going on, not to block the force of a major incursion. After all, we're on private land, so we didn't need to worry overmuch."

"Twelve bodies," Pearl said thoughtfully. "Disposing of them is going to take some planning. First, however, let me get a doctor for Brenda. Brenda? Do you want me to call your father?"

Brenda blinked. "Uh, maybe not. Do we need to right away?"

"Only if you want him," Pearl said. "You're over eighteen, so the doctor won't need permission from your parents to treat you."

"No, then. Not now. There's a lot more we need to handle."

Pearl looked approving. "Good. I have my cell phone. I'll try Dr. Andersen."

"I'm going to check on Waking Lizard," Des said. "Honey Dream is assiduously ignoring him, and Flying Claw has been standing guard over our prisoners."

Riprap arrived back then, driving a secondhand passenger van that had been Pearl's most recent acquisition. Without apparent difficulty, he lifted out several bulky bags.

"Flying Claw," he said, "I bought more than yogurt. Grab the bags?"

Flying Claw, a handsome Chinese man, apparently somewhere in his twenties, nodded, sheathed his sword, and crossed to the van without comment. Brenda looked after him with an unsettling mixture of emotions.

Pearl left one alive. Des two. Riprap one. That means of the dozen killed, Flying Claw was probably responsible for most. I didn't kill anyone. I have the impression Waking Lizard was out of it from the start. I think Pearl killed one. Righteous Drum couldn't have killed more than one, not with his arm cut off. Honey Dream might have killed several, but I remember bodies all over, and she stayed by her dad. I knew Flying Claw was dangerous, but this . . .

Riprap had paused to drop several packages over by where Honey Dream sat by her father, then to give others to Des. They talked for a moment, then Riprap came over to Brenda.

She remembered when she'd been nervous about meeting Riprap. Now the big black man seemed much like a perfect older brother. He hunkered down next to her and proffered a carton of peach yogurt and a plastic spoon.

"Des says you have mild ch'i depletion from helping Pearl with the spells. Eat this. I'll bring you some water."

Brenda accepted the yogurt.

"You okay, Riprap?"

"My brain hurts more than my body," he said, keeping his voice soft. "One minute Flying Claw is telling me about this Wolf Teeth staff that he thinks would be a great weapon for me, next I'm learning really fast why wooden baseball bat against sword isn't a good combination."

Brenda thought of the smashed head she'd glimpsed when walking over to offer to help Pearl, and had to fight to keep her yogurt from coming back up. Only vivid memories of what ch'i depletion felt like kept her from pushing the container away.

"You fought, though," she said, trying to sound encouraging.

"I killed one man," Riprap said. "Injured a bunch more. Flying Claw's the one who saved us. That man really is a tiger. I've never seen anything like it. I'd have been dead three times over without his help."

"Me, too," Brenda said, and wondered why she didn't feel more grateful—only scared.

Riprap rose to bring Brenda the promised water, and Pearl came back.

"Nissa will be here in a few minutes. She's going to drive the compact, and take you to the doctor."

"And this?" Brenda said, indicating the bodies.

"We'll deal with it," Pearl promised. "We'll deal with the dead and the living alike."

II

The land on which they had come to practice was one of several parcels that Pearl owned throughout the immediate area.

Most of her properties were rented out, contributing immensely to her wealth. However, there were always those that were between tenants. This park was attached to Colm Lodge, a large house—or small mansion—which until a few days before had been rented to the company of a traveling circus that was performing at various venues throughout the area.

"Jugglers and such," Pearl had explained when she'd suggested they use the place, "acrobats, high wire. Very few animal acts, but they did have horses and some exotics. The barn worked well for them, and they kept props and stage settings in one of my warehouses."

When the circus had moved out, Righteous Drum, Honey Dream, Flying Claw, and Waking Lizard had moved there from the somewhat expensive hotel in which they had spent the last few days.

Now that the initial chaos was over, and no new attack seemed to be in the offing, Riprap brought the van around, and the human casualties—for none of the captives were in ideal health—were moved up to the house. Then he and Flying Claw departed, taking the van so they could move the bodies to the shelter of the barn.

When she entered the house, Pearl felt the presence of wards that were not her own, but, true to their initial agreement, Righteous Drum had not done anything to bar her or her associates. What he had done was make the house infinitely more secure. Given the circumstances, Pearl could only be grateful.

"Honey Dream," she began, "shall we take your father to his room?"

A weak but completely clear voice broke in from where Righteous Drum lay on the collapsible stretcher that had been one of Riprap's purchases.

"No!" he said. "I must be present for the questioning. I must know . . ."

Pearl glanced at Honey Dream and the young woman nodded.

"He would only fret," she said, her tone cold and analytical. "Although in his weakened state I could make him sleep, I would not wish for the consequences when he awoke."

"Me either," Des said with a grin. "Right. As I recall, the living room has several sofas. We'll put him on one, Waking Lizard on the other."

Honey Dream drew in her breath with a sharp hiss and looked as if she would spit.

"Him! That traitor should be with the other prisoners, bound and gagged, not treated as if he were an ally."

Pearl frowned. She could understand the young woman's reaction, but she thought it unmerited.

"Honey Dream," she said sharply. "You forget yourself. Waking Lizard is no traitor—a tool almost definitely, but not a traitor. Were he such, we would all know. If you could reach beyond your passion, you would realize this."

Waking Lizard, who like Righteous Drum lay on a stretcher, stirred, opened his eyes, and tried to speak. The words were so garbled that they might have been the form of Chinese spoken in the Lands Born from Smoke and Sacrifice, might have been the English he spoke courtesy of a spell.

Pearl pressed her fingers into his arm.

"Quiet now. Rest. We will require you to speak later."

The patients were moved onto sofas, Honey Dream assisting with her father, but refusing even to touch Waking Lizard's stretcher. Fortunately, despite his height and long limbs, Waking Lizard was not very heavy, and between them Pearl and Des managed to move him.

The kitchen of Colm Lodge had been freshly stocked when the four from the Lands had taken up residence. While Des sat and spooned yogurt into Waking Lizard—live foods were one of the best cures for ch'i depletion, and now was not the time to worry whether Waking Lizard shared the modern Chinese tendency to be lactose intolerant—Pearl went out into the kitchen.

There she found the makings for simple refreshments: tea, rice balls, pickled vegetables, and almond wafers. Most of their group had not eaten yet. In any case, Pearl—part Chinese, part Hungarian Jew—had been indoctrinated from childhood that food would make any situation better.

She had just finished making tea when Riprap and Flying Claw came into the house through the kitchen door.

"We've got the bodies under cover," Riprap said, "and locked the barn. We're going up to wash. Flying Claw's going to loan me some clothes."

Pearl nodded, wondering how Riprap, both taller and broader than Flying Claw, would be able to wear the other man's clothing, but she said nothing. She suddenly remembered her own bloodied and stained clothing and felt a strong desire to change.

She carried tea and refreshments into the living room, and said to Des, "I'm going to change. Happily, I store some trunks of old props and costumes in the attic for a local little theater company. There's probably something that would fit you. Shall I bring you down something?"

Des nodded. "Thank you."

Pearl did not make the same offer to Honey Dream. The young woman was working very hard at ignoring them all, and Pearl was growing rapidly tired of her. However, Pearl also felt a certain amount of sympathy. After all, Honey Dream had just seen her father brutally mutilated, and unlike Pearl, whose relationship with the late Thundering Heaven had been complex, Honey Dream liked her father.

When Pearl returned from washing off in one of the spare bathrooms, and donning a neat dress that had been one of the mother's costumes in a recent performance of *The Glass Menagerie*, she found Honey Dream gone from her father's side.

"I sent her to wash," Righteous Drum said. "And to dress decently. I apologize for her lack of manners."

"She's had a shock," Pearl said.

"So have we all," Righteous Drum said, twitching his right shoulder as if seeking to move an arm that was no longer there.

Des accepted the loose trousers and sports shirt Pearl had brought for him.

"Waking Lizard's sleeping naturally now," he said. "He needs it."

"We'll let him sleep," Pearl promised. "Go get clean."

Flying Claw and Riprap came thundering down the stairs at that point. Both were damp and shining clean. Riprap wore a pair of sweat pants that were a bit short in the leg and a tee shirt that stretched alarmingly over his broad, muscular chest.

Theoretically, there should have been nothing alike about the two men. Flying Claw was tall and muscular for a Chinese, but next to Riprap's towering height and build he looked merely average. Flying Claw wore his shining black hair long—today, for practice, bound in a knot at the base of his neck, but often in a long ponytail. Riprap wore his soft, tightly curled hair in a short, almost military cut. Flying Claw's skin was golden brown, Riprap's a dark brown that left no doubt as to his primarily African heritage.

Yet there was something alike in their dark brown eyes, a clear alertness that spoke of military training and the attendant alertness.

Both young men accepted Pearl's offer of tea and refreshments, and as soon as he'd swallowed a large rice ball in about two bites, Riprap said, "Pearl, I know we're going to wait to discuss what happened today until everyone is here, but I wanted to ask about the bodies."

"Yes?"

"Those people who attacked us, they were from the Lands, right? I don't suppose the bodies will just sort of fade away, eventually, will they?"

Pearl laughed. "You mean deliquesce into some eldritch goo like in a horror film? I fear not. They came over a bridge, and so they were as much here as you would be if you traveled by a similar means to the Lands."

"So we have twelve bodies on our hands," Riprap said. "Any idea how we'll deal with them? Can you magic them away?"

"I would prefer not," Pearl said. "We have used enough magic today that I fear there will be consequences. I am open to suggestions."

Riprap thought his way through another rice ball, then said, "Do you have anything against burying them here? I worked in construction after I got out of the army—the pay was good, but at the end of the day I was too tired to coach so I switched jobs. I can operate a backhoe. You can rent really cute little ones—footprint on them isn't much bigger than a standard pickup truck."

Pearl was interested. "There's the spot near the barn where we have the manure pile. If you could move the manure to one side, dig there, and then pile the extra dirt and manure there, no one should notice."

Unsaid was the fact that the manure would also excuse any especial greenness in that area as the bodies decayed.

"I can do that," Riprap said. "The barn isn't really visible from most of the surrounding houses."

"On purpose," Pearl said. "Barns and stables are not considered ornamental, even if horses are. In any case, a minor warding spell will turn attention away from your work and not raise any additional questions."

She could see that both Riprap and Flying Claw wanted to ask about those "additional" questions, but knew she would insist on waiting until their group was reassembled.

"It would be best if the bodies were buried without their armor and weapons," Pearl said. "Can you handle stripping them?"

Riprap paused almost inadvertently, but Flying Claw said without hesitation, "I can. What do you want to do with the clothing, armor, and weapons?"

"Using magic to clean those," Pearl said, "won't raise any flags. I'll handle that later. Then we can store them in boxes in the attic neatly labeled Props for Chinese Historical Drama."

"Very good," Flying Claw said, inclining his head in acknowledgment that in no way indicated deference.

"I phoned Albert Yu," Pearl said, "when I was making the doctor's appointment for Brenda. Albert should be here quite soon, and even if the young ladies have not arrived by then, I believe we can start without them. They know the beginning of the tale, whereas Albert does not."

Riprap surged to his feet. "And so do I. Since we're going to be here for a while, I'll go and see what I can scare up in the way of a more solid meal than pickles and rice. I just happened to buy some sandwich makings when I was out."

Flying Claw said, "I will go out to the barn and start my own job. Please let me know when the discussion is to begin."

Honey Dream descended the stair at that point, and Pearl saw her looking between the young men and her injured father. Given Honey Dream's feelings for—even obsession with—Flying Claw, Pearl gave her a point for filial piety when she chose to resume her seat on her father's bedside rather than following him.

Of course, Honey Dream might not have liked the idea of courting among corpses.

Des had not yet rejoined the group downstairs when the doorbell pealed.

"That will be Albert," Pearl said. "Time to lay plans for our counterattack."

☆

"Were you scared?" Nissa asked.

Nissa Nita and her two-and-a-half-year-old daughter, Lani, were the remaining residents of Pearl's household. Shorter than Brenda, round-figured, with fluffy strawberry-blond hair worn slightly longer than shoulder-length, Nissa was a comfortable person despite—or perhaps because of—the immense strength of will that underlay her otherwise peaceful nature.

Unlike Riprap and Brenda, Nissa had not been interested in learning anything at all about swords or fighting. Pearl had not pressed Nissa to do so, saying that the amulets should suffice.

Pearl had added, "Nissa is the Rabbit, and since time immemorial Rabbits have been associated with healing. Let her be. I've seen she's no coward."

Brenda leaned back in her seat in the car and considered. "I'm not sure. It was too much, too fast. I think I felt scared when I realized it was real. After, I just felt sick."

"When you saw the bodies, you mean?"

Brenda nodded. She glanced over at Nissa. Nissa was only a few years older than Brenda, but there were times she seemed infinitely older. Part of this was because Nissa was a mother.

"Have you ever seen someone dead?"

Brenda regretted the question immediately. She knew that Nissa's mother had died in a car crash only a few years before, and that Nissa still missed her mom.

"Yeah," Nissa said, "but never like that, never dead from violence. Dead in a funeral home. Dead in a hospital. Not like what I saw when I pulled the car up to get you. And that was after they'd cleaned up a bit."

"I'd seen the same as you," Brenda said. "Funerals. Not even much there. At first this didn't seem any more real. I didn't actually kill anyone, but later, when I went across the field . . . It was the smell that got me. That and the flies. They came from pretty much nowhere."

Brenda raised her hand to her throat as if she could hold down the surge of revulsion.

"You know, you asked if I was scared. I don't think I was then, during the fight. There was too much going on. But afterwards, I was scared, but not of what you might think."

"What of?" Nissa asked softly, her Virginia accent coloring the simple phrase with a soft lilt.

"I was scared of the others, especially of Flying Claw and Honey Dream. They took it all as if it were so . . . normal. Des and Pearl and Riprap, they were wired, each in their own way, but those other two, especially Flying Claw, it was like 'business as usual.' "

"Yeah," Nissa said. "Well, we've heard that where they come from war is a lot more common—and a lot more personal. I guess we can't blame them."

"I don't," Brenda said. "But I think I'm scared of them now, scared in a way I never was before."

As she drove, Nissa had been consulting directions she'd stuck on the dashboard with a bit of the same adhesive tape she'd used to freshly bandage Brenda's wound. Now she turned in to a small shopping center anchored at one end by three short buildings bearing the sign SAINT JOSEPH'S MEDICAL CENTER.

"Here we are," she said, parking the car. "Ready?"

Brenda undid her seat belt and felt at her middle. "Just

great. I think you did such a good job rewrapping the cut, I probably could have skipped coming here."

"Sorry," Nissa said with a grin. "No copping out. I think you're going to need a few stitches, and I'm absolutely not doing those, not without a proper kit."

Dr. Andersen, Pearl's mysterious contact, had offices on the second floor. Brenda and Nissa were shown immediately into an examining room. A nurse came in, did preliminary checks of blood pressure, pulse, and temperature, asked a series of questions about medical history, but the doctor himself was a while coming.

In person, Dr. Andersen proved to be completely un-mysterious, and astonishingly devoid of questions about how Brenda had gotten such a remarkable injury well before ten in the morning. Tall, slightly paunchy, and somewhere in his sixties, he looked exactly like the second lead in a television drama about hospitals—the handsome lead's best friend, mentor, and confidant.

He apologized for keeping them. Unwrapping Nissa's bandaging, he began carefully inspecting the injury. He cleaned the wound again, complimenting Nissa on her first aid. With the aid of a mirror, he showed Brenda why one end of the slice needed stitches.

"It's superficial enough, but without stitches you're going to have a scar. With stitches there should be none. You're too young to start accumulating interesting scars, so I'll call my nurse and then we'll get started."

Thanks to an injection of some numbing drug, the stitching felt more interesting than anything else. Dr. Andersen told them to keep the stitches moist by applying a light coat of petroleum jelly twice a day, and then turned to Nissa.

"You seem to know a great deal about first aid. Have you ever removed stitches?"

Nissa grinned a bit sheepishly. "A few times. My sisters and I live out in the country, and sometimes it was easier than driving one of the kids into town."

"And," Dr. Andersen said with an answering grin, "it

spares you the co-pay, too. Good. In about three days, these should be ready to come out. Check by pulling softly on the edges of the wound. If they seem clean and tight, go ahead and take the stitches out."

Nissa nodded, and Brenda thought her friend looked rather flattered.

Dr. Andersen supplied a room where Brenda could change into the fresh clothes Nissa had brought for her, and they were on their way within an hour.

By now Brenda was feeling tired and light-headed.

Shock, she thought. *I'm in shock. Someone tried to cut me—to kill me.*

Brenda felt herself starting to shiver, and reached for something—anything—to anchor her in the present, to escape from memories of that man coming at her with raised sword, his face concentrated, seeing her as just a thing, a target.

"Wow," she said, looking at the dashboard clock. "Can you believe it's only slightly before noon?"

"Hungry?" Nissa asked. "I told Lani if she would stay with Wong and help him in the garden I'd bring her something. I think a kid's meal would about fit the ticket."

"Cold?"

"Sure. I won't get fries, and the rest will reheat. It's the little toys and the bright box that matter."

"I'd love a cheeseburger," Brenda admitted. "Breakfast was light because we were going to work out, and I've only had a yogurt since."

They stopped for fast food, and Nissa amused Brenda with tales of how her health-conscious sisters had reacted when they learned Nissa intended to let her daughter eat other than home cooking.

Brenda laughed, but there was no relief. She knew she and Nissa were both dragging their heels about returning to Colm Lodge because when they did, they would be facing something far more serious than whether trans fats contributed to a host of deadly ailments. They'd be facing a war—a war they'd thought they had weeks to plan for, but that had come to their door.

☆

Honey Dream watched as Albert Yu came through the front door, bent slightly to embrace Pearl Bright, and then turned toward the living room. Unlike most of the Thirteen Orphans Honey Dream had seen, Albert Yu looked like the sort of person Honey Dream had grown up thinking of as "real."

As was also the case with Des Lee, Albert Yu's ancestor from the Lands Born from Smoke and Sacrifice had married a Chinese. So had the only son of this union—Albert Yu's father. Therefore, Albert Yu did not have any of the features Honey Dream had found so startling, such as Nissa's bright blue eyes or Riprap's rich brown skin. However, Albert did not look like a person from the Lands, either, and most definitively, he did not look like the great-grandson of one who had reigned as emperor from the Jade Petal Throne.

Honey Dream could not quite figure out why this should be so. Albert Yu's grooming was impeccable, even if his hair—worn just to his collar—was too short, and his small, almost pointed beard was of no style she knew. Her father had cut his hair short, and wore no beard, but he still looked like a man from the Lands should.

She decided the difference had nothing to do with length of hair or stiff business suits rather than the flowing elegance of embroidered robes. It had to do with body language. Albert Yu carried himself with a certain dignity, but it was not the dignity of one who rules, who has studied the manners of court and temple. The ease in his shoulders as he took off his suit jacket—the fact that he moved to hang it up himself rather than handing it to someone else—were all wrong.

Even lesser generals and workers of magic had attendants who did such things for them. Her father had found adjusting to having no servants very difficult.

Honey Dream looked down at Righteous Drum, wondering if he would shrink from meeting this stranger in his current, mutilated condition. Instead, she found him watching Albert Yu's entrance with a certain amount of eagerness.

Still hoping to find a new emperor there, she thought with disgust. *Can't he realize how hopeless these people are? No real magic, limited knowledge of what's important. We need sanctuary of some sort if we're to get home, but didn't Father see that today Flying Claw was twice as useful as any one of them?*

This was not the time to raise the point. She'd tried yesterday, when they were alone, but Father hadn't been willing to listen. So Honey Dream schooled her features to polite listening while Pearl—assisted by Des, who had come down a few minutes after Albert's arrival—related the events of the morning.

Riprap came in bearing a huge tray of sandwiches, then went back for a couple of bowls of chips, and even some fruit. By the time the tale ended, everyone had eaten. Albert went out to the barn to see the bodies. As he was coming back inside, his features grave, Brenda and Nissa drove up. Flying Claw was called in, went upstairs to wash, and came down in his third set of clothes for the day.

Waking Lizard was awakening, as the group reassembled in the living room. He was still weak, but the inability to speak clearly had vanished with the worst of his exhaustion.

Albert turned to him. "Waking Lizard, my understanding is that the attackers owed their ability to cross not only into a warded area, but also into our world, to you."

"He is a traitor!" Honey Dream hissed.

Pearl gave her a very cold stare. "I told you before, young woman, the treaty we all signed—the treaty that was sworn to on my blade of that same name—would make it impossible for Waking Lizard to break our agreement without my knowing."

Albert interceded. "Pearl, Honey Dream does have a point. These people have magics of which we know only parts. Perhaps there are ways around Treaty our ancestors did not anticipate."

"Ancestors!" Pearl sniffed. "My 'ancestor' was my own father. He was determined to cram into me every iota of knowledge he could."

"Nonetheless," Albert said, "I would like to hear Waking Lizard's explanation for how this could have happened."

"I suppose," the old man said in a voice far softer than was usual for him, "that in some sense Honey Dream may be correct. I may indeed be a traitor, but if I am, I am an unwitting one. I told you how I decided to flee the Lands when I realized that our side—Righteous Drum's, Honey Dream's, Flying Claw's, and mine—was losing.

"The bridge by which Righteous Drum, Honey Dream, and Flying Claw had crossed from the Lands to here was still intact, although inactive. As is usual in these cases, one point of the bridge is physical, the other is a powerful mage. As the mage moves toward his destination, the bridge is drawn out behind him, enabling others to follow."

Honey Dream looked around. She could see that several of the Thirteen Orphans wanted to ask how a person could travel on a bridge of which he was also an endpoint, but they had learned something of manners in the few days since the alliance had been signed, and held their tongues.

"As one of our emperor's allied Twelve," Waking Lizard continued, "I had a link to Righteous Drum and the others— but most powerfully to Righteous Drum, because his magic was the most powerful."

Is! Honey Dream thought angrily. *Is! Even without his right arm, my father is more powerful than any of you.*

"I used that link to place myself upon the bridge of which he was an endpoint, and was drawn through to him. Shortly thereafter, the bridge was destroyed at the other end, thereby making it useless. I thought I had escaped, but now I suspect that I was *permitted* to escape."

"And that," Riprap said, showing predictably doglike

eagerness, "instead of your enemies destroying the bridge entirely, they did something that changed the link from Righteous Drum to you."

"Actually," Waking Lizard said, "I think they did destroy the bridge, but that they had set in place the means to create a new bridge. I wonder now if the reports I was brought of our complete losses on the battlefield were correct, or if, in fact, they . . ."

He stopped, took a deep breath, and went on, ". . . counted on my fleeing. I then would become an unwitting endpoint for their own bridge, one that would take them directly to those they desired to find—and within any protective wards as well."

"I wonder why they waited this long?" Brenda said. "I mean, six days have passed since your arrival, long enough for us to work out the treaty, to free the remaining Thirteen Orphans from your crystals, and do a bunch of other things."

"I suspect," Waking Lizard said, "that they were not in a position to do so until recently. Remember, if the battlefield reports were indeed false, then their position was even less secure than we thought—and we thought they would need at least a month to consolidate and send forces after us."

Flying Claw said, "That was when they would have had to create their own bridge, even so . . . I think you may be right. I think they have spent these days consolidating their conquest, and rather than waiting, they have actually moved quickly. Several of the bodies I undressed showed cuts and bruises older than could have been received today, but still fairly fresh."

Brenda gave a short, hard laugh. "Wow! Did they ever pick a bad time. I mean, what if they'd come through when we weren't here and all of you were asleep? Instead they came through not only when you had reinforcements, but when we were all wearing at least some magical protection, and several people were holding weapons."

Desperate Lee had been unusually silent for him—normally

he was almost too chatty. Now he looked over at Righteous Drum.

"Honored Dragon, is there any possibility that the treaty might have had anything to do with their bad timing? Waking Lizard did swear to do everything in his power not to bring harm to any of the signatories. Therefore, he would have been under conflicting obligations. From his condition, it's apparent they drew heavily on his ch'i to power the bridge. Therefore, the bridge could not be established unless he thought—even unconsciously—that no harm would come to us."

Righteous Drum's eyes lit with the scholarly fire that Honey Dream knew all too well. He was forgetting that he'd lost an arm, that harm had definitely been done. All he thought of was the fascinating problem.

"That is likely, Desperate Lee. The unconscious mind is closely allied to the vital energies. Some theorists argue that dreams are needed for ch'i to truly replenish, which is why even if a spellcaster is loaned ch'i to enable him to work a complex spell, still he cannot go on indefinitely without being depleted. Yes. That theory is sound."

Waking Lizard's brief speeches had tired him, so that he had sunk back against the pillows, but now he pushed himself up onto one elbow and met Righteous Drum's eye.

"I didn't manage entirely, I fear. I am sorry."

Righteous Drum smiled bravely. "As Brenda Morris has noted, we were very fortunate in the timing of the attack. We could have all been slain in our beds."

"They weren't taking any chances, though," Riprap said. "All sixteen wore armor. All had weapons. Flying Claw says that several were capable of casting spells. Certainly whoever attacked you came armed for Dragon."

"That brings me to another question," Albert Yu said. "Did any of you recognize any of the attackers, living or dead?"

"I didn't get a very good look," Righteous Drum admitted. "I was down almost immediately. I did not know the man my spell killed, even though he was a sorcerer of some power."

"I didn't," Honey Dream said, "but I also didn't see much because I protected my father."

Waking Lizard shook his head, but Flying Claw, who had been waiting with the admirable patience of a Tiger who knows the kill is his and sees no need to spring prematurely, nodded.

"I knew several among the dead. Good soldiers all. All ones I heard had joined the other side. Among the living, I knew one. I don't know what he is called these days, but when we were in school together, he was called Twentyseven-Ten."

"Twentyseven-Ten?" Brenda asked. "That's a weird name."

Flying Claw grinned at her. "We all had names like that. The first number is the order in which you were enrolled in your year. Mine was three. The second was the number of years you had completed in training. The examination at the end of the tenth year is particularly difficult. Candidates are fifteen by then, and those who do not show promise in both magic and fighting arts are not permitted to continue. Ten, therefore, is an admirable designation, and therefore he may have kept that name."

Honey Dream thought that Brenda probably had a lot more questions. She'd been sniffing after Flying Claw since the poor man had been an amnesiac captured by Pearl Bright's trickery, and held as if a fair prisoner of war. They'd called him "Foster" then, as if he were some little bottle-fed lamb.

Today had been the first time Brenda Morris had seen what a student of the hard school from which Flying Claw was an honored graduate could do. Honey Dream had thought Brenda's ardor dampened, but now she wasn't so sure.

Albert Yu broke in before Brenda could ask any more of her doubtless insipid questions.

"Shall we question this man, Twentyseven-Ten?"

"We can try," Flying Claw said. "Each of the four captives

is being held separately. Would you like me to bring Twentyseven-Ten to you?"

"Please do so," Albert responded. "Let's see what we can learn about the nature of our enemy."

"And," Pearl said, "about how immediate is the danger we face."

III

Superficially, Twentyseven-Ten resembled Flying Claw. There was something of the same combination of strength and grace in how he moved. There was confidence in his bearing. He was even handsome. But there were differences as well, differences that had nothing to do with him being brought before them wearing what Brenda guessed were the padded shirt and trousers he had worn under his armor.

He walked into the room, head held high, chin slightly raised. Defiant. Arrogant, even in defeat. And despite admiring the courage that let him show that arrogance, Brenda felt there was something coarse about Twentyseven-Ten, something hardened.

Flying Claw introduced the captive to the group.

"This man is Twentyseven-Ten. He says he is willing to answer your questions, but first he would like to know what is intended for him and the other three captives."

Pearl said quickly, "That will depend on what we learn."

Brenda noticed that Twentyseven-Ten did not seem surprised to see an older woman asserting herself in such a fashion. It was another reminder that just as the Lands did not operate by the same rules as did her own world, so they were also not China.

In China, only rare women rose to positions of power, but in the Lands Born from Smoke and Sacrifice duality was taken very seriously. Six of the original Twelve had been women, yin to the six male yang signs. Twentyseven-Ten would be accustomed to women in positions of authority.

"Ask your questions," Twentyseven-Ten said. "I will endeavor to be worthy of my life."

Pearl inclined her head to Albert, letting him take the lead. Brenda suspected that in a game of "good cop/bad cop," Pearl would much prefer to be the "bad cop."

Albert asked, "When you and your associates came here, what was your goal?"

"Our orders," Twentyseven-Ten said, putting a slight stress on the second word, as if to distance himself from personal intent, "were to capture the three renegades who had come here from the Lands."

"Then?"

Twentyseven-Ten paused. Brenda thought he was considering disclaiming any other knowledge, but a flickering glance in Pearl's direction showed that he had decided this would be unwise.

"Then, based upon what we learned from the renegades, we were either to take them back to be interviewed by our gracious emperor, or to remain here and enable the renegades to gain favor in our ruler's eyes by assisting us in achieving our goal."

"And that goal?"

"Regaining the Twelve Earthly Branches that had been lost when the twelve advisors of the emperor were exiled a century ago," Twentyseven-Ten replied promptly.

"What were your specific duties?"

"To use any combination of my abilities, both magical and martial, to facilitate the action. Our goal was to bring back alive at least one of the three renegades, preferably Righteous Drum, on the assumption that he would be the most useful."

"Then the others were considered disposable?" Albert asked.

Spontaneously, a really nasty look flickered across Twentyseven-Ten's face. His gaze flickered toward Flying Claw.

"Yes," he said, triumph in the single word. "They were disposable."

Albert paused a moment to let that sink in, then asked, "Who was in command of this expedition? Is he still alive?"

"The commander was killed by Righteous Drum's spell."

There was something odd in Twentyseven-Ten's tone of voice when he said that, Brenda thought. *He's both frightened and somehow relieved. Is it because he's glad the boss won't be around to yell at him? Is it because the boss went down so hard, so fast?*

Brenda didn't ask. She didn't think she was the only one to have noticed Twentyseven-Ten's reaction, and Albert's next question showed she was right.

"Tell me about your commander. What was his name? How did he come to be in charge of such an important expedition? Righteous Drum said he did not recognize him."

"I did not," Righteous Drum agreed, "and the more I think about that, the more peculiar it seems. I thought I knew my enemies—I thought I knew my peers. But this man was a stranger. I am sure of it."

"He . . ." Twentyseven-Ten faltered. "He told us to call him Captain. He gave us no personal name. He was a stranger to me as well, to me and to all but two of our company."

"Are either of these alive?"

"No. The Tiger lady killed one. The Tiger lord killed the other." Twentyseven-Ten hurried on, volunteering information for the first time. "My master—he who will be the new Horse—knew this man, and so assigned thirteen warriors to accompany Captain. We were to follow Captain's orders, and if, by chance, anything happened to him, to continue the mission on our own."

"How," Albert said, "did you intend to return to the Lands once you had your captives?"

"We were each given an amulet," Twentyseven-Ten said, "keyed to us personally. It does not create a bridge, but rather enables recall for ourselves and any we touch."

Riprap cut in. "When Flying Claw and I stripped the captives down, Flying Claw found the amulets. We took them off before we gave them back their underclothes. The same amulets were on the bodies."

Riprap reached into his pocket and took out a small sandwich bag with a zip closure. It held four small items. Leaning for a closer look, Brenda saw the amulets were jade carvings of birds, their wings outstretched in flight.

Albert Yu turned to Twentyseven-Ten. "Are these what you are referring to?"

Twentyseven-Ten nodded, his expression showing a moment of longing. "Those are the amulets."

"Then is the bridge anchored in Waking Lizard no longer active?" Albert asked.

"It is not," Twentyseven-Ten said, "or so we were told. I have not tested that for myself."

Trying to keep us from trusting Waking Lizard, Brenda thought. *Well, why should he help us more than he must?*

"And the amulets will only work for you?" Albert asked.

"One to each one of us," Twentyseven-Ten said. "You can read the inscriptions yourself."

That's right, Brenda thought, swallowing a grin. *Keep yourself alive at all costs. Don't you think we'll figure out the weakness of using those amulets? Even as eager as Righteous Drum is to get back to his family, he's got to have seen it.*

"So you were sent here to retrieve the 'renegades,' as you term them," Albert Yu said. "And what were your orders regarding the rest of us?"

"Sir?" For the first time Twentyseven-Ten looked flustered.

"Come now," Albert said, his voice hardening. "You told us your task was to retrieve the Earthly Branches. Myself and my associates are the current affiliates of those Branches. What were your intentions toward us?"

Twentyseven-Ten tightened his lips into a thin line, and refused to say anything.

Pearl laughed, a hard, throaty growl more like a tiger's cough. "It's obvious, isn't it? If three from the Lands—three whose only crime was supporting the wrong candidate for the throne—were considered disposable, what do you think our value would be? If Righteous Drum had not succeeded in stripping us of the Branches, then Twentyseven-Ten and his associates would have taken over the job—and somehow I have the impression they would not have cared what happened to us when they went about the extraction."

"Still," Albert said. "Even if Twentyseven-Ten was less than helpful about this one point, he has been useful. I believe he may continue living. Do any of you have other questions?"

Brenda had several, but they would have given away too much of their own weaknesses, their own ignorance. She shook her head.

Nissa asked Twentyseven-Ten, "Are you injured? Are any of the other captives injured?"

Twentyseven-Ten blinked in astonishment. He seemed to have a bit of trouble focusing on Nissa. Well, no great surprise there. If all the people he knew were dark-haired and dark-eyed, a strawberry blonde with really bright turquoise eyes would be startling. He might never have seen freckles before.

"A few bruises," he replied with a manly shrug. "I do not know about the others."

"The one Pearl clubbed at the back of the neck," Riprap said, "seems a bit stiff. Any way short of an X-ray you can tell if she broke something?"

"I can try," Nissa said doubtfully, "but neck injuries are tricky at the best of times."

She looked reproachfully at Pearl.

Pearl said, "He was going to cut Brenda in half. I did manage not to kill him."

"Ah." Nissa considered. "I'll check him out. Are we done here?"

Albert looked at the others, offering courtesy approaching deference to the four from the Lands. "Any questions?"

"Later," Righteous Drum said. "Perhaps. This has given us much to consider."

The other three nodded agreement, and Flying Claw led Twentyseven-Ten away.

"In answer to your question, Nissa," Albert said, "we seem to be done with the interview, but not with planning. We have much to decide."

"And I have a backhoe to order," Riprap said, "and a big hole to dig. Those bodies are going to get nasty in July heat."

Des rose. "I can help with that. I'll set a north wind to keep them cool. It's not refrigeration, but it's also not the sort of spell that will draw much attention."

"'Attention,'" Brenda repeated. "You and Pearl keep hinting that this morning's fight is going to have brought some sort of attention on us—and I don't think you mean the nosy supernatural creatures you taught us to ward against before you taught us our first spells. We'd set those sort of protections before we started the practice. What's going on?"

Des smiled, a thin smile without a great deal of humor in it.

"Brenda, we've told you that there are other magical traditions in this world. Do you think the indigenous magical traditions were particularly happy to have thirteen—well, twelve, actually, since the Cat was but a child—twelve highly trained, highly skilled adepts suddenly emerge into their world?"

"I hadn't thought about it," Brenda frowned, "but I guess not. Did those indigenous types notice then?"

"Indeed they did," Des said, "especially when, not long thereafter, our ancestors' enemies came after them and some rather violent magic came into use."

"You didn't mention this in your earlier account," Nissa said, her tone mildly accusing. "You made it sound like the only opposition the Twelve had to deal with came from the people who had exiled them."

"You had enough to take in," Des said, "without that."

Thinking back to the cascade of events that had begun shortly after her own arrival in California, Brenda had to admit that this had been only too true. Nissa nodded.

"As I indicated a moment ago," Des said, "the Thirteen Orphans met with hostility from the start. Beginning with the indigenous magical traditions of China, where the bridge that took them into exile had deposited them, they were treated as if they were invaders rather than refugees.

"Eventually, an uneasy truce arose between the groups, with the Thirteen assuring their unwilling hosts that they intended to do nothing to change the current balance of power. However, this truce was still young when enemies from the Lands Born from Smoke and Sacrifice—the home of the Thirteen—the very ones who had sworn to leave the exiles in peace if they would agree to leave—came after them."

Des paused as if to give Righteous Drum and Honey Dream an opportunity to speak up for their homeland, but both maintained studiously polite listening expressions. Waking Lizard had fallen asleep again.

"When the Thirteen—twelve really—used their magics to defend themselves, the indigenous magical traditions, this time not only of China but of other parts of the world as well, viewed this as an indication that the Thirteen Orphans were willing to break the parameters of their truce. The Thirteen pleaded to be left to deal with the invaders themselves, saying they wanted no one else involved with their quarrels. When the battles were over, the Twelve did their best to prove to the indigenous magical traditions by their actions that they were willing to live in peace—as long as they were not threatened."

"Are you saying they gave up using magic?" Brenda said incredulously.

"No," Des replied. "I am not. What I'm saying is that they pretty much gave up the more aggressive forms of magic—except in highly controlled practice sessions. Look, Brenda, we can talk about this later. The indigenous traditions are something we can't avoid. Is it enough to say that our battle this morning is going to have set a bunch of idiots worrying that we're about to try and conquer the world?"

Brenda blinked. "I guess so. Conquer the world, huh? I thought we were only trying to stay alive."

When offered a chance to go lie down, Brenda decided to take it. The slash across her middle was at least eight inches long, and the shock of realizing that her best had not been enough, that if Pearl hadn't been there, Brenda would have been dead, was sinking in.

I was lucky that the sword that cut me hadn't been spelled like the one that took off Righteous Drum's arm. I was lucky Pearl was there. Why don't I feel lucky?

Brenda knew perfectly well, why. She didn't want to be lucky. She wanted to be admirable, extraordinary. This morning, she'd been neither.

About an hour later, somewhat rested in body, but not the least in spirit, she rejoined the others as the group reassembled in the living room.

Both Waking Lizard and Righteous Drum looked better for having had a rest. Riprap reported that a backhoe would be delivered in about an hour, and that the newly cleaned arms and armor were stored in a trunk in the attic.

Nissa had apparently driven back to Pearl's to check on Lani, and reported that everything at Pearl's house was fine.

"I'd meant to bring Lani back with me, but she and Wong were busy potting a dwarf pomegranate tree, and I couldn't budge her. Wong said she could take her nap in the apartment over the garage—Hastings is out—and Lani was as enchanted as if he'd offered her a trip to the circus."

Pearl smiled. "Hastings came to me yesterday and said that he's been offered a job with a touring company—lead for the role he'd been understudying. I suppose I'll be looking for a new chauffeur soon."

Her expression grew serious. "But perhaps I should wait to interview until after our situation is more settled. I maintain a driver mostly to avoid having to worry about the car when I have meetings, and I don't think I'm going to be attending many committee meetings for a while. In fact, I think I should make reservations to go to New York and see Shen."

Albert Yu had changed his suit for tailored slacks and a collarless shirt that, judging from their outdated style, probably came from one of the props trunks. Despite his change in attire, he looked no more relaxed. He sat on the edge of his chair, leaning slightly forward, fingertips steepled.

"Yes. Both Shen and Deborah need to be updated, and we certainly cannot mention most of this over the telephone or even in an e-mail. Moreover, although they have verbally agreed to the treaty, I want their signatures on it as soon as possible—as we noted earlier, the conflicting duties imposed on Waking Lizard may have diluted the force of the attack. I want them protected as well."

"What about the others?" Nissa asked. "All of us here have signed, as has Brenda's father. You've mentioned Deborah Van Bergenstein, the Pig, and Shen Kung, the Dragon. What about the other five members of the Thirteen Orphans? Don't they have to sign as well?"

Albert's expression became very unhappy, but Brenda didn't think the unhappiness was directed toward Nissa.

"The situation with those five—our Ox, Snake, Horse, Ram, and Monkey—is complex."

"I know they're among the lineages that were lost or have lapsed or whatever," Nissa said, "but still, shouldn't they sign? Don't we need them?"

Albert held up a hand in an eloquent gesture that begged for forbearance. "Please. You're absolutely right, but first we must deal with the complications resulting from this morning's attack."

Nissa did not look pleased, but she nodded. "All right. What's first?"

"Well," Albert said, "Pearl has already mentioned getting Shen and Deborah to sign the treaty. Pearl, if you're willing to make the trip to New York, I'll go to Michigan and see Deborah."

He looked at the four from the Lands. "Deborah lives near Ann Arbor. As you may recall, that is not precisely near New York City."

Honey Dream and Flying Claw looked blank with the blankness that indicates an unwillingness to show embarrassment. Righteous Drum, however, nodded without any discomfort—even though the reason for his knowing where Deborah lived was that he had gone there to attack her.

"Both states are more part of what you call East than West, but, yes, they are not close. Still, you should be able to reach there easily."

"That is not the difficulty," Albert said. "The treaty is. Currently, we have one copy. I would prefer we not ship that, but neither do I wish Pearl and myself to add to our travels. In your magical tradition, is it the document, or the sense of the document that counts?"

Righteous Dream answered promptly. "In the case of a treaty, the sense of the document. Ideally, everyone would sign the same piece of paper, but when this cannot be done, multiple copies are made and linked."

"Good," Albert said. "We might as well leave the original safely here. I recall Honey Dream is an excellent calligrapher. Perhaps she would . . ."

The Snake gave a graceful inclination of her head. "I would be pleased to make copies."

"Another problem," Riprap said into the pause that followed, "is the prisoners. We can't bury them like we can the corpses."

And we don't dare leave them here, Brenda thought, *in the custody of the four from the Lands. The prisoners aren't protected by any treaty, and I wouldn't trust Honey Dream not to poison them. Or seduce them into a new alliance.*

Brenda was certain at least a few of the others shared her thoughts, but no one voiced them.

Instead, Pearl said, "While I don't want the prisoners in my house, I suppose we could put them in the garage apartment. It isn't large, but it is covered by my general wards, and we could put up other spells. Hastings said he would be moving his things out today."

"He already has," Nissa clarified. "That's why Wong thought Lani could take her nap there."

"Sounds like a plan to me," Riprap agreed. "We'll put them where we can keep an eye on them, but not where we'll have them underfoot."

Everyone else agreed. Some further discussion refined that the prisoners would be moved later that night, and how their food and other necessities would be handled.

Then Pearl and Albert went to call their travel agents. Riprap went out to watch for the backhoe. Honey Dream went upstairs and got her calligraphy materials, and a copy of the treaty. Waking Lizard and Righteous Drum were content to continue convalescing in the living room, where they wouldn't miss any interesting developments.

Brenda looked around for Flying Claw, but he had vanished. Perhaps he was standing guard to make sure no one disturbed the bodies. Maybe he'd just wanted to get away from all of them.

She went out to the kitchen and helped Nissa clean up the remaining mess from lunch.

Pearl came in shortly after. "I managed to get an early flight tomorrow morning, although I'll need to drive up to San Francisco. I'll let Hastings assuage his guilt about leaving by having him drive me up. Would the two of you like to come back to my house? I want to start packing."

Nissa nodded. "Did Albert get a flight?"

"For tomorrow afternoon," Pearl answered. "He has a meeting tomorrow morning he preferred not to cancel."

Brenda looked around, hoping for an excuse to linger.

Then she remembered how much of her survival she owed to luck.

"I'd like to go back," she said. "If I concentrate, I can make an amulet bracelet or two. Hopefully, we're not going to be attacked at tomorrow's practice, but I've given up trusting luck."

☆

"Shen."

Pearl embraced her old friend and wondered precisely when time had turned the boy she had run and jumped and played infinite games of chase with into an old man.

Shen still stood straight, but his once dark brown hair was mostly white and had thinned considerably from the curly mop he had inherited from the English beauty who had been his mother. His face was seamed, lined especially around the eyes from hours spent reading or peering through a microscope. His long fingers were gnarled until they held their pose curled around a writing brush even after the brush had been set aside.

Was it because Pearl had spent so much of the seemingly eternal flight between California and New York immersed in memories that the sight of Shen's lined face and thinning hair startled her? Or was it because she had spent the last several months associating almost exclusively with people decades younger than herself?

Probably the former more than the latter. Memories and dreams of memories could be potent drugs, ones Pearl had refused to indulge in when she saw how they could devour the soul. She'd first learned of the destructive power of memory during her Hollywood days, watching those for whom memories of past triumphs were more real than the food they ate or the air they breathed.

Tragic enough when the victim was an otherwise healthy adult, terrifying when the dreamer was a child so young that there should be no past at all, only a future.

Then there had been her father's friends, many of the

original Twelve, a dozen men and women for whom regaining lost cities, families, friends, pets, treasures meant more than those they lived among, loved among, touched and pretended to cherish.

Yes. Memory could be horribly dangerous.

This trip, though, encapsulated in the humming aluminum tube of the airplane's body, Pearl had let herself give in to dreams. The Tiger within her sensed that if there was a solution to their current problem, those twisted jungles peopled by the dead and sometimes not so dearly departed must hold it.

But now she must leave memory and face the present.

"Ming-Ming," Shen said, releasing Pearl from his embrace, her childhood nickname sweet and familiar in his mouth. "How was your flight?"

"Long and, even in First Class, tedious. At least it was direct. Layovers are the worst part of any flight these days."

Shen agreed, although Pearl knew that it had been years, decades even, since Shen had left the comfortable curving lair he'd built for himself within the environs of New York City. Dragons could become creatures of habit, coiled around what they treasured. Although Chinese dragons were not as closely associated with treasure hoards as were their Western counterparts, still, they were very much creatures of place, spiraling along foci of water or air, making themselves one with the rocky bones of earth and stone.

Pearl tried to shake off the threads of dream, but she kept hearing the Dragon who had been Shen's grandfather lecturing about the nature of creatures real and imaginary. Exile Dragon had been a good man, kind in his way, much more accepting of Pearl and her gifts than Pearl's own father had been.

"Ming-Ming?"

Pearl forced herself out of the inwardly spiraling paths of memory, broke the webs that held her within herself, and smiled.

"I am sorry, Shen. Tired. All I have done today—at least since I boarded that plane—is be gently shaken . . ."

"Not stirred?"

Shen grinned at his own joke, and Pearl saw the boy she had known so well in the tilt of his smile, the way his eyes narrowed as he swallowed a laugh. She saw then that the Shen she had known wasn't gone at all. He was there more than ever, his expressions etched with loving care onto the face of the old man.

"Not stirred. Well . . . Stirred to go to the ladies' room. The stewardess . . . No, wait. They're flight attendants, now. Really a much better name. She was very kind, kept bringing me little cups of tea or really darling bottles of water. I kept drinking them, then trotting down the aisle. I suspect I must have greatly amused the business travelers, all bent so industriously over their computers."

"I was going to offer you tea," Shen said almost apologetically.

"I'd love some," Pearl said, "but with dinner. I catch hints of something that smells wonderful."

"Umeko," Shen said, "is very happy for the excuse to cook something elaborate. She has been slicing meat and vegetables, and mixing rare marinades since last night."

Pearl had guessed. Like his grandfather, Shen had married late, and to a woman somewhat younger than himself. The marriage had been not so much happy as warmly content. Umeko was not an intellectual like her husband, but an artist. They had met over calligraphy, separated over how and why ink and brush and elegant paper touched their souls, become streams running side by side, blending, falling back into their own beds, running along again in babbling contentment.

Pearl liked Umeko. Liked Geoffrey their son. Was very glad to be here, but the Tiger that was her soul growled and rumbled, warned her that the jungle waited.

I know, I know, she said. *And Shen does also, but let us move into that tangled darkness slowly, find the trails, else we may never walk out again.*

The Tiger quieted, but Shen did not.

"You have told me some," he said after they were settled in their office. First, they had put Pearl's luggage in her room, then gone into the kitchen and spoken with Umeko.

Umeko chased them from her kitchen—but not without first giving them a tray of tiny, elegant appetizers to sustain them until dinner.

"But because we spoke over the phone," Shen said, reaching for a savory, "you were careful—as you should have been. Now, begin again."

And so Pearl did, telling Shen how Gaheris Morris had brought his daughter Brenda to California, and how almost from the moment of their arrival, nothing had gone quite right.

"Not because of Brenda, though," Pearl hastened to clarify. "She did as well as almost anyone could ask, better than many, especially after her father was attacked."

"You e-mailed a picture of her," Shen said. "She is not much like her father—or her mother, either."

"No," Pearl agreed. "She's a throwback to the old line, most definitely: almost black hair, skin tinted with gold not pink, long eyes. Slim as a reed and resenting it just a little. Right now, she would like to be full-figured and gorgeous."

"If her soul matches her appearance," Shen said with a small smile, "Brenda has reason. Our ancestors liked fat babies and women with curves. Yet Brenda is not wholly a throwback to the Chinese."

"No. Brenda looks like a Morris, but one rendered with ink and brush rather than with oil paints."

"You like this Brenda Morris," Shen said, his inflection making his words almost a question.

"I do," Pearl said, "but she puzzles me. There is something that neither Des nor I can understand about her . . . a capacity, a dimension she should not have."

"You told me," Shen reminded her, "that you thought Gaheris might have done something in an effort to aid Brenda when he felt himself endangered."

"That was the best answer either Des or I could arrive at," Pearl said, "but Gaheris is fully himself again, and he has no memory of doing anything of the sort. Indeed, he vehemently denies it. I think we would all let those events drift, but for Albert . . ."

"Yes. I have heard from him about this matter. He is less than happy with the unresolved mystery. He wants answers."

"So do we all," Pearl said. "So do we all."

"Well, perhaps you and I will find them," Shen said comfortingly. "Go on with your tale, and do not forget to pause now and then to help me eat some of this before it grows cold. Umeko will scold me if she thinks I have starved a guest."

Pearl ate a bite or two, arranging her thoughts, then went on with her tale, putting flesh on bones that Shen had already been given. She should have felt settled, for here was another to share the burden, but as she continued her narration, she became increasingly aware of the Tiger growling, warning her they did not have much time. They could not skirt the jungle forever.

IV

Honey Dream sat dutifully listening as Righteous Drum and Des Lee—her elders, but not her betters, she kept reminding herself—dismissed the amulets they had captured along with their four prisoners as a means of returning to the Lands.

"It's pretty obvious," Des said, "that wherever the recall takes them it won't be somewhere we'd be particularly welcome."

"Or rather," Righteous Drum said, "we would be very welcome—but I fear that the welcome of people who came after me with spells prepared to disable me is not a welcome I care to accept."

They talked for a while about who their enemies might be. Honey Dream had heard much of it before within the privacy of their own circle.

Des Lee seemed to have an infinite hunger for the history of the Lands and the various rivalries and coups that had colored its history. Much of it was new to him, but very familiar to Honey Dream, and as her father lectured on, Honey Dream almost couldn't blame Flying Claw for volunteering to babysit in order to get out of it.

Almost.

Especially since Honey Dream couldn't help but suspect that Flying Claw's desire to babysit had nothing to do with any lingering fondness for that annoying little brat, Lani.

Honey Dream had asked Flying Claw that morning while they were still at the mansion if he—strong, young Tiger that he was—didn't find it insulting that he should be set to child-minding. He was dining on bacon and fried eggs, a meal for which he'd acquired a fondness during his imprisonment.

Flying Claw had considered, a piece of bacon halfway to those lips whose touch she remembered in exquisite detail. "I wouldn't be insulted if I was asked to guard a lesser approach to a stronghold, if that was the best place I could serve my general. This is much the same. Nissa must be free to learn her skills, otherwise she will be of little help to us. She cannot learn with the babe nagging after her. I am a novelty. Lani will behave for me as she will not for others."

Honey Dream had to agree—even if grudgingly—that Nissa was certainly attending to her studies. The attack had created an acute urgency among the three apprentices, among them all, if Honey Dream was honest with herself—an urgency that had not existed when they had signed their treaty and had believed they had a month at minimum to plan.

That had been on July fourth. July fifth had been spent on

various tasks, including moving the four from the Lands into their current residence. July sixth had brought the attack. On the seventh, Pearl Bright and Albert Yu had left to brief their associates. Nissa, Brenda, and Riprap had turned to their studies with the avidity of the truly terrified.

That was where the three apprentices were now, closeted with Waking Lizard, who was attempting to explain the complexities of focusing one's ch'i under less than ideal circumstances.

Yes. Honey Dream wanted to believe Flying Claw's explanation, but she didn't. She thought Flying Claw's willingness to babysit arose from a hope that at some point Lani would insist on seeing her mother, and then he would have an excuse to see that horrible Ratling, Brenda Morris.

Brenda Morris. That woman—girl, really, for all she was only a few years younger than Honey Dream herself—was an enigma, a horrible puzzle. There was ample evidence that Brenda had done things she should not have been able to do. Brenda's ability to work magic wasn't the puzzle—even in the Lands, there were hedge wizards and wise women, minor sorcerers of all sorts. The same appeared to be true here in the Land of the Burning.

Very well. That Brenda Morris might have some native magical talent unconnected to the Branches, Honey Dream could accept. What plagued Honey Dream was the mystery of how Brenda had managed to manifest even a very little Rat.

Flying Claw had told them about this occurrence the morning after Honey Dream had rescued him from his foul captivity.

"There is something I must tell you about," he had said, his voice tight with urgency, "something that occurred on the night I went to gather the Rat from Gaheris Morris."

Flying Claw had paused, and they had indicated that they remembered, although this event was not something either Honey Dream or her father was likely to have forgotten.

That night had been the beginning of the end of all their plans, if they had but known the truth at the time.

Flying Claw went on. "I had expected Gaheris to be able to see me. We have never had a great deal of success in shielding ourselves from others who are affiliated with one of the Earthly Branches. I was startled when the man with Gaheris also saw me—I had not yet scouted the Dog—but I felt the Dog's paw on him and immediately knew why. But Brenda saw me as well, clearly enough that she attempted to distract me."

Did Flying Claw look a little embarrassed when he said that last? Honey Dream wondered. What had the tart done? Pulled down her blouse or tried to kiss him? Just the thought of it made her burn with contained fury.

"In the hours since my memory returned to me," Flying Claw had said, "I've puzzled over why Brenda should have been able to see me. Then I recalled something I overheard, the day after Pearl's house was brought to the attention of the Three-Legged Toad. I heard Des and Pearl discussing quite excitedly how Brenda had manifested what they called 'a little rat.'

"Apparently, this is as unheard of for them as it would be for us. That ability seems to grant Brenda powers like, but not like, those of an Earthly Branch."

What plagued Honey Dream even more than that Brenda Morris should be in the least ways anomalous was that the anomaly didn't seem to bother anyone else. Honey Dream had tried to bring the matter up with her father over the days they worked out the details of the treaty of alliance.

Righteous Drum had dismissed the matter with a careless wave of his hand. "No doubt there was a flaw in the spell that Flying Claw used to entrap Gaheris Morris. Perhaps a signal was sent that gave the Rat the momentary thought that he was dead. At that instant the most minor fragment of Ratness could have slid from Gaheris to his daughter."

Honey Dream didn't like that explanation. None of the

other capture spells had malfunctioned in that way. Why should this one have done so? She knew her father suspected that Flying Claw had been lax in some way. Righteous Drum did not especially care for Flying Claw—surely a father's petty jealousy, for until Flying Claw had entered their circle of associates, Honey Dream had honored no man other than her father.

When Righteous Drum had refused to take her warnings seriously, Honey Dream had tried to talk to Waking Lizard. That annoying old man had only laughed and waggled his beard at her.

"Envious, Snake of my heart? Beware strong emotions. They cloud the judgment."

When she had protested that there was nothing in Brenda Morris for Honey Dream to envy, Waking Lizard had laughed even harder.

Honey Dream had turned on her heel and stalked away. After all, why should she care about a cowardly Monkey's opinion? Waking Lizard only knew Brenda Morris as one of those who had saved him when he had fled to this world and collapsed covered in cuts and bruises. No doubt gratitude clouded his judgment—so who was *he* to talk about taking care to guard against strong emotions?

Honey Dream hadn't tried to discuss the matter with Flying Claw. He still hadn't forgiven her for expecting him to accede to her plan to retake the Rat's memory from Brenda Morris. He seemed to feel it was a slight on his honor.

Demons take his honor! What sort of honor could a babysitter claim?

Abandoned by her allies, her wisdom eschewed—even though the Snake was only second to the Dragon in offering wise counsel—Honey Dream resolved that she would solve the Brenda Morris puzzle herself.

She liked the idea. Once she'd shown that Brenda Morris was in some way corrupt, the girl would be sent away.

Yes. Honey Dream smiled softly to herself. Let the others

fuss over history. She would act as a Snake should and set her powers to root out that nasty sneaking little Ratling.

"Honey Dream!" Righteous Drum snapped.

Honey Dream realized with a quickly hidden blush that he had spoke to her at least twice.

"I'm sorry, Father," she said meekly. "My thoughts wandered."

"No doubt. Attend, would you? These matters apply to you as well. We were speaking of the obstacles that face our return."

"Crossing the guardian domains?" Honey Dream said, dredging up a fragment of partially heard conversation.

Des gave Honey Dream a sympathetic smile that burned, if possible, more harshly than had her father's reprimand.

"That's right," Des said, "those regions that enable us to touch—although there must be a better word than 'touch'—various planes of existence."

Honey Dream knew why Des had clarified. His command of the form of Chinese spoken in the Lands was good, but far from perfect. Equally, translation spells were fine for simpler ideas, but often bungled theoretical concerns.

Righteous Drum nodded. "The footings of the bridge we used to get here were not only in the Lands and here, but between, in those interstitial areas."

"How did you manage that?" Des asked.

"Essentially, we contracted with denizens of those areas and employed them to set our footings. The last footing—the one that was wholly in this world—was the most difficult, but we managed to create it by invoking a dragon who belonged to this world as well as to one of the interstitial zones."

"So if we choose to use a bridge to return, we'll need to do the same in reverse?" Des asked.

Flying Claw shook his head. "It will not be that simple, for now the four of us are barred from the Lands as surely as your ancestors—and by extension yourselves—are. Creatures like that dragon would not make pacts with us."

He motioned toward the stump of his missing arm. "Nor do I have the power to compel them as once I might have done. It will be a long time—years, perhaps—before I can cast spells as effectively."

Des frowned. "I don't understand. Why wouldn't we able to make it work? It seems to me the situation is a simple reverse."

"A reverse, yes," Righteous Drum agreed, "but not simple. We did not belong to your world, but we could claim—through the Earthly Branches that had been removed from the Lands—a kinship with this place. It was that kinship that persuaded the dragon to aid us—that, and many other things too complex to bring up at this moment."

"I suppose," Des pressed, "we could claim the same type of kinship to the Lands, more strongly even, since you four were born there and the rest of us have ancestral claims."

Righteous Drum shook his head, sorrow on every line of his dignified features. "I wish that were so, but we cannot eliminate the fact that your ancestors were exiled—barred, banished—by simply choosing to ignore it. Not only were your ancestors exiled, they were exiled with their own concurrence. That makes the severance even stronger. We did not agree to our exile in the same fashion, but we have been barred nonetheless."

"You have checked?"

"We have," Righteous Drum said.

His tone was level, holding nothing of the fury and despair Honey Dream recalled from that horrible day, the one immediately following Waking Lizard's arrival with the news that their allies had been defeated, the day they had tried to connect to the Lands and failed.

"Still," Des said, his tone almost pleading, "surely since you did not agree to be exiled, you could provide the final footing for the bridge. Isn't that possible?"

"Perhaps," Righteous Drum agreed, but he looked as if

he was tasting something very sour, "but highly unlikely. Our enemies in the Lands will have taken actions to prevent that very thing. We might fight our way to the very borders of the Lands only to find ourselves blocked. This is one reason why seeking to establish the Nine Gates, rather than constructing another bridge, might be a better course of action."

Honey Dream was astonished to hear her father's normally resonant tones drop, so that he sounded as if he were making a confession. "Remember, Honey Dream and I have left family behind in the Lands. I have living wives, children. She has sisters and brothers. Waking Lizard has outlived his wives and children, but he has relatives and friends."

"So does Flying Claw," Honey Dream said, hearing the defiance in her own tone and moderating it. "And since our enemies have apparently risen to power, we must fear for those we have left behind. At best they could be held as hostages against our good behavior. I don't want to think about the worst."

Des Lee nodded, and Honey Dream remembered that although he was divorced from his wife, he had children about her own age.

"I understand your urgent desire to return home, but since we've eliminated the amulets we captured from the prisoners, and the option of building a bridge seems less and less possible, then we are left with the Nine Gates."

Des took in a deep breath. "And making those is going to be more difficult than you might imagine."

"Why?" Righteous Drum said. "Albert Yu spoke as if the creation of these gates was among the lore your ancestors had preserved."

Des shook his head, not in disagreement, but indicating that he could not speak further.

"Wait until the others return. Shen Kung is our Dragon, and our greatest authority on the odd variation of magic we inherited. Pearl may be a Tiger, but she is far more magically sophisticated than she often leads one to believe. And

Albert . . . Well, the Cat has always been a little outside of the usual."

There was that in his tone that made his polite refusal quite final, and Righteous Drum did not press. The discussion turned to purely theoretical matters.

Fine, Honey Dream thought. *Then while you discuss theory, my father, I shall pursue fact. I shall do my best to learn what it is that Brenda Morris is hiding from us—and if I can, transform it into our own best advantage.*

☆

Having been severely injured only a week before, and still suffering from ch'i depletion, didn't permit Waking Lizard to lecture for nearly as long as Brenda had expected.

Nissa caught the signs that the old man was fading well before he did himself harm, and insisted that he go lie down.

"There are plenty of bedrooms," she said firmly. "The ones on this floor are all occupied, but Flying Claw's former room is empty—the one he used when he was Foster."

Riprap nodded. "I'll take you up," he said. "Don't worry. We won't waste our time. Des gave us homework."

Waking Lizard's unwillingness to argue told Brenda how tired the man must be, for even on a week's acquaintance she had seen that when rested the Monkey was as energetic as his namesake.

While Riprap settled Waking Lizard, and Nissa hurried out to the garden to check on Lani, Brenda went across the hallway to her room.

The second floor of Pearl's house was divided by the stairwell into two suites, each consisting of two bedrooms connected by a common bath. The open space at the front of the house had been converted into a comfortable sitting area. At the back was a door that led to the stairwell to the third floor of the house. This was where Des and Riprap had their rooms—and where Foster had stayed when he had lived with them.

Brenda, Nissa, and Lani occupied the suite to the right of

the stairwell (if one faced the front of the house), while Pearl had the front room of the other suite. Soon after their arrival, the other room in Pearl's suite had been converted into a cross between a classroom and an artist's studio. Like any classroom, it had a blackboard, but it also had a whiteboard. The other furnishings belonged as much to the realm of art as to that of pedagogy.

A long, wide table of scuffed mahogany was the dominant piece of furniture. Stacked in its center were four oblong boxes covered in the type of black vinyl that is supposed to resemble leather but never really does.

Grouped around the table were a half-dozen comfortable chairs. A bookshelf on the back wall held a variety of books, mostly dealing with various aspects of Chinese art, calligraphy, and culture. Other shelves held a half-dozen or so large boxes of white polymer clay, a selection of rectangular molds, bottles of ink in black, red, and green, a jar of fine-tipped brushes, and assorted modeling tools. A smaller table, set near a window, held a large toaster oven.

The room's ample natural light was augmented by an electrical fixture overhead. Small lamps were arrayed on the top of the bookshelf, mutely testifying that the work done here demanded fine attention to detail.

But on this sunny summer afternoon, Brenda felt no need for an extra light. Riprap was already settled in his accustomed chair. He had an open box of polymer clay in front of him and was vigorously kneading the clay to make it pliable. Nissa had her notebook open and was checking a list.

Today's lesson, Des had told them, would be choosing one of the more elaborate spells and encoding it into an amulet bracelet. Making such bracelets had been one of the first lessons they had learned, but the more complex patterns remained time-consuming and demanding—and they were none of them ready to cast more complex spells without physical tools.

"I'm kneading enough clay for all of us to get started,"

Riprap said. "Want to grab some molds and dust them with cornstarch?"

Brenda did so, preparing enough that each of them could make a complete set of fourteen tiles. She also took down the jar of modeling tools. The incising tools were the most important, but there were tools that made smoothing the clay easier. Then, too, the same tool that fit her hand comfortably vanished into Riprap's big mitt. Better to let each pick out what worked best.

In any case, the tools weren't what mattered, rather the end result—and the one who did the crafting.

When the Thirteen Orphans had been exiled from the Lands Born from Smoke and Sacrifice, they had faced an almost insurmountable challenge. Each of the twelve adults was a skilled adept in a peculiar form of magic. However, in their new environment, they lacked anything but their essential knowledge. How could they preserve what they knew?

A new insight interrupted Brenda's review of this now-familiar tale.

"Hey! I just had a thought."

Nissa looked up from her notebook. Riprap gave her an encouraging nod, his hands still busy working the clay. Neither teased her as her brothers would certainly have done, remarking that this must be a landmark day because "Breni had a thought!"

Fleetingly, Brenda missed her family, her friends, the relatively normal life she'd left behind in South Carolina. She shoved the emptiness away, letting enthusiasm take its place.

"Remember how Des and Pearl told us the Twelve wanted to find a way to encode their magic so it would be preserved, but so at the same time they wouldn't be tied to any particular book or staff or whatever?"

The other two nodded. Riprap inclined his head toward the oblong boxes in the center of the table as he spoke.

"They encountered mah-jong. It was already around, although a relatively new game, played as often with cards as with tiles. Its five suits, three standard, two of honors—as well as the flower and season tiles—offered a wealth of possible symbolic significance. So they decided to create a sort of mnemonic tied to the mah-jong tiles in which they could record their knowledge."

"A book," Nissa added, "that couldn't be taken from them because it was being mass-produced all over. Des hinted that some of the Orphans had something to do with the trend away from using cards to tiles for mah-jong, that they were looking to make sure the symbols would be preserved in a more permanent form."

Brenda had let their words wash over her while she let her insight take firmer form. She realized she was bouncing lightly on her toes with barely contained excitement.

"That's right. But I bet I know why the Twelve were so eager to encode their lore—and why Pearl and Des are so wiggy about our writing things down."

The other two looked at her, their expressions showing they were a step behind, but only that. Brenda hastened to articulate her revelation.

"It must have to do with these other magical traditions— the indigenous ones that Des mentioned earlier. I bet the Twelve didn't want to write anything down in a form that could be stolen, so they did this instead."

Nissa put her hand over the open page of her notebook as if suddenly fearing a spy could read what was written there.

"I think you're right, Breni. We know that the various spells take a lot of concentration. Probably back in the Lands when they wanted to do some complex working, they had tomes they could use as an aid to memory. They probably planned to reproduce those tomes as soon as they were settled here, then realized how easily their knowledge—the one really unique thing they had in their favor—could be stolen."

"And how vulnerable they would be," Riprap said, "if someone stole their tricks. Wow. Byzantine."

"Chinese," Brenda corrected with a grin. "Which, the more I learn about their history and philosophy, the more I believe means thinking in a fashion more twisted and convoluted than those Eastern Europeans ever could imagine."

"So the Twelve did write their magic book," Nissa said, "but not only did they write it from memory, they wrote it in code. I wonder . . ."

She trailed off, her hands stilling, her expression growing serious, her turquoise eyes widening a little in fright.

"What?" Brenda prompted.

"I wonder how much they forgot," Nissa said slowly. "How much they left out because they couldn't remember all the details or find a way to fit them into the mah-jong code." Nissa shivered, and suddenly got very businesslike. "I wonder how much more the people from the Lands know, and how much more they've invented in the past century."

Riprap started tearing the white clay into three roughly equal segments.

"A century," he said, reaching for the tool jar, "during which they've been busily at war while our ancestors were forgetting almost everything they ever knew."

Brenda slid into her accustomed seat. "Why don't we each do a set of the Twins?" she suggested. "They're about the most powerful and yet versatile spell any of us knows, and right now I'd feel a lot better if we replenished our armies."

The Twins to which Brenda referred were a triplet of associated spells. Like all the spells they had learned from Des and Pearl, the names came from mah-jong limit hands. Brenda wasn't quite sure whether the spells had given the limit hands their names or the other way around. It didn't really matter—or maybe it did, because when the spells manifested they often resembled their names.

The Twins were, respectively, the Twins of Heaven, of Earth, and of Hell. The spells were rendered as a series of figures corresponding to those found in a mah-jong hand: fourteen in all. Not surprisingly, given the name of the hands, they consisted of pairs, but not of the same pairs.

"Who wants which?" Brenda asked.

Riprap opened one of the boxes of mah-jong tiles and spilled them onto the table. These were all modern sets, the tiles cast in plastic. Traditional sets were made from bamboo and ivory—or bamboo and bone.

Each of the Thirteen Orphans had a family set, handmade, each slightly different from the others. These antique sets were surprisingly durable, the bamboo and bone worn smooth from the caress of many fingertips. Brenda had the Rat family set in her bedroom. Sometimes she opened the box and shuffled the tiles around on the small desk that sat in front of the window in her room. They moved easily, and occasionally she would find herself drifting into a wakeful sleepiness, a wonderful receptivity, but nothing ever came to fill that space that couldn't be explained as the waking dreams of an overtired mind.

And certainly they'd been kept busy enough lately what with lessons and meetings and a house full of people to be kept fed and clothed. Pearl had both a maid and a gardener who came in a few days a week, but as the Orphans' business required a certain degree of privacy, everyone else pitched in to do laundry, prepare meals, and run errands.

Brenda broke from her revery as Riprap snapped three tiles—one printed with black, one with green, one with red—down onto the table. "Pick," he suggested, shuffling them. "Red is Hell. Black can be Earth. Green Heaven."

Nissa darted out her hand. "Green. Heaven. Let's see. That's the one that depends on honors pairs or terminals. Doesn't leave me too many choices."

Brenda pulled one of the remaining tiles. "Black. Okay. I get Earth. I never can remember . . . When I'm making pairs, can I have more than one set of a number? There are four of each tile."

Des's voice came from where he'd quietly opened the door, his entry covered by the sound of the mah-jong tiles clattering against the table.

"You could," he said, "but only if you're looking to invoke

the symbolic strength of a particular number. Since we haven't gotten to that aspect in much detail, why not spread out the numbers?"

Des hadn't really meant the last as a question, but Brenda couldn't resist a flippant answer.

"Because it's easier to inscribe ones and twos than it is to do eights?"

"Do 'em," Des said in his teacher voice. "You need the practice. In fact, in your case you might want to concentrate on the characters suit. It remains your weakest."

"Because," Brenda muttered, not really disagreeing, "it's so much harder to draw those Chinese numbers than it is dots or bamboo."

"Not when you practice," Des said. "Nissa, you're going to do the Twins of Heaven. You might consider crafting your terminals as dots since they can be imagined as resembling the heavenly bodies."

Like the Moon, Brenda remembered with a shiver.

"Riprap," Des went on, "Hell works better when everything is a little chaotic."

"And no honors or terminals," Riprap agreed. "Pity. I like doing those. They're hard, but somehow satisfying."

Des grinned. "Don't try and show up Brenda, Riprap. She's not really lazy. She's a Rat and knows the value in being underestimated. Look, I didn't come up here to chivy you. Righteous Drum and I are taking a break from discussing history, bridges, and gates."

He turned to go, then stopped. "Nissa, I hope you don't mind, but Flying Claw took Lani over to the Rosicrucian Museum gardens."

"Not at all," Nissa said. "She's safe there with him, and when I checked on her a few minutes ago, I thought that even with Flying Claw in tow, she was probably keeping Wong from getting anything done in the gardens this morning."

"Probably," Des said with a smile that meant "definitely." "Now, remember, concentrate. Don't race and—Riprap, Brenda—no getting competitive."

They promised, Brenda all the more easily because Des had called her a Rat. She wasn't really. The Rat was her dad, but for a little while, when her dad's memory had been stolen, she'd been the best Rat they'd had. She hadn't quite gotten over suddenly not having a place.

Maybe, she thought as she packed the first bit of polymer clay into a rectangular mold, smoothing the exposed surface so her finished tile would be perfect, *I wouldn't mind so much if there were other heirs apparent here—like there would have been in Shen Kung's school—but here where everyone is formally affiliated, it's hard to be the only trainee.*

Brenda banished those thoughts from her mind as she picked up her favorite inscribing tool and forced all her concentration into the "one character" she was drawing. The little eddy of ch'i trickling from her into the tile reassured her that she had achieved proper focus and concentration, and of something else.

She might not be the Rat, but she certainly wasn't nothing either.

V

Pearl woke in the guest room of Shen's house and was pleased to find herself feeling rested. That wasn't always the case these days. A shift in time zone, a long day's travel, could wear her out. But today she felt good, strong, even happy.

She could hear Shen and Umeko moving around, but didn't go out to say good morning. A shower first, then makeup and clothes. Image was important, not only to herself, but to others. Pearl had learned that when as hardly more than a toddler she'd gotten her first role dancing and singing in a local musical.

When she was dressed, Pearl went out and found her hosts in the kitchen. The money Shen had inherited from his grandfather had assured that even with New York's escalating prices, they could own a house rather than rent an apartment. They lived in a part of Queens that had once had an active Chinatown, and still had shops that sold a wide variety of "Oriental" foods and goods.

It was a pleasant area, but after San Jose's more moderate temperatures, Pearl could feel the difference in the heat and humidity that crept past the air-conditioning.

"Good morning, Ming-Ming," Shen said, setting aside his newspaper. "Have you eaten?"

The traditional Chinese greeting, even spoken as it was this morning in English, was familiar and heartwarming.

"Even after last night's wonderful dinner," she replied, "I could eat."

"Tea?" Umeko asked. "Or coffee? We have both."

"Tea," Pearl said.

Her hosts were in bathrobes, their casualness a welcome in itself. Pearl settled into one of the chairs around the kitchen table and accepted the fragrant green tea gratefully.

"How did your class go last night?" she asked.

"Fairly well," Umeko said, placing an assortment of ready-prepared breakfast foods on the table, then shaking cereal into a bowl for herself. "There's one young woman I think has real vision—if only she'd trust herself enough to let it out."

They talked in this fashion for a while. All of them were old enough and secure enough in their professions to have done at least some teaching, whether formally or not. After the meal was ended and they had all assisted in the clearing up, Umeko announced she was heading up to her studio.

"The morning light doesn't last long this time of year. I want to take advantage of it."

Pearl suspected she was politely making herself scarce. It was kind of Umeko, but she really must assure Shen that she didn't mind.

When they withdrew to his study, she raised the subject.

"Oddly," Shen said with a sad smile, "it's not so much that Umeko thinks you would mind, as that for the first time since I confided our family's odd history to her, Umeko is uncomfortable with it—even resents it."

"Because of what was done to you?"

Shen looked very uncomfortable. "Umeko has told me that when my memory was stolen, my personality altered—so much so that she and Geoffrey feared that I might have had a stroke."

Staring down at his gnarled hands with the same embarrassment that Pearl remembered from when he had been forced to admit some boyhood transgression, Shen went on.

"For the first time since Umeko and I married, I felt like an old man—felt the difference in our ages. I was forced to admit that I might subject my wife and son to caring for some drooling, senile idiot. That the truth is that someone had the gall to steal my memories—only making me *seem* on the verge of senility rather than actually being there—does not make the situation easier to forgive."

"For either of you," Pearl said softly, understanding Umeko's reaction perfectly. "Or for Geoffrey. I'm sorry, Shen."

He straightened, and managed a twisted grin. "The phone call that came earlier this morning didn't help Umeko's state of mind either."

"Phone call? Is something wrong in San Jose? Has something happened to someone?"

Shen raised a hand to reassure her. "No. The call was local. We have been requested to attend a meeting of the Rock Dove Society today."

"That's hardly unexpected," Pearl said, "but they've certainly moved quickly."

"I believe your arrival in New York was noted," Shen said. "In any case, the East Coast organizations have always been more aggressive than those on the West Coast."

Pearl knew the Rock Dove Society all too well. Publicly, they were an association of bird-watchers. They hosted weekly talks and slide shows, even the occasional lecture series in conjunction with eminently respectable zoological and ornithological organizations.

Privately, the Rock Dove Society served as a cover under which representatives of the various indigenous magical traditions could meet and discuss matters related to the Art—and the very human politics that arose when traditions conflicted.

"The Rock Dove Society is having their public meeting at the Enid A. Haupt Conservatory of the New York Botanical Garden in the Bronx," Shen went on. "Then they are moving on to one of their usual places."

"Usual" in this case meant secured against intrusion, magical and mundane. A public garden might seem an odd place to hold a private meeting, but hiding in plain sight was a lesson of which more than one covert society had learned the benefits—and the Rock Dove Society, under a variety of names and guises, was older than most.

"But the meeting isn't until this afternoon," Shen said. "I had the impression last night that you had more that you wanted to discuss."

Pearl nodded. "Trust. I have never trusted easily, and this situation is demanding more than I find myself capable of giving. For example, right now I have five people living in my house—one of whom I hadn't even met before this spring. I knew Nissa and Brenda, but in a very different context. Des is the only one who I would have called a friend. Then I've had to open my house to four people—three of whom I would have called enemies until a few weeks ago."

"From what you have told me, the four from the Lands fought very fiercely when you were all attacked a few days ago," Shen said mildly.

"I know, I know . . ." Pearl waved one hand through the air in a gesture of dismissal. "The point is, all these people now have free run of my house. I think only Des suspects how many wards I put in place before I left."

"And I remember," Shen said with a chuckle, "how many

there were twenty years ago. You're right. You've never been a very trusting Tiger. Do you think there is reason beyond your natural inclinations to be less so now?"

"There is the matter of whoever informed on us," Pearl said. "We know for certain that someone—one of the Thirteen—was advising Righteous Drum. I suspected this was so from how well Righteous Drum and his allies navigated our world, how efficiently they located their targets. Later, Righteous Drum as much as confirmed that such a person existed."

"And?" Shen leaned slightly forward.

"And he asked leave not to reveal who their informant had been," Pearl said. "He swore that the reasons that person had cooperated were no longer valid, and said that since we needed all our number intact, such a revelation would be unwise. His reasoning seemed sound at the time, but now . . ."

"Now the Tiger is even less at ease than she was before," Shen said. "She sees a potential enemy even among those she should view as friends."

Pearl felt her cheeks suddenly heat with embarrassment. Shen had made his last statement with the oddest of inflections coloring his words, a slow trailing off that invited speculation.

"Shen! I don't mean you . . . Surely it couldn't have been you."

Shen gave her a very dry half smile. "For their informant to have been of any use to them, he or she must have had knowledge of the Thirteen. That rather narrows down who they could use. Who knows of all Thirteen?"

The question was rhetorical, but Pearl felt duty-bound to answer. "Myself, Albert, Gaheris, Des, yourself, Deborah."

"And of those six, we can rule out you, Pearl, since you seem to have been untouched. Des appears to also have been later on their list. Albert was attacked on the very day he was to have begun Brenda Morris's training. Gaheris was attacked a few days thereafter. This argues that the informant was either myself or Deborah."

"I can't believe it was you," Pearl said.

"But," Shen said relentlessly, "it is hard to believe that it could have been our sweet, maternal, yet unremittingly fierce Deborah either. And so we return to your matter of trust."

Silence dominated, a very uncomfortable, unhappy silence. At last Pearl took a deep breath.

"There are a couple other possibilities," she said, "although they are hardly preferable. Both you and Deborah have taken care to train your heirs apparent very carefully. They also know about the Thirteen and their locations."

"True," Shen said. "But from what you told me, the strongest control Righteous Drum and his allies could assert would be through the use of the affiliation each of the Thirteen has with one of the Earthly Branches."

"Yes," Pearl agreed.

"So they would have a harder time with either my son or Deborah's daughter."

"Or easier," Pearl protested. "There are ways of influencing those who have magical gifts without touching Earthly Branches."

"True." Shen relaxed a little. "I tend to forget that, especially since, given the pact our ancestors made with the indigenous powers of this world, we rarely use such magics."

Pearl nodded. "Righteous Drum said the informant should remain unnamed. When we start talking like this, I understand why. I sometimes forget that Righteous Drum has lived seeped in intrigue, probably since he was Flying Claw's age or even younger. Maybe he's right. Maybe we're better off not knowing."

"I want to agree, and yet my mind turns in circles," Shen admitted. "Is it better to know and have doubt ended—but to forever feel less trust? Is Righteous Drum attempting to do us—and his former tool—a favor or is he attempting to divide us from within?"

"And divide and conquer," Pearl said, "is a very, very old tactical principle."

"And two of us, at least," Shen said softly, "will be divided from within. Not to know if one was a tool for betrayal is very hard."

Pearl reached out and squeezed his hand. "Shen, even if it was you, you weren't ever a traitor. What is that saying, 'Guns don't kill people, people kill people'? It's the same sort of thing. Even if you were used—and I cannot imagine anyone could use you—you did not agree willingly."

"Then you trust me?"

"I do," she said. "With all my heart."

But that heart whispered traitorously in itself: *Shen is the Dragon. Righteous Drum is also the Dragon. Could Righteous Drum have employed this sympathy in their natures to use Shen? Worse. Could he do it again?*

Pearl kept those thoughts from her eyes and released Shen's hand, leaning back in her chair with affected ease that came naturally after so many years as an actress.

"I am also very worried about how far we can trust the members of the Rock Dove Society," she said, "and those they represent. My associates among the Rosicrucians have indicated that their association is willing to let us deal with our own problems. Will the others feel the same? Will they honor that century-old treaty they made with our ancestors?"

"The treaty that said the Exiles could remain as long as they didn't cause any trouble?" Shen said. "I hope so. We did not invite this trouble. Still, there is one way to find out, and we will not by sitting here. Shall we go to a meeting?"

Pearl rose. "I'd like to get there early enough to hear the lecture—and get a look at the audience—before some of them take it upon themselves to become our judges."

☆

"Pearl called earlier," Des said, when the household assembled for breakfast, "while you were running, Riprap, and you were in the shower, Brenda. She wanted us to know that she and Shen have been contacted by the indigenous traditions."

Riprap looked up from putting a layer of apricot jam on his toast. "We expected that, didn't we? But why in New York?"

"The Rock Dove Society," Des said, "is the current name for one of the older mixed-tradition societies."

Brenda felt a charge go through her that had nothing to do with the caffeine in her coffee.

"Will Pearl be all right?"

Des smiled reassuringly. "Better ask if the Rock Doves will be all right. Sure. Pearl will deal with them just fine."

But as Brenda ate her breakfast—she was actually coming to like rice congee and pickled vegetables; it wasn't that far from grits except the toppings were spicy rather than sweet and oily—Brenda thought that Des looked worried.

"Riprap, will you drive over to Colm Lodge and pick up Waking Lizard and Righteous Drum?" Des asked. "Waking Lizard is going to continue teaching you. I'm going to get Righteous Drum to tell me more about the guardian domains, since we're going to need to cross them to get to the Lands."

Brenda really wanted to ask what Honey Dream and Flying Claw were going to be doing, but didn't dare. Nissa did, however.

"Physical training," Des said, completely deadpan. "Seriously. Both have lost a lot of tone, and with Righteous Drum out of action, we're going to need them in perfect shape."

"Do the rest of us get to do more than jog?" Riprap asked.

"Absolutely," Des said. "We're going to resume training as soon as Pearl and Albert are back—one or two days at most—and I'm sure that Flying Claw would be happy to work out with you if you have the energy after your lessons are done."

"So they'll be by later?" Nissa said. "Good. Lani's going to be asking after her buddy."

Brenda felt relieved that the morning was starting with a lecture. Between envisioning Pearl embattled by mysterious Rock Doves—her mind's eye dressed them in hooded, cowled robes wearing bird's-heads masks, even though she knew that was ridiculous—and Flying Claw wrestling with Honey Dream, she would have botched any spell she attempted.

She answered the door when Riprap dropped his passengers off, and found Righteous Drum in front. He had adopted local clothing styles in place of the ornate, multilayered attire of his homeland long before they had met him. But, even after Des had taken him shopping and shown him all the options available to a modern man in California, Righteous Drum had refused to lower his dignity and wear shorts, favoring instead neatly pressed trousers and a short-sleeved button-down shirt. However, despite his interest in personal dignity, Righteous Drum saw nothing in the least strange about a man in his fifties choosing all his clothing in varying hues of yellow. Even his trousers were a sort of bright khaki, his shoes a very pale tan.

Brenda knew that yellow was the Dragon's color, but she thought that Righteous Drum carried this proclamation of his affiliation a bit too far. With his somewhat dumpy figure and short, unimaginative haircut, she thought Righteous Drum looked like Chairman Mao costumed as a dandelion.

Righteous Dream half bowed to Brenda as he passed over the threshold, but Waking Lizard shared none of Righteous Drum's concern for dignity. He was evidently feeling a lot more energetic today, and had dressed to express this.

After the shopping expedition, Des had reported that Waking Lizard had been delighted with modern clothing, especially the more casual styles. Unlike Righteous Drum, Waking Lizard appreciated shorts, especially the baggy styles favored by skateboarders and surfers. The pair he wore today were bright blue, embellished with waves. His loose sports shirt was of a roughly matching shade of blue, embellished with pink and yellow hibiscus flowers. He wore thong sandals in bright pink.

The outfit might have looked great on a teenaged boy,

especially one with thick, shoulder-length, curling golden-blond hair, but on a man in his eighties, one whose long, monkeylike legs and arms were accented by knobby knees and elbows, the effect was not so much eye-catching as eye-straining.

Unlike Righteous Drum, who had shaven his beard and mustache before leaving the Lands Born from Smoke and Sacrifice in order to better blend in, Waking Lizard had come through in a rush. Now that he was here, he perceived no need for concealment. Therefore, he continued to wear his white hair and beard both trimmed after the fashion usually seen in pictures of Confucius, long and sort of pointed at the ends.

Brenda blinked and felt certain the glaring colors left an afterimage on her retina, but she waved Waking Lizard in over the threshold, even remembering to offer a polite bow.

The morning passed quickly, and after lunch Des sent his three apprentices up to work on tiles.

"From what I'm hearing about the guardian domains, not to mention the Lands themselves, we can't have too many amulets."

Brenda looked to see if he was joking and decided he wasn't.

A high, shrill keening interrupted their conversation, carrying even through the closed door. It resolved into words.

"No! No! No! No nap! Wanna play w' Foster!"

"Tough," Nissa said distinctly. "I told you you are not to open the front door. I think you need some quiet time."

The howl rose into inarticulate fury, then muted somewhat as the door to the bedroom Nissa shared with Lani closed behind mother and daughter.

"Wow," Brenda said. "Who ever thought a rabbit could have so much passion?"

She and Riprap grinned at each other. While he kneaded the clay, Brenda set out the other tools. Nissa joined them as they were about ready.

"Overtired. Overstimulated. Sometimes I think I should

ship her back to my sisters in Virginia, but I have this gut feeling it's important that Lani not be isolated from events."

"Is Lani going to sleep?" Riprap asked. "She sounded right worked up."

"She was out before I finished the story of the Bunny and the Golden Shoes, and that's her favorite right now. She really was overtired, and I think she has a crush on Foster."

Nissa gave Brenda a sly look. "Not that she's unique in that."

Brenda, who had had more than one sisterly chat with Nissa on the subject—having no sisters of her own, she was finding Nissa's automatic assumption of female camaraderie novel and pleasant—stuck out her tongue at Nissa.

Riprap rolled his eyes. "Okay, partners. Yesterday, we did some pretty tough spells, and I for one can still feel it. Shall we do something more routine today?"

"Definitely," Nissa said. "I was considering a nice new Dragon's Tail sized for Lani."

"Wriggly Snake here," Riprap said.

"I, for one," Brenda said, "want nothing to do with snakes. I was thinking about a Knitting. Waking Lizard's lecture reminded me how useful it is to be able to combine our abilities, but we're not always going to have peace and quiet in which to compose our minds."

Like the peace and quiet of a battlefield when the battle's over, she thought, remembering when she'd last done the Knitting for Pearl.

They discussed briefly what combination of tiles would be most effective. Although Riprap argued that Brenda should again practice her characters, Brenda countered that she didn't want to forget how the dots and bamboo were arrayed. Riprap sighed and gave in.

For a long while, the classroom was silent. Focusing on the designs, Brenda inscribed one bamboo, one dot, then two bamboo and two dots. At first she was peripherally aware of the others working at other parts of the table, the faint clatter as they reached for a tool or pinched off a bit of soft clay and packed it into a mold. Then she only heard their breathing. After a while, she was so absorbed that she didn't hear even that.

Consequently, Brenda was surprised to finish her last tile—a seven bamboo—and find the other two still absorbed in their work. Nissa was working at half scale, which explained her relative slowness with a simple spell, and Riprap's big hands made crafting tiles harder for him.

Brenda raised her head, craning back to ease a stiffness in her neck and shoulders, then reviewed her work. Each tile was a tidy match—although in her own "handwriting"—for one of the fourteen tiles she had set up for reference.

She felt the pleasant lassitude that usually accompanied the cessation of intense concentration, and thought that she could use this relative lack of desire to do anything or go anywhere to practice the routines Waking Lizard had been lecturing them about. Although some involved hand gestures meant to help with concentration, the real heart of them was mental, and she thought she could manage without disturbing the others.

She stretched again, and as she was lowering her arms, folding her hands in her lap, she heard movement from the other side of the door.

Damn. Lani's decided to end her nap early, and if she comes in here hollering for Mama, Nissa's spell might be ruined.

Carefully, making as little noise as possible, Brenda slid her chair back and moved to the door into the hallway. She opened it with equal stealth, and glanced across the hallway. To her surprise, the door to Nissa and Lani's room remained closed, but the door to her own room stood ajar.

Okay. I bet Nissa locked the door and Lani decided to leave through my room.

Brenda closed the door to the classroom and moved with quick purpose toward her open bedroom door. If she handled this right, she could catch Lani and shush her before she disturbed Nissa.

She slid the door open only wide enough for her to get in, her mouth already shaping words. Then she stopped in astonishment. The person in her room wasn't Lani.

It was Honey Dream.

VI

TWO NEW members of the public, an older man and woman, slid into chairs in the back as the meeting of the Rock Dove Society was getting under way.

Sitting side by side, they listened with perfect attentiveness to an interesting and informative lecture by a Shakespeare professor from Fordham University, the campus of which was located across the street from the Botanical Garden, about the introduction of numerous invasive bird species into the United States by a well-meaning but ecologically underinformed devotee of the Bard's plays.

If the pair didn't take notes, or if their gazes seemed to travel restlessly over the assembly, observing who was there with at least as much interest as they watched the brightly colored slides, well, newcomers to an established group are often that way.

After the lecture ended, that same older man and woman were among those who chose to skip fruit punch and cookies in order to go for an undirected tour of the patch of virgin forest that was the Botanical Garden's heart. Those two were among the first to walk up to—and then directly *into*—a large glacial boulder that was situated a few steps off the trail.

Passing through solid stone was momentarily disconcerting, but then they found themselves in a large round room that was almost prosaic—if one could ignore the fact that the lighting was indirect and appeared to come directly from the stone itself. The room also appeared to be empty.

"I remember when there was a rather lovely Eye of Horus out there," Pearl said, "painted on the rock to mark the door."

Shen chuckled dryly. "I suppose someone thought the Eye qualified as graffiti. Or maybe that it attracted a little too much attention to this spot."

"Maybe," Pearl agreed, "but I still liked it."

"So did I," came a new voice from the apparent emptiness.

Conversation halted in midbreath as a woman emerged from shadows they hadn't noticed until that moment. She appeared to be somewhere in her late forties. She was clad in neat khaki slacks, a pink polo shirt, and walking shoes.

"I am Billi Rockshaper," the woman said, extending her right hand. "One of the custodians of this particular warren. You are the first to arrive. Welcome."

No one would call Billi Rockshaper pretty or even handsome. Her nose was too strong, her upper lip too thin, her lower lip very full. Heavy, coarse, brown hair hung from a straight center part, not so much framing her face as defining it. However, her expression as she came to meet them was pleasant, giving credence to her words of welcome.

"I remember you," Pearl said, meeting the handclasp. "You ran the slide projector."

"Digital," Billi said with a laugh. "I remember when a major feature of running one of those things was fixing them when they jammed. Make yourself comfortable. The others should be along soon. They take care not to leave the meeting all at once."

"Wise," Shen said. "It might be noticed."

A few folding chairs—the expensive type with padded seats—had already been set up. Shen moved to open another, and seated himself with a slight sigh. Pearl was again reminded that although they both had aged, her role as the Tiger had encouraged her to remain far more physically fit than the sedentary Dragon.

Billi moved to continue setting up the chairs, arraying them in a crescent several rows deep. Pearl went to help her.

"How many do you expect to attend the meeting?" she asked.

"At least a dozen," Billi said, "but not more than two dozen. However, I always try and arrange for both more chairs and more refreshments than we will need. As you probably already know, this can be a touchy lot. There are always one or two eager to imagine a slight."

Pearl did not disagree, although after her experiences with Hollywood egos, those of the adepts of the magical community were hardly a challenge.

As Billi had predicted, the others began trickling in soon thereafter. Pearl had counted nineteen and no more had followed for some five minutes when a sixtyish man clad in ironed blue jeans and a red sports shirt rose to his feet. His most distinctive features were his neatly cut black hair, worn quite a bit longer than was usual for a man of his age, and a short curling black beard, both lightly touched with silver.

"Judd Madden," Shen said softly, speaking underneath the man's opening comment. "He's this year's chair. Modern Kabbalist tradition."

Pearl nodded. For all the Thirteen tended to refer to the "indigenous" as if they were one group, there were many magical forms and traditions still active in this world. Some traditions were the last remnants of cultures long vanished. Magic had proven to have a peculiar resilience that resisted time.

Judd Madden was finishing his opening comments, light words thanking those who had organized the earlier entertainment. He ended by thanking Billi and someone called Hadley for arranging the refreshments for both that meeting and this one.

The routine comments created a veneer of normalcy, but Pearl was not in the least fooled. Tension emanated from the nineteen men and women arrayed on the folding chairs, each a coiled vine from which sprung leaves and branches, a jungle of human emotion and reaction through which the Tiger must find her way.

"Today we have a visitor from California," Judd Madden went on, "as well as the pleasure of the company of a local who does not join us as often as we might wish. They are both here in response to rather special—almost unique, one might say—circumstances that arose a few weeks ago.

"These circumstances were brought to our attention by Harriet LaTour on behalf of the Rosicrucians," Judd Madden inclined his head in a gesture of thanks to a sixtyish woman clad in austere white who sat on the right-hand horn of the crescent, "and were discussed in some detail at our last meeting. In response to those discussions, Shen Kung agreed to come to this meeting, and also agreed to ask one of those more closely involved in those events to attend as well. We are pleased and honored to welcome Pearl Bright of the Thirteen Orphans."

Pearl half expected a patter of applause, for in tone and meter Judd's introduction was very like those she had heard hundreds of times before. This time the conclusion of his speech was met only with silence and a growing sense of expectancy.

This was broken at last by a large black woman wearing a full-length dashiki printed with elaborate patterns in red and bronze over khaki trousers. During the public meeting of the Rock Dove Society her close-cropped head had been bare, but now her wooly curls were covered by an elaborately folded kerchief cut from the same red and bronze fabric.

"I am Renata," she said, rising to her feet and turning to face Shen and Pearl. "I represent the West African into modern American traditions. According to what we learned at our last meeting, you folks have brought some trouble onto us . . . Or something like that, anyhow. You want to explain it yourself?"

Renata's tone was friendly enough, but there was a challenging note beneath. Pearl rose to her feet and, without being invited, crossed from the back row where she and Shen had seated themselves up to the front. She'd learned long ago about commanding an audience's attention, and knew you couldn't do nearly as well if they were concentrating on craning their necks, trying to get a clear look at you.

Shen half rose as if to join her, but Pearl shook her head.

"I was there," she said. "I can answer their questions."

Shen stayed and she sensed his relief. If he had been up front with her, he'd have to keep explaining how he didn't remember even the parts in which he must have been intimately involved.

Once up front, Pearl studied her audience without appearing to do so. At least for now, she had them. The Thirteen Orphans, true to their original vows, had always kept pretty much to themselves. Therefore, much of what she had to say about the Orphans and their history would be new.

She swallowed a sigh as she recalled how her efforts to get to know other traditions had been viewed with hostility, both by many of the indigenous traditions she tried to study and by her own people. The Rosicrucians, her neighbors to this day, had been one of the marked exceptions. Their traditions included welcoming the seeker.

Pearl couched her reply to Renata's question in a reflective, reminiscent note that would invite sympathy.

"I can see why you're worrying about our bringing trouble on you, Ms. Renata. That's pretty much the response the Thirteen Orphans have always met with. The Exiles left their homelands to preserve those homelands, only to be greeted with fear and suspicion before they had hardly done more than take a few steps on the soil of their new home.

"Then they were attacked by those who had exiled them. They bravely sought to defend not only themselves, but their new world from contamination. After the attacks ended—as we all hoped, forever—they retired to quiet lives, comporting themselves as very normal citizens.

"Today, we, the descendants of those original Thirteen Orphans, find ourselves in a strangely similar position to that of our ancestors in those early years following their initial arrival. After many decades of relative peace, we were attacked by those from the Lands Born from Smoke and Sacrifice."

Although many of the members of the Rock Dove Society must have heard some version of this already, still there was an indrawn gasp. Pearl acknowledged it with a slight inclination of her head, and went on, her tone serious.

"In response to those attacks, attacks that went to the very heart of who we are, we have done nothing but defend ourselves. Yet, here this afternoon, the present echoes the past. Shen and I find ourselves asked to justify our actions when we have done nothing other than that which the least insect would do if placed in a similar situation."

Pearl saw an uneasy stirring, marked out a few whose very lack of response showed they were listening only so that they would be permitted to object, and moved to her conclusion.

"Moreover, we have done nothing that violates the pacts made between our ancestors and your predecessors. What magics we have used were used for self-defense. Nor have we done anything that would draw the attention of the nonmagical to our magics—or to the large presence of magic that is still extant in this world."

Pearl could see Shen bending his head forward, burying his face in his hands, but she could not tell if his expression was one of dismay or amusement. Never mind. His reaction would not have changed Pearl's approach. She and her own had done nothing wrong, and she wasn't going to offer the members of the Rock Dove Society an edge by starting with apologies.

Judd Madden had taken a seat in the middle of the front row of the crescent. Now he rose and scanned those still seated.

"Are there any questions? Yes. Myron?"

A short, round-bodied man who looked as if he belonged behind the counter of the best sort of Greek diner rose to his feet.

"Hattie LaTour's report," he said, "ended by noting that

although you and yours had dealt with the immediate threat to yourselves, another threat may yet emerge. Could you speak to this point?"

Myron's words made Pearl amend her assessment of him. He sounded like the CEO of some large corporation. That didn't surprise her. Talent in matters arcane did not rule out success in other areas of life.

"You are correct, sir," Pearl said politely. "The threat may not yet be ended. Initially, three adepts came through from the Lands. Their intention, so we learned much later, was to strip from the heirs of the Thirteen Orphans affiliations that our ancestors had retained despite the Exile. They wanted these because they believed they could use them to strengthen themselves so they could win against enemies who besieged their homeland.

"About a week ago, these first three were joined by a fourth, an ally from the Lands. This fourth—one Waking Lizard— reported that the cause for which he and his three allies had fought had been lost. Their armies were disbanded—the re- maining members of their Twelve killed or captured. Two days ago, during a practice on my private lands, we were again attacked. Through a combination of magical and mar- tial arts, we were victorious."

"Yes," Judd Madden said quickly. "Faint reverberations of that conflict were detected and reported."

Pearl guessed that "And discussed ad infinitum" might be added, but Judd had no desire to open that matter again.

Instead Judd looked into the gathering and acknowledged a hand that had been waving energetically.

"Erick?"

A tall, thin Scandinavian-looking man rose, but despite his appearance, when he spoke his accent was broad New Jersey.

"Erick Swenson. Icelandic tradition. You spoke of affilia- tions. Can you explain what you mean by this term?" Erick glanced around the stone chamber with a slightly apologetic air. "Sorry. Missed the last meeting, and since we're barred from using e-mail or anything to communicate about these matters . . ."

There were a few grumbles, and Myron could be heard saying quite distinctly, "You could have contacted someone."

Pearl cut in before bickering could start. She had hoped for a chance to explain matters from her point of view. There were certain advantages to be gained by establishing the emotional slant.

"Erick, if these others do not mind . . ." She glanced around and saw various—although certainly not universal—nods of encouragement. "I will be glad to explain further."

"Please, ma'am, do," Erick said.

"The Lands Born from Smoke and Sacrifice," Pearl began, "originated in 213 B.C., when the first Ch'in emperor, Shi Huang Ti, took the advice of his minister Li Szu and attempted to wipe out all knowledge that did not support his particular political point of view.

"China's is not the only tradition in which the written word is accorded magical power independent of the meaning of whatever is being written. Norse runes and Egyptian hieroglyphs come immediately to mind. Therefore, it is unlikely that the destruction of the written texts alone was responsible for what happened. Almost certainly, what contributed to the creation of an entirely new universe was the deliberate murder of scholars—four hundred and sixty according to the scholar Ssu-ma Ch'ien—that accompanied the burning of the books. Another form of destruction that may have added ch'i—psychic energy, magical force, whatever you choose to call it—was the intellectual suicide of those who chose to accede to the Ch'in emperor's edict rather than risk their lives and secure positions."

Pearl saw someone stir restlessly, and held up a hand to forestall questions. "I am not avoiding the point. I am supplying the foundation necessary if Mr. Erick here is to understand what has happened—and why our magic is unique."

The man rose and walked over to where a coffee urn had

been set up, as if this had been his intention all along. Pearl did not believe him, but did not choose to press the point.

"Because of the creation of the Lands from this conflagration, the magical and mystical traditions of the Lands resemble in some ways those of the Chinese. This includes the recognition of Twelve Earthly Branches and the association of those branches with one of twelve animals of the Chinese zodiac.

"Within the tradition of the Twelve Earthly Branches, I am the Tiger, a place I inherited from my father, who was one of the original Thirteen. Shen Kung is the Dragon, a position he inherited from his grandfather, through his mother."

Erick was nodding, but his expression made clear that he was waiting for more details. Not seeing overmuch impatience on the faces of her small audience, Pearl went on.

"Even before the Exile, I suspect that some of our ancestors hoped that if they were exiled without being formally severed from their various affiliations, they might carry at least part of those affiliations with them. Indeed, I suspect that they took steps to assure this would be so. However, the representative of the Chinese traditions who is here with us tonight can confirm that, whatever else they might have done, the Thirteen Orphans in no way imposed upon the indigenous magical traditions of China."

A tall, straight-backed Chinese-American who was famous for expanding his father's restaurant chain into a line of canned and frozen foods sold under the name "Deng's Delights," nodded stiffly in confirmation, but offered no other support. Pearl did not expect him to do so. Shared cultural heritage had made Franklin Deng a rival, not a friend.

Pearl went on. "Erick, my understanding is that those who remained in the Lands did not—for various reasons far too complex to go into here—immediately realize that in exiling the Twelve they had exiled their own ability to tie into the full power of the Twelve Earthly Branches.

"There were theories, of course, to explain why their powers were less than they thought they should be, but those theories did not become important until the group of which Righteous Drum was one of the leaders found itself hard-pressed. They decided to come after us in an effort to reclaim exclusive affiliation with the Twelve Earthly Branches. As I mentioned before, we learned of this, resisted, and that led us to our current situation."

"And that is?" Erick asked, his expression as open and eager as that of a child hearing a good story.

Pearl was about to answer when she was interrupted by a woman who had not spoken before, a thin woman, lean as a rail and somehow as rough and splintery.

"The Orphans have invited invasion of our world by some nasty folks who probably would like to get back those Earthly Branches—which probably should have been left behind in the first place."

"Tracy!" Judd Madden objected, starting to his feet, offended by this violation of proper protocol and good manners.

The woman waved him down and kept talking. "I'm thinking this impending invasion endangers far more than the current Thirteen Orphans—I think it endangers all of us, maybe our whole world."

The words were spoken in a very nasty tone of voice, offering not the least doubt that they were intended as an attack.

From a very young age, Pearl had learned the futility of answering attack with either defense or counterattack—for those were precisely what an attacker would expect. In some cases, falling back was far more useful. In others, a sidestep that put the attacker off-balance did the trick.

The latter was the tactic she chose now.

"You are afraid of our enemies, then," Pearl said with a soft smile that defused any possible accusation that she was being insulting. "Wise. Even in my father's day, the Lands were a place of war and conflict. From what I have learned from our enemies turned allies, war and conflict remains the common situation in many, many regions."

The splintery woman—Tracy, Judd had called her—paused, evidently taken aback, as Pearl had intended her to be. Tracy looked to be in her late thirties, perhaps early forties, her demeanor weathered and rough. Her aspect was of a wholesomely muddled mixture of races—all-American, to be precise. Balked by Pearl's reply, Tracy bought herself a moment to regroup by remembering her manners.

"Tracy Frye," she introduced herself. "Generalist. If I represent anybody but myself, I guess it's my kinfolk back in the Appalachians, but they'd be the first to kick me around a hill and up a tree for setting myself up as their voice. Now, before you think me a coward, I've got reason to speak like I did.

"My great-grandsire was around when your people arrived here and he liked to tell stories. I heard 'em when I was a sprout, and my own grandpa told them after. Both of them especially liked telling how your pa and those 'Thirteen' threw everyone off balance by showing up here and revealing that there was a whole world or universe or something out there that nobody had suspected existed—a universe that was birthed by this one, but didn't belong to it.

"Grandpa was a bit of an existentialist in his way," Tracy went on, "and the idea that a world could be born from a disaster fascinated him. In the threads of Great-Grandpa's tales was something else too—the suspicion that your folks could draw on powers nobody else could touch. Didn't make folks happy, I'm guessing. Grandpa implied your folks were pretty tight with what they knew."

Pearl gave the slightest inclination of her head, a motion that could indicate agreement or merely be an encouragement for the other to continue speaking. Tracy went on.

"I'm thinking, seems those Earthly Branches have been split once, between the Lands and here. Why not split them again? Share a bit of what you've been hoarding, and we can help you fight your enemies. Fair trade, as I see it."

Shen spoke from his seat at the back of the room. "Are your own traditions not enough?"

Tracy shrugged. "Like I said, I'm a Generalist. My tradition has always been to take a little from all the traditions. We've always found that like answers like best, so when it's a West African boogie, we answer with a little voodoo. When it's a Native American spirit, we take a dance and a puff of pollen. A leprechaun answers best to Celtic song and charm. Stands that the same would be true here—and I think that Miss Bright and her friends are being pretty selfish keeping all the right sort of magics to themselves when this situation puts us all in danger."

Tracy seemed so reasonable, so folksy that had this been any other gathering Pearl would have suspected her of spinning a bit of a charm into her words, but such would have been instantly detected here. The woman wouldn't dare.

Natural charisma, Pearl thought, *and very strong indeed if she can make me listen to the idea of chopping up our powers and passing them around.*

"An interesting tactic," Pearl responded, appearing to reflect, "but one I fear will not work. You see, the original Thirteen made sure that each Earthly Branch would be bound irrevocably to one adept—and pass only to that adept's own bloodline. Believe me, if the powers could be split and passed around, my father, for one, would have done his best to make certain whatever he could take from me would have been given to my brothers. He found even the idea of a Tiger Lady abhorrent."

As Pearl had expected, most of the women and a majority of the men here gathered were clearly shocked by this. Even those who had come up in conservative traditions remained modern Americans. They felt a knee-jerk antagonism to gender prejudice—even if they practiced it themselves.

"But," Judd Madden said, "that first group of invaders—the three you spoke of earlier—they *did* manage to separate the Earthly Branch from the, uh, host. Isn't that the case?"

"They did," Pearl agreed, "and the cost was loss of memory of anything connected to the Branches. Albert Yu's personality changed so much that even someone who had never met him—a girl who had never even heard of him—was able to realize that Albert Yu must have been altered. Shen . . ."

Pearl paused. She knew she was being cruel using her friend's personal tragedy as an emotional lever, but they needed all the sympathy they could create.

Shen took his cue and spoke, his voice thin and tight. "When I was severed from the Dragon, my family thought that at best I had suffered a severe stroke, at worst that I was suffering from rapid-onset Alzheimer's. My wife and son's relief at my recovery has not quite alleviated their anxiety. Indeed, the event, brief as it was, has irrevocably scarred our family. I do not believe the Earthly Branch can be separated from its affiliated initiate without at least some damage to the initiate—nor do I believe it can be split."

Fleetingly, Pearl thought of Brenda Morris. What had happened with that girl after her father had been attacked? There had been times when Brenda had seemed a little bit the Rat, even though the Rat had been stolen from Gaheris. This was surely neither the time nor the place to mention that anomaly. It was a mystery for the Orphans alone.

Erick sprang to his feet, physically facing down Tracy, although his bright blue gaze fastened on Pearl.

"Is what Tracy's saying true? About a possible invasion? It sounds like she means something bigger than what you were talking about before, right? More than three or four people, I mean. It sounds like she's afraid of an army."

Pearl met his gaze with equal directness. "That is quite likely, Erick. The three who came a few months ago with the intention of separating the Orphans from their memories were—as I have mentioned—part of a larger group that has since been defeated. We have every reason to believe that those who may now attempt to come after the Earthly Branches will be a more powerful group, for they have won their war. Therefore, they will be able to spare more resources—and probably more adepts."

Renata, who had given Tracy a very nasty look when the Generalist had spoken so flippantly of banishing West African "boogies," turned a sympathetic face toward Pearl.

"I'll tell you because no one else seems to be doing so," she said, her tone defiant, "but there's been talk since Hattie LaTour here passed on what the Rosicrucians had learned, that the easiest solution would be to give the invaders what they want and send them off home.

"From what I'm hearing, though, it wouldn't be as tidy a solution as some were making it out to be, would it? Seems that if you lost contact with those Earthly Branches, we'd be lobotomizing you."

Pearl nodded. "Those who were attacked lost any memories connected to their lives as associated with the Earthly Branches." She let a note of steel enter her voice for the first time. "And we are not going to let it happen again."

"Even to save a world?" asked Myron in a soft voice.

"Let us fight against invasion of this world," Pearl said, "as our ancestors fought before. After all, although you may have forgotten, this has become our world, too."

VII

"What the hell are you doing in my room?" Brenda asked indignantly.

An irreverent voice in her head said, *I sound like something out of "Goldilocks and the Three Bears."*

Honey Dream swung lightly around to confront Brenda. She'd been standing near the small desk where Brenda's laptop and a few books rested. The motion brought her almost back to the doorway.

Today Honey Dream's attire was almost normal: short shorts, a tee shirt cut so that her navel (and the Snake tattoo that surrounded it) showed, and long, teardrop earrings of polished green jade. Her feet were bare, but her toenails were perfectly manicured. Brenda's feet never looked so good.

Honey Dream's long hair was caught up almost casually with a couple of polished sticks—not chopsticks, though. A while back, Brenda had made the mistake of trying to be friendly, and in complimenting Honey Dream's hairstyle had referred to the sticks as "chopsticks." She had been informed in a very frosty tone of voice that Honey Dream would never put eating utensils in her hair. These were hair ornaments.

Normal as the rest might be, the expression in Honey Dream's narrowed eyes was anything but normal. For a moment, she reminded Brenda of a snake about to strike: cold and focused. The Rat within Brenda quailed, but she forced herself not to step back, holding her position in the doorway.

This is my room, dammit.

Then Honey Dream's expression softened. Her lips curved in an embarrassed smile. She looked almost friendly.

"I needed a bathroom," she said softly. There was a embarrassed note to her voice that Brenda felt certain was affected. As far as she could tell, nothing embarrassed Honey Dream.

"There's a powder room downstairs," Brenda said. "Why come up here?"

"I thought the powder room was in use," Honey Dream said. "The door was closed. Why are you so upset?"

Because you're on my turf. Because you're snooping in my room, Brenda thought, but she knew Honey Dream would deny any such intention. *Because the door to the bathroom is nowhere near my desk. Because when I came in I think I saw your hand reaching for my computer.*

"Because Lani's taking a nap," Brenda said aloud, "and she needs her sleep."

"Ah . . . I think I heard her screaming a while back. She wanted her 'Foster.' Poor child." The curve of Honey Dream's lips seemed to accord pity to Brenda as well. "I would not wish to wake the child. I will go downstairs."

Brenda stepped out of the doorway to let her pass and watched as the other woman walked—no, undulated—down the stairs. Brenda heard the door to the powder room open and shut.

Well, she'd have to go there after what she said, wouldn't she? Doesn't prove anything.

Brenda went into the bathroom that linked her room with Nissa's and opened the door a crack, until she heard Lani's quiet breathing. Then she pulled it shut again, and reentered her own room and gave it a minute inspection. The way Honey Dream was dressed, she couldn't have hidden much on her, but it was worth checking to see if anything was gone.

As far as Brenda could tell, nothing was missing. She thought some of her things had been moved: a hairbrush, some of the loose items on her dresser, her pillow. She couldn't be sure, though. She was honest enough with herself to admit that she might be being paranoid.

When Brenda left her bedroom, she closed the door firmly behind her. She wondered if she could make a ward of some sort—not a damaging one, but one that would let her know if someone, namely, Honey Dream, was prowling.

Brenda had seen wards etched into the soft wood of doorways and along stairs. She didn't want to do anything destructive here. This was Pearl's house, after all, so she shouldn't be putting graffiti on it, but maybe she could make an amulet bracelet and hang it on the doorknob.

Later, she'd ask Des if such things were possible.

Turning from contemplating her door, Brenda realized Riprap and Nissa were standing in the doorway to the classroom, their expressions showing they knew something was wrong.

"Is Lani all right?" Nissa asked.

"Sleeping like a baby," Brenda promised. "I checked."

"What happened?" Riprap asked.

The lines of the big man's body were tight, as if he were containing an impulse to go after someone: an attack dog, waiting to have his target pointed out to him.

Brenda motioned them back into the classroom, and when the door was closed, quickly told them everything that had happened. As she did so, her heart started beating far faster than it had done during the actual confrontation—rage and indignation flooding to the fore.

"I'm sure Honey Dream was poking around in my stuff, not just looking for a bathroom," Brenda concluded. "But what could she have been looking for? I mean, I'm not even one of the Thirteen."

Riprap looked uncomfortable. "Even if you're not technically one of the Thirteen, you're still an adept." He gestured with one broad hand at the array of tiles waiting to be baked, evidence that Brenda was capable of making magic. "You're also our contact to your father."

"Or Honey Dream's snooping might have nothing to do with magic," Nissa said, her turquoise eyes bright with laughter. "She might be interested in finding out other things about you—like just how close you and Flying Claw are."

Brenda felt herself blush. Then she got angry.

"We're not close at all," she said. "Honey Dream's the one who says Flying Claw is her beloved."

Nissa shrugged. "Since when has what someone says about a relationship mattered? Isn't what's really going on what matters?"

Riprap wasn't about to get distracted from the main point. "Whatever the reason, I don't like Honey Dream prowling around like that. She's proven before this that she doesn't exactly respect our privacy. This is a violation of hospitality, if not of our formal treaty."

"So you two think I should tell Des and Pearl," Brenda said. "I mean, I was planning to tell Des eventually, but I was figuring I could wait until the four from the Lands had gone back to Colm Lodge."

"Tell Des," Riprap agreed, "and he can decide if we should distract Pearl. However, I think your report can wait until the four from the Lands leave—but I don't think it should wait a moment after."

"We're working with Righteous Drum and all them," Nissa agreed, all her former merriment gone, "but that doesn't mean we can trust them. In fact, given the circumstances, we'd be stupid to do so. They need us. That has to hurt given that they came here hunting us. I'm sure that all of them would give anything to have the upper hand again."

Brenda nodded. "I'll tell Des then. You're right. Waking Lizard is so friendly, and Flying Claw and Righteous Drum so cooperative that I sometimes forget that not long ago they were our enemies—and that their being our allies doesn't make them our friends."

☆

"Your world, too," Tracy Frye echoed. "But you're willing to let a war the like of which we've never seen come here—and expect us to stand by and let you do the fighting while everyone and everything we care about is endangered. I don't think so."

Pearl shook her head. "You misunderstand me. Deliberately, I think. We have intended from the start that we will take the battle to them—anticipate the invasion—intercept it before it can reach this place."

"And how," Judd Madden said, interest mingled with fear tightening his voice, "are you planning on doing that?"

"I am not going to detail our plans," Pearl replied a touch haughtily, hoping that hauteur would cover the reality that, as of yet, she and her allies did not have any concrete plans. "However, the Exiles told us that there are several ways between the Lands and here. The recent invaders—intruders—came via a bridge linking the universes. All of these bridges have been destroyed."

She had their attention now, and was determined to hold

it. "As you know, the Exiles' main hope was that someday they could return home."

"They planned to break the terms of their exile," Tracy Frye said. There was no mistaking the sneer in her voice. "Probably even as they accepted it."

Pearl did not let her annoyance show. "The Exiles left children and spouses, parents and friends, pets and property. Of course they hoped to return home. This does not mean that they did not intend to honor the terms of their exile, only that they hoped circumstances would permit its repeal."

Tracy looked no less hostile, but Renata set a firm hand on the other woman's arm, and Tracy sank back into her chair.

Pearl continued. "The Exile Dragon left records of the Nine Gates that could be passed through in order to reach the Lands. These gates are not so much in the Lands as they are potentially of the Lands. The higher the potential, the closer the link. We are researching that route now."

Erick leaned forward, all eagerness. "And how can we help?"

Pearl shook her head. "I thank you for your kindness, but our belief—and our research supports this—is that no one who does not carry the blood of the Lands can enter there. This is not something that the Exiles accepted lightly—especially after spouses and friends were acquired who belonged wholly to this world."

Pearl wasn't sure the assembled Rock Doves accepted this restriction, but no one was going to challenge her—at least not until they had a chance to do research of their own. For a moment, Pearl thought Tracy might make another nasty comment, but although the other had raised her chin pugnaciously, she lowered it without comment.

Tracy Frye made her interest in acquiring our particular lore too apparent, Pearl thought with satisfaction, *for her to play disinterested patriot now.*

Hattie LaTour, the Rosicrucian representative, raised a

hand. Judd Madden, his relief obvious that someone remembered the rules of polite discussion, acknowledged her.

"Hattie LaTour?"

"We of the Rock Dove Society," she said, her light voice strong despite its softness, "have rules of our own. Ever since the ugly internal conflicts that arose during the Second World War, we have all sworn to refrain from using our powers except in the most personal of ways. This has kept us from internecine battles for over fifty years, and is not a regulation to be lightly broken.

"I have known Pearl Bright personally for a decade. There are members of the Rosicrucians who have known her far longer. We have always found her reliable and trustworthy. Indeed, we have found the scions of the Thirteen Orphans very willing—even eager—to keep the pact they made after they found themselves in our world. I suggest we give them the opportunity Pearl requests."

Tracy muttered, "Demands, you mean."

Myron the Greek raised a hand. "I second Hattie's motion."

"I third it," Erick said. "If motions get thirded, I mean. Give them a chance. We can always step in later if they can't handle it. I mean, we won't have any choice, right? Anyhow, this seems like a personal matter between two branches of one tradition, and we don't want the Rock Dove Society to get involved in mediating those, do we?"

This Erick is cunning, Pearl thought. *I begin to understand why he is here as a representative. That open expression along with a devious mind is a devastating combination.*

Erick's words had evidently hit home. Billi Rockshaper came forward with a box and slips of paper. A quick vote was taken. Judd Madden counted out the results.

"Eighteen for," he said, "two against. Very well. For now the matter will be treated as one between segments of a single tradition and the Rock Dove Society will not interfere—and will recommend noninterference by related societies as well."

Pearl glanced back at Shen. Their gazes locked and it was clear to her that he shared her mingled relief and dread.

We have permission to go ahead, Pearl thought. *I hope to whatever Heaven listens to a Tiger's prayers that we can pull this off.*

☆

"I cannot, simply cannot, believe you did something so foolish! You have endangered our treaty! You may have made it impossible for us to return home!"

Righteous Drum didn't shout. He didn't even raise his voice, and that made his fury all the more terrible.

Honey Dream fought not to shrink back as Righteous Drum continued his tirade. She reminded herself that she was the Snake. Although Righteous Drum was her father, in this they were equals. She was the Snake. He was the Dragon. Would he have yelled at Waking Lizard this way?

She considered and was forced to admit that probably Righteous Drum would have done so, but then the Monkey—like all Monkeys—possessed a playful streak and often did impulsive, childish things that deserved such reprimands.

Honey Dream's confidence shrank a little. Had she behaved like a Monkey, rather than a Snake? Did she deserve her father's—the Dragon's—anger?

No. Honey Dream straightened her shoulders, fleetingly wishing that she was wearing the impressive robes that would have been hers back home in the Lands Born from Smoke and Sacrifice rather than these flimsy but ever so comfortable shorts and cropped top. It was difficult to be haughty and impressive when nearly naked, but then again, if one relied upon clothing . . .

She waited for Righteous Drum to pause for breath—or perhaps to find an appropriately cutting phrase—and slid her own words smoothly into the gap.

"You are overreacting," she said calmly. "As doubtlessly this Cat, this Albert Yu, intended when he phoned you. He is sly and manipulative, that one, for all he is but a pretend emperor—his blood three generations attenuated with that of this poor excuse for a land. Who is a candy merchant to criticize me?"

"Whoo!" Waking Lizard gave a laughing cheer. "Nice words! Dare you repeat them to his face? For all your sneers, Albert Yu smells of more than chocolate. He has power and has been well trained in how to use it."

Honey Dream lifted her head and looked down her nose at Waking Lizard. "I have no desire to antagonize one for whom we have a use."

"Then why," Righteous Drum said, "did you risk antagonizing the entire lot of them by prowling around in their private chambers?"

Honey Dream shook her head. "I have admitted to doing no such thing. I was looking for an empty bathroom. I thought the one downstairs was in use."

Waking Lizard gave another gusty laugh. "By all means stick to your story, dearest Snake, but you know, and we know, and most importantly of all, our associates know that you were snooping. And not snooping very effectively either, since you were caught. Would you care to tell us what was so important that you would take such a risk?"

Honey Dream glowered at him. "I tell you. There was no risk. Indeed, none at all. Brenda Morris overreacted. My question is this. Why should she be so guarded? Why should she care if someone walks through her room in order to get to a bathroom? What is it that she has to hide? If Nissa had been concerned, that might have been reasonable. Her little girl was the one who was napping, but, no, it was Brenda Morris who came hurrying out, so worried about my 'trespassing.' I say her actions, not mine are the suspicious ones. I say it again. What is it that Brenda Morris has to hide?"

Honey Dream tried not to hold her breath, not to show how carefully she was watching their reactions. Would they accept this explanation? Would they transfer their suspicions from her to the one they should feel suspicious about?

Righteous Drum looked thoughtful. Waking Lizard maintained his expression of amused superiority. He really *was* annoying.

Honey Dream sneaked a glance toward Flying Claw. She still was not certain about his feelings for Brenda Morris. There were times she thought he might care for her, others when she was almost certain that indifference was his strongest emotion toward the other woman.

At this moment, Flying Claw was leaning back in his chair, his eyes half closed in the manner that meant he was considering her challenge. This was good. At least he hadn't rejected it right off. Still Honey Dream felt a faint sour burn in her gut that he hadn't immediately leapt to take her side.

"Tell me again," said Waking Lizard, his expression suddenly serious, "why it is you have such a great suspicion regarding Brenda Morris. Remember, unlike you other three, my interactions with her have been completely harmonious. Your first treaty with these people was made before my arrival. The second and more detailed one soon after, while I was still recovering from my injuries. Perhaps I have missed something."

Honey Dream did not think that Waking Lizard thought anything of the sort. That mention of the "first treaty" was enough warning. It hadn't really been her fault that Righteous Drum had been forced to agree to terms that limited their freedom of action. It had been Brenda Morris's fault. If Brenda had stayed asleep as she was supposed to do, everything would have been fine. Flying Claw would have been free, and no one the wiser as to the manner of his departure.

But, no, Brenda Morris had to wake up and come wandering out into the hallway, ruining all of Honey Dream's carefully laid plans. She had to have the gall to grab those bracelets and dare defend herself when Honey Dream had tried to settle things quietly.

Honey Dream found herself struck by the coincidence. That Brenda Morris really had a thing for wandering out whenever she wasn't wanted. Could that be coincidence or might it be an indication of something else, something suspicious?

She voiced this new thought to the others.

"Oh," said Waking Lizard with a dismissive wave of one of those knobby-knuckled hands, "that's nothing. She probably had a ward up."

"There were no wards," Honey Dream responded promptly, "except for the household ones that warn Pearl if unauthorized magics are being done."

"Strange," Waking Lizard said with another annoying chuckle. "You checked for wards when you were going to the bathroom?"

Honey Dream realized she'd been caught out, but she sniffed.

"Of course. I knew those amateurs were studying. I didn't want to risk disturbing them. Those amulet bracelets they so rely upon are ruined if the caster loses concentration while creating them."

"How considerate of you," said Waking Lizard dryly. "You really are an example to us all."

"Stop this bickering!" Righteous Drum snapped. "We have a serious problem confronting us. Whether or not Honey Dream was snooping is not the issue. The issue is that the people upon whom we are relying to help us return to our homeland believe that was her intention—and for good reason. Honey Dream has not exactly built a reputation for trustworthiness among them."

"Unfairly," Honey Dream said, "because this time I wasn't snooping, and the other time I was trying to effect a rescue. If anything, that first time should have shown them how very trustworthy I am. After all, we were opponents then, not allies."

She regretted her outburst once she had begun, because, after all, the comrade she had been seeking to rescue had been Flying Claw, and no man—and especially no Tiger— would like to be reminded that he had put himself into a position where he had needed rescue. She glanced over at Flying Claw, but he did not look angry, only thoughtful.

He sat straighter, crossing his arms loosely across his chest. "Although overall I think Honey Dream is overreacting," he said, his words measured, "I did report that there is something odd about Brenda Morris, but whether that means she is a threat to us or whether her oddness presents us with an additional asset remains to be seen."

Honey Dream wanted to scream, wanted to yell out at the unfairness of it all. She wanted to say, "If she wasn't a girl and didn't look at you with those great big adoring eyes, would you be so 'balanced' in your outlook?"

She didn't say it though. She was, after all, the Snake, and had been trained in diplomacy and tact. However, the inside of her mouth tasted of blood from where she'd bit her lip in her fury. She hoped the red didn't show against her teeth.

"So what do we do?" repeated Righteous Drum. "Do we seek to make amends or do we side with Honey Dream's version of events? She is my daughter, and I admit that I am not the best judge where she is concerned."

When Waking Lizard and Flying Claw turned their gazes upon her, Honey Dream did her best not to fidget. Then Flying Claw passed judgment.

"We side with Honey Dream," he said. "We are too small a band and too much in need to be divided."

The triumph that welled within Honey Dream's breast was quickly quelled with his next words.

"But she'd better not do anything so stupid again."

☆

A horrible shrill growling roused Brenda from a sleep she hadn't even known she'd been sleeping.

Last she remembered, she'd been sitting in Pearl's downstairs front parlor, dutifully reading a chapter in a rather dull book on the evolution of Chinese culture. She must have nodded off.

Brenda leapt to her feet, letting the book drop to the floor, hearing it thud against the thick parlor carpet. Her fingers slipped beneath the tile bracelets on her wrist as she calculated what she needed to do.

First, Dragon's Tail as a ward, although whether that would do any good against something that could get through Pearl's existing wards, then . . .

A whirlwind of yellow and orange, striped in black, still emitting that horrible shrill growling burst through the open parlor doorway that let out into the entry hall. The whirlwind sprang upon her, wriggling and snarling.

Brenda let the Dragon's Tail amulet bracelet snap back on its elastic threads to rest against her wrist. Then she scooped Lani up and held her at arm's length. The little girl kept growling, but now the growls were more than half giggles.

Lani was dressed as a tiger in a black-striped orange tee shirt, slippers with tiger faces embroidered on the toes, a beanie-like hat with tiger's ears and eyes, and, crowning glory, a black and orange tail stuffed into the back of her elastic-waisted pants.

"Down! Down! Down!" Lani shouted gleefully. "I'm a tiger, like Foster."

Brenda put the girl down—she was really hard to hold on to when she kicked and wriggled like that. Brenda was afraid she'd drop her. Lani reciprocated the kindness by crouching down and biting Brenda on one bare calf.

"Hey!" Brenda howled, kicking out and knocking Lani back none too gently. "That hurts!"

"But I'm a tiger," Lani explained in a very small voice, as if the insanity of excitement gone, she realized how far she'd overstepped.

"Never mind that," Brenda replied grumpily, examining her calf where a little crescent of red marks showed quite distinctly. "Human tigers don't bite. Have you seen Pearl bite anyone?"

"No, but I saw . . ."

A sound from the hallway distracted them both. Foster—

Flying Claw—was standing there, arms crossed over his chest, an expression of mingled amusement and something like apprehension on his face. His eyes met Brenda's, then dropped to her calf. The expression on his face became a definite grin.

"Lani," he said, the snap of reprimand in his voice, "did you bite Brenda?"

"I'm a tiger," Lani tried one more time, although her tone said she was perfectly aware the explanation wasn't going to work.

"That is not an excuse," Flying Claw said. He spoke the short phrase in English. Unlike the others from the Lands, his command of the language was the result of hard study enhanced by sorcery, rather than sorcery alone. "Tigers are dangerous. They must learn to sheath their claws and bite only their enemies."

That sounded like a lesson Flying Claw himself had been forced to learn, Brenda thought. She wondered if Lani, now on all fours, prowling among the legs of a chair, had heard.

"Did you give Lani the tiger outfit?" Brenda asked. "It's really cute."

Flying Claw shook his head. "I didn't. There are similar outfits in my homeland. Parents evoke the tiger to protect their children from the five poisonous creatures: the scorpion, snake, centipede, lizard, and toad."

Brenda had a fleeting thought that being a tiger hadn't protected Flying Claw from a certain very poisonous Snake, but she didn't say anything. For the moment, Flying Claw was relaxed and smiling as he watched Lani prowl among the chair legs. Brenda didn't want to ruin the mood. She turned to Lani.

"Lani, did Des give you your tiger clothes?"

Lani emerged from under the chair and bounced a few times to show off her stripes, although the quick glance she gave Brenda's leg showed she hadn't forgotten her transgression.

"Nope. Grr-Harris did. A present."

"Harris?" Brenda guessed this might be one of Pearl's

friends, and she wondered that she hadn't heard the doorbell.

"No! No! No!" Lani said indignantly. "Grr-harris. You know. Your dad."

"My dad!" Brenda looked side to side, as if Gaheris Morris might appear from thin air. "Is he here? I didn't know he was coming. I mean, I thought he was coming next week. He's here now?"

Flying Claw took mercy on her. "Gaheris arrived a short while ago. We let him in via the garden gate because Nissa said you had fallen asleep in here. I came in hoping to catch Lani before she could disturb you. She wanted to see herself in a mirror."

Lani jumped up. "Mirror! I forgot!"

She dashed out of the room and Brenda heard her making her laborious way upstairs to where a floor-length mirror adorned the bathroom door.

Flying Claw took a step back so he could keep an eye on the child, but he didn't follow her. Instead he gave Brenda a smile that mingled friendliness and concern.

"Did she hurt you? Human mouths are very dirty. If she broke the skin . . ."

Brenda extended her leg so he could see. "No harm. Let's not tell Nissa. I think Lani got overexcited, and she's not likely to do anything like that again."

Flying Claw looked doubtful. "Should we undermine the authority of a parent?"

"This once," Brenda said. "Nissa's got enough on her mind without worrying that Lani's biting people."

"If you say so," Flying Claw said.

Then, before Brenda could react, he knelt and ran his hand over the place where Lani's tooth marks were already fading. The touch was perfectly clinical, but Brenda felt her skin tingle.

"No broken skin," Flying Claw said, rising to his feet. "So I will not tell Nissa, but I will speak to Lani about the responsibilities of being a Tiger."

The back door from the patio into the kitchen opened and Nissa called, "Lani?"

"She's upstairs," Brenda called. "Growling at herself in the mirror. Flying Claw just told me my dad's here."

Nissa came in and stood at the bottom of the stairs. The sounds of Lani being a tiger drifted down.

"Gaheris arrived about a half hour ago. I knew you were worn out from this morning's lesson, so we decided to let you nap. Sorry about Tiger-paws up there."

Nissa started mounting the stairs to retrieve her daughter. "Did your dad give you and your brothers presents like that?"

"And worse, sometimes," Brenda admitted with a laugh, "at least from the point of view of order and peace. There was the Fourth of July he gave us water balloons and slingshots for throwing them. Then there was the Thanksgiving we got things like kazoos that were supposed to be turkey calls and . . ."

Nissa laughed. "I don't envy your mother."

"Oh, Mom had the last word on everything," Brenda assured her. "We soaked each other with the water balloons outside, and she confiscated the slingshots before we could get any bright ideas about throwing more than water balloons. The turkey calls were restricted to outside, too."

Flying Claw had been listening avidly. For a moment, Brenda saw a wistful look cross his features, a look that had been practically omnipresent when Flying Claw had been Foster and had lacked a memory. It made him curiously familiar again.

Brenda realized she'd been so busy being shy, fearful, and disoriented around Flying Claw that she'd never asked about his family and childhood—something she'd always wanted to do when he was Foster. She was about to ask when the back door opened again.

Des's voice called, "We're getting ready to have a conference. Grab Lani and bring her out. Everyone else is already here."

Brenda glanced over at Flying Claw, but the moment of

gentle rapport they had shared had vanished. Once again he was the young warrior, his lean body alert for the call to duty. He gave her a polite nod, and headed for the patio without a backward glance.

VIII

Brenda realized that staring forlornly after Flying Claw was going to get her less than nowhere, so she reached down and scooped up the book she'd been reading from where it had fallen to the floor. Dull as it was, it was a book, and the already strong love she had for the written word before she'd come here had only been enhanced by her studies.

"Nissa?" Brenda called up the stairs. "Did you hear what Des said?"

"We're coming," Nissa said, "as soon as Lani and I take care of a rather embarrassing accident."

Brenda understood. Lani had been toilet-trained before her arrival at Pearl's house, but she was still not even three years old, and accidents did happen.

Brenda thought about offering to help, but Nissa would have the matter under control. Instead, Brenda dove into the ground-floor powder room, rinsed the staleness of sleep from her mouth, and ran a comb through her hair. Before finishing her business, she glanced down at her leg. The little tiger's bite had almost vanished, but the skin still tingled when she thought of Flying Claw's touch.

Outside, Brenda made a beeline for where her father sat in one of the deck chairs, a beer in one hand, listening to something Waking Lizard was explaining. Gaheris Morris was a good listener, so he didn't leap up and greet his daughter when he saw her. He did give her a slight grin to let her know he'd seen her.

Gaheris Morris looked no more Chinese than did Shen Kung, who had arrived yesterday from New York with Pearl—and for similar reasons, although the divergence from the ethnic Chinese had come later in the Rat's family. Exile Rat had gotten his heir on a mainland Chinese woman. Second Rat, therefore, had been ethnically Chinese. However, like many of the Orphans, who were eager to hide within the general populace once they emigrated to the United States, Second Rat had used magical arts to alter his appearance.

Pictures Brenda had seen showed Second Rat looking more like an Eastern European. He had married an American woman of mostly German heritage. Their son—Brenda's grandfather—had been reared American, and had been very resistant to learning any of the Orphan's arts. If asked, he identified himself as German-American, never mentioning his father's contribution at all.

Second Rat—Brenda actually found it easier to think of her great-grandfather like that—had told his son—Third Rat, Grandpa—that if Gaheris was not taught the Exiles' traditions Grandpa would be disinherited.

The Rat's love for gain had overcome rebellion—as Second Rat had certainly known it would. Even so, Gaheris had not had an easy time with his dad where Gaheris's training was concerned.

Gaheris's mother, Brenda's much-loved Grandma Elaine, was Scotch-Irish and as romantic-minded a soul as ever walked through a cornfield and imagined it the rolling hills of Eire. Grandma Elaine was the one who had insisted on naming her son after an Arthurian hero. When she heard of Second Rat's demand, she had strongly supported the idea of Gaheris learning arcane lore—even if she would have preferred that lore to have been one that involved Sidhe folk under the hill and harps of gold to one that centered around making and breaking mah-jong tiles.

So mothered by a Celtic Romantic, fathered by a German-Chinese American, the current Rat of the Thirteen Orphans looked in no way the scion of the heritage from which he drew his power. Curling reddish-brown hair framed a face ruddy with the sun and lightly freckled. Gaheris's bright, active eyes were hazel green, and his body lean and wiry. When he rose to hug Brenda, she realized once again that they were nearly the same height—she might even be a little taller—and the realization made her curiously protective of her dad.

Brenda pulled a pillow over next to her dad's chair, snagged a beer from the ice chest, and was pleased that Gaheris didn't question her right to a drink—even if she was still, technically, underaged.

Sipping from the beer, Brenda scanned the group. Happily, even with the refreshment table that dominated the center of their loose circle, the brick patio provided ample space beneath the grapevine-overgrown ramada for the large group that had gathered there. In addition to the seven now residing at Pearl's house, there were the four from the Lands, Albert Yu, and the newly arrived Gaheris Morris.

And that totals thirteen—or twelve adults, one Lani, Brenda thought. *It's funny. When I learned about the Thirteen Orphans, they sounded like such a small group, so tightly knit that I never considered all the disagreements they would have. When we're all grouped up like this, thirteen seems like a pretty large number, so large I find myself hoping that we'll reach some sort of agreement—especially since the Landers refusal to admit that Honey Dream was snooping has caused some pretty hard feelings.*

Albert Yu began the meeting by the simple expedient of clearing his throat and saying, "Now that we're all here, and relatively settled, Gaheris says he has something rather disturbing to tell us."

That's why I didn't know Dad was coming, Brenda thought. *This visit wasn't planned. This isn't going to be good.*

☆

Pearl saw worry on the faces of the three apprentices, and tried to make her own features look confident and serene, as if nothing—not even something that would make Gaheris Morris spend the money for an emergency airfare—could disturb her. Nonetheless, a sense of dread spread through her gut.

"Yesterday morning," Gaheris began, "I was working in my office back in South Carolina when my secretary rang through to say someone wanted to speak with me about a possible deal.

"Now, with what I do, this sort of approach isn't really common—at least not these days. Unique Wonders produces personalized promotional items: anything from a gross of keychains to a thirty-foot-high plastic replica of a team mascot. Our business comes in mostly through two different streams—big deals I drum up in face-to-face pitches to clients, smaller but steady deals that come in through our Web site. These days, clients don't just drop in cold and offer to do any business that's worth my time, so I told Etta to tell the caller I was engaged.

"Etta got this strange look on her face, and said, 'The lady said she thought you'd say something like that, and I was to tell you that she was here about the Thirteen Orphans.'

"Well, I guess Etta probably thought I was as crazy as my caller, because when the Thirteen Orphans were mentioned I told Etta to show the lady in. My caller proved to be a woman I've met in passing, a member of the Rock Dove Society by the name of Tracy Frye."

Pearl raised her eyebrows. "I met Ms. Frye during my recent trip to New York. A difficult person. An ambitious one as well."

Gaheris nodded. "I agree. Tracy came in, and once Etta had left, Tracy turned around and made certain the door was shut all the way. Then, without so much as a 'by your leave,' she cast a ward for privacy. Did it so easily, I was glad she didn't have anything nastier prepared—though since my 'return' after my first encounter with our new friends here in that LoDo parking garage . . ."

Gaheris shot a grin at the four from the Lands, but his

gaze rested particularly on Flying Claw. "I'll admit I go about a bit more prepared."

"There is wisdom," Flying Claw said, his voice so level that Brenda couldn't be sure if he was serious or teasing, "in learning from past experience."

"Is there any other kind?" Gaheris asked. "When you figure out how to get future experience, let me know. We'll cut a deal.

"But, to return to my visitor . . . After casting her ward, Tracy plopped herself down in my client chair and gave me a smile that wasn't in the least friendly. She's a tough woman, reminds me of a railing in a split-log fence. She has a reputation for figuring that anything that isn't nailed down is fair game for those grasping fingers of hers.

"Tracy Frye swallowed that nasty smile and tried to look nice. Then she said, 'Mr. Morris, I'm not here to buy any of that plastic garbage you sell—although I might stretch the point if you were selling mah-jong sets and the rules to a certain form of the game.'

"Well, I don't know if you'll believe me, but she was so rude and so full of herself, that I wasn't even offended. When I got done laughing, I said to her, 'Sorry, Ms. Frye. I don't sell mah-jong sets with any but the standard set of rules. Now, I can get you a nice line on some good-looking molded plastic sets straight out of China, but adapted for the Occidental market with the winds, dragons, and numbers marked. They even come in vinyl cases that look like nothing so much as tacky vinyl. Retail price runs between sixty and seventy dollars apiece, with wholesale price set by the size of the lot.'

"She gaped at me, and said, 'I didn't think you'd be so slow, Gaheris Morris. It's the rules I want, not the board game. My understanding is that if you have the rules, you can play with any old set—or none at all. I like that, and I think that with the trouble you people have brought on yourselves, you'd be eager to have some friends.'

"And I said, 'Friends understand the meaning of "no,"

and my friends and teachers Pearl Bright and Shen Kung tell me you folks from the Rock Dove Society have already been told "no." What makes you think I'd be any different?'

"She said, sneered, really, 'Because you're a man who knows the value of making a profit, Mr. Morris, and since I've set my mind on getting these rules, I figure you'd see the value in making something rather than nothing from my determination.'"

Gaheris blew out a theatrical sigh. "I'll spare you the rest of it. She coaxed and she threatened, and she offered me various things in trade—including some tempting samples of various bits of lore she'd picked up over time—but I held the party line, and didn't give an inch."

Albert Yu said dryly, "I am sure. Now, you're not the first to get asked to sell our secrets, and I'm certain that—if we survive to the next generation—you will not be the last. What makes this encounter so special that you flew all the way here—spending considerable money to do so, I am certain—to report this incident?"

Gaheris grinned, and Pearl knew that grin for the one that hid when Gaheris was actually really pissed. She wished Gaheris would give up his childhood rivalry with Albert.

"I had frequent-flyer miles," Gaheris said, "and a favor or two I could call in to get on a direct flight, but I would have come even if I had to take a red-eye and pay full price, because when I refused her a final time, Tracy Frye got nasty.

"She made very clear that she was the mouthpiece for a consortium that, as she put it, 'thinks far too much time has passed without the Thirteen Orphans showing appropriate gratitude for the hospitality extended to them.' She added that the impending crisis has brought others over to her point of view, and was pretty convincing in her claim that even if everyone in the Rock Dove Society wouldn't join her, there were a good number who would look the other way, and a very few who would defend us."

Albert looked appropriately serious at this. "Did she provide proof that this was more than an idle threat?"

"She named some names," Gaheris said, and recited them. Pearl recognized a few. No major players, but then Tracy Frye would be careful not to mention any major players, too much on the line there.

Des said, "So we're pressured on both sides: enemies in the Lands, adversaries here. If we effectively deal with the threat of invasion from the Lands, then Tracy's faction would lose a lot of support. People tend to lose their ethics when they're scared. I think all but the most ambitious of those who are part of that 'consortium' would remove their support if they decided we could deal with our own problems."

Riprap shook his head.

"But until we do that," Riprap said, "I see a lot of potential for trouble. What if the Lands get someone through into this world—make a bridge like Righteous Drum and his crew used and we don't notice—and Tracy's faction gets to them first? We could find even those with ethics pretty eager to turn us over to our enemies as a means of forestalling invasion. That's how Hitler took a lot of his early conquests, remember . . . Give Germany back what should be hers anyhow, and we'll rest content."

"You'd think they'd remember that lesson," Pearl said acidly. "Many of the current Rock Dove Society rules and regulations grew out of the aftermath of arcane involvement in Hitler's war. They should remember how appeasement only feeds the hunger of the invaders."

"Ah," Riprap said, "but this wouldn't be appeasement in the British sense—more like the deals the Soviets cut for themselves with both the Germans and, later, the Allies. I'm betting that the Tracy faction would insist on a cut for themselves. From what you and Shen told us, it seems that almost from the start, the Thirteen Orphans have faced envy and covetousness regarding the unique nature of their magical abilities."

"The link to the Lands," Shen agreed, "a connection to a universe that—although not entirely unconnected to our own—is unique and filled with its own power. Yes. Some have envied us that for as long as they have known of its existence. Only our relative peacefulness barred them from being more active in their coveting. And yet, I assure you, the coveting has always been there. Quiescent but present."

"So what do we do?" Brenda asked, a high, tense note of fear in her voice. "Is it true that we'll need all Thirteen Orphans to get back? Because, if it is the truth, then we might as well roll over and quit."

"I am not very good at quitting," Pearl said softly. "And neither are you, Ms. Morris. Neither, I think, are any of us here gathered. If that was the case, we would not be here. Therefore, let us put by any talk of rolling over and examine what we can do."

Pearl saw Brenda straighten in response to her challenge and smiled, but she could not let her pleasure in the younger woman's bravery show. Waking Lizard had made clear that he, at least, was not completely certain that Honey Dream had not been snooping. However, he had noted that certainly Pearl must agree that Brenda was a bit of an anomaly, one to whom attention should be paid.

Pearl had said she disagreed—although in her heart she did not—but she had thought it wisest that she not draw attention to Brenda.

Righteous Drum spoke. "Why is it that you believe that all Thirteen Orphans would be needed to effect the return? I understand that this is what your ancestors believed. Although it is right and proper to revere the wisdom of those who came before, still, sometimes it is even more right and proper to understand why they decreed what they viewed as the right and just course of action."

Although the question had been addressed to them generally, all attention shifted to Pearl.

"We," Pearl gestured to Shen as she spoke, "agree that although there were varying reasons for the insistence that all thirteen must be involved, the dominant one was this. Twelve had been exiled, but not as twelve individual people—as a unit, a wheel of the years, a cycle of the Earthly Branches.

Therefore, that single unit would be needed to form the key that would once more unlock the way into the Lands Born from Smoke and Sacrifice."

"A wise precaution," Righteous Drum said, "on the part of those who negotiated the exile. Otherwise, were there a difference of opinion between the Exiles, a smaller unit might attempt to renege on their contract—to make the return on their own."

"One or two," Des said, "might not have proven to be much of a threat to the Lands, but if three or four or more decided that they were now strong enough to challenge those who had once conquered them . . ."

"And were willing to risk the families they'd left behind?" Riprap's question was almost a statement. "Remember, you said that the reason the Twelve agreed to be exiled was that not only did it save their hides, it saved their families and property."

"True," Des agreed, "but people change, priorities shift, even ideals lose their shine. Some of the Twelve had more reason than others to want to return. The Ram, for example. She didn't know she was pregnant when she'd left the Lands. Now she had a baby she fiercely wished to be able to reunite with its father."

"In any case," Honey Dream said, hissing a little on the s's in a fashion Pearl found infinitely annoying, "we stray from the central points. A unit was exiled, and so the Twelve believed that unit must return. Did their research uphold this belief?"

"Yes," Shen said, and Pearl realized with a hot spark of delight that he was struggling not to hiss in imitation.

Shen wouldn't have been being either mocking or cruel—the elongated sibilants were nearly irresistible—but he was wise enough to know that a sensitive, arrogant young lady like Honey Dream would take any teasing as mockery.

Shen went on, "My grandfather told me how a few—Ram, Dog, Rabbit—investigated the possibility of making a return on their own. They could get as far as the guardian domains, but no further."

Nissa tilted her head to one side, as if listening to something far away. It was a very rabbitlike gesture, so much so that Pearl almost expected to see that Nissa had grown long ears.

"I have a question," Nissa said. "I understand about the Twelve having been exiled as a unit. I understand why everyone thinks that the Twelve—or in our case, the Thirteen—need to return as a unit. Still, how would having that unit reassembled make a difference? Wouldn't the exile still hold?"

Waking Lizard grinned and stretched his long arms so that knobby elbows cracked. "Drummy and I think we have a way around that little problem. It's a technicality, but one that should at least let us slip you all back into the Lands long enough for us to establish a foothold. The four of us who are here will formally rescind your exile."

"Rescind?" Albert asked, the momentary astonishment that lit his face shifting almost immediately to calculation.

"Rescind," Waking Lizard repeated. "After all, our bridge may have been broken, and our way back home barred, but we didn't agree to it. We didn't take any vows to support the new government. As far as we're concerned, we are still the duly constituted officials of the Emperor's court. In that capacity, we can pardon the Twelve."

"We are even willing," Righteous Drum said with a sidelong glance at Albert, "to view the descendant of a certain unjustly deposed emperor as the due heir to the Jade Petal Throne, should we return and find that throne no longer in the possession of the emperor to whom we have sworn our service."

To Albert's credit, he looked shocked and appalled rather than pleased.

"I don't know if that is necessary," he said. "I have hardly trained to be an emperor."

"Think about it," Righteous Drum replied, his smile showing that he thought Albert was merely demonstrating due modesty. "That is not a matter that needs to be resolved all at once."

"But," Brenda said, and Pearl noted that the fear that had made her voice shake was gone, replaced by purpose, "for any of that stuff about emperors and the rest to matter, we'd still need to reassemble the Thirteen Orphans. The Ox, Horse, Ram, and Monkey are so alienated from their heritage that I don't see how we can hope to train them and educate them. I mean, I know how hard it was for me to accept all of this, and my own dad was there to explain it to me."

Riprap leaned forward and scooped up a massive handful of chips. "Like Brenda said. Even with my father's stories and the letter he left me, I might have had more trouble accepting everything that Brenda and Gaheris had to tell me if Flying Claw hadn't chosen that same night to come after Gaheris."

He gave Flying Claw an apologetic grin. "Sorry, buddy, but you did us a favor there."

"Unintentionally, I assure you," Flying Claw replied with an answering grin.

"Anyhow," Riprap went on, "does anyone have any idea how we might work around the fact that we only have eight of the original twelve? Could Albert stand in?"

"No," Albert said. "The Cat is indeed a wild card, but not a Joker in the deck. The Cat will provide added strength, all the more so because he—I—may not be expected. However, I cannot be anyone but the Cat."

Pearl cleared her throat. "Shen and I may have worked out a possible solution—but making it work will not be easy. Teaching the lost four might be easier. However, this could be faster, and speed may be important. Shen, you're better at explaining arcane matters than I am. Would you take over?"

Shen inclined his head in agreement. "First, I must note that what we are about to suggest is quite likely to seem at the very least distasteful to some of you. To others it may seem completely revolting. I want you to know, we would not suggest it if we thought we had another good option."

To this point, everyone had been listening politely. There had not been even the background ripple of whispered conversations that would usually accompany such a large gathering. Now, however, the listening silence became absolute.

"The answer," Shen said slowly, "may be found in the family mah-jong sets—or rather in what they are made from."

"Bone and bamboo," Riprap said promptly, "or ivory and bamboo."

"Bone and bamboo," Pearl said, placing the slightest emphasis on the first word. "Bone and bamboo. To be precise, human bone. To be more precise, bone from the original Exile who represented that Branch."

"That's disgusting!" Nissa exclaimed.

Brenda's hands flew up—one to cover her mouth, one to hover over her gut, as if she were fighting down a sudden surge of nausea. Riprap's expression went suddenly blank.

Des, Gaheris, Shen, and Albert already knew this little fact, of course. It was usually related to each Orphan as he or she took possession of the family set. In the case of Riprap and Nissa, Pearl and Des had thought this information unnecessary. There were too many skills the new Dog and Rabbit had needed to learn without making them squeamish about what would, eventually, become a specialized tool of their craft.

Pearl glanced over to where the four from the Lands sat, seeking to gauge their reactions. Righteous Drum looked interested, as if he were already seeking the ramifications of her announcement. Honey Dream's expression was torn between fascination and revulsion. Most interesting of all, both Flying Claw and Waking Lizard seemed more interested in how the others were reacting, as if the information meant nothing to them personally.

And yet it does, Pearl thought, *for this may be their only way home.*

"Human bone?" Brenda repeated, as if hoping she might be wrong.

"That is correct," Pearl said. "As you may recall, the thirteen original exiles did not survive very long as a group. Within five years, First Horse had been slain. This raised some serious questions about whether there was any chance that the group would return to the Lands. They all had hopes that their continued affiliation with the Twelve Earthly Branches would be enough, but what if it wasn't?

"They decided to make certain that even after death some part of each of them could remain with their heirs apparent. Mah-jong had already been selected as the means by which they would encode their magic. In China at that time, the game was played with either cards or tiles. The remaining Twelve knew they could not hope to carry a body around with them. Even a body part or ashes might raise difficulties, for the Thirteen were often on the move. However, a set of game pieces might escape greed or seizure, and although a mah-jong set is heavy, it is not impossibly so. In a pinch, it might be broken down, the various tiles distributed."

"More hiding in plain sight," Riprap muttered.

"More like hiding in plain hiding," Des laughed. "Gambling has been frowned upon by the civil authorities in China for generations—centuries—yet the Chinese remain a people who love games of chance. The Twelve had ample resources for hiding their special mah-jong pieces. Remember, too, initially they did not have twelve sets to worry about, only a few."

Pearl frowned reprovingly at Des. "You are taking us away from the main point. Shall I continue?"

"Sorry," Des said, but he didn't look particularly sorry, and Pearl was pleased with him. His casual manner was easing the remaining strain from Nissa's and Brenda's faces.

Pearl went on. "First Ram was, as many Rams are, a skilled artisan, and so she came up with the logistics of the plan. Several of First Horse's bones were, let us say, cleaned and cured. When next the Exiles were relatively settled, tiles were shaped from segments of bone and backed with bamboo.

"As each of the original Exiles died, the same course of action was followed, although, of course, First Ram could not make all the sets, for eventually she also died. The difficulties the Thirteen encountered in following this course of action are interesting, but not particularly germane to our course of action."

"Which is?" Righteous Drum said politely, although his eyes were shining with eagerness.

Pearl inclined her head toward Shen, indicating that he should answer. She'd already said more than she intended, but family history was close to her heart.

"If we can get our hands on the mah-jong sets belonging to the missing four Exiles," Shen said, "we may be able to use them as a stand-in of sorts."

"Dry bones rather than living men and women?" Flying Claw challenged. "How could that work?"

"Not so much dry bones," Shen said, "as the spirits who can still be summoned from them. I am hoping that, if we are lucky, we may be able to draw upon our ancestors' counsel. In the research I have been doing, the Nine Gates must draw upon the power of the Nine Yellow Springs."

He glanced at Righteous Drum, who nodded.

"Yes. This matches the lore of the Lands."

Shen looked pleased. "I hoped it did. I have been reading my grandfather's notes, but he was a great scholar of traditions other than those of his homeland, and I was concerned that his notes were contaminated."

"No," Righteous Drum assured him, "the Nine Yellow Springs and the Nine Gates are intimately connected."

"Well," Shen went on happily, his expression reminding Pearl of the boy he had once been, "the Nine Yellow Springs are in the underworld, and who better to advise us how to find and utilize them than ghosts?"

"Interesting," said Righteous Drum, "but why do we need

these four sets? I understood that each of you is in possession of your own family sets."

"That is so," Pearl agreed, "but we have more than merely consulting our ancestors in mind. We had hoped that with proper and respectful approaches, we might convince the original Ox, Horse, Ram, and Monkey to lend enough of their spirit to our cause that our group of thirteen would be complete."

"Necromancy?" asked Des with marked disapproval. "Let the dead remain dead."

"Consulting the ancestors," Shen countered, "is very Chinese. I thought you out of all of us would understand, Des, or are you more American than you'd like to believe?"

Des frowned. "Honoring the ancestors is very Chinese, yes, but asking them to manifest again in the world of the living? I'm not certain I agree."

"What greater honor," Pearl said, cutting in before matters could become too theoretical, "could we do our ancestors than fulfilling their greatest desire—their desire to have their exile rescinded, their desire to return home?"

IX

Honey Dream enjoyed watching the Orphans argue. It was a balm to her own still-bruised soul.

Although Shen and Pearl had explained their point of view quite logically, Des's frown did not diminish. Pearl pressed her point.

"Des, when you assumed the Rooster's place and were given her mah-jong set, you were told that there were two reasons that these sets were made. One we have already mentioned—so that the Thirteen Orphans would remain together, even after death. What was the other?"

Des might have taken on the responsibility of teaching the newest Rabbit and Dog, but clearly he had not forgotten that once Pearl and Shen had been his own teachers. He responded promptly and in good form.

"So that offerings could be made to their spirits, as is right and proper."

"And why was this seen as important?" Shen took over the catechism.

"Because their exile isolated them from their kin," Des said, "from those who would in more normal circumstances have made offerings at their graves. The mah-jong sets were meant to serve, in a manner of speaking, as portable graves."

Des turned to address Brenda, Riprap, and Nissa directly. "None of you were raised Chinese, so you can't know how important those offerings are to the dead. Every family makes offerings to their dead at least twice a year, on Ching Ming and at the New Year. Even when immediate family members move on, there's usually someone to make at least a token offering. Without those offerings the afterlife would be unpleasant for them."

Shen, whom Honey Dream resented because in his unskilled hands rested some of the power that should be her father's alone, shook his head reprovingly. "Let us be blunt, Des. Precisely because they were skilled in the magical arts, the Exiles knew how horrible the afterlife could be for an unsustained spirit. My grandfather had met ghosts. Some were creatures to fear, others to pity. None were anything he wished to become."

"Yes," Des said, "and we have cared for our ancestors, but I do not see how this permits us to abuse their spirits now that they are at rest."

Pearl rose abruptly, unsettling the cat Amala, who had settled in her lap. The cat jumped to the patio and dashed out into the garden. Lani shrieked in delight, but no one else paid the least attention. They were all focused on Pearl.

"Des, aren't you listening? This has nothing to do with theory, nothing to do with necromancy in the usual sense.

We are not inflicting an indignity upon our ancestors. They did this to themselves. First Ram cleaned and flensed the bones of her friend, First Horse, at his behest. My father requested the same be done to him. We are not doing anything they would not have wanted. They did it to themselves!"

"Well," Des admitted slowly, "I suppose you're right, but still, this is unsettling."

Honey Dream tuned out the incredibly dull discussion of ethics and morality that followed, focusing on keeping her appearance calm and yet alert.

Hands remained her greatest difficulty. Ever since she was a little girl, she'd twisted her fingers into each other when she was excited or angry. Her mother had noticed and had warned Honey Dream against giving her inner thoughts away—and then had reinforced the point by using those tics against her.

Despite the sometimes painful memories that accompanied this training, it was all Honey Dream could do to keep her hands still in her lap as Shen Kung and Pearl Bright revealed the source of the bone in the heirloom mah-jong sets and their plans for it.

Honey Dream wondered if her father, Waking Lizard, and Flying Claw saw the possibilities as clearly as she did. Pearl and Shen spoke of using spirits to fill in for missing members of their consortium of thirteen.

(Twelve, really. Despite all the respect everyone kept paying to Albert Yu, this Cat was really discardable. No matter what her father implied in an effort to flatter these strangers into cooperation, there was no way a candy maker would be elevated to emperor.)

Why stop with filling in for the *missing* members of the Twelve? Why not eliminate their descendants entirely from consideration and seek alliance with the wellspring of the line? Why not bring the Twelve Exiles home again?

Surely such an act would be right and even virtuous. Honey Dream did not think the dead Exiles could be resurrected as such. However, if their spirits could be drawn back to the vicinity of these remnants of their bodies, then held there, the act of transporting the mah-jong sets to the Lands would also return the Exiles' spirits to their homeland. This was what the Exiles had desired, so they should be willing to cooperate.

Of course, there would be difficulties. For this to work, the ancestral spirits must have priority over their descendants in their alliance with their affiliated Earthly Branches. If they did not, then the power would be further fragmented just when concentration was what they needed most of all.

Honey Dream wondered if the others had thought of this. For a moment, she considered being subtle, then shrugged and decided to take guidance from the Thirteen Orphans and practice the subtlety of hiding in plain sight. Direct interest in one thing could hide her deeper interests.

"Pardon," Honey Dream said when there was a pause in the discussion. Her hands were completely still in her lap, although she had a strong desire to fidget with her writing brush. "I have no desire to interrupt this interesting discussion, but a difficulty in this otherwise admirable plan has occurred to me. I may be but young and foolish. My ignorance may be the source of confusion on one point that is apparently clear to heads wiser than my own."

Everyone fell quiet during her little speech. Riprap and Flying Claw both looked relieved at the break in the increasingly esoteric subject matter of the earlier discussion. Nissa moved slightly, golden lashes fluttering over those impossibly blue eyes as if she had been nearly asleep until Honey Dream's words roused her.

But Brenda Morris did not look pleased at Honey Dream's interruption. Brenda quickly schooled her features to immobility, but her teachers had not been as strict as had Honey Dream's and a hint of suspicion shaped the angle of her brows.

Honey Dream ignored the annoying Ratling, and focused on Shen Kung. Old men liked pretty girls, and Shen had no reason to dislike her. She also gave her father a respectful nod, acknowledging that he was also a Dragon and therefore a master of arcane lore.

She very carefully did not look at Flying Claw. If her future plans were to work, she knew that he must not dismiss her as merely trying to impress him. She would need an ally, and she would like that ally to be him.

"You speak," Honey Dream continued, her inflections very formal, "as if you believe that—at least in the case of the four unfaithful families—the spirits of the departed ancestors could somehow substitute. How could this be? Didn't you tell us that the Earthly Branches were bound to pass down the family lines? Wouldn't those bindings have held even when the lore that enabled the Branch holder to exploit the connection was lost?"

Shen Kung looked at her with approval. "You have anticipated a point that we were going to bring up, Honey Dream. Des, are you willing to let this ethical discussion go for now?"

Des Lee tugged at one edge of his beard. "For now. I admit, I'm interested in the answer to Honey Dream's question."

Shen returned his attention to Honey Dream. "As circumstances now stand, you are correct. The bindings between the Earthly Branch holders and the Branch persist—even if those who hold it are completely unaware of the relationship. However, there may be ways to undo those bindings. The best solution would be to ask the ancestors themselves to do so. They may be willing to work the unbinding, especially if we explain that the continuity of lineage they sought to assure has become so attenuated as to be useless to them."

"We would need to promise," Des said, "that we would bear their bones back to the Lands."

"Of course," Shen said. "We would need to take them with us in any case so that the Thirteen would be complete."

Honey Dream listened with half an ear to the ensuing discussion on what course of action might or might not be followed. She'd already learned that these Americans would talk any matter to death before reaching a decision.

Seductive and enticing, other possibilities claimed her attention. Shen Kung seemed certain that contact could be established between them and the spirits of the original Orphans. Very well. She would take his word for it and learn the details of how this could be achieved later.

What interested Honey Dream was what might be done once that contact was established. Shen and Pearl were concerned solely with rounding out their set of Thirteen Orphans, as if they were indeed playing mah-jong, drawing from a wall that grew shorter and shorter, their options becoming more limited with every tile drawn.

But why play that game at all? Why set out to break the wall with tiles that had been drawn before Honey Dream herself became a player? Might she not shuffle the tiles, build the wall anew, play a fresh game?

If four of the Exiles might be brought back, why not the other eight?

Why deal with these annoying Americans and their strange magics at all? Why not return to the source? Why not bring back the Exiles, offer them a remission of their exile, a chance to go home?

Yes. The extant group would not like this at all, but they could be eliminated from consideration. There was the spell Righteous Drum had designed, the one that robbed memory, that separated the power from the person.

There were other options, more direct. Could she say "murder" even in the quiet of her mind? Honey Dream dared herself, and found that she could.

Her father had been reluctant to take this course for a variety of reasons: foremost, the difficulties that might arise for them if law officials realized murder had been done. Honey Dream had been here in the United States long enough to realize how silly this worry had been.

Magic did exist in this world, but most considered it a matter of superstition. Those who had magic kept themselves hidden away. The law would not detect a magically done murder, and from what she was learning about the Orphans' relationship with the various indigenous magical traditions, the locals would probably not care if the Orphans were wiped out.

The simplest course of action would be to eliminate (a nicer word than murder) those who were affiliated with one of the Earthly Branches. It might even be necessary to eliminate an heir apparent, if that heir apparent had received training in arcane matters. Then, when this was done, Shen Kung's plan for persuading the ancestral spirits to join their cause could be put into action.

Raise them. Speak with them. Show them how useless their descendants were, explain how the bindings must be broken. Then, when this was done, all should be simple. How much easier it would be to establish the Nine Gates with the spirits of twelve powerful sorcerers as allies, rather than with these pathetically weak American imitations.

Ah, but there would be problems in carrying out this tidy little plan—doubtless why her father and Waking Lizard were so involved even now, even when another course should be clear to them, in discussing how to make do with partial measures.

In short, there were the treaties. The first had been signed when Honey Dream herself had been caught some weeks ago during her attempt to rescue Flying Claw. It had bound Righteous Drum and Honey Dream from expanding their aggression to include the relatives, allies, and even friends of Pearl Bright and her associates. Later, when Flying Claw's memory had been returned to him, and after Waking Lizard's arrival, they had been "requested" to also sign the treaty and had done so.

Then there was a second treaty, more detailed, more complex, that protected both sides of their uneasy alliance from betrayal.

They were good treaties. Honey Dream knew this better than most, for as the Snake she had been called upon to help design them. Moreover, both treaties had been sworn to over the blade of Pearl's sword, the sword called Treaty, a sword that seemed to have a will of its own where such bindings were concerned.

Fleetingly, Honey Dream wondered about the genesis of that sword, for it had been forged not for Pearl Bright, but for her father, Thundering Heaven, one of the original Exiles. Tigers such as Thundering Heaven had been were not usually concerned with treaties, but with what happened before there were treaties and when treaties failed. Perhaps the sword had been forged when he was an old man, disappointed in his girl-child heir, tired of war.

Honey Dream shrugged, and saw Brenda Morris looking at her oddly. No wonder, for the current conversation was not one to which a shrug could be considered a fit response. Honey Dream raised her eyebrows, endeavoring to look wise and inscrutable. Brenda rolled her eyes and very deliberately looked away.

Honey Dream settled herself to seeming attentive, dipping her brush into the ink, making a few characters on the page before her. Already, though, her thoughts were drifting back to her nascent plans.

The treaties might seem an insuperable obstacle, but Gaheris Morris's report had revealed those who might be willing to ally themselves with Honey Dream in return for new magical lore—or merely because they feared what horrors might ensue if the battles of the Lands Born from Smoke and Sacrifice spilled into their world.

She could use this to her advantage, turn others into her tools, make allies of her own. If she did it right, they might even be protected by the very treaties that bound her own hands.

That would be a delicious irony.

Let the others make their limited, ridiculous plans. She would dream bigger dreams, she would be like Chang-o, who reached for immortality and not only became immortal, but became Queen of the Moon as well.

And unlike Chang-o, who shared her realm with a Toad and a Rabbit and a certain amount of notoriety, Honey Dream would share her triumph with a Tiger, with Flying Claw, and they would dwell together in glory, among the highest in all of the Lands Born from Smoke and Sacrifice.

The thought was so delicious that Honey Dream could have purred, but being a Snake, she settled for hissing.

☆

"Right," Des said, and Brenda could tell he was trying to sound enthusiastic when he was anything but, "it looks like our first move is going to be trying to get those four mah-jong sets. Any idea how we go about it?"

"Buy them," Dad said. "Simple and direct. Might even be able to get them for a reasonable price—they're bone and bamboo, common materials, not Bakelite or jade or something."

"I agree, Gaheris," Albert Yu said. "I would further suggest that I be the one to go out and do the buying. Although I am a second-generation Californian, my Chinese heritage is obvious. Well-established businessmen of a certain ethnic background are known for peculiar collecting habits, for reconnecting to their 'roots.' I don't think my wanting to purchase antique mah-jong sets will raise any flags. I might even work through an agent."

Brenda could tell that Dad wasn't exactly thrilled by the ease with which his plan had been adopted. She couldn't figure out why. It seemed as if Albert got on her dad's nerves without even really trying. Was it that bit about being a "successful businessman"? Did Dad feel challenged?

She really was going to have to ask Auntie Pearl—the old manner of address seemed right in this context—about what there was between those two. It might be important later, when they all had to work together.

Inadvertently, Brenda glanced over at Honey Dream. She didn't believe that slinky Snake's excuses for being up in Brenda's room that day—not for one minute—but if Brenda was supposed to pretend they were buddies and work together for the good of the Cause, well, Dad could learn to do the same.

Pearl cut in, as aware as Brenda of the tension between her two former students.

"Very good, Albert, you work out the details. I'm wondering if we should try to get our Snake's mah-jong set as well. She is very old, and is not likely to be a great deal of help to us in this. Certainly, we could not ask her to help establish the Nine Gates. The best we could hope for would be that she would be willing to make the journey to the Lands with us— and to expect such of a somewhat senile octogenarian . . ."

Her pause was eloquent of the dangers and disasters that could be involved in that journey. His expression thoughtful, Riprap paused with his hand partway to the chip bowl he had nearly emptied during their conference.

"I've been wondering about something related to just that matter, Pearl, ever since Des told us how old the Snake is. The Snake and the Monkey are two of the Thirteen we're going to have trouble including in our plans, but it occurred to me—we have a Snake and a Monkey: Honey Dream and Waking Lizard. If I understand how these affiliations work, they even represent versions of the same Branches that we do—attenuated versions, but the same. Why can't Honey Dream and Waking Lizard stand in?"

Neither Pearl nor Shen, who might have been expected to reply, were the first to answer. Surprisingly, the one who did so was Righteous Drum.

"I thank you for your affirmation of the bond between us, Riprap. However, much as my associates and I would be delighted to spare even some of your company the dangers that will be part of involvement in these matters, most of us lack one essential element to fulfill the role. We may be affiliated with the same Earthly Branch, but we lack the blood tie."

Riprap's head lifted, like a hunting dog questing after an elusive scent. "Most of us, you said . . . Who?" Then his expression cleared. "Of course, it must be Flying Claw."

Brenda heard the sudden intake of breath from Pearl, saw the older woman's knotted hands tighten in her lap, sending the cat who had just returned to settle in once more shooting off into the shrubbery.

But this only registered in her peripheral attention. Like the others, her attention had been drawn to Flying Claw, as suddenly and irrevocably as if he were a powerful magnet and they all iron filings.

The young man sat very erect in a cedar patio chair, a long-necked beer bottle held loosely in one hand. His expression was remote and serious, without a trace of the humor it had held when they had spoken in the parlor only a short time before. Although all eyes were on him, his attention was focused on Pearl, gauging her reaction and apparently finding little in it to surprise him.

Riprap broke the tension with the same skill he had used professionally to defuse brawls.

"I don't know why I took so long to consider the probable closeness of the relationship," he said easily, his tone holding only interest. "Pearl knew who Flying Claw was even before she spoke to you because you so strongly resembled her father. How close is the connection?"

"My grandmother," Flying Claw said, "was Thundering Heaven's sister. Pearl is my second cousin, if I understand how you people use the terms. The relationship would be considered a close one in the Lands."

He said this last almost apologetically, and Brenda knew why. Although Pearl had softened somewhat toward Flying Claw, her resentment of him—because he resembled the father who had rejected her, because he was the male Tiger she could never be—had caused a considerable amount of tension in their little household only a few weeks before. Indeed, it had taken Nissa threatening to walk out—and the other three agreeing that they felt Foster deserved better treatment—to get Pearl to moderate her stance.

Since then Flying Claw had done nothing to give Pearl

reason for maintaining her poor opinion of him, and even a few things to earn him points with her. But this reminder . . .

Brenda bit her lip, wondering how Flying Claw would deal with Pearl. He surprised her by giving Pearl a gentle, almost whimsical smile.

"My family is a large one," he said, almost inconsequentially, "but we have never forgotten to make offerings to Thundering Heaven's spirit—certainly for many years before his actual death. We did so privately, because his role as a member of the Shamed and Defeated—as the Twelve were publicly referred to when I was a boy—is still remembered. An official imperial decree made it a crime to remember them at all, but after a few years no one looked too closely at what was done at private memorials.

"But we could not forget that what prosperity, indeed, what freedom and life we possessed, had been given to us because Thundering Heaven and his associates surrendered and accepted exile to protect us. In public, we agreed that they were all cowards and wrong-thinking scoundrels. In private, we revered them. For this reason, at least one male in each line was trained after the arts of an adept, in the hope that one day one of us might again bear the Tiger's mantle.

"I am not an only child," Flying Claw continued. "I have an older brother who will make sacrifices to our ancestors and care for our parents. I have an older sister who is considered something of a wise woman, despite the fact that she is not much older than I am. I have two younger siblings as well. However, I had the good fortune to be the one chosen to go into training. I left my family when I was only a small boy, and was dedicated to the task of becoming one of the Twelve—and most especially to becoming the Tiger."

He looked at Pearl as if expecting her to say something scornful, but Pearl's lips were pressed tightly together. Brenda recognized this for what it was—an effort to hold back tears—and spoke quickly to give Pearl a moment to compose herself.

"So that's why you didn't remember anything about your family—I mean, after your memories were stolen away by the spell. Even before you went away to be taught, you must have been set on trying to be the Tiger. You couldn't remember one without remembering the other."

Flying Claw nodded. "I was, I have been told, a very focused child. My favorite bedtime stories, even when I was smaller than Lani, were about Thundering Heaven—or rather about heroic Tigers. I fear that my imagination compressed them all into one impossibly heroic man."

"That's how myths are made," Nissa said almost inconsequentially, "according to my English teacher, at least."

"I know now," Flying Claw said, "how great a legend I created. I have learned for myself how difficult it is to be a heroic Tiger—and Thundering Heaven was even younger than I am when he was recruited into the Twelve. I wonder if the circumstances were similar?"

Pearl had control of herself now, and when she spoke her voice was the gentlest Brenda had ever heard it. "So your idolizing of my father was what got you into this mess, was it?"

Flying Claw responded to the tone, not the words. "I was idealistic, yes, and when I was approached with the opportunity to restore to the Jade Petal Throne the line of the very emperor who Thundering Heaven himself had served, I was not in the least difficult to convince. The previous Tiger had been friend and mentor to me, and I also wished to carry out his dreams."

Brenda held her breath, waiting for Pearl to say something cutting, but Pearl surprised her—and perhaps herself—by looking Flying Claw squarely in the eyes and saying, "Thundering Heaven would have approved of you. You can be certain of that."

There was no bitterness in the words, although Thundering Heaven had never approved of Pearl, and that lack of approval had blighted Pearl's entire life.

Flying Claw talks about fulfilling his mentor's dreams,

about living up to his family's expectations, Brenda thought. *I wonder if he's ever allowed himself a dream that was all his own. I wonder if it would be entirely bad to have everything so neatly laid out for you.*

She glanced up at her father. Gaheris Morris had that absent look in his eyes that she knew so well. He was planning something. It probably had to do with one-upping Albert over those mah-jong sets. What was it with those two? She decided that she'd ask Pearl if she could get her alone later.

Their meeting broke up shortly thereafter. Even though he'd rushed out to the West Coast, Gaheris wasn't one to waste a business opportunity. He had an appointment in San Francisco the next morning, and was taking the train up that night.

"Means I have to pay for a hotel room, Breni," he said, when she drove him to the station in the small car, "but it also means I don't need to deal with rush hour, and that's a bonus. What do you think of our grand plans?"

"Kinda shaky," Brenda replied honestly, "and not much for me and the others to do but make more amulet bracelets while Albert runs around buying mah-jong sets."

"Learn the techniques that will make those bracelets backup, rather than your entire arsenal," Dad advised her.

Brenda nodded. She'd had a reminder when she'd caught Honey Dream prowling in her room of just how little she could do, just how vulnerable she was.

"Dad, do you really think we can pull this off? I mean, can we get to these Nine Gates and back to the Lands before whoever in the Lands comes after us? And once we're there, can we actually do anything? I mean, it seems so impossible."

Dad answered sideways, an annoying habit of his.

"Actually, Breni, we're not going to need to 'get to' those Nine Gates. We're going to need to build them."

"What?"

He ignored her and went on. "As to whether we can do it or not, if there's one thing that Ms. Tracy Frye's visit to my office the other day proved to me, it's that we'd better make every appearance of trying very hard to do so. Otherwise we're going to find ourselves under a lot of pressure."

"From the Rock Dove Society?"

"From them, and from people who are a whole lot less pleasant—people who don't pretend to be a bird-watching club when they want to meet. When I brought you out to meet Albert—god, was it only a little over a month ago?—I knew that what I'd be introducing you to was a whole new worldview. I admit, I'd hoped that we could concentrate on our traditions for a while before being forced to explain the complexities of this world within a world that we're part of."

Brenda had pulled into the commuter train station while he was speaking, and Dad leaned over and gave her a peck on the cheek before reaching into the backseat for his overnight bag.

"My advice to you, Brenda Morris," he said, suddenly serious, "is to do your best to concentrate on your immediate studies. Learn what you can—what you need—and leave worrying about the big picture to us."

"To us 'grown-ups,'" she said, trying to make a joke of it and feeling pretty certain that she'd failed.

"To those of us who have a bit more training," he replied seriously as he got out of the car. When a Zhi Pig is coming at you is *not* the time to wonder if the sequence you need is 'dragon—dragon—wind' or 'wind—wind—dragon.'"

"What's a Zhi Pig?" Brenda called after him.

"Ask Des," Dad called back. "Ask Des. I'm going to miss my train."

He jogged toward the platform, and Brenda watched him go. Then she pulled back into the stream of traffic and drove thoughtfully along the now-familiar streets to Pearl's house.

X

Honey Dream was coming out of the downstairs powder room when she heard Brenda Morris's voice drifting down the stairs. From the location of the sound, she guessed that Brenda must be in the upstairs classroom, and that the door was open. That must mean that whatever lecture or work session had been going on was ending, because the door was invariably kept shut otherwise.

"Des? What's a Zhi Pig?"

"Where did you hear about Zhi Pigs?" Des's voice sounded surprised.

"Dad. When I took him to the train station yesterday, he told me that I needed to concentrate on my studies, because when a Zhi Pig was coming after me, that was no time to worry about the sequencing of a spell."

"He's right," Des replied. "The spells need to come quickly, the images to flow through you like . . ."

"Des!" Brenda interrupted. "We just finished that lecture. I agree. Really. I'm working on it. What's a Zhi Pig?"

The voices were coming closer now. Footfalls hit the stairs. These were made by more sets of footsteps than two. Probably Nissa and Riprap were present as well.

Honey Dream thought about drawing back, but she wasn't doing anything wrong, and she *was* interested. Where had Gaheris Morris learned about Zhi Pigs? They weren't precisely common.

"A Zhi Pig," Des said pedantically, "is a denizen of the Floating-Jade Mountain. Despite its name, it more resembles a tiger than a pig, although its tail is like that of an ox. It is carnivorous, and a known man-eater."

He and Brenda, walking side by side down the staircase, had turned toward the back of the house and so saw Honey

Dream standing in the hallway. Brenda—predictably—stiffened, although Honey Dream had done nothing to merit such a reaction, but Des gave an easy smile.

"Hi, Honey Dream. Have you ever seen a Zhi Pig?"

"I have not," she admitted, turning to lead the informal procession—for Nissa and Riprap were indeed coming down the stairs a few paces behind their teacher and classmate— toward the back of the house. "Once, at a festival there was a man displaying what he said was the skin of one, but I had my doubts. The ox's tail had clearly been stitched on to the tiger's skin. When I challenged the man, he refused to be shaken from his lie. He said that the tail had come loose during the curing process, and he had simply returned it to its natural place. I did not press him further. Argument with a fool makes one a fool oneself."

"I can see why you wouldn't bother," Des agreed.

They had all arrived in the large back area of the house that combined kitchen, informal dining area, and what was, for some reason Honey Dream couldn't quite fathom, called the "family room." The name seemed odd to her, especially in light of the fact that until recently Pearl had apparently lived alone in this large house without even a niece or nephew to attend her needs, only a few paid servants—and these about only during the day.

Riprap had, inevitably, crossed to the refrigerator and was pulling out a bowl of cherries. The big man could eat more than any grown man Honey Dream had ever met, and he always seemed to be hungry.

"Have you ever seen a dragon, Honey Dream?" Riprap asked. "I mean living wild or in its natural habitat or whatever, not summoned by a spell."

"Of course," she said. "Dragons are easy to find if you know their habits."

"Must be something," he said. "I mean, even with what we can do with our spells, even with what we've seen, I can't really believe that there are places where dragons live the way squirrels and rabbits live around here."

"Dragons," Honey Dream reminded him, "are much more intelligent and dangerous than squirrels and rabbits."

Riprap nodded and extended the bowl of cherries to her. Honey Dream took a small handful, glad that she hadn't offended Riprap with her unnecessary reminder. Having watched him in action during the attack, she felt sharply aware that for all the big man's eager cooperation so much of the time, he could be quite dangerous.

Honey Dream knew perfectly why she kept digging at the Orphans. She felt so out of place here, and kept trying to remind them—and herself—how much she had to offer.

The bowl of cherries was placed on the long table. Riprap seated himself within easy reach. Nissa and Brenda had vanished, probably outside to check on Lani. Honey Dream was internally debating whether she should remain here or return to Pearl's office, where she had been taking notes for her father, when she saw Des looking speculatively at her.

"I'm thinking," he said, when she raised her eyebrows at him in mute query, "that Riprap is right. Dragons and all the rest are far too unreal to all of us. Yet, if we are going to attempt to establish the Nine Gates, we will need to adjust our worldview—to widen it. Otherwise, we're not going to be much help."

Honey Dream didn't know how to respond to such an odd statement, but Riprap made that unnecessary.

"So what are you thinking? Adding zoology to our lessons? I'm not sure I can handle much more memorization."

Des reached for a cherry and used one long fingernail to split it and remove the stone.

"I was thinking of something more immediate than memorization," he said. "I was considering a field trip into the guardian domains. We're going to need to enter them eventually. Why wait to acclimate you three until after Righteous Drum and Shen agree where and how to set the first gate?"

"Have you been there?" Honey Dream asked.

"A few times," Des said. "My grandmother took me in,

just as far as the edges, when I was a boy. What she showed me was interesting, beautiful sometimes, but not exactly where I'd choose to go on holiday."

Honey Dream had to agree. She had done some training in the edges of those lands herself, but had not cared to venture in very deeply. Her teachers had not pressed her. Later, when passing over those lands via the bridge, she had been relatively safe. Even so, she had seen things that continued to transform the most benign dreams into nightmares.

She was impressed that Des had been there. His training had been more rigorous than she had thought.

Riprap looked excited and pleased—a clear indication he had no idea how dangerous what Des proposed might possibly be.

"When would we go?" he asked.

"I'll need to talk with Pearl," Des said, "but I was thinking tomorrow. I thought I'd request that Flying Claw—and Honey Dream, if her skills as a researcher are not needed here—accompany us, so that we will have a mixture of talents and a certain degree of experience."

Riprap looked momentarily disgruntled, as if he were going to protest the need for a caretaker, then what Honey Dream had come to accept as his basic good sense took over.

"You're right. Brenda, Nissa, and I are all novices. It would be too much to expect you to cover for us all if there was an accident."

"And Zhi Pigs," Des reminded him, heading in the direction of Pearl's office with his usual directness of purpose, "are noted man-eaters. They're not the only creatures to have cultivated that taste."

Following the inevitable discussion that Honey Dream was coming to accept as part of anything the Orphans did, Des's suggestion of a field trip was not only agreed upon, but viewed as a very wise preparation for the tasks to come.

Pearl retreated to her office to make a series of phone calls that somehow related to the planned journey. Nissa had her own series of phone calls to make, these involved with keep-

ing Lani occupied while they were away. It had been agreed
that this was not the time to take the child along.

Brenda vanished upstairs and Honey Dream heard the
door to the studio/classroom close firmly behind her. Des
and Riprap left—inviting Flying Claw to go with them—in
order to do some shopping in preparation for the trip.

Seeing them all so purposeful, listening to them discussing arcane items like ultralight Coleman lanterns and collapsible cooking pots, Honey Dream felt so out of her depth
that she considered making an excuse to remain here. However, if she didn't go, she had a feeling that she'd regret it.
There was too much she didn't know about these guardian
domains, too much she needed to know.

And, if she stayed behind, Brenda would have Flying
Claw to herself in the cozy intimacy of shared danger. That
wouldn't do. That wouldn't do at all. . . .

That night, Pearl and Shen sat in her office waiting for the
Double Hour of the Tiger—or less poetically put, for three
o'clock in the morning. After assisting with arrangements
for what Des persisted in calling the "field trip," both of
them had taken afternoon naps, agreeing that going to bed at
their normal hour, then expecting to get up at 2:00 A.M. and
function with clear minds would be more difficult.

Clear minds were what they would need, for the reason
they were waiting for the Double Hour of the Tiger was that
they were going to set wards and protections on the warehouse from which Des and his students would be making
their departure for the guardian domains.

The household had begun settling in to sleep at 7:00 P.M.,
when a protesting Lani was taken up for her bath. The adults
had stayed up longer, of course, but by midnight, reminded
that tomorrow would be a very busy, very unusual day, the
last rushes of water through the pipes, the last muffled thuds
of motion from above, had indicated that all but Shen and
Pearl were asleep.

They had filled the remaining time sitting in her office

with the lights turned low, alternating between conversation and meditation, gathering the ch'i they planned to spend in lavish wards, enjoying the luxury of time when of late there had been so much rush.

Pearl was leaning back in her favorite wingback chair, grey Bonaventure purring lazily in her lap, when she felt one of her household wards go off.

She rose, pushing Bonaventure to the floor, reaching for her sword Treaty, which rested—polished, shined, and sharpened—on top of her desk.

"Pearl?" Shen pushed himself to his feet, hands on the arms of the wingback chair that matched her own. "What's wrong?"

"Something's set off one of my wards, one of the ones on the garage apartment."

"Where the prisoners are?"

"Exactly."

Pearl had kept moving as she spoke, and now she was heading toward the back of the house. The garage was a separate small building that could be entered either from the walled backyard, or from the street. The ward that had alerted her had been on the street side.

"Should we call the others?"

"I'm not wasting time to run upstairs," Pearl said. "Might be perfectly normal thieves, and, if so, the wards will stop them, but if it's someone else, I don't think we should let them know we've detected them by shouting upstairs. There are windows open all through the house. The sound would carry."

Shen nodded. "I'm coming with you."

Pearl glanced back and saw he had a long-handled ink brush in his right hand. She smiled.

"Glad to have you."

The brief exchange had carried them to the door that led out of the kitchen onto the patio. Pearl undid locks both mundane and otherwise, pocketed the key, and left her wards in place. The door had a spring fastener and would lock behind them.

Together Pearl and Shen picked their way down the three stairs that took them onto the patio. Then Pearl led the way onto the path that led to the garage. Like all the paths in the overgrown but carefully tended jungle that was her garden, it twisted and curved, dispersing natural ch'i where it would do both the plants and the house they sheltered the most good.

Usually, Pearl liked her twisting paths, but tonight she could have wished for straighter lines, more direct access. A portion of her attention was anchored within the wards, and what she was receiving was very interesting.

Unlike a normal thief, who would find himself suddenly apprehensive and bored, who would wonder why these old wooden doors were so hard to force, who would decide there must be easier pickings elsewhere, and who would never know that these impulses were not generated by his own mind, whoever had touched Pearl's ward had recognized it for what it was and had withdrawn.

However, in the time it had taken for Pearl and Shen to cross from her office to the back door, the would-be intruder had returned. This time he—and Pearl felt very certain her opponent was a male—had set out to render the ward quiescent, not so much deactivating it as muting it.

Pearl tasted his magic as it glided through her own, probing, tweaking, loosening. One of the indigenous traditions. Pearl didn't know which, but there was nothing of the taste of the Lands here.

If I hadn't been awake, Pearl thought uneasily, *I might have been unaware. That first impulse might have dissolved into an uneasy moment in a dream.*

They had reached the garage door. Before opening it, Pearl paused, extending her awareness to her other wards. She, Des, and Albert had set their protections in layers, since the garage itself would need to be used during the day—not only to park vehicles, but because if they sealed the garage, inevitably they would discover that they needed something stored within.

Therefore, the lower level of the garage was warded so that the residents of Pearl's household could go in and out without setting off alarms.

The upper level, where the apartment was, however, had been sealed so that no one but Pearl, Des, and Shen could gain access. The prisoners had been given a supply of food, and had running water and basic comforts. They were checked on twice a day—first thing in the morning, and last thing at night. Sometimes, over Pearl's protests, Shen went out and talked to the prisoners, saying that isolation was horribly cruel. It was not an ideal situation, but it had worked for the six days—*Seven now*, thought Pearl—since the attack.

Whoever had triggered the ward had only touched the lower level. Pearl stood on her toes and looked through the glass window into the garage interior. Nothing. And that nothing was something. The street side of the garage had motion-sensitive lights. Whoever was out there—and she was certain someone was out there—had taken care not to activate them.

They're good, Pearl thought. *But I'm better.*

Her nerves hummed happily, the way they had before stepping before a camera, before breaking into a song she knew would be listened to by hundreds of thousands of people. It was a very good feeling, but Pearl knew the danger of overconfidence, knew the abundant ch'i she had stored was humming in her veins, urging her to foolish action.

No "Take Two," here, she thought. *Make every step count.*

Pearl looked over her shoulder and found Shen distant and abstracted, his ink brush dangling loosely from his fingers.

"I have them," he said softly. "Three. One is infiltrating the wards. I traced back through him and found the others. One female. Another male. They are standing back across the street, waiting for the one who is working on the wards to finish."

Pearl did not ask how Shen knew this. Dragons were far better at magic than were Tigers—and even if this had not been the case, Shen's grandfather and teacher had been from the Lands, and had lavished knowledge on the grandson who had been the only good to come out of his daughter's death in childbirth. Shen had always been better than her at magic.

Shen went on. "I've woken Des, sent a surge up through one of the wards he helped make. He knows to be quiet, not to make a light."

Pearl nodded. A suspicion was seeping into her ch'i-charged nerves, a warning that told her that nothing was as simple as it seemed. Yes. Whoever was out there would probably like having their prisoners, but what if their goal was more complex?

We must be very careful, Pearl thought. *They are across the street. That means they are technically not invading my lands, even if I know one is meddling with my wards. That meddling is skillful, would be hard to prove.*

Pearl had great respect for their opponents. Unlike her father, she did not scorn the indigenous traditions of this world. She had not formally studied them, not learned their arts, for to do so any teacher would have demanded that she trade away some of the Orphans' knowledge, and that was taboo, but Pearl had learned what she could.

And there is power other than magical power, she thought. *There is manipulation other than skillful defusing of a ward. What if I was meant to feel that first intrusion? What if we are meant to do something impulsive, something that will withdraw even more of the tenuous support we have from the members of the indigenous traditions?*

Pearl looked at Shen and saw from his slight nod, from the character he traced in the air with one fingertip, the one for "trap," followed by the very usual question mark, that he, too, had his doubts about how to handle the situation.

Pearl glanced down at her watch: 2:15 A.M., about the time she and Shen had planned to leave the house in any case. The probing had loosened, although not broken, one of her wards and had come up against another. Their opponent's laborious unweaving must begin again.

Pearl smiled a wicked tiger's smile. *Traps may be sprung, snapping closed, catching nothing. True, we will not catch those who set it, but then I don't believe we wish to do so. I will know this one's signature if we meet again. I expect Shen will recognize all three. That is something. Let us spring their trap.*

She looked at Shen and grinned mischievously, then she slipped back along the garden path and opened the kitchen door, this time not bothering to do so quietly.

Reaching around the doorjamb, she switched on the array of lights that lined the paths and edge of the patio. They glowed quietly enough by the standards of polite company, but glaring after the nighttime darkness.

"Time to get going, Shen," Pearl said, as if her companion was still inside. "I know it's early."

He had followed her back, and now he replied, his tones natural enough to demonstrate that the amateur theatrics they'd done as teenagers hadn't been forgotten.

"It's earlier for me than you. I'm still on New York time, remember? There it's five-fifteen, early, but not quite god-awful."

Des had descended the stairs. He was wearing a bathrobe of dark red Chinese brocade, his hairy calves and bare feet poking out under the hem.

The Rooster nodded at Pearl, his lips shaping a smile of greeting, but his eyes preternaturally solemn. Then he moved into her office, where a window gave a good view of the side street. Otherwise he gave no indication that he was present.

"Hang on," Pearl said. "I've forgotten something."

She hurried back into the office, and gathered up the already prepared bag of tools she and Shen would need to craft the wards at the warehouse. Treaty still rested in her hand, and she grabbed the sword's sheath, but left the case behind.

The feeling of pressure on her wards was easing. Since

they had not been broken, they tightened back into their usual effectiveness.

I suppose I could be grateful that I don't need to reset them, Pearl thought, *but I'm still pissed.*

Shen took the bag of tools from her, freeing her hands so that she could get to her car keys. Once in the garage, she switched on the light.

Leave them wondering if we knew they were there. They certainly didn't expect us to be awake.

In a moment, Pearl was backing the town car out onto the narrow street. She was out of practice, but at this early hour the cars that would later crowd the edges—overflow from the museum—were not yet there and she managed not to clip anything.

Shen peered out the window, New Yorker nervous about cars in tight spaces, calling occasional warnings to her as she backed. When they were straightened out and on the road, he poked her in the ribs.

"Gone, Ming-Ming, but they were there. I wonder if they wanted the prisoners or for us to do something foolish?"

"I suspect they would have settled for both," Pearl said. Her phone rang. "Get that for me, would you? I bet it's Des."

It was. Shen held the phone so Pearl could listen in.

"Our visitors left as soon as the garage light went on," Des said. "Two men and a woman. I didn't get a clear enough look to be sure, but I think I recognized one of the men from his walk as a member of the Finch Society. Hot-tempered fellow, Polish nationalist, terrorist connections."

Pearl nodded. The Finch Society was the local version of the Rock Dove Society. The trend for using bird-watching groups for cover was nationwide, enabling various local branches to invite visitors from out of the area without arousing suspicion.

Shen answered, "Sounds good. The wards seem to have reset, but you should check them."

"Them and the prisoners both," Des said, "but I think we're safe for tonight."

"I agree," Shen said. "I think they were pushing, testing, seeing what they could manage. Maybe they got wind of the prisoners. Maybe they figured we would have taken less care with the garage than with other parts of the house, but Pearl and I think they may have been trying to prompt something rash."

"At two in the morning?" Des said doubtfully.

"Never underestimate your opponent," Pearl said.

"Pearl, Shen," for a moment Des's voice, even distorted as it was by a cell phone, sounded more like that of the little boy she had once taught, "do you think this is a coincidence? I mean, we plan a trip to the guardian domains, and then next thing we know, we're being attacked—or at least Pearl's house is."

Shen replied after a thoughtful pause. "It is possible that this is no coincidence."

"Does that mean," Pearl asked sharply, "there is still an informant among us?"

Shen shook his head. "Not necessarily, Pearl. For one, whoever informed the Landers about the Thirteen Orphans was almost certainly coerced to do so."

"That's what Righteous Drum implied," Des agreed. "He also said flat-out that the informant would have no reason to continue doing so."

"And so requested that he not need to reveal who it was," Pearl concluded. "And we agreed. Shen, if it isn't that same informant, do you suspect another?"

Shen shook his head again. "No. We are not the only magical tradition to practice divination, Pearl. What I suspect is that in addition to setting purely human watchers on us, our adversaries—that consortium of which Tracy Frye boasted—has been regularly doing divinations or auguries. Such could not tell them precisely what we are doing, but it could indicate that we are intending on taking a major step, even, if they are clever enough to ask the right questions, that we are planning on setting up a gate."

Pearl was so interested in what Shen was saying that she

nearly drove through a red light, an easy thing to do at this hour when the streets were nearly deserted.

"And if," she said, "they could have prompted us to do something impulsive, something the paranoid would interpret as an attack, then they might be able to stop us, to insist on an observer, any number of things. Gates and bridges make people very nervous."

The light changed to green, and Pearl resumed driving.

"Des," she said, "we're nearly to the warehouse. The Double Hour of the Tiger is nearly upon us, and more than ever Shen and I have work to do."

XI

The next morning, directly after rush hour, they picked up Flying Claw and Honey Dream at Colm Lodge. The van was crowded, especially after Honey Dream and Flying Claw had added large duffel bags to the pile of gear already stacked in the back.

From his place at the wheel, Des said, "Trivia time. There are four guardian domains, each oriented to one of the four cardinal points. Our group would have an advantage in one of the four. Anyone want to guess which one?"

He'd directed the question to Brenda, Nissa, and Riprap, which was only fair. Honey Dream and Flying Claw probably already knew the answer. In fact, based on the smug expression on Honey Dream's face, Brenda was willing to bet that the Snake, for one, certainly did.

Brenda thought quickly over what she'd learned about the Chinese perception of the universe. Four areas. Directionally oriented . . . In Chinese cosmology, there was a fifth direction—center—but that direction belonged to the Lands.

Wait! Brenda remembered something about the Tiger.

Both Tiger and Dragon were not only associated with signs of the zodiac, but with directions as well. Tiger was Guardian of the West. Dragon was Guardian of the East.

She blurted out her answer, eager to wipe that smirk off Honey Dream's face. "West. Tiger. Tiger is the Guardian of the West. That's our advantage. Foster . . . I'm sorry, Flying Claw is the Tiger. Somehow that will give us an edge."

"Two points," Des said, marking with two fingers on an imaginary board.

Brenda was pleased by the praise, but she was even more pleased by the flicker of disappointment that went over Honey Dream's face. She guessed that Honey Dream had been looking forward to lecturing their ignorant selves.

Brenda hoped Flying Claw hadn't been annoyed by her lapse—referring to him as Foster, not Flying Claw—but right now she felt too shy to look over at him.

Riprap had flashed an approving smile at Brenda when she'd answered, but now he was looking serious again.

"Our larger group," he said, "I mean, when you include Pearl and Shen and the rest, has not one but two Tigers, and not one but two Dragons. Has that been taken into those calculations you keep mentioning?"

Des nodded. "It has, and that's one of the reasons that it's taken so long for the appropriate formula to be constructed. I spoke with Pearl this morning, and unless they turn up something new in their work today, the plan for when we set out to set up the Nine Gates is for us to enter in the West, then place the gates in a sequence that will enable us to make our final exit from the guardian domains into the East. Righteous Drum has something of an acquaintance with either the Dragon or a dragon—I'm not really sure which—in the East. He hopes that will facilitate our final transition into the Lands, even if various barriers have been erected specifically against any of our return. But that's for later. Let's get on with now."

"And 'now,'" Nissa said, "includes setting up the first of the Nine Gates, earlier than planned."

"Last night's little adventure," Des said, "makes that necessary. We need to establish a gate into the guardian domains before enough of the indigenous traditions are stirred up and start insisting that we do nothing to perforate the integrity of what they see as 'their' domain."

Brenda glanced at Nissa. The other woman's turquoise eyes were very round and her expression far from reassured. They traded worried looks, but obviously the time to argue was long passed.

"But we're not constructing the gate at Pearl's house?" Nissa pressed. "Won't that make it vulnerable?"

"Pearl," Des said, "does not welcome the thought of a series of gates beginning in her house, and she extended the same courtesy to Colm Lodge. Instead, she suggested we use some commercial real estate she owns. There's a building not currently rented that should be perfect for our needs.

"The building we'll be using," Des went on, sensing their need to be reassured, "is fenced. Equipped with locks. Pearl and Shen came out this morning at the start of the Double Hour of the Tiger and secured the premises further."

That's three in the morning, Brenda thought. *And they came over after dealing with our "guests." I hope they get some rest before Righteous Drum and Waking Lizard arrive to fuss over the intricacies of magical formulae.*

The area in which Pearl's rental property was located was in one of those nice commercial/industrial areas that are so well groomed that they look more like parks than warehouses. Even the unmistakable security fences were nicely made. The ones guarding Pearl's property had a light growth of bramble roses on them—ornamentation and deterrents in one.

"Classy," Nissa said with approval. "But then if Pearl's involved, I'm not surprised."

"Pearl's parents—her mother in particular," Des said, pulling the van in front of a gate and reaching out to press a code into a keypad, "had a good eye for real estate. Pearl sometimes gripes that she supported her family far more than her father ever did, but unlike many child stars, her parents made certain there was plenty left over for her."

The gate slid open, and Des eased the van through. A moment later, the gate closed again.

"Classy," Nissa repeated.

Des parked the van under a steel ramada around the side.

"Everybody grab a bag or two out of the back," he said, taking up a small case he'd had resting next to him on the front seat. "I'm going to open the warehouse."

They did so. There was a pack for each of them, none overly large, but holding between them a wide variety of camping and medical gear. As Des had put it the evening before, he didn't expect them to need ninety percent of what they'd be carrying, but he'd hate to have them wishing for bandages or water-purification tablets or the means of making a fire merely because they were too lazy to carry them.

"After all," he'd said, "we're not going for a walk in the park."

There was another package, too, something large, wrapped in a tarp, that Riprap and Des had stowed with teasing solemnity. Riprap took charge of this, moving it with ease, despite its bulk and evident weight.

There were packs for Flying Claw and Honey Dream already made up, so Brenda wondered what they'd brought in their duffels. When Flying Claw moved his, it emitted a faint but distinctly metallic clank, and she thought she knew.

Des was standing in the doorway of a medium-sized prefabricated building too small to really be classified as a warehouse, but too large to be a shed.

"Come on," he called. "Grab the stuff and get a move on. Riprap, make sure the van's locked up tightly. I don't trust these beeper things."

Riprap did so without comment, and Brenda, who'd been about to make some joke about old people and electronic devices, fell silent. He was being a perfect Dog, the ideal strong team player. They might not have crossed into the guardian domains yet, but this was none too soon to start taking things seriously.

There's just one problem, she thought, sliding her pack onto her shoulders. *I don't really believe we're going to do this. Despite everything I've seen, I don't really believe that in a few minutes or hours or whatever, we're going to be walking somewhere that isn't in this world.*

The interior of the warehouse smelled of animal feed and burnt sugar. Although no air-conditioning was running, the interior was cool.

"Pearl rented this space to the same itinerant circus that was using Colm Lodge," Des explained. "They only picked up their gear last week. There's another small room in addition to this large one. It's basically a closet, lined with shelves, but you . . ." he glanced at Honey Dream and Flying Claw, "might find it useful as a changing area. You can leave your duffels in there on the shelves. You won't want to carry them."

"No," Flying Claw agreed. "Honey Dream can change first. I would like to help orient the gate."

Brenda held her breath, waiting for Honey Dream to say something provocative, but the Snake did not. She didn't even look disappointed.

She also realized this is work time, not flirt time, Brenda thought. *I've got to get my head on straight.*

"Change?" Nissa asked.

"Into my working clothes," Honey Dream said, hefting the duffel slightly. "The robes of the Snake."

Nissa looked impressed. "Of course. That makes sense, but you wouldn't have wanted to wear them over here. Someone might have seen and noticed."

"Do you think someone is watching us?" Brenda said. "I've been looking, but I haven't seen any cars following us."

"I think it's likely," Nissa replied. "We know Tracy Frye and her associates are interested in what we're doing. As far as they know, we've come here for some sort of training exercise, but if Flying Claw and Honey Dream had been seen in elaborate robes, someone might have wondered."

"And Pearl would prefer to keep people wondering," Des said. He was kneeling on the floor, next to the case he'd brought from the van. "In this, she and Righteous Drum are in the fullest agreement. Brenda, you've got to remember, there are more ways for our adversaries to watch than by physically trailing us."

Brenda felt dumb.

Honey Dream was heading for the closet. Nissa called out after her.

"If you have any buttons that need to be done up or ribbons tied or whatever, let me know."

"I am not Lani," Honey Dream began sharply, her words snapping in the empty air. Then, perhaps hearing how bitchy she sounded, she softened. "I'm sorry. Thank you. I can reach almost all the ties, but I will call if I need help."

"We'll be here," Nissa promised.

"We will indeed," Des said.

He had pulled out a compass and was checking the directions. Flying Claw was standing next to him, using a compass of his own. The design was somewhat different from the one Des was using, the dark wooden case elegantly carved with elaborate symbols.

It seemed to work the same, though, because both Flying Claw and Des oriented on the same wall, almost as if performing steps in some slow, solemn dance.

"Okay," Des said, making a mark on the floor with red chalk. "Here's due west. Do we want to set up directly against the wall or out a bit?"

Flying Claw went and ran his fingers over the ridged metal of the walls.

"We could set up here, but I would prefer if we did not. That would put two liminal zones in against each other."

"Liminal zones?" Brenda asked, forgetting her shyness now that the project was becoming real.

"Borders," Des explained. "Space between space. Walls may look solid, but they are what create inside and outside. Gates open inside and outside of the space between here and somewhere else. That's what Flying Claw means."

"Can we set up here?" Flying Claw asked, taking a few paces back from the wall and consulting his compass. He bent and made a few marks on the floor with a perfectly normal yellow pencil. "It feels like the proper place."

"We can try," Riprap said. "Des and I experimented in the hardware store last night, and picked up what we'd need to make this stand on its own."

With that, he stripped off the tarp, and Brenda saw with a little shiver of amazement that what he'd carried in was a complete door assemblage in unfinished pine, frame and all.

Within a few moments, the door was standing on the bare concrete floor, looking very odd. Riprap put his hand out and gave the doorframe a solid shake. It vibrated, but remained steady. He opened and shut the prehung door, kicked another shim under the doorframe when the door didn't swing neatly shut, then tried again. This time everything worked perfectly.

"All right," Riprap said. "We have a door. However, I don't think it's going to take us anywhere without some further modifications. What do we do next?"

Des was holding a folder he'd taken from his case, and now he opened it to display two colorful prints depicting heavyset, red-faced Chinese warriors in elaborate if obviously stylized armor. Each bristled with weapons, and each held what Brenda decided must be lanterns.

"These," Des said, "are the Men Shen. That simply means Door Spirits or Door Gods. A more accurate translation would probably be 'door guardians,' because that's what they do. These are modern depictions, so their costumes and the way their faces look owe a lot to Chinese opera, but the tradition is quite old. Records exist as far back as the second century A.D., but they are probably far older.

"There are several different stories as to how the door guards originated, but these two are based on actual historical people, ministers of the T'ang emperor T'ai Tsung. The story is that whenever T'ai Tsung tried to get some sleep, he was plagued by supernatural visitations. Some versions of the story call them demons, others ghosts or goblins. What's absolutely clear is that T'ai Tsung couldn't get a decent night's sleep. This was good neither for the emperor, nor for the lands he ruled, and especially not for his ministers."

"Yeah," Riprap said with a grin. "They'd be on the front line if the emperor got cranky."

"So two of those ministers," Des continued, his answering grin fading into storytelling solemnity, "Ch'in Shu-pao and Hu Ching-te, offered to guard T'ai Tsung's door—some stories say they guarded the palace gates, but the point is the same. They put on their most elaborate armor and all their weapons before taking up their posts. In the end, they were so ferocious-looking that whatever supernatural creatures were bothering Emperor T'ai Tsung decided to back off. The ministers kept watch for several more nights, and the creatures did not return.

"Eventually, T'ai Tsung, noticing that two of his key ministers weren't quite up to their duties, since they weren't getting very much rest, thanked them for their services. However, he asked if, before they put off their armaments, would they permit the court artists to make life-sized portraits of them. These portraits would be placed on the palace gates to remind the supernatural creatures how well the emperor was guarded.

"The tactic must have worked, because there is no further record of the emperor's sleep being troubled. A continuing New Year tradition is to hang portraits of the Men Shen on the door to keep evil influences at bay. I picked up these two when I was in San Francisco last week."

"Nice," Riprap said. "So I guess Ch'in Shu-pao and Hu Ching-te will guard the first of the Nine Gates for us. I admit it's a relief that our backs will be guarded, but how will they help us get into the guardian domains?"

There was a slight rustling of silk behind them. Brenda turned to see Honey Dream, clad in elaborate robes of pale golden yellow, elaborately embellished with snakes and other, less immediately recognizable things, coming over to join them. Across the large room, the door to the storage closet was closing behind Flying Claw.

Honey Dream was trying to fasten one of the ribbons that bound her thick, black hair into an elaborate twist, and Nissa moved to help her. Perhaps in gratitude, Honey Dream spoke almost politely, certainly without her usual condescension, her reply showing that she had been attending to Des's lecture.

"Doors—and gates are simply a kind of door—are considered dangerous because they make an opening that introduces chaos into the system of order. In their role as guardians, the Men Shen make the choice as to what—and who—are to be guarded against, who to be admitted. We will request that the Men Shen open the gate into the Western guardian domains for us. Then, unless the White Tiger of the West refuses our appeal to enter, they will let us pass."

"Because," Nissa said, tucking an edge of Honey Dream's hem so that it hung straight, "if the White Tiger admits us, we will not be introducing chaos into the ordered system."

"Correct." Honey Dream nodded approval.

The Snake moved restlessly to join them, shaking down a long sleeve. Brenda had a sudden insight that made Honey Dream humanly vulnerable.

She wants a mirror. She can't tell if she's gotten everything on so it looks right.

Des seemed to realize the same thing. His folder containing the pictures of the Men Shen still in his hand, he moved over to inspect Honey Dream's costume with a detached professionalism he must have acquired when working as an artist's model.

"That's a wonderful shenyi," he said. "Very classic in style, with little influence from the later garments that evolved from it."

"Among our Twelve," Honey Dream said, "all our ceremonial attire takes its form from the fashions of the days when the Lands were created. The robes conform in shape and style to the regulations and rituals as set down in the Book of Rites."

"I've read the Book of Rites," Des said, "or at least the version that came to us. The shapes that make up the shenyi express a balance of square and round, reflecting the balance of the universe. The hem must be cut perfectly, long enough to conceal the ankle, but never touching the ground. This creates a garment laden with symbolism, practical as well as elegant. I notice, however, that your embroideries show the influence of protective charms from later ages, as well those that were common at the time of the Ch'in Dynasty."

Honey Dream actually grinned. Brenda couldn't believe how approachable the expression made her seem.

"Well," Honey Dream said, brushing a hand along one section of her skirt. "When one is working with dangerous elements—and magic can be very dangerous—one does not limit the protections one can gain. My robe is dominated by snakes, of course, but there are both bats and clouds to bring happiness and good fortune, and crabs to repel evil magic."

"Can you move comfortably swathed up in all that fabric?" Nissa asked.

"Easily," Honey Dream replied. "Indeed, until I came to your world, I would have wondered why you asked."

Brenda noticed that in one way at least Honey Dream's elegant shenyi was clearly a working garment. The waist was cinched with a leather belt—the bronze buckle worked in the twisting form of a snake, of course—and various tools hung from the supple, polished leather. There was a curved dagger Brenda had only too good a reason to remember, as well as three bottle gourds whose surfaces had been elaborately painted with stylized Chinese characters. Tucked on the right side, a bit toward the back, was a small flat case that Brenda thought might hold inkstone and brushes.

Brenda had seen how Honey Dream could do magic

through written characters, so she understood why the Snake would carry the means for writing. She was momentarily puzzled by the bottle gourds; then she remembered that bottle gourds were often featured in Chinese fairy tales or folk legends as containers that held magic.

"I've already discussed this next part with Flying Claw," Des said, "and with Pearl. She reminded us how on the Night of the Three-Legged Toad, she had reason to draw rather more strongly than usual upon her Tigerness. Therefore, the White Tiger of the West may already be aware of us. This could be good, but it also could mean trouble. Much will depend on whether the Tiger will feel we have honored the connection between him and our own tigers or exploited it. When we open the gate, I want everyone to let Flying Claw invoke the Tiger. No matter how rough things get, don't interfere unless Flying Claw directly asks."

Brenda thought Des gave Honey Dream a particularly meaningful stare, but the Snake only smoothed one of the folds of her shenyi and looked mysterious and serene.

Riprap seemed about to ask a question when the door to the storage closet opened, and Flying Claw emerged. His appearance was so remarkable that all conversation stilled.

Flying Claw was wearing armor. It wasn't the body-enclosing armor of a medieval knight, but a torso-covering tunic made from thick leather scales, studded with iron. The leather scales had been embossed so that they created a relief portrait of a snarling tiger's face, the details enhanced with a few carefully placed metal studs.

The armor was worn over a long-sleeved, knee-length tunic of heavy green brocade. The brocade was elaborately worked with various designs in which the tiger predominated: sometimes prowling, sometimes pouncing, sometimes leaping among clouds. Bats flew overhead. Crabs scuttled beneath.

Flying Claw's neck was protected by a heavy scarf or cowl made from fabric dyed a rich, dark red. Fabric of the same color cuffed the sleeves of his undertunic. It provided a nice contrast to the green brocade.

And, Brenda thought, *red is a great color for hiding bloodstains.*

Flying Claw's long hair was worn in an off-center knot, bound at the base with more of the red fabric. He carried a helmet under one arm, so apparently he didn't go bareheaded into battle. His sheathed sword was worn at his waist, as were a dagger, a pair of gourds, and a writing case.

I thought I heard his sword rattling in that duffel, Brenda thought. *But for some reason I never thought of armor.*

Brenda found herself thinking that, dressed this way, Flying Claw looked somehow familiar. That was absurd, since the only other time she'd seen him in his Chinese costumes had been shenyi-style robes.

Then she realized where the sense of familiarity originated. This was the same sort of armor and hairstyle worn by those famous terra-cotta warriors. For the first time, Brenda felt the connection between a series of events in Chinese history, rather than knowing them as dry, memorized facts.

The emperor who had ordered the elaborate tomb in which the thousands of terra-cotta warriors had been found had been Shi Huang Ti, the first Ch'in emperor. That was the same man who had ordered all those books burned, all those scholars murdered, and who had in doing so inadvertently created the Lands Born from Smoke and Sacrifice.

Wasn't Shi Huang Ti also the same man who had ordered the Great Wall of China built? Hadn't he simplified the writing system, passed hundreds of new laws, ordered connecting roads to be built, and sent out expeditions beyond China's borders? And hadn't his reign lasted only fourteen or fifteen years? Shi Huang Ti must have been an extraordinary individual—but not, Brenda thought, someone she'd necessarily want to know.

But he created not one new land—the empire of China—but two, and the Lands Born from Smoke and Sacrifice could be said to be an entire universe, not merely a land.

I wonder if Shi Huang Ti knew. I wonder, if he knew, what he would have thought.

Des gave Flying Claw an appreciative once-over.

"You look very martial," he said. "If you folks will excuse me for a moment, I'll get myself ready, and then we can go."

"Ready?" Riprap said. "You mean you have robes like these?"

"Closer to Honey Dream's shenyi than to Flying Claw's armor," Des replied. "My grandmother insisted."

Des wasn't gone long, and when he emerged he was wearing a shenyi cut from silvery white brocade, so heavily embroidered with roosters and other lucky signs that the color beneath was almost lost.

"White," Des said, shaking his head so that his long braid hung straight between his shoulder blades, "is the Rooster's color. However, it is also the color associated with loss. Grandmother thought the coloration of this robe provided a good compromise. You'll notice that in addition to the crabs, clouds, and bats that adorn our friends' robes, I also have any number of other symbols. I'll explain them later, if you'd like, but they're mostly for wealth and longevity. That's because, elaborate as it is, my shenyi is a general-purpose garment, meant as much for ceremony as for anything else."

Des turned to Honey Dream and Flying Claw. "I mention this specifically as a reminder to the two of you. You've donned your working clothes and so may forget that with the exception of Riprap's miliary service, the four of us have fought very few battles in our lives."

For me, really only two, Brenda thought, *the one against Righteous Drum, and the one during our practice session—and I pretty much stood around during that second fight and got attacked. Our encounter with Flying Claw in that parking garage was more a situation of mutual shock than a battle.*

Honey Dream preened, smug and pleased, as if his admission improved her somehow, but Flying Claw looked very serious.

"I will not forget. We have had too little time to practice since our first session was so rudely interrupted by Twentyseven-Ten and his associates. Let us all rely on what we know best."

"And most of all, let's hope all this talk about fighting is unnecessary," Des added.

He was holding three small brocade bags in his hand, and now he handed one each to Brenda, Nissa, and Riprap.

"We haven't had time to order your own robes," he said, "and in any case, I agree with Flying Claw that now is not the time to add new complications."

"Walking in skirts," Riprap agreed, "would definitely be an unwelcome complication—at least for me."

Riprap had been opening his bag while he spoke and now he shook the contents out into his hand. It proved to be a satin cord from which hung a translucent stone pendant that, despite its yellow hue, Brenda was certain had to be jade.

"A dog!" Riprap said with delight. "A fierce fellow, too. I'm so glad it's not a Peke."

"It's a Tibetan mastiff," Des said. "I commissioned it a few weeks ago and have been waiting for the auspicious time to give it to you. I'm glad you like it."

Nissa had shaken her own pendant out, and happily displayed the figure of a green jade rabbit. This was no cuddly bunny, but a watchful creature sitting up on its haunches, ears raised, nose tilted back to sniff the wind.

"It's lovely!" she exclaimed. "Did you commission this one, as well?"

"I did," Des said. "Rabbits are pretty easy to find, but I wanted this one to be unique."

Brenda had hesitated to open her own bag, knowing that since she wasn't the Rat, such a charm would be presumptuous. However, as attention turned to her, she did so. Her pendant was cut from a shining black stone—the Rat's color—but as she expected, it was not a rat, but a frog.

"The Frog," Des said, "is associated with both wealth and

protection." He indicated one embroidered on the sleeve of his shenyi. "I chose this over many other symbols because I wanted to remind you of your encounter with the Three-Legged Toad. You did very well then—unpredictably well—and I didn't think you should forget that."

Brenda ran her thumb over the smooth black stone. She hugged Des, quick and hard, taking care not to squash his elegant robes or to let the tears welling up in her eyes stain the silk brocade.

"I suggest," Flying Claw said, reaching out and stopping Nissa in midmotion, "you hang those charms from a loop on your belt rather than around your neck. It is never good to give an enemy an easy means to strangle you."

Nissa looked momentarily startled, but complied. Brenda followed suit. The stone frog hung heavier than she'd expected, so that she felt it even through her jeans. She touched the array of amulet bracelets she'd strung around her wrists that morning.

Des looked approving. "I had time to put some minor protective magics in these, but nothing else, so don't count on them replacing your own abilities."

"Right," Riprap said. The two women nodded.

"Ready?" Des asked, opening his portfolio, and removing the pictures of the Men Shen. "Then let us begin."

XII

From the moment Pearl opened the front door of her house to admit Albert Yu, she knew something was wrong.

The Cat's grooming was meticulous, as usual, but somehow he still gave the impression of having dressed hurriedly.

"Come in, Albert. Righteous Drum and Waking Lizard

arrived about ten minutes ago. They're out on the patio with Shen, having tea and discussing our next move."

Albert accepted her invitation with a slight bow that did nothing to remove Pearl's impression that something was wrong.

"And Des and the others?"

"They left about an hour ago, according to plan. My guess is that they are establishing the first of the Nine Gates even as we speak."

"And Lani?"

Pearl smiled slightly. "She is having a playdate combined with another screen test. My friend Joanne is taking her. They will be gone until slightly before Lani's bedtime."

"Good," Albert said. "I have some disturbing news."

"I thought as much," Pearl said. "Have you eaten?"

"Not much," Albert admitted. "If you have something easy . . ."

Pearl smiled again, every iota the gracious hostess. She had learned long ago that acting what you wished others to believe often created the very mind-set you were trying to achieve. Right now Albert needed her to be the strong, calm Tiger, and although she wanted to shake his news from him, that strong, calm Tiger was what she gave him.

"With Riprap living here," she said, "there is always something to eat. This morning they made some sort of egg pie with cheese and chile. We can heat you some. There's coffee and fruit set out on the patio already."

They joined the others in a few minutes, Albert carrying the plate with his breakfast, Pearl with a tray holding more coffee and tea. She had a feeling they were going to need it.

After greetings were exchanged, Albert began, ignoring the meal he'd said he wanted.

"As planned, I set out to acquire the mah-jong sets representing the lapsed branches. I also decided that the recommendation that we acquire the Snake's set was not a bad idea. She is not wholly senile, but she does have a rather scattered focus at times. In any case, an eighty-three-year-old woman should not be asked to make the journey we are contemplating."

Pearl bit back a sarcastic comment, but she and Waking Lizard shared conspiratorial glances. Ability, not age, should be the basis for such judgments. It wasn't that Pearl didn't agree with Albert's assessment. It was simply that she'd prefer he didn't make age sound like something that could be measured by one of those signs they put up by amusement-park rides. She imagined this one as a sort of timeline, "Those over this date cannot participate in this activity."

Unaware of Pearl's reaction—or perhaps politely ignoring it—Albert went on.

"Because I have kept in contact with the family, I went to Justine Bower, the Snake, myself. She's living in an assisted-care facility in Duluth. Her daughter, Katie Dunham, lives nearby, and she is actually custodian of the set.

"I went to talk with Justine, and found her quite lucid, if inclined to talk about the past rather than the present—and I can hardly blame her. Her present—she has very bad knees and so cannot get around easily—is not exactly dynamic. I was pleased to find her quite happy to discuss our shared heritage. When I requested a loan of the set, she phoned Katie right off and asked her to bring it over.

"Katie came by about two hours later, with the set. To my surprise, she had a good many questions of her own. It appears that her mother's reminiscences have made Katie more interested in the family lore, more inclined to think there might be something to the stories her mother—and more particularly, her grandmother—once told her."

Shen leaned forward. "But did Katie let you have the set?"

"Yes," Albert assured him, "but only as a loan and only on the grounds that we get together at some point so we can discuss those 'family fairy tales' in more detail."

Pearl nudged Albert's plate toward him, waited until he had taken a few bites, and then said, "Normally, I'd consider this all good news, but there's something bothering you. Why don't you tell us about it?"

Righteous Drum, very conscious of Chinese politeness regarding guests and food, added, "But, please, finish your breakfast. We would not have you go hungry."

He then made it impossible for Albert to continue his report by the simple expedient of excusing himself for a trip "inside."

When he returned, Albert had finished his breakfast casserole and first cup of coffee, and was slicing sections from a pear. As soon as Righteous Drum settled into his chair and warmed his own cup of tea, Albert resumed.

"So, I have the Snake set. We acquired the Ram's mahjong set with relative ease."

"We?" asked Waking Lizard.

Albert made an apologetic gesture. "I am sorry. I hired an agent to make some of the inquiries for me—a reliable man I've used when seeking pieces for my business. Matt Bauminger is a good negotiator, and, more importantly, famously discreet."

"Very good," Waking Lizard said. "I recently learned about what is called 'the royal we' and I wanted to be certain I understood."

"Quite so," Albert said, ignoring the indication that he might have been speaking as royalty. He ate a slice of pear and continued.

"The Ram's family moved from California in Third Ram's adulthood—back in the forties. They moved several times thereafter, following work. Third Ram died a few years ago, and her daughter—the current Ram—is presently settled in New Hampshire. My agent purchased the Ram mah-jong set from her for a fair price, and delivered it to me by hand. He had less luck thereafter.

"Clotilde Hilliard, the current Ox, has recently moved to Boston, in order to live closer to her daughter, who lives in Cape Cod. Since Matt was already in New Hampshire, he went to her next. He contacted Clotilde via phone, prepared to explain in some detail what he wanted. To his surprise, she interrupted him almost before he had begun.

" 'That? Yes. I have it. Had it. I sold it a few days ago.' " Matt then requested an interview with Clotilde, and she granted it. Her daughter is in a relationship with an artist, and so Clotilde is more aware than most of the competitiveness in the world of art collecting.

"In short, Matt learned that a woman had called inquiring after the mah-jong set. She was very specific about what she wanted, up to and including a description of the ox depicted on the lid of the case. Due to her recent move, Clotilde not only knew where the set was, but was familiar with its condition.

"They met, negotiated, and, although Clotilde set a considerable price for the set—again as a result of her experience with collectors—the woman paid without a demur. That was why Clotilde was interested in meeting with my agent. She wanted to pump him for information as to what price she could have gotten. He assured her that she had done very well indeed."

Shen had been methodically eating grapes while Albert spoke, and now he set the bare stem aside.

"This woman who purchased the Ox mah-jong set, did your agent happen to get her name?"

"Name and description," Albert said, "both. He let his chagrin show, and hinted that a commission might be in line if he managed to buy the set from the first comer. The buyer called herself Tracy Highlander, but her description matches that of the Tracy Frye who is a member of the Rock Dove Society."

"The same woman," Righteous Drum asked, "who attempted to get Gaheris Morris to come over to her?"

"The same," Albert said. "When my agent learned that someone else was after the sets, he switched his tactics. He phoned both Fourth Horse and the son of Third Monkey who—despite not being the current Monkey; it's a long story—has charge of the set. He received mixed news. The son of Third Monkey lives in upstate New York, near Ithaca. He had sold the set earlier that day to the same Tracy Highlander. Like Clotilde, he was curious as to the sudden interest in something that had been collecting dust in his attic, and so was willing to talk.

"However, Matt didn't talk long. Once he realized that he had again been beaten in the chase, he called the Horse. Her name is Ainsley O'Reilly, and she lives on an isolated ranch in Montana where she raises quarter horses and exotic livestock with her husband."

For the first time, Albert looked amused. "Her husband's name is Ricardo O'Reilly. He's part Puerto Rican, part Irish, and all American West. Ainsley was out when my agent called, and Rico insisted on knowing what some man was doing calling his wife. Matt explained, and Rico got really suspicious, because this was the second call that day about that same mah-jong set."

"Oh, no!" Pearl said.

Albert nodded. "Matt realized that if Tracy Highlander—as he knew her—had been in upstate New York earlier that day, it was unlikely that she could be at some ranch in Montana until the next day, maybe even later. Matt called me and got permission to charter a plane. He got to the ranch before Tracy Highlander, but he found Ainsley and Rico unwilling to sell the set until they'd heard the other offer."

"Reasonable," Shen admitted reluctantly.

"Very," Albert said. "In the meantime, I've had someone do a check on Tracy Frye, a.k.a. Tracy Highlander. She's comfortably off, but not rich, so either she's taken out a loan to enable her to go art shopping—oh, I forgot to mention, she paid for both of the sets in cash—or she has backers. My detectives haven't found evidence of a loan."

"So at least one member of her consortium," Righteous Drum said, "is wealthy. As wealth often translates into power, that is not a good thing."

"I agree," Albert said. "Matt should call today—tomorrow at the latest—to say whether he managed to get the set."

"If money is a problem," Pearl began delicately, knowing how proud Albert could be.

"I don't think money is what's going to win this bidding war," Albert said. "Tracy Frye's backers must have financial resources to match our own. However, I'm hoping they won't be able to match what I can offer."

"And that is?" Waking Lizard asked, his eyes crinkling with amusement.

"Star power," Albert said, bluntly. "Right now Matt is operating for an anonymous patron. However, he has my permission to indicate who the buyer is if he thinks that will help."

"And will the prospect of selling to a candy merchant," Righteous Drum asked with obvious confusion, "make such a difference?"

"It might," Albert said. "I'm a pretty important 'candy merchant.' The access to my more exclusive lines—most of which are never for sale even in my own shopfront—might tempt. However, I can offer more than that. I have some pretty high-profile clients, and I can offer the O'Reillys connections to markets for their horses and cattle like they've only dreamed."

Pearl, who had been trying to guess who Tracy Frye's backers might be, said, "But can't the other side do the same? There were at least two men at that Rock Dove Society meeting who could have similar connections."

"Ah," Albert said, looking very catlike in his satisfaction, "but while they can give Tracy Frye money anonymously, high-profile backing, by definition, cannot be given that way. And since the official position of the Rock Dove Society and its associates is to give us a chance to deal with the incursion from the Lands before they intervene . . ."

"Brilliant!" exclaimed Righteous Drum. "You are offering the one thing they cannot: patronage. Truly, you have the mind of an emperor."

Albert looked very pleased. He reached for the coffee carafe, but even before he had filled his cup, his air of tension had returned.

"But even if Matt gets the Horse's set for us, we have lost

the Ox and the Monkey sets. Once again, we are balked in our efforts to assemble the full Thirteen."

"And without that," Pearl said, "no matter if we establish the Nine Gates, our hopes of gaining access to the Lands Born from Smoke and Sacrifice are slim indeed."

☆

Honey Dream stepped forward to assist as Des pulled the two pictures of the Men Shen from his portfolio. He looked mildly surprised, but accepted her help without question.

"We're going to glue them up," he said, producing from one pocket a small white bottle with a cylindrical orange top. "You want Yu Che or Ch'in Shu-pao?"

"I'll take Yu Che," Honey Dream said, then watched carefully as Des twisted the orange top to open the container of glue.

One of the few things Honey Dream loved about this Land of the Burning, mutated as it had become since it gave forth the Lands, were all the interesting items for tasks related to writing: pens, inks, pencils. Now it appeared there were glues that didn't smell bad or come in awkward ceramic pots.

Des squeezed the creamy white glue directly onto one of the upper panels of the wooden door, then smoothed it out with a forefinger. Honey Dream heard no incantations, sensed no magic being worked, so when Des handed her the glue, she imitated him carefully, trusting that the white goo alone would be enough to hold. The printed depiction of Yu Che was beautifully done, the intricacies breathtaking, but there was no magic in it.

Well, that was how it should be. No matter how many people—and she had found them in her own world, and suspected they were in this world as well—wanted to believe that magic was some sort of system, something that could be learned merely by memorizing the correct series of gestures, magic was something that came from deep within the liver, the seat of the soul.

That was why ghosts occurred when the soul fragmented after death and the various parts were not ushered on to their next incarnation. The inner self, not the gestures or items used to give it focus, was the wellspring of magic. Honey Dream knew that the greatest sorcerers could work miracles with no more effort than they breathed, but that was the purview of saints and mystics. Here and now, they had before them the relatively direct task of opening a way between two different and yet related universes.

Honey Dream smoothed the air bubbles from beneath the print of Yu Che, then turned to listen as Des, giving the portrait of Chin Shu-pao an affectionate pat, addressed them all in his best "teacher voice."

"Our ancestors left us a limit hand they named with admirable directness 'Nine Gates.' It consists entirely of characters."

Brenda Morris gave a small, barely audible groan, and Des shook his head reprovingly at her. Honey Dream felt appropriately superior, but did her best to hide her reaction. Still, she suspected Brenda guessed.

"Sorry, Des," Brenda apologized. "It's just that I have so much trouble drawing the characters that I have difficulty concentrating."

"You need to stop worrying," Des said sternly, "and use the very fact that you find characters difficult to help you concentrate."

"I know. I know."

Brenda looked appropriately contrite, and Des returned to his explanation.

"The sequence for Nine Gates begins with three ones, then contains at least one of the numbers two through eight, before concluding with three of the number nine."

"That's only thirteen tiles," Riprap said, rather predictably in Honey Dream's opinion. He was such a Dog, so eager to prove how attentive he was. Des didn't seem to mind.

"The fourteenth tile in the sequence—the fourteenth

number, actually, since we're not going to make tiles for this spell, but inscribe the numbers directly on the door—will be keyed to which door in the sequence we're opening."

"So this door," Riprap said, "will have four ones instead of three. That must make this a stronger sequence than most."

"So I thought," Des said, "when I first learned Nine Gates, but when my grandmother taught me the sequence and its uses, she corrected that misapprehension. Because the one and the nines already begin as sequences of three, the additional 'tile' actually adds less force, even though it completes the set."

Nissa nodded immediate understanding, and Honey Dream was reminded that Nissa was a student of medicine and chemical formulas.

"I see," Nissa said. "Adding a fourth tile to a sequence of three only raises the percentage of 'ones' by thirty-three percent. When we get to the middle sequences, although we will only be adding one 'tile,' it will actually be a fifty-percent increase in the force of that number. When we reach the Ninth Gate, we will face the same diminution of force again. That's really interesting."

"But dangerous," Des said. "Theory aside, that danger is what we must remember. None of the Nine Gates will be precisely simple to establish, but the first and ninth contain that additional fillip of risk. That means that we're going to all need to obey Flying Claw without question when he negotiates with the White Tiger of the West."

Honey Dream found herself fascinated by this first close look at the Orphans' peculiar way of focusing magic. It was both brilliant and yet oddly childish, simple yet fraught with hidden complexities. Her respect for the Twelve Exiles who became the Thirteen Orphans rose once again.

"We must remember," Honey Dream said, hearing her own eagerness, "that the numbers you are referring to as 'one,' 'two,' 'three,' and so on actually must be perceived as multiplied by ten thousand. In the Lands, at least, there is a tale that the character for 'ten thousand' is a representative of a scorpion, because these creatures are rarely found alone."

"Another theory," Flying Claw said so mildly he did not seem to be contradicting, "is that the character has its source in a depiction of a field full of grass. That is the image I wish to invoke for this first gate, since tigers are very at home in tall grass and I wish the White Tiger to feel welcomed—and that we are not in the least afraid of it."

Des nodded, but he flashed a smile at Honey Dream. "However, I think we will invoke your scorpions when we first contact Hell and seek to link to the Nine Yellow Springs. I think we'll welcome the scorpion's protection then."

Brenda Morris was looking confused again, but, although Des looked over at her as if inviting questions, Brenda kept her silence. Her right hand drifted down to where the polished black stone frog hung against her thigh as if seeking reassurance.

Honey Dream hardly blamed her. This was too complex for an ignorant novice.

"We're ready, then," Des said. "It would be best if each of us took a part in the opening. Brenda, you do one and two."

Brenda touched the little frog again, but stepped forward boldly enough. Des handed her a stylus shaped like a pen, but where the nib for the ink would be, the stylus was tipped with hard, sharp steel.

"Cut the numbers into the door alongside the left panel," he instructed. "Relax and concentrate."

Brenda tested out the tip of the stylus against the surface of a pine packing crate, its broken side testifying why the prior tenants had left it behind.

"Cuts well," she murmured. "Right. I can do this. Start with four ones, then one two."

She moved to the door and rested her arm against it, striving for the correct angle.

"Is it okay if I touch the picture of the Men Shen?" she asked.

"Fine," Des said. "Start as high up as you can comfortably reach. Now concentrate. Everybody, stop staring at her. You'll have your turn soon enough."

Honey Dream turned away from the temptation to stare, knowing without a doubt that she could make Brenda feel her skin creep where Honey Dream's gaze rested. But what would be the point? Honey Dream wanted these gates opened, wanted the opportunity to return home, to take revenge on those who had overthrown their emperor, claimed the Jade Petal Throne for themselves. If she had to accept Brenda Morris's help to do so, well then, she would.

However, she would not accept Brenda Morris.

Flying Claw had gone off into a corner by himself. He had drawn his sword and held it point-down against the floor. As Honey Dream watched, he knelt in one graceful fluid motion and pressed his forehead lightly against the hilt, focusing his ch'i.

Seeing his intensity, Honey Dream was momentarily ashamed of her childish impulse to sabotage Brenda Morris's efforts. Then she regained her composure, and looked over toward where Desperate Lee, formal and flamboyant as a Rooster should be, stood in his robes of heavily embroidered silver, watching as Brenda carefully completed the third of her four ones.

"Who will be next?" Honey Dream asked Des, moving to where she could speak in the softest possible voice.

"Nissa for three and four," Des said equally softly. "Riprap for five and six. I'll do seven. I want you to do eight, and Flying Claw to conclude with nine. In this way, we who belong to this side of the gate will begin, and you who will be crossing a little closer to your home will end it."

Honey Dream nodded acceptance and made a slight, formal bow that acknowledged the elegance of the plan. Doubtless Des had arrived at this arrangement after consultation with Shen and Righteous Drum, but he spoke as if the plan was his own. He was very much a Rooster, for they were among the most solitary of signs and yet could be good leaders, even as a rooster was the sole male of his flock, and yet commanded the hens.

By the time Brenda finished her two sets of characters, her forehead was lightly beaded with sweat. Prompted by Des, Nissa stepped forward and accepted the stylus, pausing only long enough to give Brenda an approving squeeze on the shoulder before moving to take her place.

Brenda gave a wan smile, then moved to seat herself on the edge of a short stack of shipping pallets that stood off to one side. She took a water bottle from her pack and drank deeply.

Honey Dream glanced over to where Nissa was now scribing in three and four, her hand on the stylus firm and confident. Perhaps she should have trained as a surgeon rather than a pharmacy assistant.

Taking a deep, full breath and calling on the Snake who coiled against and within her, Honey Dream asked her eyes to see the ch'i present in the room. Pale light immediately glowed blackly from where Brenda had cut her characters. Below it, Nissa's characters were shaded with the green of fresh grass. In the corner where he still meditated, Flying Claw was surrounded by an aura the darker green of jungle foliage.

Honey Dream let the sight lapse. It was easy enough to summon, and she had no wish to have her small magic disturb the current building around the doorway.

Confident that Des had matters well in hand, she composed herself into a light meditation that would enable her to focus her ch'i while leaving sufficient awareness so that she would know when her turn to inscribe the doorway had come.

When Des finished, Honey Dream was ready, her ch'i so finely focused that she knew she glided across the floor as if her feet were a fraction of a finger's width above the concrete floor. The metal stylus was warm in her hand, and seemed to glow faintly with the colors of those who had used it before her.

She settled herself in to draw the shapes of the number eight, two simple lines that nonetheless had a sense of motion to them. As she drew the character for "wan" or "ten thousand," she concentrated on evoking the deep grass of a never-mown field. The inscription took very little time, and so little effort that she was tempted to continue and draw in the "nine" as well, but Flying Claw was waiting close at hand.

She could smell him, clean and fresh, yet somehow rank with the odor of a tiger, and knew this was not the time to cross him.

Flying Claw took the stylus from her hand and padded forward. He had to bend slightly to fill in the bottom of the panel, but his hand moved surely. As he set the last of the three nines in place, a sharp cracking sound echoed through the confines of the warehouse, the door swung open, and through it they saw not the other side of the warehouse, but a field filled with waist-high, lush green grass. In the distance, beyond the field, could be seen the edges of a jungle, a wall of living vegetation splashed with flowers in such brilliant hues that they startled the eye.

But before the last echo from the door's opening had faded, the view beyond was blocked by two towering figures in warlike armor and bearing weapons that, for all the gems that bedecked their hilts and hafts, looked very sharp and completely deadly.

Without a pause, Flying Claw stepped forward and bowed. The motion was full of respect, but without the least hint of groveling. It was a greeting between warrior and warrior, minister and minister, not youth and figure out of legend.

Honey Dream felt her heart tighten with pride and delight, an emotion that in no way diminished when Flying Claw addressed Yu Che and Ch'in Shu-pao.

"Greetings, legend-sung guardians of a thousand doors, a hundred thousand gateways. I have come to speak to my father-self, brother and uncle, the White Tiger of the West. I am in no way in disfavor with him. Will you grant me passage into his lands?"

Yu Che turned ponderously, hand resting on the haft of the whip which he used to scourge demons, and faced Ch'in Shu-pao.

"Do you see your way to granting this petition, minister who is faithful through the night?"

"I might," replied Ch'in Shu-pao, "but a guard is always wisest when he asks leave of the master of the house. I will watch the door if you will bear this message to Pai Hu, the White Tiger of the West."

He unslung a mighty battle-axe, and swung it down so that it barred the open door. The sharpened edge of the blade cut the air with a hiss, but Flying Claw did not step back.

"I admire your axe," he said, courtly yet conversational, "but I assure you, it is not necessary. I will not force entry, for I feel sure of my welcome here."

"Sure?? Sure??" came a roaring, growling sound, terrible and yet with every word perfectly clear.

The air shimmered around where the incised door stood, then both doorway and Men Shen vanished. In their place was the head of an enormous tiger, fully as high and then twice as wide again as the doorway it had replaced.

The tiger's fur was white, its stripes black, its eyes the hot golden brown of a burning coal. Its fangs were like sharp-tipped spears of bone, and its breath as hot as the wind that comes forth from a furnace.

Honey Dream stepped back despite her best intentions, then tried to cover her moment of panic by acting as if she had been trying catch a glimpse of the rest of the white tiger's body, but although she had the sense that it was there, monstrously huge, crouched as if to spring, she could see nothing but that enormous head.

The burning eyes focused on Flying Claw, but the young warrior stood tall, head thrown back, a faint smile on his well-shaped mouth. He did not touch even the hilt of his sword, but held his hands in a relaxed posture at his sides.

"I know you," said Pai Hu, the White Tiger, and his words made Honey Dream's eardrums ache from the vibration of his growls. "And yet . . . Were you not a woman the last time I saw you?"

"You are remembering my aunt," Flying Claw said conversationally, ignoring what must have been a deliberate insult with incredible poise. "She who is called Pearl Bright. She sends her greetings, and asks if you enjoyed your game with the Three-Legged Toad."

There was a moment of silence, then the great Tiger huffed and sneezed in what Honey Dream realized must be laughter—but laughter whose gusts could sink ships and level forests.

"It was a good game," the White Tiger admitted when its laughter had stilled. "I enjoyed it. For having only three legs, the Toad hops very quickly. Where is Pearl Bright? Why does she send a little he-cub to bring her messages?"

Again Flying Claw ignored the insult, although this one was more pointed than the last. His hand did not even stray an inch toward the hilt of his sword.

"My aunt will be coming to visit you in a short while," he said, "that is, if you will grant us access to your realm of the West."

"And why should I do this?"

"Perhaps for family feeling, perhaps for the amusement that will come," replied Flying Claw.

"Is that all? Can you not do a favor or so for me?"

"If such is within my power, and if such is not in violation of oaths I have already sworn."

"Wisdom and prudence both," the White Tiger rumbled, and Honey Dream was almost certain Pai Hu was pleased. "But you may need more. You may need courage as well. Tell me, do you seek passage only for yourself, or for that mob I see behind you?"

"For these and for others," Flying Claw said. "In the end, we may be as many as thirteen plus five."

"Thirteen," rumbled the White Tiger. "I remember a certain Thirteen quite well . . . Yes. That could indeed be amusing. Still, amusement is not enough. If you wish to pass through my lands, to anchor your gates through my realm, then you must do me a favor. If you should do that, I will grant you passage from your world into the West, passage for yourself and your entire thirteen plus five—but I do not promise you any help beyond that. These are unsettled times, even for the White Tiger of the West."

Flying Claw straightened and looked pleased, as well he should, but a touch apprehensive as well—as indeed he should. The type of favor the White Tiger of the West would want granted would not be a light one.

"By the terms already mentioned," Flying Claw said, "and within the restrictions already placed upon me, I will do this favor for you."

"And we," said Des, speaking for the first time, his gaze warning the others to keep silent lest a chance word get them into more than they desired, "will help him to the extent of our abilities and our honor."

"You will, will you, cockerel?" The White Tiger laughed again and stretched his jaws. "You will need more than pretty words if you are to satisfy me."

The jaws stretched yet more, becoming all of heaven and the edge of Earth, but the fangs looked no less sharp for their great size.

"Come. Show your courage, all of you," the White Tiger rumbled. "Come and walk between my jaws."

XIII

Albert Yu's cell phone rang while they were discussing what alternatives remained open to them. Albert answered the chime (it sounded rather like temple bells) and listened intently. They all did, for Albert made no attempt to hide his side of the conversation.

"Very good, Matt. Thank you. Yes. Send it to my e-mail and I'll review the details and fax back a signed copy, then get the original in the mail. How soon? Hang on."

Albert lowered the phone and spoke to Pearl. "Can I use your fax and printer?"

"Certainly."

Albert lifted the phone back to his mouth. "Within a few hours of your getting me the contract. Great. Phone me when you e-mail the document and I'll get right on it. Thanks again. Yes. I'd prefer you bring the set in person. After all of this, it would be stupid to lose it in shipping. Bye."

Albert flipped closed the phone and slipped it back into his pocket.

"That was Matt. We'll have the Horse's mah-jong set probably by tomorrow. Tracy Frye could match us in money, but not in favors. Ainsley and Rico, however, insisted on a contract."

"Contract?" Righteous Drum asked. "For favors?"

"Something like that. Matt's going to work out the details. They're thinking of some sort of event promoting their ranch, with me as a sponsor."

Pearl frowned. "Can you do that? You've done a great deal to protect your reputation for exclusivity."

"And it's what makes my candy so expensive," Albert agreed. "Don't worry. We're not doing anything tacky like peanut butter mint pinto ponies." His narrow face grew very serious. "And Aunt Pearl, how exclusive my chocolates are won't matter much if we don't win. I know that, and so do you."

"I do," Pearl said, "and when this is done, if the inclusion of one attenuated child movie star will make a difference in the guest list, count me in."

"Thank you, Aunt Pearl." The warmth of Albert's smile faded as quickly as it had risen. "But even if we have the Horse's set, we are still without the Monkey's and the Ox's."

Waking Lizard waggled a long finger. "You have mentioned this Monkey before, and always with a peculiar note to your voices. What is the problem caused by my Branch cousin?"

"Well," Albert said, looking a bit embarrassed. "We lost him for a time, and when we found him again . . ."

"Lost?" asked Righteous Drum indignantly. "I thought you had the means for tracing each Exile's line."

"We do and did," Pearl said, "but after a while, this seemed less and less important. Really, the problem goes back to Exile Monkey himself."

"How so?" Waking Lizard asked, leaning back and looking quite interested in this bit of history.

Pearl wondered if Waking Lizard, like Flying Claw, had made a fetish of his Exiled predecessor. She decided not to ask, but instead launched into her tale.

"The Exile Monkey was in his fifties when the Exile occurred. He was both highly irresponsible and highly sexed. Neither of these traits mattered when he was in service to his emperor, but they made him a problem after the Exile.

"By all accounts," Pearl continued, "and I overheard far more than the 'grown-ups' might have imagined, Exile Monkey would have sex with anyone—male or female—who proved even vaguely willing. Despite this, he showed no interest in tracking the possible issue of those liaisons. In his defense, Exile Monkey may have had no real desire to return to the Lands Born from Smoke and Sacrifice. He had no established family or commitments there, and may have viewed the Exile as a tremendous adventure."

Righteous Drum hrumphed, but Waking Lizard only grinned.

"Monkey's more responsible associates," Pearl went on, "Ram especially—kept track of Exile Monkey's bastards. In time, a boy child born to a peasant girl in China was clearly shown to be the next Monkey. They bought the child from his mother and began carting the boy around with their increasingly large nursery. To everyone's surprise, Exile Monkey showed some interest in assisting with the education of the child. Indeed, I think he honestly loved the boy.

"In the 1920s, Second Monkey was killed in mysterious circumstances—probably due to one of the attacks issuing from the Lands. First Monkey was so hard hit that he actually married for the first time, wedding a lovely Polish immigrant much younger than himself. She bore him a son. A much-changed Monkey doted upon this boy, tutoring him and telling him many tales about the wonders of the Lands. Exile Monkey didn't have much time to indoctrinate the boy. He died about five years later, from old age and the side effects of a dissolute life.

"By the time First Monkey died, circumstances had changed. The Thirteen Orphans were less certain they would ever return home. Moreover, under United States law, Third Monkey's mother had complete custody of her son. She had no particular desire to have her child taught strange lore by her late husband's odd associates. She took him away to where her own people had settled somewhere in the Midwest. Illinois, I think.

"The Cat kept track of the Monkey's family, as was his duty. Therefore, we knew when Third Monkey's first child—a girl—was born. We also knew when she died of complications related to childbirth while she was still a relatively young woman."

Albert cut in, still looking ashamed. "No one bothered to see who would replace her. By then, ambitions to return to the Lands were at an ebb. Third Monkey was still alive and had other children. Those who bothered to think about the matter at all assumed the Monkey's line would pass to one of these.

"When Third Monkey died of pneumonia ten or so years ago, Shen, Pearl, and I did an augury merely to keep in practice. That's when we got a shock. All the evidence showed that Monkey's lineage had not passed to any of Third Monkey's children."

"Who then?" Waking Lizard asked.

"It took us a long time to find out," Albert said. "Eventually, we traced the lineage to a boy of twelve who is apparently a descendant of one of the Exile Monkey's later bastards. We don't know how the confusion occurred. My theory is that the man we knew as Third Monkey never really was his father's heir, and that First Monkey deceived us. What matters to us here and now is that the Monkey line rests with a twelve-year-old boy who knows nothing of his heritage. The Monkey mah-jong set was in the custody of one of Third Monkey's sons."

"Are you certain about that?" Righteous Drum asked.

"We researched both matters carefully," Albert said, his tone making quite clear that he realized that this had probably been too little, too late. "The 'real' Monkey knows so little of his heritage that his disconnection from the Monkey Branch apparently affected his behavior not in the least."

"This is not good," Righteous Drum said. "Are matters as bad with the Ram's line?"

"Almost," Albert admitted, "except that we never lost track of that lineage."

Shen took up the account. "First Ram's situation was unique among the Exiles. She was already pregnant when she was exiled from the Lands Born from Smoke and Sacrifice.

"Exile Ram's daughter was born some months after her mother's arrival in mainland China. Exile Ram's passion to return home to her husband and other children was a drive she used to whip on the rest of her contemporaries—with guilt if not desire—when their devotion flagged even momentarily."

Righteous Drum, who was probably using similar tactics to motivate Waking Lizard, looked very neutral.

Shen pulled at his lower lip, as if the action would help him in concentrating his memories, then said, "Second Ram was a close contemporary of First Cat and Second Horse—one of that handful of small children who were shuffled from place to place, country to country, apparently at the whim of her mother and her mother's friends. Even so, Second Ram did not become as great a disciplinary problem as First Cat— probably because she was not as indulged. She was taught by her mother and seemed obedient.

"However, in addition to her mother's passionate desire to go back to the Lands, Second Ram was also deeply influenced by the 'Hua Problem.'"

He glanced at the others. "Pearl has told you about that?"

"Yes," Waking Lizard said. "Hua was the adopted daughter of the Exile Ox, but the other Orphans came to—disown her, I suppose is the right way to put it—because they feared she lacked the appropriate bloodline to tie her to the Lands."

"That's it," Shen agreed. "Hua had been like a big sister to Second Ram and the other small children, and eventually Second Ram came to resent 'Big Sister's' second-class status with many of the Orphans."

"So Second Ram didn't," Waking Lizard guessed, "put a lot of energy into educating Third Ram. Did Third Ram learn something of your history despite her mother's indifference?"

Pearl nodded. "Third Ram learned a bit because her grandmother—the Exile Ram—survived until Third Ram was a little younger than Brenda Morris is now. The Exile Ram made certain her granddaughter learned whatever she could teach. However, Second Ram's ambivalence played its own part. After her grandmother's death, Third Ram drifted away from the society of the Thirteen."

Albert, keeper of the contemporary roster, took over. "To the best of my knowledge, Fourth Ram—the woman we would need to deal with—knows a few legends, but has no training. She married late and has a teenaged son who is, according to what Pearl and I have observed, very spoiled."

"Almost as bad as the Monkey's line," Righteous Drum agreed, a note of something like hope in his voice, "but perhaps not quite as bad."

Albert's phone rang again. Everyone fell silent as he answered it.

"Matt? Got the contract so soon? Something else?"

There was a long silence as Matt explained something on the other end. From the small notes of sound, not really words, Pearl caught from the other end, Matt was apologizing. Albert responded decisively.

"No. No. You didn't do anything wrong. Yes. I'm acquainted with the woman you mentioned. I think she's stretching matters to say we're friends—oh, associates?—well, perhaps. Let's leave it that I know her."

There was another pause.

"Yes. You can give her my phone number. Yes. This one is fine. No, not my private office line. I'm not there in any case and probably won't be today."

Pause.

"Right. Oh, and Matt, take good care of that mah-jong set. I have no doubt that this woman represents the competition, and I don't think she's above trying to get a third set."

Pause.

"Fine. And don't forget to call me when you have the contract done with the O'Reillys. Great. Thanks."

Albert terminated the call.

"Tracy Frye isn't giving up. She cornered Matt and demanded that he put her in touch with me. I've agreed. She should . . ."

The phone chimed again. Albert flipped it on and held it to his ear.

"Yes. Yes, Ms. Frye. Yes. I know who you are. Yes. Ms.

Bright and Mr. Kung did mention your thoughts on this matter, so did Mr. Morris. That surprises you? It shouldn't. Gaheris Morris has always been more complicated than most imagine."

Pause.

"No. I'm not discussing this further on the phone. None of this. If you want to meet with me and my associates, you're going to need to come to San Jose. No. Not San Francisco. I'm currently in San Jose. Yes. That is convenient."

Pause.

"Call when you get into town. I'll see if I can arrange a neutral meeting place. Yes. I mean neutral. I was thinking about our meeting under the auspices of the Rosicrucians."

Pause.

"Yes. Many of them are friends with Pearl Bright, but do you think that changes their neutrality in a matter such as this? No. I didn't think you'd go that far. Fine. I'll talk with them, and when you get into San Jose, call and we'll meet. Yes. I'm aware that it's not likely you can arrive any sooner than tomorrow, possibly the day after. No. I will not discuss this further over the telephone."

He disconnected the call, and when the phone chimed a second later he glanced at the caller ID and gave a tight, thin-lipped smile.

"I think all of you could follow that."

"The woman who has the mah-jong sets," Righteous Drum said. "She is willing to trade."

"That's what she said." Albert nodded. "However, she started dropping hints, and I'm not certain that we're going to be willing to trade with her."

Shen looked very worried. "But that would mean doing without the sets."

Albert's expression was saturnine. "You were the one who taught me, good teacher, that there are simply things we do not do. Not for anyone. Not for any reason at all."

"But we shall speak with her," Waking Lizard said. "Good.

I've wanted to meet this lady since Gaheris Morris first mentioned her. She sounds interesting."

"Interesting," Albert said, "seems like a supreme understatement to me."

☆

The White Tiger's jaws gaped. Brenda could feel his breath: warm and moist, like a humid day back home in South Carolina.

The rush of homesickness that washed over her at that moment didn't help her courage. She wanted to go home. What was she doing here in California? She should be back working a summer job, hanging out at one of her friends' pools in the evening, talking about books and boys and bosses.

What was she doing here, being told she had to walk into a tiger's jaws to get somewhere she wasn't sure she wanted to go? Why wasn't her father here, doing his part? He was the Rat. She was just Brenda Morris.

Brenda felt herself taking a step back, turning to head for the door. She could go wait in the van. She wouldn't mind. Wait. They might be gone for days. Fine. She had her cell phone. She'd call her dad, explain things, tell him she didn't want to do this anymore.

She just wasn't ready.

Flying Claw was standing in front, obviously prepared to lead the way into danger. Nissa was moving up to join him. She didn't look happy, but she wasn't turning back either. Des was adjusting a strap on his backpack to accommodate the wide sleeves of his silver robe. Riprap was shouldering his own pack, and Honey Dream . . .

It was Honey Dream who—inadvertently—saved Brenda from embarrassing herself beyond retrieval. From the corner of her eye, Brenda caught Honey Dream staring up at the White Tiger's gaping mouth, her lips moving slightly as she counted every fang.

Then Honey Dream's fingers tightened around the hilt of

that curved dagger she wore at her waist, and as clearly as if she'd spoken aloud, Brenda could tell her thoughts.

"Fine. Go ahead. Swallow me whole if you want, but I've got fangs of my own, and I'll give you a stomachache to remember me by."

Brenda couldn't bear to be less than Honey Dream in anything, even in stupid courage. She slid one of the amulet bracelets—one that held the Dragon's Tail protective spell—down into her fingers. That might make it harder for the White Tiger to chew on her.

She didn't activate the spell, though. Des had repeatedly reminded Brenda, Riprap, and Nissa that their ability to work magic would be limited by the dozen or so bracelets they could wear. It wouldn't do to use one up before she needed it.

Brenda reached for her pack and tried to act as if her momentary retreat had been nothing more than getting it adjusted. She didn't know if she fooled anyone—or if anyone had noticed her moment of funk. It was possible that, faced with walking into that yawning red cavern with its stalactites and stalagmites of gleaming white, no one had noticed.

But something in Riprap's brown velvet eyes, something in how he stood waiting for her, made Brenda think that one of their company, at least, had indeed noticed.

Flying Claw glanced over his shoulder.

"I will go first," he said. "Follow as you choose."

Two people? Brenda thought. *Did Flying Claw notice, too?*

She felt her face grow hot at that thought as it hadn't when she thought Riprap might have caught her out. Embarrassment firmed her resolve, and Brenda moved up alongside Nissa.

The Flying Claw stepped onto the red tongue, paused for a moment, and then strode forward. Light, or maybe it was perspective, grew weird after he had progressed a few steps, and a sensation like vertigo made it impossible to track him further.

Nissa looked at the area where short middle teeth between two dominant fangs made an obvious gap.

"I have a feeling," she said, stepping forward, "that we're supposed to enter one at a time."

"At least the jaws haven't moved," Brenda said, and was astonished to hear her voice sounding perfectly normal. "I'll be right behind you."

"Great," Nissa said. "See you in the tiger's den."

She stepped over the smaller teeth—each still the size of a paving block—and onto the tongue. A few steps and she was as impossible to focus on as Flying Claw had been.

Brenda moved forward, and felt a hand on her arm. Des was looking at her with almost fatherly concern.

"Want me to go next?" he said. "Boy-girl-boy-girl? Yang-yin-yang-yin?"

His tone was light, but his eyes showed his concern.

Oh, damn. He noticed, too, Brenda thought.

She was beyond blushing.

"I told Nissa I'd be right behind her," she said, "so unless you think the balance needs me to wait . . ."

Des shrugged. "Hey. I'm a male Rooster. You're a female Rat. If you want to go, go right ahead. I'll come behind."

Brenda nodded, momentarily sorry he hadn't overruled her. Then she forced a grin.

"See you in the tiger's den," she said. "I'll save you a chair."

The step over those lower teeth was more of a reach than she'd thought, maybe because Brenda didn't trust her footing on the other side. The tiger's tongue provided surprisingly firm footing, not in the least slimy, the texture underfoot like sand on the beach right after a wave had pulled back, damp, but not really wet.

The roof of the Tiger's mouth was ridged in a way vaguely familiar to Brenda from giving the family cat pills when it had a urinary tract infection, but that familiarity did nothing to make the experience any less horrible.

Claustrophobia washed over her, combined with the certainty that any moment now those jaws were going to close and crush her. Or maybe she'd be swallowed instead. Didn't the great cats usually skip chewing and gulp stuff down?

Brenda could see neither Nissa nor Flying Claw, and if Des had kept his word and entered right behind her, she couldn't hear him either. She was alone in the mouth of a tiger, and as many times as she tried to tell herself that it was all an illusion, all a dream, all some sort of magical trick, her mind knew the truth.

This was real, and reality was far stranger than she had ever been prepared to accept.

At last, she emerged, not as if from a tunnel or even from a mouth. One moment she was pacing along, trying to keep moving, trying not to give in to screaming fits or the urge to run back the way she had come, the next she was walking on thick grass, pale green light filtering through the leaves of towering trees.

Flying Claw was there, and Nissa, and from how they turned to look at her, Brenda sensed they hadn't reached this place much before her.

"Where are . . ." Brenda began, and then Des was stepping out behind her.

She turned to see from where he had emerged, half expecting to see the back of a tiger's head, like the archway in an amusement park, but seeing only more of the same grass.

"Where are . . ." Des said, and seemed astonished when the three who were present started laughing uncontrollably, but only until Riprap arrived and asked, "Where are . . ."

Honey Dream came last, and Brenda, knowing that the Snake had experienced her own moment of fear, respected her for having the courage to wait until last and still coming on. She had to have wanted to stay back, to come up with excuses.

Brenda didn't much like respecting Honey Dream, even for this, but she was too stripped to her bare emotional bones to deny it.

With Honey Dream's arrival, a hoarse sound, somewhere between a growl and a cough, demanded their attention. They turned as one to see the enormous—if not so completely overwhelming—form of the White Tiger of the West before them.

"You have entered the West," he said. "Now let us see if you can earn the right to remain. Make yourselves comfortable. Have you eaten?"

"We have," Des said politely.

"Still," the White Tiger said with equal correctness, "something small would not be amiss after your journey. Be seated and make yourselves welcome."

Shrubs that a moment before Brenda would have sworn held nothing but leaves and the occasional starlike blossom now bent beneath the weight of aromatic berries. They looked and smelled like blueberries, one of her favorite fruits, but the berries were easily the size of her thumb.

Around their feet the turf seemed to grow somehow more inviting, the grass not so much thickening as becoming mossy plush in its density. Rises and falls Brenda had not noticed appeared, comfortable spots that invited sitting.

Des gathered his skirts and seated himself. Without pause, he reached out and plucked a berry, eating it with every sign of enjoyment. With a touch more hesitation, the others followed his example. What Brenda ate tasted like a blueberry, and she suspected left the same blue-grey stain.

Surreptitiously, Brenda sucked at her lips to make sure they were clean. Des had blotted his own mouth with a handkerchief he removed from his sleeve, and addressed Pai Hu.

"You told Flying Claw there might be a favor we could do for you, great White Tiger of the West. Now that we are refreshed, would you care to explain what humble mortals like ourselves might do for an immortal of your stature?"

The White Tiger's ears twitched back and forth, forth and back. His nose wrinkled slightly so that his whiskers twitched, but Brenda had the impression that Pai Hu was amused rather than otherwise.

"For several months now," the White Tiger began, "I have

been walking through a recurring dream. It begins with fire. Small flames lick first at the pads of my paws, then rise to leap to the height of my shoulders and then over my head. I feel the heat, smell the flames, but I remain untouched, unharmed. At least initially . . .

"Then I feel the ground beneath my feet growing hot. It does not singe or burn or otherwise catch fire, but rather begins to soften and then to melt. Soon the ground is gone. I am swimming in a sea that is silver, eddied with gold and bronze. It is deep, so deep that I know it is bottomless. Infinite, so that I know it has no shores.

"I swim and feel no tiredness, for the White Tiger of the West does not ever feel tired, but as I swim I realize that I am also beginning to melt. As with the lands that had been my domain, I neither singe nor burn, but rather I begin to soften, then to lose shape, and finally I see myself as black streaks among the silver of the endless ocean.

"The ocean spreads, and although there are no shores for it to lap against, no bottom to its depth, yet it comes to an edge. The water falls over that edge, falling into a Void that contains nothing, even the water that empties into it. The water falls, and as it falls I know no more."

"But then," Brenda blurted, "you wake up, right?"

She clapped her hands to her lips, horribly embarrassed, but right at the end there Pai Hu had sounded like Dylan or Thomas back when they were young enough that they'd still come and climb under the covers with her, or, when they were a little older, sit on the edge of the bed, their feet trailing on the floor as they told her about nightmares that seemed more real than the carpet brushing their toes.

"Sorry," Brenda said, softly. Then she straightened. "But you do wake up, don't you?"

The White Tiger twitched his ears at her. His tail, which had started thumping when she'd spoken, stilled into a black and white striped curve in the thick grass.

"As I do not sleep," Pai Hu said, "I cannot wake up, but, yes, I do become aware of myself and know this for a vision rather than reality, yet there is a fear within my viscera that rather than a foreboding, this is a foretelling, so that each time the vision comes to me, I do not know whether this is merely a vision or the coming of my end."

"But," asked Riprap, "can you end? I mean, you're an immortal principle, not a mortal creature."

"All things can end," the White Tiger said. "Between mortals and immortals it is only the manner of that ending that differs. Some sages teach that even the nature of that ending is less different than we might imagine."

"I can see why you're worried then," Riprap said.

The White Tiger's tail twitched, as if not wanting to admit to ever worrying, but he did not gainsay Riprap.

Brenda glanced at the others. Flying Claw and Honey Dream were sitting very still. Neither of them looked as if they wanted to attract the White Tiger's attention. Nissa was also silent, but hers was a silence of listening, not of dread.

I guess the four of us who aren't from the Lands, Brenda thought, *are too dumb to know how dangerous this conversation is. Still, we're not going to learn anything by trembling and hoping the White Tiger will deign explain himself.*

Des, who despite his robes was now lounging in a manner both comfortable and decorous, stroked his beard. Brenda thought he looked like a Taoist sage in an ink-brush painting, finding wisdom among the glories of nature.

"Pai Hu, is there any interpretation you would place upon this vision or dream?"

The White Tiger's tail lashed. "I have my thoughts, but I would like to hear yours—if you have any."

Tiger, Tiger, Temper Bright, Brenda thought. *Be careful, Des. Pai Hu didn't like admitting that he had a bad dream, much less that it has scared him. Be very, very careful.*

XIV

Des inclined his head respectfully. "I have some thoughts, mighty White Tiger of the West, but my knowledge is slim and secondhand, learned from books and mortal teachers."

"I know you are limited," the White Tiger growled. "Even so, I would hear you speak."

"Very well," Des said. "Two things occurred to me. When you first spoke of seeing flames, I recalled that the Lands Born from Smoke and Sacrifice were created through fire. I wondered if you might be having a vision of those days, but this did not quite fit. What your flames led to was dissolution, not creation."

"I know that well enough," the Tiger growled. "Have you anything more?"

"I do." Des did not seem in the least disturbed by that growl. "I recalled that in the manifestations of ch'i within the physical world, West is associated with the element of metal, the color white, and the season autumn—and, of course, the Tiger.

"In the cycle of creation and destruction, metal is destroyed by fire, but gives rise to water. This is very much the character of your vision. When, within the vision, the flames begin to have an effect on your land and yourself, neither burns. Instead, there is melting. In the end, there is a sea, so Metal although destroyed by Fire is not gone. Rather, Water remains, and you within that Water.

"What disturbs me—and you as well, mighty Pai Hu, I am certain—is the next part, for instead of Water giving rise to Wood, Water tumbles over the edge of the precipice and falls endlessly into the Void, thus interrupting the cycle of creation from destruction. You say your vision ends there. Do you have any sense of the water's final destination?"

"None," the White Tiger rumbled. "The water falls, first

as a wave, then as a sheet, then as droplets, finally as mist. My awareness of myself as myself fades with each attenuation, until I believe the vision ends not because there is nothing left to see but because I am no longer sufficiently aware to have any sense of anything at all."

"So you are seeing a vision of your dissolution," Des said.

"I agree," the White Tiger said. "But what I do not know is whether this is an unalterable vision. If it is a warning, then I will have the chance to fight."

From slightly out of Brenda's line of sight, Flying Claw spoke. He sounded tense and a little bit angry.

"Who would send you such a vision? If someone wishes to warn you, why would this well-wisher not come in person?"

"I can think of several possibilities," the White Tiger said. "Not everyone would dare come before me as you have dared. Or the 'well-wisher,' as you term him, might be afraid of his giving warning being discovered. After all, one who has the power to attempt to destroy me might take nasty vengeance if he learned of his plans being bruited about."

Brenda started to automatically correct the exclusive use of the masculine pronoun, then bit her words back unspoken. This was *not* the time to emphasize the use of politically correct diction. She'd have to remind herself that the White Tiger's enemy could be female as easily as male.

"But," the White Tiger continued, the glance his burning eyes gave Brenda making her wonder if he might be able to read her thoughts, "the reason I think that the well-wisher has not come to me is that I think the source of my vision is Shang Ti."

"Shang Ti?" Nissa said. "I'm sorry, but I don't know who that is. I'm afraid I didn't grow up with Chinese lore."

"Brave Rabbit," the White Tiger said, clearly amused, "to walk in this world and yet not know of Shang Ti. He is the first emperor, Lord of the Center. Many legends credit him with the creation of the universe."

"I thought that was P'an Ku?" Brenda asked, feeling very confused. "I'm sure I read about P'an Ku creating the universe."

"Yes. Later legends told how P'an Ku created the world," Pai Hu agreed, "and set the White Tiger, Vermillion Bird, Azure Dragon, and Dark Warrior as guardians over the four directions, but those are very late legends."

Des nodded. "Yes. I believe most scholars credit the P'an Ku tale to the Taoist recluse Ko Kung in the fourth century A.D."

"My head hurts," Brenda said, and meant it. She thought she remembered Pearl or Des refering to the Red Bird of the South, not the Vermillion Bird, but she wasn't going to make a fool of herself by asking. After all, vermillion was red, wasn't it?

Nissa, however, wasn't to be distracted.

"So this Shang Ti, is he God?" Nissa said.

"Not 'God' as you mean the term," Honey Dream interjected, "at least within your monotheist cultural view."

Brenda swallowed a sigh of exasperation. Apparently, although Honey Dream couldn't quite bring herself to speak directly to the White Tiger, she couldn't resist correcting one of them.

Honey Dream continued, her tone pedantic, "Shang Ti is a very old deity. Sometimes he is called T'ien or Sky. Another name given to him in later writings is Yu Huang or August Jade. Whatever the name, Shang Ti is acknowledged as supreme ruler of the celestial hierarchy, the one to whom all the other deities must answer."

"Sound like God to me," Nissa muttered, "but I think I see what you're saying. Whatever Shang Ti is, wherever he is, he is not someone we're likely to meet casually—even in a place like this—but he is someone who might send a message to Pai Hu."

Honey Dream nodded. Brenda couldn't quite decide if the Snake was pleased or miffed that Nissa had caught on so quickly, but a whole new set of gods was a lot easier to accept with a tiger that would dwarf an elephant lolling in the grass in front of you, discussing his dreams.

Nissa returned her attention to the White Tiger.

"Is it because of the divine hierarchy," Nissa asked, "that Shang Ti would need to contact you through a vision rather than coming to visit?"

"Close enough," the White Tiger said, and Brenda felt certain they were not getting anything like the full story. She decided she was relieved.

"What may we do to serve you, Pai Hu?" Flying Claw asked.

"Your next destination will be Hell," the White Tiger said matter-of-factly. "As Hell connects all places, there you may find some indication, some rumor, of the source of this danger of which I have dreamed. If you learn anything, no matter how vague, I ask you to report to me."

"We will do this gladly," Des said.

"Additionally," Pai Hu said, "since you intend to travel into the other three guardian domains, I request that you ask my counterparts if they have had any similar warnings. You may share what I have told you if they seem reluctant to speak."

The White Tiger looked over where Flying Claw was sitting. Brenda turned and saw that Flying Claw seemed distinctly uncomfortable.

"You are surprised I would admit this vulnerability, Brother Tiger?" asked Pai Hu.

"For a moment, I was," Flying Claw said sheepishly.

"There is no shame to admitting truth," Pai Hu said. "I do not think this vision a sign that I fear something, but rather that something has designs on myself and my domain. True shame would be refusal to admit this until it was too late to act."

"Then why," Riprap cut in, "don't you go talk to the other three yourself?"

The White Tiger's tail lashed, but apparently at the casualness of Riprap's approach rather than at the question, which he answered politely enough.

"I forget you do not know. Our domains do not touch. We are separated by the Center. If I did not believe there was a threat, I might go and call upon one of my neighbors, but because I do believe there is a threat, I will not diminish my presence in my own lands."

"Reasonable," Riprap said. "Thank you."

The White Tiger seemed amused, but since Brenda thought cats of all types usually looked amused in a sort of lofty way, she couldn't be certain.

Des rose to his feet and bowed deeply. "Great White Tiger of the West, we will do all you request of us. You are gracious beyond belief to make us your messengers."

"You arrived in so timely a fashion," the White Tiger said, "that I cannot help but wonder if your problems and my vision are somehow intertwined, but speculation on such before we have more information would be idle."

"Right," Riprap agreed, shouldering his pack and making a fairly tidy bow, his hands pressed together in front of him.

The bow should have looked stupid with Riprap dressed as he was in jeans and hiking boots, but it didn't. Brenda imitated him and noticed the others doing the same.

Riprap was looking to where a path had opened in what had before been trackless jungle. "I'm guessing that's a hint. More walk, less talk."

Brenda looked back from the trail, meaning to thank the White Tiger one more time, but, perhaps predictably, the White Tiger of the West was nowhere to be seen.

☆

Tracy Frye called the next morning to inform them she would be arriving in San Francisco that afternoon. Pearl, Shen, and Albert were finishing breakfast in the informal dining area of Pearl's house.

"Very well," Albert said into his cell phone, his fork playing idly with a piece of cantaloupe on his plate. "Shall we meet this evening? I have spoken to the director of the Rosicrucian Museum, and he has requested that we hold our meeting when most of the tourists will be gone for the day. I, of course, agreed."

Tracy's reply was apparently less than perfectly polite, because Albert wrinkled his nose fastidiously, as if smelling something unpleasant. His tone when he replied, however, showed nothing of this.

"If you would like, I can arrange for a car to pick you up. No? You would rather arrange for your own transportation? Very well. Shall we say seven o'clock? The worst of the heat should be ebbing by then. And would you like to leave me a number where you can be reached in case something changes?"

Albert paused and rolled his eyes. His fork started squashing the square of cantaloupe into orange mush. "Very well. Nothing had better change. I understand. Have a good day's travel, Ms. Frye."

He thumbed off his phone and said conversationally, "Why she thinks being so acid will do her any good escapes me."

Pearl gave a knowing smile. "Because Ms. Frye believes she has the upper hand. Bullies always get rude when they believe they are in charge."

Shen, who had been looking tired and worried ever since Des and the others had departed, looked up from his hardly touched meal.

"But doesn't she? Without the Ox and the Monkey's sets, our only remaining option is to try and educate two complete novices. Even if we didn't train them in any element of our particular arcane skill set, even getting them to believe enough that they would accompany us into what is likely to be a very dangerous situation would be difficult."

Albert nodded. "And I would feel very uncomfortable about taking a boy and a woman of mature years into a such a situation without giving them any training."

"I suppose," Shen said, with what was clearly an attempt at humor, "that we could knock them out, then carry them along. They couldn't get into trouble that way, and we could protect them more easily."

Albert continued mashing cantaloupe. "I'm desperate enough that that idea sounds almost attractive. Thirteen people—seventeen when we include our four from the Lands—is an enormous group. It's too large for stealth, too small to be an army."

"They say there is strength in numbers," Pearl tried to encourage him.

Albert shook his head. "Not in this case. Too many of us have too little training. I feel uncomfortable about what risks we're asking our three apprentices to take. As matters stand, I am strongly inclined to leave Brenda Morris behind, but I know her father thinks that this is the opportunity of a lifetime."

Pearl nodded. She decided not to mention that Brenda actually raised the size of their group to eighteen.

"Taken at its most literal," Pearl said, "this is the opportunity of a lifetime—of many lifetimes. It's a journey none of our ancestors ever had the opportunity to make. However, let's worry about whether or not we take Brenda along after we know there will be a means of reaching our destination."

"Right," Albert said. "After all, even if we manage to get the two remaining mah-jong sets, we still have four ghosts to summon and convince to assist us."

"Five," Shen said, not completely helpfully, "if you include the Snake."

"As we must," Albert said in the tones of one repeating a lesson he'd rather forget, "unless we wish to include a barely trained, rather absentminded, eighty-three-year-old woman in our entourage."

He stopped mutilating the cantaloupe and started rubbing his hands up and down over his high cheekbones. It was a habit he had had since childhood, and while it indicated agitation, it also indicated a desire to concentrate.

Pearl, meanwhile, had felt a shred of an idea when Shen had mentioned something. What had it been? Something about knocking out the boy Monkey and the Ox . . . That had made her think of some kidnapping farce and . . . Got it!

"What if," she said, "we anticipate our meeting with Tracy Frye, try to take the mah-jong sets from her?"

"Steal them?" Shen said, appalled.

"If you're worried about the ethics of it," Pearl said, "we can leave her cash. I'm sure Albert's Matt could give us an estimate of the purchase prices."

"No," Shen protested. "It's not that. We've gone to a lot of effort not to give the various indigenous traditions an excuse to rally against us. Now you want to attack Tracy Frye and perhaps others."

Pearl shook her head. "I don't want to attack anyone, but neither do I want to be walked all over. I believe we could justify the—let's call it 'reacquisition'—of the mah-jong sets by arguing that Tracy Frye and her allies are acting not only counter to our needs, but counter to the desires and ideals of the larger indigenous magical community."

"We would have witnesses," Albert mused, "purely non-magical witnesses, to the fact that Frye et al. went after the ancestral mah-jong sets *after* the Rock Dove Society, of which she is a member, had agreed to let us have a chance to deal with the potential invasion ourselves. Matt could confirm that Tracy Frye offered to make a deal in exchange for the sets before we ever asked—showing that she did not go after the sets because she desired to own them."

"So, Albert," Shen said resignedly, "do you also think we should go ahead with Pearl's idea? Are you sure we should steal them before we find out what Tracy wants to trade?"

"We might do better if we do," Albert said. "After we've refused, they're going to be more on guard."

Pearl waved a dismissive hand. "In any case, we know what Tracy Frye will want to trade for already. She told Gaheris. She wants to have training in our specific type of magic. She's very proud of being a Generalist, remember? It's not only our style of magic she wants—although I bet she wants it pretty bad—it's being able to add another notch to her bedpost."

"Notch to her bedpost?" Albert asked bemusedly. "Is that the right idiom?"

"I don't care about the idiom," Pearl said. "Arrow to her quiver. Thorn in her crown. What I mean is that she wants the bragging rights that she was the first to get her hands on a form of magic that no one else in all the affiliated and unaffiliated magical orders of this world has ever possessed. That is what she wants. Even the magic, I suspect, comes second."

Shen sat quietly, obviously considering, then he shook his head. "No, Pearl, Albert, I'm sorry, but I think this would be absolutely the wrong thing to do."

"But you're not saying we should trade away our lore!" Pearl protested, horrified. "What would your grandfather have said?"

"He would never have permitted it," Shen replied without hesitation, "not even to stop an invasion. He would have argued that we would have been inviting our own dissolution, perhaps even endangering the Lands. However, he would also have said we should not stoop to theft—and so take the risk of weakening our position with the indigenous magical traditions."

Albert had stopped rubbing his face and was looking intently into the middle distance. Pearl had seen him do this before, usually in business meetings, when calculating precisely how much the market would stand.

"Very well. Aunt Pearl is right. So are you, Uncle Shen. We know what Tracy Frye wants. We also know that it is something we cannot give her. The first question we must ask ourselves is does she know we will not give in to her demands?"

"No," Pearl replied immediately. "She thinks she has the upper hand. Her rudeness to you on the phone proves that."

"Good. Now we move on. We will not trade, but we will not attempt to steal the mah-jong sets. What options does that leave us?"

There was a long silence, a very long silence as each of them weighed the options. At last, Shen spoke.

"Our only other option is to include the Monkey and the Ox."

Pearl said, "But as we already discussed, training them is hardly an option. We would need to have their involuntary cooperation."

Albert said hesitantly, "There is Righteous Drum's spell, the one he used to steal some of our connection to our Earthly Branches. Could we use that?"

A look of purest distaste crossed Shen's features, but he spoke politely enough. "I think not. Remember, Righteous Drum's goal and our own are different. He wanted only the Earthly Branches. We want the ability for some or all of us to reenter the Lands."

"So that won't work," Albert said, "and I don't think we can expect to gain the cooperation of the current Ox, and especially the current Monkey because in his case not only would we need to get his cooperation, but that of his parents as well. Uncle Shen, I'm starting to think that Aunt Pearl might be right—that our only option is to get back those sets."

"Hmm . . ." Shen said. He leaned back in his chair, folded his hands over his midriff, and closed his eyes. "I need to think. I'll walk out to the garage and check on the prisoners. They're still grateful enough not to be dead that they're behaving well, but I promised to bring some books out."

Pearl did not protest, but let herself work through the various options, looking for a way around this problem.

The best solution, I suppose, would be for us to drop out altogether, let Righteous Drum and the others find their own way home. If we did that, we would be breaking a promise—and thereby invalidating the treaty that protects us from them. The attack a week ago is ample proof that not all those who are eager to go after the Thirteen Orphans would be nearly so interested in our physical welfare as Righteous Drum was.

Eventually, Shen returned. "Sorry I took so long. I had to unclog a toilet and explain the pipes couldn't dispose of just anything."

He sighed and settled into his chair. "I can't think of another option—not another good one at least. I considered the possibility of having representatives of the indigenous magical traditions witness our meeting with Tracy Frye in the hope that they would somehow rein her and her allies in, but we would have no assurance that they would do so. In fact, they might decide to change their minds about not interfering in our private business, might decide that we are not competent. Then, in addition to dealing with the problems in the Lands, we would be facing well-organized opposition here."

"So you agree that we need to reclaim the Ox and Monkey mah-jong sets?" Albert asked.

"On one condition," Shen said, "that we meet first with Tracy Frye, and hear her conditions."

Pearl stirred, and Shen turned an engaging grin on her.

"Pearl, it's not that I don't believe you're right about her goals. I do. However, if we anticipate her, she can always claim that she never intended to try and force us to do her will. This way, it will be certain."

The urge to move, to attack, to get something *done* was very strong, but Pearl forced herself to consider.

"All right, Shen. I agree. You're probably right."

"Very well," Albert said, nodding that he agreed to Shen's condition. "If we're going to have to go after the mah-jong sets, we should consider who our opponents might be. We know about Jozef Ski, the Polish nationalist, but we didn't get a clear look at the two who were with him. Any thoughts as to who they might have been—or who else might be involved?"

"I can think of one," Pearl said, "who might be involved,

although I doubt he was one of those lurking by my garage. However, he has the money to be Tracy Frye's financial backer and has ties to this coast. He made himself notable to me by how he went out of his way not to speak to either Shen or myself at the Rock Dove Society meeting, even though he has known us all his life."

Shen looked mildly annoyed, as if he were going to demand that Pearl stop talking in riddles, then his face lightened. "Franklin Deng. Now that you mention it, I think you could be right. Franklin's own magical tradition is Chinese in source, so he has been very interested in our tradition for a long time. So was his father. I believe the father called on my grandfather, pressing for shared information. He did not like being refused even what he called 'theoretical discussion.' "

"Another reason," Albert said, "Franklin Deng might be backing Tracy Frye is that he doesn't like me, personally. Some years ago, he was putting together a line of frozen dinners built around Chinese menus. He even included a tea bag containing the jasmine tea so many restaurants serve. Knowing Americans have a sweet tooth, he wanted to include a dessert, but Chinese sweets don't translate well to an American palate."

"What about fortune cookies?" Shen asked.

"Oh, he already had that covered, except that in addition to the fortune, the cookie was also going to contain a coupon for another Deng's Delights product."

"So he came to you?" Shen asked, puzzled. "Wouldn't chocolate as good as yours suffer from freezing and thawing?"

"My point exactly," Albert agreed. "His idea was that he include a square of hot pudding cake, like you find on buffet steam tables—but to differentiate his product from the mob and maintain a Chinese cache, he wanted to have it be official Your Chocolatier pudding cake."

"Not really!" Shen laughed.

"Really," Albert said, "and Franklin didn't like it when I turned him down. He pressed, pointing out all the free advertising I would get in addition to his licensing fee. He didn't like when I pointed out that I got more business from not advertising, from being so exclusive that you already had to be 'in the know' to get access to most of my product line."

"I take it Deng didn't care for that," Shen said.

"He didn't," Albert agreed. "I think Des Lee has also annoyed him, back when they were both on a committee for some festival in Chinatown—something to do with accurate period costuming for some float."

Shen chuckled. "With Des on the side of accuracy, no doubt. So several of our number have annoyed Deng on numerous levels. Do you think Tracy Frye will be staying with Franklin Deng?"

"She did say she was flying into San Francisco," Pearl said, "not San Jose, although her ostensible reason for coming to California was to meet with us."

"So you think he will be here, too," Albert said.

"I think so. If we are correct, she is carrying two pieces of art Franklin has paid a great deal of money to possess."

"Do you think he doesn't trust her?" Shen asked.

"Would you?" Pearl said reasonably. "I wouldn't, and if I can read her personality, I am certain Franklin can as well. He didn't rise to his current prominence merely by being his father's heir. He earned it."

"How do we confirm our guesses?" Albert said. "Do we attempt mundane means? I could have someone find out what flight Tracy Frye is on, and then track where she goes from there, if anyone picks her up, things like that."

"That might be best," Pearl agreed, "and easier than tracking her magically. Do you have anyone in mind?"

"There's a security firm I've used," Albert said, pulling out his phone. "They're reliable and discreet. Excuse me, and I'll see if they can get on this right away."

He took the phone into another room, and in a moment they could hear the murmur of his voice.

"Pearl," Shen said, "do you think we should tell the others what we plan? Righteous Drum and his crew, I mean?"

"I think we must," Pearl said. "They deserve to know we're working on a solution to our mutual problem. Also, if something goes wrong, someone should know."

"So you don't think we should include them in our . . ." Shen pondered for a moment, then grinned. ". . . strike force? After all, they're probably more powerful than you or me."

"Absolutely not," Pearl replied. "Doubtless they are powerful, but they also might do something just plain dumb like setting off an alarm system or leaving fingerprints. Also, right now this is the Thirteen Orphans against Tracy Frye and her consortium. If we include Righteous Drum and Waking Lizard, then it could be argued that instead of stopping an invasion, we're aiding and abetting one."

"You have a good point there," Shen agreed. "I notice you didn't mention Flying Claw or Honey Dream. Do you think we should move ahead, even if Des and the others aren't back yet?"

"I do," Pearl said. "Des planned to be gone only a day or so, but who knows what they will encounter? Our window of opportunity may be small. If Des and the others are back, great, but otherwise we need to move ahead."

Shen looked at Pearl, shaking his head in mock dismay.

"To think we are contemplating something like this, at our ages."

"You're only as old as you feel," Pearl retorted, "and right about now I feel like a kitten—a tiger kitten."

XV

The first day in the guardian domains—or rather half day, for their meeting with Pai Hu carried them into the afternoon—passed quickly and enjoyably.

The twisting path led them through marvelous landscapes,

eventually ending in a glade that all but begged to be camped in. They took the hint.

Here Des changed from his elaborate shenyi into clothing more fit for travel. Honey Dream decided this was a good idea. However, she didn't change into the casual clothing she had acquired in the Land of the Burning, but opted instead for a short upper tunic and loose trousers tied below the knee, attire such as she might have worn at home.

They woke at dawn the following morning, refreshed. Flying Claw had taken off his armor while they were in camp, but redonned it in the morning.

"The White Tiger of the West has been hospitable thus far," he said, tightening a strap and rotating his shoulders to make certain the fit was right. "However, I would not put it past him to decide we need testing. In any case, sauntering around as if we were in some great park is so arrogant as to nearly invite such tests."

Honey Dream wasn't certain she agreed. Didn't Pai Hu want their help? What good would it do him if they were all killed by his own denizens? She didn't argue, though. Tigers might understand tigers better than snakes could do.

A path no one remembered having seen the night before had appeared to one side of the glade, and Des Lee decided to take a hint. They walked down the path slowly, letting breakfast settle, and trying to identify the various unseen birds by their songs.

"Does anyone," Honey Dream asked, trying very hard to keep the apprehension that warred with annoyance in her breast from showing in her voice, "have the least idea where we are going?"

Des Lee, who was, along with her, the rear guard of their little band—Nissa and Brenda were in the middle, Riprap and Flying Claw in front—glanced over at her.

"We are going wherever the White Tiger of the West wishes for us to go," Des said with cheerful mildness.

"Yes," Honey Dream hissed. "I know that, but do any of you have the least sense where our own gate into this place is to be found? I cannot imagine you have forgotten how we entered the West."

"Through the White Tiger's jaws," Des said, "and I dearly hope he'll spare us that journey on the return."

Honey Dream shrugged as if that was of no import to her, although she wondered if she could make herself pass into that gaping maw again. It had been bad enough the first time, but the first time she could convince herself that the mouth was only illusion, that stepping through would be like passing through any more usual door. Knowing that it would not be, knowing she would be forced to tread that red tongue, pass beneath that ridged mouth top, between those fangs . . .

She caught herself as she was about to start wringing her hands, covered by moving to adjust the hang of one of the gourds on her belt.

"I hope so as well," she said calmly, "but that will hardly matter if we cannot find the location of the gate. I do not think any of us would importune the White Tiger to come and serve us, would we?"

Flying Claw had his compass out, and was inspecting the reading. "If no other alternative suggests itself, then I suggest we use this to guide us as far west as possible, since that is where our gate is most likely to have penetrated. However, the White Tiger has use for us. I do not think he will waste our efforts—or his own—by leading us astray."

As if Flying Claw's words had been a charm of some sort (and for all Honey Dream knew, perhaps they had been), within a few steps the trail they followed curved and at the end of that curve was an open glade. Other trails left the glade, going off into the jungle in various mysterious and tangled directions. However, to one side stood a perfect prosaic unfinished pine door, the bar code from the hardware store still visible where it was stapled into the wood on one side.

"There is our exit," Des said. He reached out and touched the doorknob. "Nicely locked. I can feel the Men Shen within. If any of us ask, they will open it for us, but I'm willing to bet that anyone else entering this glade won't even see there is a door here."

"Good," Riprap said. "That's one problem solved. Now, do we go back to Pearl's and tell the others what we've learned, or do we go on?"

"Go on," Brenda Morris said with annoying certainty. "I'm not saying we should try and open another gate or anything, but part of this trip was to get me, Nissa, and Riprap a little more up to speed. After meeting the White Tiger, if there is one thing I'm sure of it's that I'm not up to speed on just about anything."

Her combination of frankness and humility made Honey Dream's blood boil, but Flying Claw looked impressed, so Honey Dream decided she had better not say anything. The last thing she wanted to do was put him in the position of explaining how admirable that deceptive little Ratling really was.

Des glanced at Nissa and Riprap and their expressions made clear that they agreed with Brenda. Nissa looked a little wistful, though. She probably wanted to go home and tell her Lani Bunny about Mama's brave adventure with the Magical Tiger.

Honey Dream tried not to gag. These people were completely without dignity. Nissa was the Rabbit. Mothering concerns should no longer distract her. Although, Honey Dream admitted to herself, Rabbits did breed like, well, rabbits, and given the peculiar way power was handed down within families within the Thirteen Orphans, perhaps Nissa wasn't so out of line.

She realized that Des was looking at her, and from his expression had probably spoken to her.

"My apologies," she said loftily. "I was reading the emanations of ch'i in this place."

Des looked at his three students. "See how easily she does it? No hand gestures, no word, simply drifts off a little. Honey Dream," he said politely, returning his attention to her, "I asked if you agreed that we should continue on? If we do run into trouble, you and Flying Claw are likely to be the ones who are going to have to pull us out."

Honey Dream glanced over at Flying Claw and saw the faintest of grins playing around his handsome lips. *He* knew perfectly well that she had been caught napping—or daydreaming or brooding, whatever—but she took heart from the fact that he clearly wasn't going to embarrass her in front of these others.

"You know what your students are capable of," Honey Dream hedged. "If you think they will benefit from further exploration, then by all means, let us do so."

"We're agreed, then," Des said. "We'll take a look around. I don't want to set up another of the Nine Gates quite yet. I think I know what our direction will be, but I'd hate to get back and find out that Shen and Righteous Drum have recalculated everything."

"Now," Des continued, "if all of you have rested your feet and adjusted your packs, shall we go on? Honey Dream, you were reading the ch'i. What do you suggest?"

Honey Dream fought down a momentary flare of panic. Then she noticed Flying Claw gesturing ever so subtly toward one particular path, a bit wider than the others.

"That one," she said grandly, pointing with a gesture that made her sleeve flutter most attractively. "I think that one might prove of interest."

And "of interest" did it indeed prove.

Until the end of her life—and curiously, most acutely when that life was in danger of ending—Honey Dream would remember that "field trip" through the outer fringes of the realm of the White Tiger of the West.

For the first time since Honey Dream had crossed the bridge from the Lands into the Land of the Burning, she had the sense of being in a place that felt like home. In addition to the more usual plants and animals, she could sense dragons in the streams and dwelling in the upthrust bones of the many rises and ridges that characterized this particular region. Indeed, for all that their initial journey had taken them through jungles, here the terrain was rocky and often open, making it easier to see the creatures who made their homes here.

Honey Dream hadn't realized how much she had missed the awareness that, even if unseen, the resident creatures were there in a way they were not in the Orphans' world. She wondered if in the Orphans' land they had been driven away, of if they simply took more care to remain hidden. Either would make sense. For all the Lands were in constant governmental tumult, there was considerably more respect—even simple awareness—of those others who had their own claims on rock and water, hill and tree.

But Honey Dream was in no mood to philosophize. She gloried in this living, breathing realm. Indeed, she felt more kindly toward her companions than ever she had before, taking every gasp of awe, every expression of wonder and pleasure as if she were a householder and they were admiring her manse.

The White Tiger of the West must have somehow communicated his—"welcome" might be too strong a word—but at least that he was not adverse to their journey. They saw many creatures Honey Dream had only read about in dusty bestiaries.

The Dugu—that curious creature shaped much like a tiger, but with its snowy pelt unbarred with black, its head more like that of a dog, and its tail like that of a horse—looked down at them from a crag on a particularly barren rocky slope. It offered neither welcome nor threat, and they followed its example, bowing politely as they passed.

When their trail through the rapidly thinning jungle emptied out in a series of rocky hills, fingered through with tendrils from a river that seemed to have its origin somewhere farther west, they glimpsed a herd of slender creatures something like a horse in shape, but with tails more like those of an ox. Their coats were all in shades of white, from pearl to ivory, to powdery chalk and translucent alabaster. Their elegant brows, delicate as those of a deer, were ornamented with a single horn.

Nissa gasped. "Unicorns! An entire herd of unicorns!"

Honey Dream heard this word through the translation spell, initially broken down into its meaning as "one horn," and again as the given name of a type of creature.

"These are Boma," she corrected. "Some say they are kin to the ch'ilin."

Flying Claw was looking after the fleeing herd, aware that unless the Boma chose to turn back, there was no way the humans could hope to catch them.

"The sage who tutored us in such things," he said, "noted that the Boma cried out in a voice that was almost human. He never said they could speak, though. In any case, these do not seem inclined to stay and visit."

Brenda and Nissa were watching the retreating Boma with shining eyes, their expressions so bright and filled with wonder that Honey Dream made a mental note to look up this "unicorn" when they returned to Pearl's house. She thought she had seen a group of creatures rather like Boma on one of the children's television programs Lani watched, but those had been plump, almost dumpy, and their coats had been uniformly of pastel hues. She did not think those would have aroused such a reaction in Brenda and Nissa.

Riprap, too, looked fascinated. His big hands kept opening and closing in the vicinity of his chest.

"Man! I wish I'd thought to bring a camera. *National Geographic* would just flip! Heck, I'd settle for doing a slide show for Pearl and the others."

Des smiled with gentle good humor. "I doubt any camera— except maybe for a very simple camera obscura made from local materials—would work here."

"Isn't that always the way?" Riprap chuckled. "But I'd still like to try."

They did not see a Zhi Pig, but when crossing a river (a fallen tree made a convenient bridge) they saw a school of

Zhi Fish. The Zhi Fish had the long, heavily scaled bodies of ocean fish, making them interesting enough as denizens of an inland river, but when they poked their heads from the water, it could clearly be seen that those heads were shaped like those of dogs.

Brenda Morris nearly lost her balance and fell off the log when she saw this, but Riprap grabbed her arm and arrested her fall. The Zhi Fish made a sound like crying babies, although whether in disappointment or amusement Honey Dream could not be certain.

That night they made their camp at the edge of a grove of trees near a freshwater spring. They did not hunt or fish, but ate from foods they had brought with them. Des insisted on adding some foul-tasting tablets to the spring water, assuring them that the tablets would make certain the water was pure. Honey Dream had her doubts as to the need—the spring water looked wonderfully clean and clear to her—but she certainly didn't want to risk the indignity of getting the runs.

Later, when they were sitting around the fire telling stories, they saw a dark-winged bird, rather like a crow, fly over their camp. It dropped a twig or some such into the fire, and in the sudden flare they all saw the bird had a human face, but surrounded by feathers where the hair would be.

"Banmao," Flying Claw said dreamily. "My teacher pointed them out to us, and said their flesh was a sovereign cure for insanity."

"No wonder," Nissa said, shivering a bit, although the night was quite warm. "Looking at one is enough to drive anyone crazy. I've been comparing Chinese cures to the ones I studied in pharmacy school. I noticed there are a great many built around symbolic correspondences."

"And I wonder which set of methods," Brenda Morris said in that voice Honey Dream hated because she knew that they were being forced to listen to the idiot girl think aloud, "would work here? I mean, Des said Riprap's camera wouldn't, but he still made sure we had to use those awful purification tablets in the water."

Des gave a rueful grin, aware but unthreatened by his contradictions. "I suppose I'd want that shot of penicillin if I got an infection, but I wouldn't turn down some traditional remedy either."

The next day they continued their progress, heading west for a few hours, then beginning to circle back in the direction that both Flying Claw and Des agreed (after much checking of their compasses and cross-referencing the results) their gate lay.

Their new route took them through lands somewhat less barren, perhaps because they were so well watered. It seemed as if they forded some brook or stream every hundred paces.

During one such ford, Nissa spotted some very odd deer with four long antlers. They had fled before the group could get a closer look, and Riprap muttered, "Okay. Maybe a camera won't work, but next time I take binoculars or at least a telescope."

Later, Brenda shrieked when she spotted a Tiaorong—a bright yellow snake with tiny wings, almost like fins. The creature was so startled that it dove into the water of a nearby stream. The resultant flash of golden light was so bright that even in daylight everyone was temporarily blinded.

"Nice defense mechanism," Des said, wiping his streaming eyes on his sleeve.

Not all the creatures were as timid as the four-horned deer and the Tiaorong. Once Flying Claw and Honey Dream had to hold off a Yayu. The Yayu had lured Nissa close by making a sound like a baby crying. The Yayu didn't look dangerous—only strange with its ox's body, human head, and horse's hooves—but the way it leapt at Nissa left no doubt as to its carnivorous intent.

Riprap grabbed Nissa and dragged her back as the Yayu reared, barely getting the Rabbit clear of the slashing front hooves. Flying Claw interposed himself, his sword out as quickly as his namesake's claws.

Brenda was fumbling for one of her bracelets when Honey Dream raced forward. Knowing how quadrupeds of all types hate serpents, she cast a sensation of snakes twining about the creature's hind legs. The Yayu wheeled and Flying Claw took off its head in a single swipe. The creature's blood was pale green, rather like sap.

No one had much room left for wonders after that, so Honey Dream didn't mention the Dragon-Turtle whose shell was one of the stepping-stones they used as they hurried back to the gate. She thought Riprap noticed though, and heard him mutter something about a camera.

When they turned their feet to return to where they would cross back into the Land of the Burning, Honey Dream had to resist a desire to stay here where things were so familiar—even as they were so strange. But then she saw Brenda gazing at Flying Claw, her expression filled with longing, and changed her mind.

I am the only one who realizes how dangerous Brenda is. I cannot be weak, I cannot give in to my own desires. Not yet, at least, and when I do, I doubt Brenda will enjoy the results.

☆

When Righteous Drum and Waking Lizard learned of the latest complication, they volunteered to carry forward with the more theoretical work, so that Albert, Pearl, and Shen could prepare both for the interview with Tracy Frye that evening, and the eventuality that the Ox and Monkey mahjong sets would not be reclaimed then.

They also agreed that they would return to Colm Lodge well before Tracy Frye was due, and that Lani could come and stay with them, since it was likely that Pearl and the others would have a busy night.

"Will the prisoners be secure?" Waking Lizard asked.

"Oh, yes," Pearl assured him. "I've tightened my wards. If you'd like, I can create a link between you and them. I'll give you a emergency phone numbers in case you sense anything amiss."

When this was done, Pearl suggested Waking Lizard and

Righteous Drum work in the family room, rather than her office.

"I may need access to my computer," she explained politely.

"We will not be in the least inconvenienced," Righteous Drum said. "Mostly we need to do some independent calculations and compare the results."

Once the two Landers were settled at the long kitchen table with stacks of books, pads of paper, and an abacus that Pearl had kept out of sentiment for her own school days, the other three carried a pot of tea into Pearl's office.

"Now that we've decided to carry on with this," Albert said, "I'd like to try and figure out what we might be up against."

"I made some careful inquiries at Franklin Deng's California residence," Pearl said. "He has a mansion and vineyard in Woodside—that's an expensive area south of San Francisco," she added for Shen's benefit.

"Did you give us away?" Shen asked anxiously.

"Not at all," Pearl said. "I posed as a member of a committee fund-raising for the restoration of a historic building in Chinatown. I learned Franklin was currently in California, but not available to come to the phone, as he was involved with guests. I then rung off politely and promised to mail my information."

"He won't wonder?" She asked.

"My guess is that he won't even hear about it," Albert said. "Not if his staff is any good. They'll wait for the materials to arrive in the mail."

" 'Guests,' " Pearl repeated. "That sounds promising."

"I agree," Albert said, "but I wish there was a way we could find out if they—or indeed he—have anything to do with this situation. If Tracy Frye is dropped off there this evening, we'll have some confirmation of our suspicions, but I'd love to know sooner."

"There are variations on the divination rite we have used for years to keep track of the Thirteen Orphans," Shen reminded him. "These can be used to trace others although what we will learn will be limited: perhaps only general location and, if we are very fortunate, something of their state of mind."

Albert smiled. "I haven't used that variation for years. It has been a long time since there was anyone I couldn't track simply by picking up the phone and making a few calls."

Albert did not mean to sound boastful, but Pearl knew with absolute certainty that if Gaheris had been present, he would have taken the simple statement as a boast.

What are we going to do about those two? Pearl thought, then let the matter go. Now was certainly not the time to let herself be distracted.

Taking Albert's expression of interest as agreement, Shen rose, took the Dragon mah-jong set from the safe in Pearl's office, and began clearing off a table.

"We won't need the marked cloth," he said, "but it would help if we knew both Franklin Deng's and Tracy Frye's astrological affiliations."

"One moment," Pearl said. "Deng's Delights has a business Web site. Let me consult it."

She crossed to her desktop and pulled up the site.

"Franklin Deng," Pearl continued, "is a Dog, born in a Fire year."

"Now," Shen said, "if we could only learn the same about Tracy Frye."

Pearl struck a few keys, feeling very pleased with herself. Over to one side, her printer hummed to life.

"Actually, after Gaheris told us about her coming to his office, I did some research. Like many of the vainer sort, she has a Web site for no other reason than she can. Tracy Frye is a Ram. Interestingly, she was also born in a Fire year."

"I wonder," Shen said, "if that affiliation will make Deng and Tracy get along better or worse? It could go either way. Dogs and Rams don't find themselves in accord. Dogs tend toward order and structure. Rams are dreamers—and they can have that trickster side, too. That really can drive a Dog crazy."

"Like the sheep that won't be herded," Pearl said.

"Fire usually intensifies Fire," Albert added thoughtfully. "Makes it burn hotter."

"Or out of control," Pearl said. "I wasn't able to find anything out about Downhill Ski, the Polish fellow. He seems to be Tracy's opposite, devoted to secrecy."

"Ah, well," Albert said. "You've done amazingly."

"I have remembered a little about Jozef Ski," Shen said. "He belonged to the Rock Dove Society some years ago—a decade or more, when he was much younger. He resigned because he felt the policies were too mild. I believe he has had similar fallings-out with some of the Polish organizations as well."

"Just Tracy's sort of man," Pearl said.

As they talked, Shen had been laying out the various mah-jong tiles facedown on the padded surface of the table. For the first time in many, many years, Pearl was aware of whose bone had been shaped into these little rectangles. She'd liked Exile Dragon. Exile Dragon had liked her, had been a far more interested and interesting teacher than her father.

Now she turned her computer off, and joined the others.

Hello, old friend, she thought, caressing the tile as she laid it down. *I hope you're well, wherever you are. Whoever you are. I wonder if you've been reincarnated? Damn. We never thought about that. What if reincarnation is the way it goes? Then even if we do figure out how to contact the spirits of the Orphans we need, they won't be there.*

Once again she put the worry from her mind as unproductive.

I'm developing a file cabinet of things I'm not thinking about: Albert and Gaheris; how far can we trust Righteous Drum and the others; what's weird about Brenda; reincarnation. I'm going to need to deal with some of these.

But not now. Now is time to build the wall, and find out a bit more about Franklin Deng and Tracy Frye.

When all of the tiles had been turned upside down, Pearl paused. "The Tiger's direction is east-northeast. The Dragon's is east-southeast."

"Cat's direction is the center," Albert said, "so I can take any seat."

Pearl looked at Shen. "What do you suggest?"

"Have Albert take east," Shen said. "That's the first seat in any case, and so, appropriate for him. I'll take south, and you take north."

Pearl's table was already aligned to the four directions, so they moved to their appropriate places.

"I suppose," Pearl said, "we're going to start with Franklin Deng," she said. She went over to the printer and took out three freshly printed sheets. "His corporate Web site included a recent photo and a facsimile of his signature."

She handed each man one of the printed sheets.

"This should work," Albert said, a slow smile spreading across his face. "The signature is a particularly good idea. Hey! You got not only his English signature and his Chinese signature, but his chop as well. Very nice."

"Thank you," Pearl said, trying to hide how much the compliment meant. "I thought perhaps a writing exercise might help us to concentrate on our goal.

"Shen," Pearl continued, "would you get out writing materials for each of us? I have spare inkstones in the cabinet, and several pads of paper."

"I have my case here," Shen said, reaching into his pants pocket for a flat, portable case. "Do you have any preferences, Albert?"

Albert shook his head. "A slimmer-handled brush is all, but anything will do."

Pearl didn't say anything. She knew that even without being asked, Shen would bring her the small, flat box that contained her preferred brushes and inkstone.

Pearl and Albert pushed the tiles to the end of the table

where no one was sitting, giving them each room to rest their writing materials in front of them.

For a long time no one said anything, each of them concentrating on the photograph of Franklin Deng while writing his name over and over again in both Chinese and English.

If you truly believe words are magic, then they will be magic. That is what Exile Dragon had taught his students, and what those students had in turn taught their own. Pearl put her imagined observer from her mind, concentrating on the flourishes contained in Franklin Deng's handwriting.

Strong strokes in both English letters and Chinese characters. A sense of power in the down sweep, a reluctance to let go at the end of the line, so there was often a little spreading of the ink, a widening of a line. Yet there was control as well. Reluctantly, perhaps, but the lines did end within the proper limits. There was no obvious stylization.

Pearl felt she knew the man better for this study. Focused. Intense. Willful. Not overly creative, but with a touch of the visionary.

That may be the Fire influence, she thought. *Fire brings illumination, but too much fire may destroy what it merely seeks to light.*

She studied the photograph, too. She had deliberately chosen the official corporate photograph, not because she thought it was necessarily more representative, but because what it showed was how Franklin Deng wanted to be seen. His hair, unsilvered, despite the fact that he was over sixty, lay neatly on either side of the right-hand part. His eyebrows showed none of the wildness that often came to men with age. Pearl suspected that he probably had them trimmed and shaped, although with such care that no one but an actress would guess.

His gaze was direct, straight on to the camera. No dreamer here. None of that Kermit the Frog vague friendliness that Silicon Valley titans like Bill Gates so often let be part of their public image. This was a Dog in charge. A Dog who herded his flocks.

Riprap's Dog—as she and Des both had separately intuited—was fighter as well as herder. That's why Des had chosen a Tibetan mastiff as the model for the charm he had had carved for Riprap.

By contrast, Franklin Deng was a border collie. Admirable. Organized. Eyes on the prize.

I think, Pearl mused, *that he and Tracy Frye will eventually come to a parting of the ways. He has herded the Sheep very neatly thus far, but she's going to be the black sheep who insists on turning and going her own way—and usually precisely when it will lose the Dog his prize.*

And maybe, just maybe, we can be the ones who create the trial where she bolts. But not, I think, until we have what we want. We must take care. She may already be resisting his control. We don't want to precipitate a sudden departure. I wonder if Franklin Deng has reached the same conclusion about her nature. I wonder if that's why she is staying at his house.

Almost in unison Shen and Albert raised their heads, the stilling of their brushes telling Pearl without the need for words that they had finished their own focusing. Brushes were dropped into a glass of water to soak, writing pads and inkstones set aside, but other than that, they did nothing to break their concentration.

Without speaking, they slid the tiles back to the center of the table, shuffling them back and forth in the gentle mixing and intertwining motion often referred to, even by those who had no idea of the potency latent in those deceptively simple rectangles, as "washing" the tiles.

They concentrated on their target, Franklin Deng's image—even more than that, his essence—trembling through them and into Exile Dragon's bone and the resilient bamboo that backed it.

With wordless accord, they knew when the tiles were fully washed. Each of the three slid a few tiles toward them and with the clattering of bone against bamboo, the wall took shape, tiles seeming to take their places by their own inclination.

Once built, the wall was broken, the tiles arrayed in elaborate patterns like and yet unlike those used to read into the well-being of the Thirteen Orphans.

"Franklin is definitely here," Albert said, with satisfaction. He turned over one tile, then another. "Interesting. Three bamboo. Three strong subordinates. One character."

"That will be Tracy Frye," Shen said, and no one questioned his certainty. Dragons tended to know things. Shen turned another tile. "Nine dots. Likely the household staff."

"If Franklin is like most of us," Albert said, "these will probably not stay on the property—or have their motions restricted—when he expects to discuss occult matters. Rules as to secrecy are even stricter among the indigenous groups than among the Thirteen."

"This would seem to indicate that we have at least glimpsed the entire cabal," Pearl said. "The three who were here and Tracy Frye."

"Our focus," Albert reminded her, "was on those we might face if we went after the mah-jong tiles. The cabal could be much larger, simply waiting for these to do the dirty work."

"True," Pearl admitted.

"Deng's state of mind is interesting," Shen said when they had turned a few more tiles. "North winds and green dragons. Cold aggression teamed with vibrant growth—the focus on profit."

"But no suspicion," Shen said. "No peacocks screaming warning. He anticipates controlling whatever game it is he has in mind—both with us, and with Ms. Frye."

Pearl leaned back, stretching like a satisfied cat.

"Well, he's in for a surprise. Let's do our best to make sure that surprise is not mutual."

XVI

Shen, Albert, and Pearl spent the remainder of the day acquiring the knowledge they hoped would help them regain the mah-jong sets.

Albert took over Pearl's computer and began searching out everything he could learn about Franklin Deng's Woodside estate. The Web yielded not only overhead photos, but a variety of views, both from various gala events and from occasional private tours of the vineyard.

Pearl and Shen reviewed various spells, for, although Albert had been well taught, there was no doubt that their knowledge was both more sophisticated and more intense.

As he researched, Albert periodically called Shen or Pearl over to see what he had learned. None of it was encouraging. Delight Vineyards was fenced. Albert zoomed in to inspect details in various photos and said he felt fairly sure that not only did the place have an electronic alarm system, it also had guard dogs.

"See," he said, showing them a detail on a photo. "That's a kennel, and those aren't Pekingese in there. More like Dobermans."

Shen had been poring over some closely written scrolls he had brought with him from New York, and Pearl recognized an increasing mood of cheerfulness, but whenever pressed, he refused to say anything.

"There's something I'm going to need to check first," he said, "when we meet Tracy tonight. It's not worth wasting your time with explanations if that doesn't pan out. Keep planning. None of what you're doing will be wasted."

Both Pearl and Albert knew better than to press, and went on with their own preparations, Albert growing increasingly more morose, but Pearl was buoyed past her own uncertainties by Shen's air of cheerful confidence.

* * *

That afternoon, the security firm Albert had hired called to confirm that Tracy Frye's plane had landed, and that she had been met by a man who met Jozef Ski's description.

"Anyone else?" Albert asked. He'd set his phone to speaker mode so Shen and Pearl could listen.

"Just a driver for the car—a big man, Eurasian, looked as much like a thug as a chauffeur."

"Did you happen to learn whose car it was—or was it just a hire?"

"Yes, we did. Private car. Registered to Franklin Deng in Woodside. Do you want the number?"

Albert punched the air with one fist, but when he spoke his tone remained level and businesslike. "Where did they go?"

"To the Hilton near the airport. I made some inquiries, and Jozef Ski has been staying there on and off for about a week. He has a suite, and sometimes a couple stays with him: a husband and wife, both Hispanic. Their names are Glorieta and Edmundo Sanchez. She's quite a looker, probably about forty, and at least fifteen years younger than her husband. He's a big guy, a bit gone to seed, but I'd bet anything he used to be a boxer—he's got the flattened ears and that nose has been broken more than once."

"Are Ski and Frye still there?"

"Yes. My partner's watching them. They went up to the suite, and when they came down Ms. Frye looked as if she'd taken time to shower and change her clothes. She looked pretty beat when she got off that plane. They're in the hotel café, having something to eat."

"Anything else?"

"One thing. It may be minor, but since it was out of line, I thought I'd mention it."

"Go on."

"When Ms. Frye got off the plane, she had two pieces of luggage, a rolling bag, and a shoulder bag that stretched the limits for a second personal item. The shoulder bag seemed pretty heavy, but when the man who met her tried to take it, she literally slapped his hand away. She's got the bag with her now in the restaurant, has it set between her feet, and keeps reaching to touch it."

"Thank you," Albert said. "That is very interesting."

"Shall we just keep watching her?"

"Her in particular," Albert confirmed, "although if you can manage to keep an eye on her companion—or companions if anyone new joins them—I'd like to know."

"No problem."

Pearl rose. "Since we know Tracy Frye is here, I'm going to take a nap."

"Nap?" Albert echoed, his tone appalled.

"Nap," Pearl repeated firmly. "I am not as young as you, and tonight promises to be a rather late one. Shen?"

"I think I might as well," Shen said, "or at least meditate. There are some interesting ramifications in what I've been reading."

Albert still looked appalled, but he couldn't protest their wisdom. "Do you need me to wake you?"

"No," Pearl assured him. "I'm sure we'll both be down with time to spare."

Shortly before seven that evening, as they were finishing a light meal, the man from the security firm called back to say that Tracy Frye and her companion had left the hotel and gotten into the limo.

"I think there was someone already in the car," he said apologetically, "I mean, other than the driver. The man who met Ms. Frye at the airport started to get in the rear seat, kinda pulled back, and then got in front next to the driver."

"Interesting," Albert said. "Follow them to their destination. If they get out at the Rosicrucian Museum, you don't need to follow them. They're supposed to meet me there."

"Do you want us to follow them after?"

"You've already had a long day. Can you handle that?"

"Sure. No problem."

"Then I'd like that. If you can arrange for relief, that's fine, too."

"No problem," the man repeated. "We've only been on since her plane came in, and hanging around a nice hotel isn't exactly rough."

"Thanks," Albert said. He flipped the phone shut. "They're on their way. Ready?"

Pearl rose and brushed down her skirts. "I am."

Shen nodded. "Let's go."

Despite a certain amount of activity near the main entrance, the Rosicrucian Museum exuded absolute tranquillity when Pearl, Albert, and Shen walked over from Pearl's house and mounted the broad, sphinx-flanked steps that led to the buildings containing the museum and lecture halls.

Pearl's old friend—and in one sense next-door neighbor— Dr. Broderick Pike, the museum's director, was waiting for them out on the steps.

Dr. Pike nodded to them as casually as if they were simply a few familiar faces among the trickle of people flowing up the steps. Then he crossed to speak with them. He was a short man somewhere in late middle age, his bearing that of the college philosophy professor he had once been.

"Our regular summer lecture series meets tonight," Dr. Pike said, "but that shouldn't interfere with your business. A few people may drift out to the gardens during the break, but Isis's alcove is reserved for you. The goddess knows to expect you, and will extend her protection."

The small side garden, a particularly lovely spot where a statue of Isis overlooked the dark waters of a perfectly proportioned reflecting pool, had the specific advantage of being magically shielded from eavesdroppers—the goddess's protection.

"Thank you," Albert said. "Hopefully, our meeting will not take long. There may be no need to interfere with the freedom of those attending the lectures to enjoy the roses."

"The roses are good this year," Dr. Pike said, "even for this late in the summer."

His mild, yet still somehow commanding, gaze flickered behind his rimless glasses to where a long midnight-blue limousine was pulling up into the loading zone in front of the museum steps.

"Excuse me while I greet your associates," he said.

"We'll go around to Isis's garden," Albert said. "Thank you again."

Pearl followed Albert's lead, but she couldn't resist a quick glance back to see who was accompanying Tracy Frye. Only one other person had gotten out of the limousine, a tall, lean man, with thick curly dark hair.

Jozef Ski appeared to be somewhere in his mid-thirties. He was not precisely handsome, but attractive after the square-jawed slim-hipped fashion of the actor who played the hero's best friend or the competent heavy in the movies of the fifties.

"Downhill Ski," Shen said softly. "One of those Yeats described as 'full of passionate intensity,' if I have the poem right."

"I believe," Pearl said, "the line is 'the worst are full of passionate intensity,' but I'm not trying to bias you."

"Downhill Ski," Albert repeated, "but no one else, yet as the detective reported, he got out of the front seat, Tracy out of the back. Do we place bets that Franklin Deng was there?"

"No takers," Pearl said.

Tracy Frye and Jozef Ski were not long in joining them. When Pearl had first met Tracy at the Rock Dove Society meeting—had that only been five days ago?—the other woman had been dressed very casually, her slightly faded but wholly presentable jeans, brown and orange madras plaid button-down shirt, and walking shoes appropriate for the setting.

Today, however, Tracy Frye must have decided that her new importance merited a change in style. She wore a beige silk dress that fell in soft folds past her knees, expensive flats in a coordinated shade of tan, and small emerald studs in her ears. Her long brown hair, worn so aggressively unstyled before, was now swept back and clasped at the nape of her neck.

But she still looks like a fence rail, Pearl thought, *so much that I wonder how she got that dress on without snagging the fabric.*

Clothing might disguise a bit of Tracy Frye's rough-and-tumble ways, but nothing could conceal the triumph that flashed in her hazel-green eyes.

Jozef Ski looked like the jeans and tee shirt sort, but for this meeting he'd put on khaki trousers and a sports shirt whose thin stripe brought out the dark blue of his eyes. He looked uncomfortable, not shy, but rather as if he were more comfortable haranguing crowds rather than in a small group meeting.

Whereas Tracy Frye was empty-handed, Downhill carried a hard-sided briefcase, wide enough to hold the two mahjong sets.

So some degree of trust has been established, Pearl thought. *Or maybe Tracy thought the briefcase didn't go with her new look.*

Unnecessary introductions were made all around, then they seated themselves on the carved stone benches that flanked the reflecting pool.

Pearl couldn't help but remember the last time a group had met there, less than two weeks ago. That was right after they had finally forced Righteous Drum into a situation where he must talk terms with them.

Why don't I think this meeting will go as well?

Because then, she answered herself, *you knew that you wanted to reach some sort of agreement. This time, you don't.*

Tracy Frye, however, clearly thought differently. She arranged the skirts of her dress, then glanced at Downhill Ski. The man inclined his head slightly.

Pearl, a student in the nuances of body language, read this as, *Go on. We'd agreed you'd do the talking.*

Tracy Frye might have changed her clothes and done her hair, but her voice held the same splintery note Pearl remembered.

"It seems we've all been shopping for the same collectibles," she said.

Albert refused to play games. "Yes. The mah-jong sets belonging to the original Thirteen Orphans. You have acquired two: the sets belonging to the Ox and the Monkey. I assume this meeting is for one of two purposes: Either you wish to negotiate to buy the other sets, or you wish to sell your own."

Clearly, this meeting was not going as Tracy had imagined it would. Pearl saw Downhill tighten his lips to hide a grin.

No doubt she has been holding forth, telling how we would grovel. Albert is far too canny a negotiator for that.

"Would you sell the other sets?" Tracy asked.

"I would not," Albert said. The momentary gleam of triumph that rekindled in Tracy's eyes faded with his next words. "For one, they are not mine to sell. I only hold title to my own and those my agent acquired for me. The others belong to those who inherited them. I am not looking to make a collection."

"So you don't want the sets?" Tracy said. "I was told . . . that is, I thought you would."

"I do want them," Albert said patiently. "I am waiting to find out if you want them as well."

"I . . ." Tracy Frye stopped.

You can't very well say you never did want the nasty things, now, can you? Pearl thought, amused. *You can't say you only went after them because you thought they'd give you leverage to get what you really want.*

"If," Tracy said at last, "I were selling the two mah-jong sets I have acquired, what would you pay for them?"

Albert considered. "My agent has established what the going rate is for the sets. He was even able to learn what you paid for the two you acquired. You have not had to hold on to them long, so I think a twenty-five percent profit would be reasonable. I can even arrange for cash."

Tracy Frye looked momentarily tempted. After all, she was not wealthy, but the temptation was reflex.

"I wouldn't be interested," she said, "not for twenty-five percent, not for a hundred percent. My price doesn't have dollar signs at all."

"Then?" Albert's mild expression didn't change in the least.

"I want to learn your lore—the lore of the Thirteen Orphans," Tracy said. "Look. I offered these two . . ."

She tossed her head in the direction where Shen and Pearl sat, her first acknowledgment of them other than when greetings had been exchanged.

"I told these two that I'd be happy to help you all, happy to lend you a hand with your problems, but they turned me down. From what I've heard about the Orphans, you're like the king. Maybe you can make a deal where they couldn't."

Albert allowed himself to look mildly interested.

"Would you clarify what you are offering?"

Pearl saw Tracy blink as if wondering just when she had turned into the supplicant.

"I'm telling you," Tracy said, stressing the middle word just slightly, "that if you want these two mah-jong sets, then my price is as follows. I want an introduction into your magical lore—and not just some empty theory. I want something with real flash."

"Flash," Albert repeated, with a nod. "Go on."

"And since I have two of your ancestral mah-jong sets here, and those sets have lots and lots of pieces, I don't think I'm out of line saying that I want to be permitted to bring a friend with me to learn what you have to teach. And I want permission for that friend and me to be permitted to eventually pass a little of your lore on to a couple of chosen allies."

"An introduction," Albert said. "That is all you want?"

"A real introduction," Tracy said, "like you've been giving those apprentices of yours—how to make those bracelets, the theory behind them, things like that."

"Why are you so certain you could learn our lore?" Albert asked. "As you must know, it has been restricted to the Thirteen Orphans and their direct heirs."

"Because," Tracy said, "if those heirs can learn it, then I figure I can. Brenda Morris isn't yet an Orphan, but she can work some of your tricks. I'm good at absorbing other techniques. I figure this is just more of the same."

"And your friend," Albert turned his gaze to Downhill, "is he similarly able?"

"I am not," Ski said, "the one who will be your other student. I'm coming in on the second round. However, the delay does not mean that I would not make myself and my abilities available to you in your fight, your noble fight to keep our world free from invasion."

Downhill spoke in a measured fashion, his voice rising almost involuntarily as he offered his services. So might a knight of old have spoken, eager for battle, any battle, as long as he could believe it just and himself a hero.

"Your proposal is interesting," Albert said, "but although you have honored me by acting as if this is a matter I can decide all on my own, I will need to consult the other Orphans."

Shen cut in at this point. "I want to see the sets. We shouldn't make any deals until we're sure she has the real ones."

Tracy Frye didn't look offended at this, but then Pearl had long noticed that deal cutters usually expected to be doubted rather than believed.

"I have them with me," she said.

Downhill lifted the briefcase up onto the bench and removed the Ox mah-jong set, immediately recognizable by the stylized animal painted in faded gold on the outside of the hinged box.

Shen opened the brass latch and began to make a deliberately fussy inspection of the contents, even going so far as to pull a jeweler's loupe from his pocket and closely inspect the carvings on some of the tiles.

When he finished, he closed the box lid and set the latch, making no comment other than to turn to Jozef Ski and say, "The other set?"

Downhill was clearly impressed, almost despite himself, and pulled out the Monkey set with deferential promptness. Tracy Frye was watching the proceedings with narrowed eyes, but she did nothing to stop her associate.

The box in which the Monkey set was kept showed some signs of water damage. When Shen sniffed disapprovingly, Tracy said, "Hey. I didn't do it. Guy I bought it from said it had been stored in a basement rec room and a pipe broke. Pieces looked okay to me, and the set's intact."

Shen gave an abstracted nod, then subjected these pieces to an even closer inspection. When he had finished and politely returned the box to Ski's custody, Shen turned to Albert.

"All is as it should be."

"What's that supposed to mean?" Tracy asked sharply.

Albert turned a cool gaze on her, his eyebrows slightly raised. "Why that these are the genuine sets? What else could Shen mean?"

Tracy clearly wasn't satisfied, but she couldn't protest that Shen had done something illicit because he had not—and Pearl would have bet dollars to doughnuts that Tracy had been using some spell to make certain that none of them were violating their agreement to refrain from the use of magic.

I wonder if that in itself constitutes a violation, Pearl mused, but she wasn't about to raise the point.

"Very well," Albert said, when Tracy did not reply to his question. "I believe we understand each other. I must contact those active members of the Orphans who are not present and explain the situation. How long may we have to come to a decision?"

Comfortable now that she believed herself in charge once more, Tracy Frye glanced at her watch. "It's nearly eight now. I think twenty-four hours should be sufficient. Let's say eight tomorrow night."

"Where may I phone you?" Albert asked.

"I'll call you," Tracy said. "Make sure your cell phone is on."

"Very well," Albert said. "I shall talk with you tomorrow."

If not sooner, Pearl thought as they made their polite farewells. *If not much, much sooner.*

☆

Despite the exotic creatures and weird landscapes—some of which could have come right out of a Chinese ink-brush painting—Brenda found herself studying Flying Claw as if the young warrior were more remarkable than fish with human faces or dogs that walked upright and wore garments that resembled bathrobes, both of which she had seen with her own eyes.

This would be their second—and last—night in the guardian domains, and Brenda had a desperate sense that if she was ever going to understand this enigmatic young man, this was the place to do it.

She knew they'd be back, but next time they'd be focused on the job, on getting the next gate opened, on finding—however one did that—the way to the Yellow Springs, springs that apparently had their source in a Chinese hell.

Brenda didn't study Flying Claw too openly, though, not after she caught Honey Dream staring at her, her hand resting on her sheathed dagger, an expression of purest malevolence making her pretty face very ugly . . . and very frightening.

Brenda wished she could talk to Honey Dream, explain that far from coveting Flying Claw, she was actually growing increasingly uneasy around him. It wasn't that Brenda was afraid he'd do any of them harm. He hadn't been anything but perfectly courteous, and his quick and skillful reaction when Nissa had stumbled into the Yayu's reach had certainly saved her from considerable injury, maybe even from being killed.

But hour by hour, even minute by minute, Brenda was coming to accept what both Pearl and Nissa had tried to tell her from the moment they had realized Brenda's growing attachment to Foster: that Foster might be a very different person from whoever he had been before his own spell took his memory from him.

And yet, Brenda thought. *The spell took his memory. It didn't transform him. Foster was Flying Claw, just Flying Claw without all the baggage being the Tiger had put on him.*

And not just "baggage," Brenda had to admit, but skills and habits, most of which seemed centered around either hunting and killing or getting into position to do so.

Or, she thought, watching Flying Claw as he skillfully kindled a fire with a bow drill, *to enable him to take care of himself while getting ready to hunt and kill. He's really a frightening sort of person. I wonder if, after seeing him out here, doing his stuff, Nissa will let him babysit Lani anymore.*

Yet Flying Claw had never harmed Lani, not even when the child grew absolutely exasperating. His kindness to her went beyond what was required by their mutual aide pact into what seemed like genuine affection.

Brenda had done a little campfire cookery when she was younger, but her skills didn't go much beyond hotdogs on a stick and s'mores. Therefore, her job was to fetch water from a nearby stream and doctor it with Des's foul-tasting tablets.

Des had advised Brenda to draw the water from where a waterfall plashed over a clean limestone face into a natural stone basin that overflowed prettily to feed the stream from the other side. The waterfall was a convenient distance from the campsite, close enough to provide fresh water without being so close that the sound of falling water would have covered the sounds of anything approaching and undermined the safety of the camp.

Almost too perfect, Brenda thought. *I wonder if this is another of Pai Hu's little "welcomes."*

She wasn't quite right, but as she learned a few moments later, she wasn't quite wrong either.

There were two buckets to fill, and the first took most of the water in the stone basin. Brenda held the second bucket to catch the water as it fell. As it grew heavy, she glanced into the bucket to see if it was full enough. What she saw nearly made her drop the bucket.

A face, like enough to her own that for a moment Brenda thought it a weird reflection, looked up at her from the troubled waters. Brenda might have screamed in surprise, but the thought of Honey Dream's contemptuous response when she learned that Brenda had been frightened by her own reflection made Brenda swallow the scream and take a second look.

That second look was no more reassuring. This time Brenda saw that this could not be a mere reflection. For one, the face was older than her own, and more closely resembled that of Brenda's mother, Keely, than Brenda's, especially in the shape of the eyes. Then there was the matter of color— for this incongruous reflection that was not really a reflection was in color.

Whereas Brenda's hair was such dark brown that it was nearly black, the reflection's hair was a golden red. Brenda's eyes were dark brown, but those of the reflection were a bright leaf-green. Then, too, the reflection's skin was peaches and cream fair, where Brenda's had a distinct ivory hue. These colors ruled out this apparition as some vision of Keely McAnally, for Keely's coloration, although similar, blended browns into the mix: auburn hair, hazel eyes, and the tanned skin of a modern American woman who liked gardening and hiking.

Now Brenda tried to scream, for in her experience visions or dreams were best handled by group participation, but her mouth was dry and her tongue stuck to the roof of her mouth.

Those leaf-green eyes studied Brenda critically, the full, lovely lips moving in a pleasant, amused smile that showed teeth as shining white as those of a toothpaste model.

"So, at last you are where we can look upon each other face-to-face. I am not entirely displeased. Nay, I believe I am quite pleased. From your gaze I can see, however, that you do not feel quite the same. Faith, child, I mean you no harm. Quite the contrary."

The voice was gentle, holding in it the lilt of an Irish accent. However, despite the reassuring words, the gentle tone, Brenda's heart hammered so hard in her chest that she thought she might pass out.

She tried to speak, and this time words came out, creaky and rusty from her dry mouth.

"Who are you?"

"I am a friend, child. Believe me in this. Your family has known me or mine for many generations, since the days your grandmother's people still walked the green hills of Eire."

"No . . ."

"Yes. Not wishing to believe will not change this, Brenda Morris."

The vision in the bucket rippled, so that for a moment all Brenda saw was water. Then the woman with the red hair reappeared. This time she was frowning.

"I had hoped we could talk longer, but I see that is not to be. Perhaps you should not speak of this just yet."

The leaf-green eyes narrowed, and although Brenda could only see the face, somehow she knew that slender fingers had moved in a complicated gesture.

"There. Be at peace. You will remember this, but it will not alarm you, nor will you think to speak of it. When you remember, you will think of it as you might a dream, a pleasant . . ."

The voice faded into splashing water. Brenda heard Des calling, "Can we at least have the first bucket? I want to mix some journeycake and get it baking."

"Sure," Brenda called. "I've got enough."

A little voice in her head said, *Maybe more than enough*, but she dismissed this as nothing but a passing daydream.

XVII

After they were back in her house and the wards stood between them and any possible eavesdropper, Pearl and Albert looked expectantly at Shen.

"The sets are the real things," he said. "My grandfather helped make both, and through my role as his heir, I have established a connection with them. I feel absolutely certain I can find them, wherever Tracy or her allies might hide them."

"Well, I'm glad you have some sort of connection to the sets," Albert said. "I've been looking at Webcam photos of Delight Vineyards, and the estate sprawls over several acres. In addition to the main house, there are separate garages and various buildings associated with his vineyard."

"I feel certain," Pearl said, "Franklin will keep them in the house proper."

"That's big enough," Albert said.

"Don't get discouraged before we start," Pearl said. "Franklin's not going to have stored the mah-jong sets in the kitchen or pantries or anything like that. In fact, I think we can be almost certain that they're either in his bedroom or in his office—especially if he has a safe there."

"Another possibility," Shen said, "is that the sets won't be in the same place. Our auguries didn't show a great deal of unanimity of spirit between him and Tracy Frye. It's likely that each has one set."

"Or neither does," Albert offered. "And that Jozef Ski is holding on to them as something of a neutral party."

"Don't get discouraged before we start," Pearl repeated. "Knowing we'd need to track the things down is why we had Shen check to make certain the resonance between him and the mah-jong sets still exists."

Albert did not look reassured.

"Okay, Aunt Pearl, Uncle Shen, I've gone along with you to this point—mostly because I think you're right. We don't have any choice but to try and take those sets back. But now that I've had time to do some research I don't know how we can pull this off."

Shen laughed. "Wait a minute, Albert. I thought I was the reluctant one."

"You were," Albert admitted, "but I tried to tell you earlier . . ."

"And Shen told us he had a plan," Pearl said. "It sounds as if he thinks he can make it work. Let's hear him out before despairing."

They had moved into the family room while they were talking, and now Albert collapsed back into one of the lounge chairs and let out an exasperated sigh that Pearl could hear even from the kitchen, where she'd gone to put on water for tea.

"All right, then you tell me how we're going to break into a private estate—one that is walled and guarded and, I have no doubt, warded—and acquire not one, but two of what are probably currently regarded as the most valuable items in the place."

"We're not going to," Shen said. "We're going to have someone bring them out to us."

Albert stared at him. "We are? Who? Downhill Ski? Are you going to bribe him to change sides?"

"Albert!" Pearl said sternly, putting a snap in her voice that she hadn't used with Albert for decades. "Don't be a child."

"Sorry, Aunt Pearl," came the immediate reply. "I keep seeing headlines: 'Stealing Trade Secrets?' 'Competition in Chocolate?' 'Tong Wars?' I know it's ridiculous to worry about my reputation when we're up against being murdered or lobotomized—not to mention having our world invaded—but it keeps bothering me."

"For good reason," Pearl said. "But for now put that aside and listen. Then we'll have tea and work out the details."

Albert turned to face Shen. "If you would, sir?"

"My pleasure," Shen said with equal formality, but his eyes were shining. "I suppose Des and the rest being in the guardian domains is what got me considering doing things this way, but I think our best bet is to summon agents who are both of this world and not—agents who have a completely physical form, but who can become disembodied to work their way past wards."

"Dragons," Albert breathed.

"You guessed," Shen said, looking quite pleased. "I have a good affinity with dragons, and even a few friends among the *lung*. However, I needed to make sure that I could give them a precise—'scent' is the best word I can think of. I can, but I fear that in order to do so, it would be best if we were as close as possible to the house."

"So we won't be able to completely avoid prowling around," Pearl said. "Still, with Windy Nines to hide us, or perhaps Confused Gates . . ."

The kettle had begun whistling. Pearl began the routine of rinsing and pouring, her mind racing as she thought through the details.

"Can we get everything ready in time?" Albert asked.

"I think we can try," Shen said. "It's only a little past nine now. I don't suppose we want to be prowling around until we can be fairly certain Deng and his guests have gone to bed."

"Plenty of time," Pearl agreed, and she hoped she was right.

Two in the morning, the Double Hour of the Ox, found them sitting in Pearl's town car on a graveled service road bordering Delight Vineyards. Behind the tall iron fence, Deng's mansion was mostly dark and entirely quiet.

Pearl had prepared the sequence for All Green, a spell that would let her see magical workings. Her enhanced vision confirmed that she was seeing the mansion as it was, not cloaked in any illusion. Franklin and his guests had indeed retired for the evening.

Dreaming of our magic, Pearl thought, *and the power it will bring to them.*

The gently curving road they were on had two main virtues: its proximity to the property, and that it had been landscaped with trees and ornamental shrubbery so as not to be noticed. This, Pearl supposed, was so that such mundane inconveniences as plumber's trucks or delivery vans would not mar the illusion of a genteel estate, independent and isolated behind the vigilance of its spike-topped iron fence.

Security had not been ignored along this service road. Indeed, it was more carefully attended to here than along the front section of the property. There a twelve-foot-tall spiked iron fence, gated and concealing a discreet electronic alarm system, was considered enough. Indeed it was enough, given that the main road was well lit, and routine patrols by local police swept the area for loiterers.

On the fence bordering this service road, the iron bars were more tightly spaced, and the electronic security was augmented with razor wire. A nice concealed dip—a sort of waterless moat—in the manicured sward would slow anyone who managed to top the fence, miss the wire, avoid activating the alarm, and drop to the other side.

The reason the slowing was advantageous was, of course, the dogs. Two of these—stern Dobermans with spiked collars—came and studied the town car soon after Albert parked it on the shoulder of the road in a spot where a shade tree concealed them from a casual observer on the main road. The dogs stayed on the far side of the moat: alert and curious, but uncomfortably silent.

"Franklin wouldn't want the dogs barking every time a car came down the road," Pearl guessed. "Their reaction might be different if we crossed the fence, but if everything goes well, we won't be crossing the fence."

"If everything goes well," Albert agreed. He'd shut off the car's headlights and engine as soon as he had parked. Now he reached to deactivate the dome light so it wouldn't come on when a car door was opened. "If you two are ready?"

"Ready," Shen agreed, opening the back door and getting out a little tentatively. He moved with more assurance once he'd tested the footing, reaching behind him to remove the case in which he'd stored the tools he'd prepared. Among these were elaborate scrolls that would enable him to remain in communication with the dragons he summoned—and them with him.

Pearl, meanwhile, had gotten out of the passenger side of the front seat and was moving closer to the main road. There she set about the routine that would create Confused Gates, that very useful spell that did not so much conceal as create a lack of desire to pay attention to a particular area. They didn't know how often the police came down the main road, or whether their patrols ever made random sweeps down the side roads, so a little misdirection seemed in order.

While Pearl was setting up her Confused Gates, Shen was placing the finishing touches on a spell with the deceptively simple name "Dragon."

Unlike "Windy Dragons" or "All Winds and Dragons" or several other spells that contained "dragon" in their names, "Dragon" actually summoned one of the resident dragons of an area. Chinese dragons were distinctly elemental creatures, associated primarily with water in the popular imagination, but integrally connected to earth as well.

Feng shui might be translated as "wind-water," but more accurately the science involved the manipulation of the ch'i of an area. In deciding to use dragons to fetch the two mah-jong sets, they were taking a great risk, for it was unlikely that a sorcerer schooled in the Chinese traditions would have ignored his local feng shui. However, Shen was certain he could find a dragon—or two, for it would be better to send a separate messenger after each set—who would be willing to cooperate with them.

"There must be some local *lung* Deng has overlooked," Shen had assured Albert. "In fact, it's likely that while he has taken care to propitiate them, he has done so without binding them. Dragons," he added, a wicked grin lighting his face, "do not care to be bound. They tend to resist bindings. When they do, you have earthquakes and tsunami to deal with."

"Or at least broken pipes," Albert replied.

Albert assisted Shen to set up a portable altar, a neat little device about the size and height of one of those trays on legs sold to facilitate the idea that eating breakfast in bed could be an elegant experience. This wasn't as easy as unfolding the legs and setting it down relatively level on the gravel surface. A feng shui compass must be used to align the altar with the appropriate forces. Reading the tiny figures on the complicated dial with only a shielded pocket flashlight was a trying task.

Once the altar was in position, Shen set thin sticks of pure incense burning at the two upper corners. Pearl, standing back from the road so that a chance car would not ruin her night vision with its headlights, caught a teasing trace of the heavy, musky odor of freshly lit incense and wondered what the still-watching Doberman pinschers thought of it.

Pearl's job at this point was to keep watch, and if by any chance a car did turn in to the road, provide a sufficient distraction that Albert and Shen could get the altar stashed away. Therefore she did her best not to pay attention to what Shen was doing, although she knew when the soft murmuring of words in the distinctive Chinese of the Lands Born from Smoke and Sacrifice shifted from rote spell sequencing to conversation.

Pearl did not hear the reply, which told her that Shen had contacted at least one dragon. Some time later—after four passes of a patrol car, and three passenger cars had all done their part to raise her blood pressure—she heard Shen's voice beginning the spell sequence once more.

One dragon, then, she thought. *Or did he fail and end up having to start all over?*

She longed to ask, but years of discipline at keeping her mark, not missing her cues, kept her at her station. Her feet, even in sensible shoes, were beginning to ache enough to be a distraction when Shen shifted to speech once more. This time she thought she heard the word "Monkey," and felt marked relief. Shen would have sent the first dragon after the Ox set, order and method being part of the Dragon's nature. If he was asking this one to go after the Monkey set . . .

She changed her angle slightly so that she could still keep an eye on the road, but also study the mansion behind the iron fence. It remained darkened as before, the same lights glowing mutedly in the same places.

Good, she thought. *Iron. I never considered that, but I bet that fence is meant as security against magic. It would provide some against most European traditions, but our abilities are unimpaired.*

Pearl glanced at her watch. This was taking a long time, longer than she had expected, longer, she thought, than Shen had expected. A quick look showed her that Shen was kneeling on the ground in front of the altar, his head bent, his arthritic fingers resting lightly on the elegant calligraphy that represented the two dragons he was guiding.

"Here comes the first one," Albert said, his softly spoken words reverberating with relief and triumph.

Pearl permitted herself a quick look in the direction of Franklin's mansion. Invisible to most, a *lung*, the Chinese dragon, swam through the air, propelling itself with the strength of its long tail and two hind legs, its front legs clasping the long, flat rectangular box that held the Ox's mah-jong set.

Shen did not stir from where he sat behind the altar, not even when the *lung* arrived with its prize. Albert stepped forward to receive the box, thanking the *lung* with exquisitely elegant politeness.

"The task was not too difficult," the *lung* replied. "The box was locked in another box. The door of the second box was locked, but that could not stop me. I went through, and carried out the box in the same way."

Pearl understood what the *lung* meant. Not being limited

to one plane of existence, the *lung* had entered the "second box"—presumably a locked safe—and then transferred the mah-jong set to an alternate plane. Still within that plane, it had made its retreat.

The maneuver avoided whatever wards Franklin had in place because the *lung* was not an intruder, but associated with the warded area.

Pearl added her thanks to Albert's and was surprised when Shen did not add some flowery speech of his own. She looked over, and saw that he remained fixed before the altar. His head was bent forward, his shoulders slumping. Even in the poor light, he looked grey and drained.

"Shen!" she said, hurrying to his side, trusting her Confused Gates to defend the road. She laid a hand to one side of Shen's face and found the skin cold and damp.

He shuddered slightly beneath her hand, but when he spoke it was not to her.

"Albert, take over," he said, his voice the merest wheeze.

Pearl began to kneel, to ease Shen to one side. "Let me. I'm already here."

Shen shook his head. "No. Albert can be Dragon."

Pearl understood. The abilities of each of the Thirteen Orphans overlapped more or less, even as the Twelve Earthly Branches overlapped, but the Cat—the one Orphan who did not belong to traditional Chinese lore—had an ability that was unique. The Cat alone could take on the aura of another Orphan, temporarily impersonating that Orphan.

"Copy-catting," Shen's grandfather, the Exile Dragon, had called the ability, laughing as he did so, although like all of the Twelve he had been distinctly astonished when the ability first became evident, for no one would admit to having formulated or designed it. It had simply happened, as if the Cat, like the original twelve, connected to some force greater than the individual.

Albert came hurrying over, understanding what was needed of him. The first *lung* had started to disperse into the surrounding elements, but as soon as Albert had taken Shen's place before the altar, Shen called after it in a voice stronger than before.

"Brother, I beg you . . ."

The *lung* paused. Pearl sensed annoyance balanced by curiosity, but the curiosity was stronger.

"Yes?"

"Your neighbor, he who also came to my aid, is in some difficulty."

"Oh?"

Pearl tensed, reached for the sword she was not wearing, for a sword would have been very difficult to explain if they were stopped by local authorities. She looked over at Franklin's mansion, but the mansion remained as before.

"He, too, was asked to bring forth a box and its contents, but the thief who took that box removed some of the tiles and scattered them throughout her chamber."

"Clever!" the dragon cheered. "But deserving of cleverness in return. How the thief will cry out when she finds all her treasures taken."

"So we thought," Shen said. "Will you assist us then?"

In answer the *lung* drew itself back from the surrounding lands and turned back toward the mansion. As it passed over the Dobermans both dogs whined uneasily, knowing something was wrong, but unable to find that wrongness with nose or ear or eye.

Pearl crouched next to Shen, reaching for his wrist so she could check his pulses. Tigers were not healers as were Rabbits, but then again, a warrior benefited from knowing how to perform basic first aid. Shen's pulses were all wrong, some too fast, others too slow.

"Breathe," she said. "You've used too much ch'i too quickly. What happened?"

"As I said," Shen said, "the *lung* was distracted when it found not one signature to follow, but something like ten. Tracy Frye not only hid parts of the mah-jong set around her room, she was sleeping with the box under her pillow, her arms wrapped around it."

"Not so good," Pearl said, opening her purse and taking out a small bottle of water. "Here."

"I think we got the box without waking her," Shen said after he had drunk. "We substituted a book about the same size, but the *lung* started growing restless after that—and I don't blame it. Ms. Frye had so many wards and charms in place that moving through that room on either plane was like swimming through water strung with barbed wire."

Pearl nodded. Since Tracy Frye wasn't of Franklin's household, her wards would inhibit a creature of the place as Franklin's own would not. Doubtless they were her assurance against treachery on the part of any of her associates, but that didn't make them any less of a problem for the Orphans.

"The *lung* won't quit?" Pearl asked.

"Not with Albert taking over," Shen assured her, "not with the other *lung* eager to show it up. Dragons can be very competitive."

"So can we all," Pearl said. "Feeling better?"

"I am." He sounded ashamed. "Theory is one thing, Pearl, but it has been a long time since I did much other than teaching or in routine practice. I'm out of shape."

"We'll get you in shape in no time," Pearl reassured him, but she was far from confident.

Shen's pulses had not felt very strong. She was all too aware that people aged at different rates. She had met people her own age who were invalids, frail and unable to move without canes or walkers. Others were active and robust. She'd always thought that Shen would be as tough as she was, but what if he wasn't?

What are we going to do if Shen isn't up to his part? she wondered. *Can Geoffrey take over for him?* She felt a traitor for entertaining the thought.

She settled Shen in the backseat of the car where he could

recover in greater comfort. He hadn't protested, only insisted that the door be left open so that he could see what Albert was doing and come to his assistance if needed.

Two more private vehicles, a patrol car, then two more passenger cars—one weaving as if the driver had drunk more than was good for him—had shown headlights over the blacktop before Albert rocked back on his heels and pointed toward Franklin's mansion.

"There," he said softly. Pearl looked and saw two *lung* swimming rapidly through the air toward them. "That was about as much fun as waltzing in a minefield, but we did it—and we have all the pieces."

Pearl had long ago resumed her patrolling of the service road, strengthening her Confused Gates, keeping herself alert for any problem that might arise. Now, as Albert thanked the *lung* and requested their silence as to the assistance they had given him—a request they were quite likely to heed, because like most supernatural creatures, they enjoyed being enigmatic—Pearl added her own thanks, then began to prepare her final spell.

It was a simple one, a summoning of the wind of the east-north-east, her own direction. Her instructions to the wind were equally simple—to dust away any physical signs that they had been here. She didn't think Franklin and his associates would call in the police, but one never knew. Better to leave nothing for anyone to work with.

Pearl had spoken to the wind earlier, and found it waiting, interested and ready. Now, as she got into the passenger side of the front seat, its kiss brushed against her cheek.

She leaned back against the upholstery as Albert drove the car out. When they passed onto the blacktop, she let her Confused Gates crumple into absentmindedness.

I'm so tired, she thought, but even through the tiredness, she found herself smiling. *We've done it! Won't the others be delighted. We've done it!*

XVIII

The pine door was waiting in the grove. As she waited for her turn to cross the threshold, Brenda couldn't decide whether the entire experience was ordinary or completely extraordinary.

After all, to get here we had to walk into a tiger's mouth. That somehow seems more right than just opening a door and walking from one world into another.

But she did, and decided that the experience was pretty wonderful after all—especially since when she looked back, all she saw was the other side of the warehouse, without a leaf or blade of grass from the White Tiger's jungle.

The clock on Brenda's cell phone—which, like the phone itself, had stopped functioning as soon as they passed into the guardian domains—now read 8:30 A.M.

That was early by some standards, but since they'd risen at dawn—prompted by some very noisy birds—eaten a light breakfast and then hiked for several miles, Brenda felt as if the day was already quite old.

Fascinating and enticing as Pai Hu's realm had been, Brenda was very glad to feel the very ordinary firmness of the concrete slab under the soles of her shoes and see the normal, dull corrugated metal warehouse roof over her head.

She'd been the second one through—Des had come first— and now she stepped clear to let the others follow. They did so in neat order, although Brenda saw Honey Dream cast a long, wistful look back over her shoulder as she stepped over the threshold.

Since he'd changed into normal clothing on the other side, Des sealed the gate, thanking the Men Shen for their continued assistance. Honey Dream grabbed her pack and headed for the large closet to change out of the Chinese-style tunic and baggy pants she'd worn in the guardian domains. Rip-rap pulled the keys to the van out of his pocket.

"We'll start loading things," he said, collecting Brenda and Nissa to him with a toss of his head. "It's going to go faster without having to fit our junk in around the door."

Des unshouldered his pack and pulled out his phone.

"I'll call Pearl and tell her we're back, and should be to the house in about a half hour."

Flying Claw grinned. "I'm not trying to get out of the heavy work, but I think I'd better change out of my armor and pack it. No need to attract attention."

By the time the van was loaded, both Honey Dream and Flying Claw had finished changing, and Des had pocketed his phone.

"Pearl suggests that since after a couple days camping, we're all probably pretty ripe, why don't we drop Honey Dream and Flying Claw off at Colm Lodge. They can shower there, brief Waking Lizard and Righteous Drum, and join us all at Pearl's a little later."

Unspoken but understood was that although they were al-lies, still their groups were separate and time to confer pri-vately would be appreciated.

So would a shower, Brenda thought, wondering if she could beat Nissa into the bathroom they shared. *Probably. Lani is going to need some mommy-time.*

To everyone's surprise but possibly Des's, they found Lani waiting for them at Colm Lodge.

"I spend the night here," she said importantly, accepting her car seat only after Nissa sternly informed her that they were not going to start the day by breaking the law. "An' Pearl and Shen and Albert have to go to a party, and Mr. Drum and Mr. Lizard babysitted."

The little girl was so excited by her own adventure that she hardly had energy to spare to ask about her mother's "camp-ing trip."

Lani didn't know any more about the "party" that had drawn Pearl and Shen away so unexpectedly, and if Des knew, he wasn't talking. Brenda, still feeling a bit vague, as if her dreams wouldn't quite let go despite a very active morning, didn't really mind.

At Pearl's house, Nissa suggested Brenda take the shower first, since Lani was still babbling happily about how Waking Lizard had entertained her with shadow pictures and stories. This wasn't very surprising, as Waking Lizard was naturally outgoing and amusing. More surprising was learning that Righteous Drum had put on a one-handed shadow play about a prince who befriended the son of the Dragon King and traveled with him beneath the sea.

But then, Brenda thought, making her heavy way up the stairs and stripping off her less than clean clothing, *I keep forgetting that he's a dad, and that Honey Dream isn't his only child. Seeing how close those two are, I really shouldn't be surprised to find out Righteous Drum is good at entertaining little girls.*

Brenda called her mom while she was getting dressed, and caught up on all that had happened over the last couple of days. Dad was on the road again, something about a contract for window stickers for a college in North Carolina. Dylan had a summer job with a lawn service, and Thomas was playing in a soccer league.

After a very funny anecdote about the argument Tom's coach had gotten into with one of the parents, Brenda realized that the sound of Nissa's shower running had been over for a while.

"I'd better go, Mom," she said. "I keep thinking there's something that I want to ask you about, but every time I nearly remember . . ."

"I know how it is," Mom laughed, "but, you're too young to claim senioritis, Breni."

"So are you, Mom," Brenda replied, laughing in turn. "I'll call later if I remember. Give the boys hugs."

"If they'll let me," Mom promised. "Now, you to your work and me to mine."

Brenda bounced down the stairs feeling more lighthearted

than she had since she woke up that morning. She found all of the household seated around the long table that stretched between kitchen and family room. Riprap was eating a second breakfast, but almost everyone else had settled for coffee or tea.

Deciding to compromise with a yogurt, Brenda got some, and listened to Des concluding his summary of their encounter with the White Tiger of the West, and of the strange visions the tiger had been experiencing.

Brenda felt a flicker of déjà vu as Des finished, almost remembering what it was she'd wanted to ask Mom about, but the memory faded before she could grasp a solid hold.

I'll remember, she thought, taking a seat next to Riprap so she could snitch a piece of his bacon. *I'll remember when it's important.*

Shen and Pearl speculated for a few minutes about what might be troubling Pai Hu. Then Pearl halted herself in mid-speculation.

"But this can wait until the others get here. No doubt the Landers will have a great deal to contribute. Let me tell you what Righteous Drum and Waking Lizard already know. We have recovered the Ox and Monkey mah-jong sets!"

When the spontaneous cheering subsided, Pearl and Shen traded off a spirited account of how they had been forced to move by Tracy Frye's confrontation, and the actions that had followed.

"I have the two sets here in my safe," Pearl said. "And Albert has driven back to meet Matt Bauminger, the antiques dealer, to get the two he purchased."

"Pearl," Riprap said, "you say the sets are in your safe, but didn't Franklin Deng think the Ox set was secure in his own safe?"

"He did," Pearl agreed, "but the circumstances are very different. He has no link to the sets as Shen did. Moreover, I have not overlooked making pacts with the dragons who are associated with this piece of land. Between them, my usual wards, and the protections the Rosicrucians have set around this entire block of the Rose Garden, those sets are perfectly safe."

"What about Albert?" Riprap persisted. "He's out in the open."

"He also has two agents from the security firm with him," Pearl said, "and, perhaps more importantly, we let several people—including Broderick Pike of the Rosicrucians—know quite off the record that an attempt had been made to force us to take on allies in our 'noble effort to forestall invasion of this world.'"

Her tone made clear that the last was a quote, and had probably been delivered with a great deal of pained indignation.

"Okay," Riprap said. "I hope Albert will be all right."

"How did Tracy Frye get back before this Matt?" Nissa wanted to know.

"She left before he did," Shen said simply. "Remember, Ainsley and Rico O'Reilly insisted on a very detailed contract laying out the provisions of their agreement with Albert. Matt stayed to supervise the negotiations. Tracy seems to have left as soon as she realized she was beaten."

"I'm surprised she didn't go after the set anyhow," Riprap said. "This Matt isn't magical, is he?"

"No. And that's why he would have been safer than one of us. The Rock Dove Society and its affiliates are quite aggressive about punishing any and all who take the risk of magic being noticed."

"Right," Riprap said. "With everything we've been through, I keep forgetting that."

"Don't," Shen said severely. "They are even stricter with those of us who are here on sufferance."

Riprap nodded and rose to clear his plate. He was pouring himself a massive mug of coffee when the front doorbell rang.

Lani went racing to answer it, yelling, "Bet it's Mr. Drum and Mr. Lizard! They said they'd come over today. Bet it's Foster, too!"

Nissa hurried after her, and after a careful check through the peephole called, "Lani's right. Shall I let them in?"

In a few minutes, the group around the long table had grown by four. Lani was sitting on Flying Claw's lap, tugging at his ponytail—Brenda noticed it was still damp from his shower—and asking if he knew how to make shadow pictures.

"I think," Nissa said, "that Wong is here and needs help in the garden. Would you like to help him, or are you overtired and need an early nap?"

"Wong!" Lani exclaimed, abandoning Flying Claw with indecent haste and pelting for the door.

Nissa watched her go, waving thanks to the gardener.

"I hate doing that," she said, "but we've a lot to discuss."

"And to decide," Righteous Drum agreed. "Flying Claw and Honey Dream have told us of Pai Hu's difficulty. This is troubling, an unanticipated complication in our plans."

Riprap held up one hand. "Wait. First things first. Should we go any further in establishing the Nine Gates? After all, we Orphans don't know if we're going to be able to get through into the Lands—and we won't until you folks have a chance to work with the mah-jong sets, to see if you can—well, work out a substitution."

Des looked reprovingly at his student. "I think we should. Even if we Orphans can't pass into the Lands, the gates will give Righteous Drum and his associates a better chance of getting home."

And, Brenda thought, *let them see we're doing our best by them—let these indigenous traditional types see that we're making some sort of effort, too.*

"I agree with Des," Pearl said. "Our return is not the most important thing."

"Perhaps not most important," Righteous Drum said, "but very important. I do not believe the four of us can forestall our enemies from coming after you. We will need help, and until we can reconnect with what allies may remain to us, you are our best hope."

Until, Brenda thought, *you reconnect. And then? I think Honey Dream figures I'm extraneous now. Is that attitude going to extend to the rest of us once you're where you want to be?*

But she didn't say anything, figuring a challenge would do no good at all, and would probably do a lot of harm.

"I'm wondering," Shen said, "if we can work on both problems simultaneously. We need to learn if we can contact and perhaps work with the ghosts of our ancestors. And, in case you've forgotten, we're going to need to link each of the Nine Gates to the appropriate Yellow Spring."

This time Brenda did speak up. "I can't forget, especially since those Yellow Springs start somewhere that people keep referring to as 'Hell.' My family wasn't exactly religious. Mom's family was Irish Catholic, but she'd dropped that I think even before she and Dad got together. Dad was even less religious. But even I know that Hell is not a nice place."

"Maybe," Nissa asked hopefully, "the Chinese hell isn't so bad?"

Unconsciously, they'd both addressed their comments mostly to Des, probably because the habit of viewing him as their teacher had become ingrained.

"I don't know precisely how it is in the Lands," Des said, glancing over at the Landers, clearly inviting their clarification, "but the Chinese view of the afterlife has evolved over time. As I understand it, at first it was a lot like that of the ancient Greeks—pretty featureless. Later, as ancestor worship took hold, the idea grew closer to that of the ancient Egyptians. How much a person enjoyed the afterlife had as much to do with the offerings left by his or her descendants than with the life he or she had lived on Earth."

"Unless," Righteous Drum agreed, "they had behaved particularly heinously. Then some argued there was punishment. Others that since punishment of the dead was fairly useless, that the condemned would suffer annihilation."

"Nasty," Riprap said.

Des nodded. "It was after Buddhism came into China from

India that the conception of the underworld really got complicated. First of all, the Buddhists were firm believers in reincarnation. Secondly, they had an elaborate system of 'hells'—different regions of the afterlife, where the dead were treated more or less well depending on how they'd behaved when alive. The Taoists got jealous, and they developed their own more elaborate, more colorful series of hells."

Shen laughed, a boisterous sound that Brenda hadn't heard before.

Their game of "Dragon" last night did Shen a lot of good, she thought. *He seems a lot more relaxed.*

Shen stifled his laugh. "Sorry, Des. I didn't mean to interrupt, but I was thinking about the uniquely Chinese twist given to this system of reward and punishment."

He turned to the rest of them. "Des already mentioned how the traditions of ancestor worship held that offerings to the dead would influence how the dead were treated in the afterlife. Well, when the various systems of hells came into fashion—I guess you'd call it that—no one, especially the various temples who benefited from the offerings, wanted them to stop. Gradually, the idea came in that those offerings would enable the dead to bribe the officials in the underworld, so that the dead could arrange for better treatment, or for remission of punishment."

Riprap laughed. "Man, you've mentioned that the Chinese were both business-minded and bureaucratic, but this takes the cake—bribes and corrupt officials in the afterlife?"

Pearl sounded mildly annoyed as she replied, "I don't see how that's much different from the prayers for the dead that many Christian sects offer. I seem to recall in my childhood people buying Masses for the dead, and the dead getting so many years off of purgatory for rosaries said for them."

"I dated a Catholic once," Nissa said. "I think all of that went out with some Church counsel. I'm pretty sure both purgatory and limbo got dumped, but I could be wrong."

Brenda didn't know either. Her Grandma Elaine was a

practicing Catholic, but hadn't put the least pressure on any of her grandchildren to attend services. Her grandfather Fritz had been what Brenda privately thought of as a habitual Catholic. He went because he always had, not for any other reason.

She looked over to where the four Landers were listening to this convoluted explanation. Righteous Drum looked quite interested, Honey Dream bored. Waking Lizard was clearly amused, and Flying Claw's brow was furrowed with thought.

Des suddenly recalled that this wasn't a general theological discussion, and looked over at the Landers.

"Righteous Drum, I think Buddhism came into China in the first century A.D.—that is, well after the burning of the books gave birth to the Lands Born from Smoke and Sacrifice. Does any of this apply?"

"I believe it does," Righteous Drum answered. "I know who Buddha is, and the influence of his teachings is present. Reincarnation is also a familiar doctrine, as is the concept of what you referred to as an 'elaborate system of hells.'"

"Reincarnation could make our trying to get in touch with our ancestors more difficult," Des said, and Brenda, remembering his initial protest, thought he was as much relieved as not.

"I think," Flying Claw said, "that it will not be an obstacle for us. As I told you, my family regularly made offerings for the comfort and care of Thundering Heaven's spirit. We, at least, do not consider ourselves Buddhist, although we do honor to the most noble of their deities."

"Like Kwan Yin," Honey Dream said, her expression softening, becoming almost wistful. "The Merciful Goddess, she who hears the cries of the world. My mother always did her honor, but otherwise, no, I do not think we believed our ancestors would be reincarnated—at least not without very good reason."

Righteous Drum's expression confirmed this. "There are many traditions in the Lands, but that which we—and your own ancestors—belong to is more Taoist than Buddhist, more animist than either, for our roots are in the old magics of the universe."

"So," Riprap said, and Brenda could hear that "sheepdog" tone in his voice, the one that said he was going to keep them on track or die trying. "We've resolved two things. One, we're going to go ahead and establish the gates, whether or not the Orphans can use them. Two, since it is unlikely that the spirits of the original Orphans have been reincarnated, they're out there, somewhere, and we might be able to use them to help us not only get into the Lands, but to do something about the Nine Yellow Springs."

"Admirably put, Watson," Des said. "Shen, which of our ancestors do you want to try getting in touch with first?"

Shen sat straighter and looked more professorial than any of the professors Brenda had encountered in her freshman year in college ever did.

"I think that we should refrain from troubling any of the ancestral spirits who have a living, trained successor since we might attenuate the power of the Earthly Branch as that power is currently invested. That leaves us four: Ox, Horse, Ram, and Monkey."

"What about Snake?" Nissa asked. "Didn't we decide we couldn't take the current Snake with us? Didn't we get her mah-jong set for that reason?"

"True," Shen said, "but that situation is going to be complicated enough without complicating it further. I say we should leave the Snake out of the matter until we are ready to return to the Lands."

"Even if her refusal to cooperate might stop us flat?" Nissa asked.

"Even so." Shen smiled wickedly. "Snakes are diplomats, attuned to the need for compromise. I am hoping we will be able to persuade her if she finds herself the last block to our success."

Riprap guffawed. "Otherwise, she might find the spirits of her former associates making the afterlife hell for her."

"Ouch," Brenda said. "That's bad."

Shen ignored Riprap's joke, his attention on Nissa.

"I'm fine with leaving the Snake out of it for now," she said. "I just wondered if we couldn't deal with three problems all at once."

"Let us stay with what we have," Shen said. "Surely that is enough."

☆

Honey Dream didn't miss the fleeting look Shen Kung gave her when the subject of the Snake came up. Nor had she overlooked that unlike her father and Flying Claw, she and Waking Lizard were in a somewhat different position.

Whereas the Dragon and the Tiger were both held by living Orphans, Orphans who—following that disgusting and highly inappropriate system established by the Exiles—would pass on their affiliation with their appropriate Branch to their designated heir apparent upon their deaths, the Snake and the Monkey were in a different situation entirely.

True, the Branches were held, but in one case by a senile old woman, in the other by a child who knew nothing of his heritage. These situations meant that the Orphans themselves were willing to try and undo the safeguards set in place by their ancestors.

If the Orphans detached the Earthly Branches from those who held them here, could she grab hold? True, the plan was that the ghost of the Exile Orphan would take over, but surely a living affiliation would be more appealing, more dynamic, more useful.

In any case, surely the Earthly Branches had never intended to permit themselves to be stolen away from the Lands.

But it seemed that Honey Dream reacquiring the full powers of the Snake must wait, for attempting to sever the Snake from its current holder was being delayed.

Perhaps the Monkey, then?

She was about to suggest this, when Shen said, "My first thought was the Horse. Not only was the Exile Horse a very fine soldier—a leader of armies—he also was the first of the

Exiles to meet his death. Initially, I thought this would mean he would have less emotional baggage, less attachment to his heirs and their rights. Then I remember how he died, and . . ."

Shen trailed off, and to Honey Dream's astonishment, he looked directly at Desperate Lee. What connection could Des have to a man who had died before the Exiles had even departed China?

Brenda Morris had noticed the odd interchange, too, and she spoke out directly.

"What haven't you told us, Des? I noticed that when you were filling us in on the various Orphans you skipped over the Horse rather quickly."

Des licked his lips, and looked both amused and embarrassed.

"This particular story touches my family, as well as that of the Horse, for the Exile Horse was in love with the Exile Rooster—my great-grandmother. Indeed, the Horse and the Rooster may have been lovers before the Exile, but they soon learned that this was a situation that could not continue."

Des looked around the group gathered at the table as if he'd be glad for someone to interrupt, but no one did. After a swallow of tea, he went on.

"When the decision was made that the various Branches must be bound to specific lines of descent, the need to keep those lineages perfectly clear became a requirement. Birth control wasn't as easy in those days, even with magic, and Exile Horse and Exile Rooster were forced apart.

"Exile Horse took a concubine—a series of concubines, really, for he would not give his sole attention to any woman other than the Rooster. Eventually, one young woman bore a child who was his son and heir. Exile Horse acquired custody of the child, keeping the mother on as wet nurse but making quite clear that he did not intend to marry her.

"Exile Rooster, however, was more creative in her choice

of a father for her heir. In order to assure a strong connection to the Lands Born from Smoke and Sacrifice, she seduced one of those adepts who had come in pursuit of the Exiles. Eventually, she became pregnant by him. The Exile Horse was slain not too much later by his beloved's lover."

"Oh!" Brenda pressed her fingers to her lips. Honey Dream was pleased to see her embarrassed by the exclamation, but no one else seemed to have noticed the Ratling's loss of control.

Des continued, speaking more quickly now. "I don't know whether Exile Horse went after the other man in a fit of jealousy, or if the reverse was true. Maybe it was just chance. Whatever the circumstances, the end result was the same."

Shen nodded. "And I suspect that those very circumstances are going to mean that Exile Horse might not have strong ties to his familial line—after all, he hardly knew his infant son. Additionally, he may hold strong resentments against his former allies. With him, as with the Snake, we may do better approaching him when our goals are nearly accomplished. Whatever else he was, he was a war leader, and will not wish to be the reason the battle is lost."

Riprap nodded. "Fine. No Snake. No Horse. We have Ox, Ram, and Monkey left. Any preferences?"

"Ox," Pearl said. Honey Dream had the distinct impression the older woman was surprised to hear herself speak, but Pearl recovered smoothly and went on. "Exile Ram was driven, obsessed even. Exile Monkey had an irresponsible streak. Exile Ox, however, was possessed of both forethought and steadiness."

Righteous Drum was nodding. "Ox, with Rat, is of the House of Construction, but being the yin representative of that astrological house, she is more concentrated on solid foundations than on aggressive gain. If I were choosing merely on astrological grounds, Ox would probably be my first choice."

Pearl smiled. "I'll admit. I'm biased. Of the three, she

was certainly my favorite, for all she died when I was still a child."

"Foundations," Shen mused, "that's just what we're looking to establish for our Nine Gates. Yes, Ox would be our best choice."

"I don't want to put a damper on things," Des said, "but you do realize that Exile Ox is also going to have some difficulties when she learns how matters have progressed with her lineage. Not only has the line of the Ox fallen away, but how Hua, Exile Ox's heir, was treated contributed to the disaffection of several other lineages."

"I think the approach to take," Pearl said, "would be to show that Hua was loved and admired by her peers, even after the Exiles had begun to fear that Hua's bloodline would make her less than perfectly suited to her role."

"That might work," Des admitted, and Honey Dream noted a grudging note in his voice. "Fine. Now that we've decided on our target, just how do we go about establishing contact with the Exile Ox? Are all of us necessary or can a few work the ritual?"

Shen responded not to the words, but to that grudging tone. "Des, from the start you have resisted the idea of our trying to contact one or more of the Exiles. To answer your question, a few can work the contact ritual, but if you are to remain in charge of the group in the guardian domains, you're going to need to get comfortable with the idea of working with ghosts."

Des looked angry, possibly for the first time since Honey Dream had met him. The expression reminded her that for all Roosters were known for their elegance and theatricality, they were fighting creatures as well.

"If I don't do it, Shen, who's going to? Certainly not our apprentices. They're willing, but they're not ready. Certainly not any of our allies from the Lands. These Gates must be Orphan artifacts. It's our spell. You and Pearl are . . ."

Des stopped in midbreath, aware he was being tactless, but Shen did not spare him.

"Too old? Too fragile? I admit, our bodies are not what they once were, but we might manage. However, remember, the situation has changed from a few weeks ago. Albert and Gaheris are no longer suffering amnesia. Deborah plans to join us fairly soon. Any one of them could take over."

Pearl nodded. "I had actually thought about asking Albert if he could accompany the first venture to the Nine Springs. His bloodline is attenuated, true, but he is still of the line of the emperors who held the Jade Petal Throne. Such things count in the afterlife."

Des had had time to recover from his outburst, and now he looked distinctly embarrassed.

"I'm sorry Pearl, Shen . . . All of you, really. I just . . ." He rested his hands on the table with an audible thump. "I guess I heard too many ghost stories when I was a kid. I'll admit it. The idea of working with a ghost makes me nervous."

Righteous Drum looked interested. "I don't know if ghost lore is the same here as in the Lands, but if it is, I think you are wrong to fear those ancestral spirits."

Des looked at him, angling his head sharply as a rooster does when it wishes to fix the focus of one eye on its subject.

"Would you explain, sir?"

Righteous Drum looked so profoundly scholarly that Honey Dream felt her breast swell with pride.

"Correct me if our traditions vary greatly from your own, but our beliefs hold that after death the soul fragments. There are various theories as to how many parts the soul has, but that doesn't matter here. What does is that the good and the bad, or perhaps the spiritual impulses and the animal impulses, separate."

"The hun and po souls," Des said softly.

"Ah, so our traditions are similar," Righteous Drum said with satisfaction. "Now, because the po soul with its more animal inclinations is what lingers with the body, we are all taught to be careful around graves, to fear ghosts. Is that correct?"

Des nodded.

"But when you go in search of the Nine Yellow Springs," Righteous Drum said, "your guide will be the hun soul, the soul purged of the more animal inclinations. So, you see, you have little to fear. Your guide—this Exile Ox, let us say—may have memories of past wrongs, old slights, but she will not be as emotionally tied to them. She will be elevated, purified. If her time since her death has been spent with an awareness that sacrifices have been maintained even after her daughter's line strayed from affiliation with the Orphans, she will probably feel gratitude as well."

He paused, and Honey Dream was gratified to see that Des was nodding, the tension that had lingered about him visibly relieved.

"Thank you, sir," Des said, bowing from the waist so deeply that his forehead touched the table. "Your wisdom has greatly relieved me of what I now see was a foolish and juvenile anxiety."

When he raised his head and faced the rest of them, his eyes held their more usual cheerful, enthusiastic expression.

"Count me in, for contacting ghosts, and certainly for working with the team that's establishing the gates. I agree that having Albert along when we try to reach the Yellow Springs would be a good idea."

Doubt dimmed the brightness in his eyes. "I mean, I'll go if people still want me to, especially after seeing me behave like such an ass."

Nissa leaned across the table and patted his hand. "Don't let it get to you, teacher dear. I think we all like you better than ever for not being quite perfect."

"When do we begin?" Honey Dream asked.

"The Double Hour of the Ox," Shen said promptly, "which begins—unfortunately, from the point of view of our getting our beauty sleep—at one in the morning."

Pearl glanced at the clock on the wall. "That gives us ample time to make preparations, choose our team, and make sure everyone involved gets some rest."

"And the rest of us?" Brenda said.

"We can always," Nissa replied, "use more amulet bracelets."

XIX

"Pearl Bright's residence," Brenda said, answering the phone from the kitchen extension.

Although the voice on the other end spoke with measured control, a rasping note underlay the words, as if the speaker was trying not to scream.

"Put her on."

"I'm sorry," Brenda said. "She's not available."

"Tell her," the voice said, "I know she was responsible for what happened, and that I'm not going to forget it. She might have had friends but now . . ."

"May I say who's calling?" Brenda said, doing her best to keep her voice level although the ferocious anger in the speaker's voice was pretty scary.

The only answer was a hard click as the phone on the other end was hung up.

Brenda stared at the receiver for a long moment, then replaced it in its cradle. Pearl really wasn't available, but Des was. When Brenda went looking for him, she found him in the kitchen, mixing a marinade that smelled of ginger and sherry.

"Man or woman's voice?" Des asked, when Brenda finished her report.

"Woman. I think. Tell the truth, whoever was on the other end of that phone hardly sounded human. I don't think I've ever heard someone so angry."

Des nodded. "Happens. If I had to guess, I'd say your caller was Tracy Frye. My guess is that she and her friends have discovered not only that the mah-jong sets are gone, but that they were removed in such a fashion that she and her associates are going to have no luck proving who took them."

"I wonder that they took this long to figure it out," Brenda said. "Didn't Shen say something about Tracy Frye, at least, sleeping with hers under her pillow?"

"True," Des said, "but I don't think Tracy trusts the others very much. There were probably a lot of accusations and checking and double-checking before they decided that—impossible as it must seem—somehow we'd removed the sets."

"Impossible? But the caller said she _knew_ what happened," Brenda said.

"Saying you know, and proving you know to, for example, the police, is another thing," Des said. "Note that your caller didn't say what precisely 'happened.' My guess is that she hoped whoever answered the phone would be tempted to do some bragging. She probably had a tape running."

"Is that admissible in court?"

"She wouldn't need to go to court," Des said, "not the type of court you're thinking of at least. She'd probably want to try the Rock Dove Society first."

"Do you think she'll go to the police?" Brenda asked. "I mean, she has receipts to prove she bought the sets."

"No, I don't," Des said. "Police tend to ask questions such as how could the sets have been removed without setting off alarms, and wonder if you're trying to pull an elaborate insurance fraud. Besides, I don't think Franklin Deng will want to raise a fuss—no more than Albert does."

"Yeah . . ." Brenda sighed. "But whoever was on the phone sure sounded angry."

"Tell Pearl about it when she comes out," Des said.

Brenda nodded. After a morning spent in various activities—including crafting amulets—everyone had scattered. Flying Claw, Waking Lizard, and Riprap were over at

Colm Lodge doing some sort of weapons practice. Nissa had taken Lani to a kids' party sponsored by Joanne—the woman who had been "stage-mothering" Lani.

Pearl, Shen, Albert, Honey Dream, and Righteous Drum were closeted in Pearl's office doing something complex and arcane in connection with raising the spirit of the Exile Ox. After some consideration, they had decided they wouldn't try the ceremony right away, not after the immense ch'i drain of last night's activities, but would wait until the next double hour of the Ox.

That left Brenda and Des to handle the various preparations for the arrival of Deborah Van Bergenstein, the Pig and the remaining "active" member of the Thirteen Orphans.

Brenda hadn't minded. She'd thought about going along to the weapons practice, but the fellows were planning on helping Riprap discover the strengths and limitations of the rather nasty-looking wolf's-tooth staff Flying Claw had found among the weapons left by the dead assassins. The mixture of spells and weapons that Pearl had been working on with Brenda when they had been attacked nine days ago had once again been postponed.

Deborah Van Bergenstein was due to arrive in San Jose from her home in Michigan shortly before dinner. As interested as Brenda was in meeting Deborah, she was more enthusiastic about the other expected arrival. Gaheris Morris was also flying in. He was due to arrive with enough time to rent a car. Then he would meet Deborah's flight and bring her over to Pearl's.

Good thing Pearl has lots of spare room, Brenda thought, heading upstairs to the third floor, her arms piled with sheets and towels.

Deborah would be staying in the room that had been Flying Claw's when he was Foster, since it had its own bathroom. Shen had moved from Foster's room in with Des. Dad and Albert had been offered sofas, but Dad had opted for a hotel, pleading the need to squeeze in a few meetings. Albert lived close enough that he could easily drive.

Even so, Pearl had asked Brenda to drag out a couple of folding cots so they could air, "Just in case."

To distract herself from the cold shiver that went up and down her spine whenever she thought about how angry that voice on the phone had been, as Brenda went about her chores, she used her cell phone to place calls to various friends. She was trying hard to stay connected to her "normal" life, but it wasn't proving easy with anyone except her mom. The problem was that between the three-hour time difference between California and South Carolina, and the added complexity of summer jobs, finding the right time to connect was tough.

Still, Brenda managed a few good chats while getting the cots out and the guest room set. When she went downstairs to make a double batch of the chocolate mousse that had become quite popular with the residents of Pearl's household, Brenda felt a relieved sense of being part of the "real" world.

Brenda didn't know much about Deborah Van Bergenstein, other than that she was from the generation between that of Shen and Pearl, and Gaheris and Albert. Now, while separating eggs and putting a scandalous amount of cream in the microwave to scald, Brenda asked Des about the impending guest.

"Deborah?" he said, his hands never pausing in their rapid chopping and slicing. "She has an interesting background. Her mother married a German immigrant—a refugee from Hitler's Germany. Deborah was born before the end of World War Two and grew up knowing that there were people who didn't like her father for no other reason than that his native country had once been an enemy of the United States."

Brenda poked the tip of her little finger into the cream and decided it needed a little more heating.

"Not nice," she said in a tone that invited Des to say more.

"Nope," he agreed. "Deborah wasn't an only child, though—Pigs run to large families—so she had plenty with whom to share the burden. Her parents encouraged education for both boys and girls, so Deborah started out teaching elementary school. She decided that wasn't for her, and trained as a nurse. Sometime in her mid-twenties, she settled down with a nice German-American boy who understood exactly what she'd been through as a child. They have—if I remember right—six kids and tons of grandkids."

"Wow," Brenda said. "And with all of that, Deborah kept up with being an Orphan, too?"

"And made sure her heir apparent—Liesel's about your dad and Albert's age, a few years younger—got her training to be the next Pig, too," Des agreed. "Liesel, by the way, is a philosophy professor at the University of Michigan. She's promised to come out if we need her, but she's teaching summer session, and with her kids out of school, she's pressed."

"How many kids does Liesel have?" Brenda asked.

"Two," Des answered, "but Liesel started late, and her kids are still quite young. Five and three, I think."

"Is Deborah nice?"

"In a drill sergeant sort of way," Des agreed. "Organized. Efficient. She's going to be a lot of help—among other things, she can help me get you three apprentices up to speed."

Brenda widened her eyes and pressed one hand to her throat in mock horror, but in reality she was pleased. Initially, both Pearl and Des had taken part in their training—although Des had always been Brenda's primary instructor. Now Pearl seemed to hardly ever be available, and Des was constantly being called on to consult on other matters.

Therefore, when the front doorbell rang shortly before six in the evening, Brenda raced Lani to the front door in high spirits. Not so high, however, that she forgot to check who was on the stoop. At first she saw only her dad, then she caught a glimpse of a shock of white-blond hair right below the peephole.

Another short one, Brenda thought, undoing the wards, spelled chain, and perfectly mundane lock that held the front door safe from intrusion.

When Brenda swung the door open, her first impression

was that Deborah Van Bergenstein resembled a fireplug. Deborah didn't seem the least bit fat, but the figure that was packed into a neat pantsuit was one long curve. Her hair, cut in one of the short, helmetlike cuts that so many older women seemed to prefer, completed the impression.

She's taller than I guessed, too, Brenda thought, extending a hand in welcome. *She was probably bending over her suitcases.*

There were two of these, canvas sides bulging. Brenda noticed that Dad carried another bag that matched the first two. Deborah obviously didn't believe in traveling light.

"Hi," Brenda said politely. "I'm Brenda Morris."

Deborah, who stood about five foot six inches tall, gave Brenda a stern look up and down as she shook the proffered hand. Then she smiled.

"I would have guessed. Your father showed me family pictures while we were waiting for the luggage."

Brenda hugged her father, then gestured him in and made sure the door was locked and warded. Behind her, she heard Deborah ask, "And who is this?"

"Lani!" the little girl answered exuberantly. Then she became suddenly shy after the fashion of children her age, and ducked behind Brenda. "Are you Deb'rah the Pig?"

"I am indeed," Deborah said. "And you are a Rabbit."

"A bunny!" Lani said, shyness gone, and hopping in demonstration.

Brenda had lifted the two canvas bags, and found them quite heavy enough that she wasn't insulted when Riprap appeared and offered to take Mrs. Van Bergenstein's luggage to the third floor.

"Deborah," the new arrival corrected, "and you must be Riprap."

"That's right, ma'am," Riprap said with a teasing smile.

"Now you stop that, or I'm going to start calling you Charles!"

Riprap looked mock horrified, collected the bags—including the one Gaheris had been carrying—and headed up the stairs. He was back before introductions were quite completed all around, for the four from the Lands were dining at Pearl's that evening.

Dinner began with elaborate appetizers, then continued through soup and various courses, sizzling hot from the wok. Des was the head cook, but to Brenda's surprise Flying Claw was his main assistant. Honey Dream, Brenda now realized, had shown no interest in anything domestic, and Brenda—feeling comfortably superior when everyone oohed and aahed over her mousse—wondered if Honey Dream even knew how to cook.

Despite the number of people at the table, conversation remained general. Part of this was because Deborah had many questions about various of the events that had begun late in May. Over and over again Deborah said, "Albert told me, but . . ."

Before long, Brenda noticed that her dad seemed to take a special delight in filling in whatever it was Albert had missed—even if the events in question were ones that neither he nor Albert had personally witnessed.

Dad's got issues with Albert, Brenda thought. She remembered how hesitant her father had been to tell her anything about Albert in advance of their first meeting, how even after it became evident that something bad had happened to Albert, Dad hadn't seem so much worried as annoyed. *But I thought they were boys together, playmates even. Maybe I was wrong—or maybe it's just my imagination. I'm overreacting because he's my dad.*

But she wasn't. After they had retired from the formal dining room to the family room, Brenda noticed that a gradual stiffening was spreading throughout the gathering, making the conversation stilted and awkward. Only Lani—who was playing Go Fish with Flying Claw—seemed unaffected. Only Lani and Dad. Dad kept smiling and talking, telling anecdotes with great enthusiasm, laughing at his own jokes.

It's like everyone is holding their breath to see what Dad will say next—and no one is willing to call him on anything

*because he hasn't actually done anything rude or mean—
he's just overly enthusiastic. Except he isn't.*

Brenda expected Pearl to be the one to call Dad on his
behavior, maybe ask him to come and help her with something, but it was Deborah who, suddenly stern, turned a smile
that managed to be both polite and freezing on Dad.

"Gaheris, I appreciate your interest in this, but really,
since you're only reporting secondhand, perhaps we should
give those who were there a chance to speak?" Her expression became conciliatory without in the least removing her
reproof. "Des has asked me to help with the teaching of our
Rabbit and Dog—and, of course, Brenda—and it would
help me to see where their strengths and weaknesses lie."

Dad blinked, but his charming smile never faded. "Sorry,
Deborah. I guess I got carried away."

"Ah, yes," Deborah said. "Always the eager one. Liesel told
me that when she studied with you and Albert under Shen you
were always first with the answers."

"Pretty little Liesel," Dad said, his smile becoming just a
touch wistful. "I had such a crush on her. I really wanted to
impress her."

He turned to Brenda and winked, "This was long before I
met your mom, of course."

And who is it you're trying to impress now? Brenda wondered. *Me? I don't think so. The Landers, maybe? Show them
how much you've learned even if they did steal your memory?
I wonder. I really, really wonder.*

☆

Pearl wasn't in the least surprised when later that evening,
after all the guests had left, and the household had settled
down, Brenda Morris came knocking at her office door.

"Can I talk to you for a minute?" Brenda asked.

"Certainly. Have a seat. Would you like some tea?"

"No. I'm fine." Brenda sat for a moment, eyes narrowed in
thought. Then she said, "Pearl, what's the problem with Dad
and Albert? There's something there. We all noticed."

Pearl sat for a moment, eyes closed, considering what to tell Brenda. The truth, certainly, but perhaps not all of it.

"Brenda, your father's problems with Albert date back to his own father. You remember that your grandfather wanted nothing to do with his heritage as the Rat of the Thirteen. Although his father could not make his son behave as he might wish, he did everything in his power to make certain that Gaheris was taught our lore."

Brenda nodded. "Great-Grandpa threatened to disinherit Grandpa, and Grandpa knuckled under."

"That's about it," Pearl agreed, "but your grandfather did not 'knuckle under,' immediately. For a while I thought we were going to have to take your grandfather to court to enforce the terms of the will. When your grandfather realized we were serious—by 'we' I mean myself, Albert's father, and Des's great-grandmother—he gave in, but it was a bad time.

"Even when your grandfather did give in, he didn't do so fully, not to the point of teaching—indoctrinating, I suppose he would have called it—Gaheris himself. But he permitted me and Shen and a few of the other elders to do so, and that was enough to fulfill the requirements of the will.

"When Gaheris joined us, Albert was already one of our students. His father—the Second Cat—hadn't rejected his role as emperor-in-waiting, but, frankly, he seemed to take the 'waiting' far more seriously than he did the 'emperor.' Most of what Albert learned, he learned from other than his father. Then, not long after Gaheris joined us, when Albert was ten, Albert's father died in a car accident that may not have been an accident. Albert's mother was severely injured in the same accident, her legs broken in multiple places. For a while, she managed to get around with a cane, but today she's restricted to a wheelchair. There were other injuries, not as visible, but at least as debilitating."

Brenda frowned. "So Dad and Albert were both pretty vulnerable when they started taking lessons from you. That didn't draw them together?"

"It did, after a fashion, and it did not. For one, Albert was slightly older, and definitely more experienced. Small differences like that matter a great deal to boys. They are fiercely competitive at that age."

Brenda laughed. "Do they ever stop? But surely you noticed that competitiveness."

Pearl shook her head. "That was a complicated time for us all. Shen and Umeko's son, Geoffrey, was born that same year. To say that Shen didn't have quite the attention for his students that he should have . . ."

Pearl smiled reminiscently. "Let's just say Shen was rather distracted and overtired. I had let my own business interests lapse to attend to the Rat lawsuit. I wasn't in danger of becoming impoverished, but those were years of rising inflation, and I had worries of my own. None of us even considered that what we were seeing was more serious than two strong-willed, intelligent boys trying to decide which one would be boss."

"But didn't Albert have the advantage?" Brenda asked. "I mean, not only was he a little older, but he was ahead in his studies, and, no matter what Dad did, Albert would be the emperor, while Dad was just a Rat."

"And," Pearl said, pleased with Brenda's acuity, "not even a full Rat. His father was still alive, even if he refused to exercise his abilities. Gaheris was a Rat-in-Waiting, feeling himself inheritor of all the Rat's responsibilities, without the full affiliation."

"I know how that feels," Brenda said. "I feel that way now that Dad has his memories, like I'm not sure where I fit in."

Pearl decided this was *not* the time to get sidetracked into a discussion of Brenda's own peculiarities. Reassurance was what was needed.

"You are doing very well," she said. "Talk with Waking Lizard. In the Lands, the Twelve mentor those who show promise, not just in the various arts, but in having a particular affiliation for a Branch. You are in a similar relationship with Gaheris, with the added certainty of your place being assured."

"Flying Claw mentioned his mentor," Brenda said. "I guess it's that Dad isn't really mentoring me, if you know what I mean. He keeps showing up, leaving, showing up again. If I have a mentor at all, it's Des—or you."

"You have us both," Pearl assured her, "and believe me, we are very happy to have you."

"Thanks," Brenda said. "So, when did you figure out that Dad and Albert's problems had gone a bit deeper than usual?"

Pearl considered. "Brenda, can I be honest with you? I'd considered holding some of this back, because it's not all very pleasant—and it reflects worse on Gaheris than it does Albert."

Brenda looked startled. She sat upright, suddenly very serious.

"Sure, Pearl. I think I sort of suspected that Dad was to blame from how he has acted. Let me guess. Dad really, really didn't like that, no matter what he did, Albert would still be emperor, and he'd be, at best, first counselor."

"Very perceptive."

"I know my dad. Competitive isn't the word for him—and he's worst when he's competing with himself. If Albert sneered at him even just a little, it would have made Dad crazy."

"And Albert probably did sneer," Pearl said, "being that he was ten years old and his father newly dead, and his responsibilities had come home to him all too suddenly. To Albert's credit, I don't think that sneering lasted long. I think the responsibilities scared him into sense."

Brenda grinned, a flash as white and hot as summer lightning. "I bet you had a bit to do with that scaring, Pearl. I can't see you putting up with a boy giving himself airs."

The grin vanished as fast as it had arisen. "But Dad wouldn't have forgotten, not even if it was just one sneer. Don't get me wrong. Dad's a great guy. Loyal and loving, but he's not as secure as he might seem. I never knew why, just sensed it there, but I guess Grandpa really hurt Dad."

"He did," Pearl said softly. "Your grandfather hurt a good many people, all because he thought himself hard-used."

She thought about how she herself had treated Foster, and had the grace to be quietly and thoroughly ashamed.

And so because your father had hurt you, you were determined to snub that boy who looked so much like him—who echoed him in that grace of motion, that inescapable masculinity that you could never have. Yes. I've been guilty of as much as Gaheris's father—but hopefully I can make amends.

Brenda was watching Pearl carefully, and Pearl wondered just how much those rat-sharp eyes had seen, how much that too-acute mind had surmised. Brenda was at that age where it was easy to misjudge her, to underestimate her, filled with wisdom one moment, mooning over an imagined wrong the next.

"We realized that Gaheris had developed 'issues' with Albert one day when Gaheris arrived just as Albert and Shen were concluding an exercise that involved projecting oneself into a manifestation of the affiliate Branch. Since Gaheris was not yet the Rat, he couldn't practice this, and while Shen finished with Albert, I set Gaheris to doing moving meditations . . ."

Brenda looked interested, but Pearl could see from how she glanced at the clock that she was aware of the lateness of the hour. Questions about "moving meditations" were obviously being filed away for another time.

"Albert and Shen finished. When they joined myself and Gaheris, Albert looked like one of those Pre-Raphaelite paintings of a knight concluding vigil over his armor: translucent, exhausted, and yet somehow transcendently powerful. Gaheris saw it, too, and I naively hoped this would inspire him to greater efforts in his own exercises. To that point, he'd been making the appropriate motions, but his focus was completely off.

"I forget what called Shen and me away just then. It might have been a phone call. Umeko might have been having trouble with the baby. For whatever reason, we both left, giving the boys the sort of general instructions that are all too easily ignored.

"We were drawn back by angry yelling from the classroom. Gaheris was shouting at Albert. 'You're not even a real Branch. You're just a Cat. Just an afterthought. I don't know why you think you're so great. The only thing you have going for you is that you're the third failure in a line of failures. Fourth, since that hotshot emperor we've all heard so much about couldn't have been much if his subjects wanted to overthrow him and his own advisors wouldn't stick by him.'"

"He didn't!" Brenda gasped. Then almost immediately, "He did. That's exactly the type of mean thing Dylan or Thomas would say. Hell, that I would have said when I was ten. That's so mean, and so dumb. What did Albert do?"

"I don't know what he would have done," Pearl said, "because I came through the door right then and I didn't feel like waiting to find out. I got them away from each other, into different rooms. Shen went to talk to Albert. I went to talk to Gaheris. We got them both calmed down, then set them to work. By the end of the day, they were talking pretty normally to each other, but I'm not sure that Albert ever forgot what Gaheris said."

"Why?"

"Because while Albert had been a good student before, from that point on he obviously started trying very hard to be a good leader as well. You've been in student government, so you know that being a leader may sound glamorous, but it often means doing things you don't want to do."

Brenda nodded. "Staying later than everyone else, making sure things are locked up, making phone calls."

"Keeping your temper when no one else is doing so, pretending to like talking to boring people, remembering that even one person is an audience. Neither First Cat nor Second Cat had been particularly responsible. One was a spoiled brat, the other a dutiful donkey. Albert was the first Cat to start acting like an emperor of any sort."

"And Dad?"

"First Gaheris tried to needle Albert. When that didn't work, he decided to match him at his own game. That made life quieter for us all, but I don't think Shen or I ever assumed that peace and tranquillity reigned in either of the boys' hearts. Then adolescence complicated the picture."

Brenda gasped. "Don't tell me that they fell in love with the same girl."

"I could only have wished," Pearl said. "Instead, Albert fell in love with Gaheris."

Pearl watched Brenda's expression as it went from surprise, to shock, and settled on curiosity.

"Albert's gay?" Brenda said. "But I thought he had kids."

"He does," Pearl agreed. "Two. A son and a daughter. They live with their mother, but their relationship with their father is relatively cordial. Their mother is far too aware of the advantages of Albert's wealth and links to power and celebrity to alienate her children fully from their father.

"Albert's own character stands him in good stead. His children know he is gay, but he keeps his liaisons discreet. He is also a devoted son, never stinting in anything that will make his mother more comfortable or content. Besides, being gay, especially in the Bay area, carries very little stigma anymore."

"But my dad grew up in the Midwest," Brenda said. "How did he feel about having a guy have a crush on him? For that matter, why did Albert get a crush on Dad of all people? From what you've said, it's not like Dad was exactly nice to him."

"I think that last was precisely the reason Albert developed his attachment. Just as his response to Gaheris's accusing him of not being worthy of being emperor made him try to develop the qualities of a good ruler, so Gaheris's rejection made him try to win him over. When they were eleven and twelve, this simply took the form of trying to get Gaheris to accept him."

"Surely Dad didn't hold out," Brenda said, her tone pleading. "I mean, he's stubborn and he's competitive, but he's not mean."

"Gaheris is not," Pearl agreed. "Not in the least, and I think that for a few years he and Albert did become friends of a sort. Gaheris grew resigned to, if not exactly happy with, the fact that he wasn't going to be able to do some of the things Albert could for a long time, but he worked very hard and caught up in other areas. It helped that they were both highly talented. Had they not been, the problems might have intensified. They are also not unalike in physical build. Both are on the shorter side of average, and rather slight. This meant that when they began training in physical arts, they could compete evenly."

"Good thing Albert wasn't built like Riprap," Brenda said, "or Dad might never have gotten over it."

"True," Pearl agreed, "although Gaheris did have difficulties Albert did not. Albert is average or above average in height and build for a Chinese. Gaheris is rather on the small side for someone of German-Irish heritage."

"Yeah," Brenda said. "It's a family joke that it looks like I'm going to be taller than Dad. I don't think he always thinks it's funny."

"His pride in you is evident," Pearl said. "I don't think something as unimportant as height will make a difference."

"But when Albert got a crush on Dad?" Brenda pressed. "That did?"

"It did. Young men are far more insecure about their sexual identities than young women. You must have noticed that."

"I have, sort of, but I've got to say that I don't think anyone has it exactly easy these days. I mean, when you were a girl, people didn't even talk about homosexuality, except in whispers, right?"

"I grew up in the theater, in the movies," Pearl said, "but, yes, even in that relatively relaxed atmosphere there were things that were known and accepted, but never, ever talked about. It's different now. I thought it would be better."

Brenda ran her hands over her admittedly less than well-endowed chest.

"I wish. It seems like half the girls in my dorm have decided that they're gay, or at least bi. I'm not, but because I'm not stacked and loaded with curves, I've had lots of people assume I'm not interested in boys. I thought that living in a co-ed dorm would mean that I'd be worrying about the guys. It's the girls . . ."

Brenda waved a hand as if the problem could be physically removed. "It's not really a problem. All but the ones who are really confused themselves and think that they need to convince you to join them take a polite 'no' for an answer, but next year I'll probably be in a different dorm and I sincerely hope that my new floor won't be so sex-crazed."

Pearl laughed. "Try being a woman who has remained single by choice into her seventies. One 'tell-all' biographer actually hired a detective to probe into my very routine romantic life."

She glanced at the clock. "The hour is growing late, so let me finish. I think it was the summer the boys were fourteen and fifteen, that Albert took to mooning around after Gaheris. Gaheris wasn't exactly quick to catch on, but when he did . . ."

Brenda winced. "You don't need to tell me. You know, I don't think I want to know. Well, I do want to know one thing."

"What?"

"Did they get into a fight over it, or did Albert catch on and back off?"

Pearl considered. "A little of both. They were both getting training in various martial arts. A few of their training bouts . . . I don't think Gaheris knew whether he wanted to throw Albert across the room or avoid touching him entirely.

Eventually, Albert caught on—I think Shen spoke with him—and realized that his interest in Gaheris was not only not returned, but was interfering with his ability to be emperor. With what I expect he thought was great nobility of spirit and self-sacrifice, Albert resigned himself to a broken heart."

"Too weird," Brenda said. "Poor Dad. Poor Albert."

Pearl nodded, wondering if she should go on from there and talk about how Albert had reacted when Gaheris—who like any normal young man had been involved in a series of romances before he met Brenda's mother—actually proposed to Keely. The matter had been complicated by more than old jealousy.

Was Brenda ready for all of that? Remembering those arguments, Pearl thought not, especially since she'd need to explain other things as well, and Brenda was rising to her feet, clearly satisfied.

"Thanks, Pearl. I'll keep this to myself. If Nissa or Riprap asks me—well, Cats and Rats don't really get along, do they?"

After Brenda had gone up to her room, Pearl poured herself a final cup of tea from the pot under the cozy on her desk. She thought back to the days when Gaheris Morris had proposed to Keely McAnally. For the first time in a long time, she found herself wondering about Keely. Perhaps, Albert had been right to oppose the marriage. Maybe his reaction to Gaheris's intended had been born from wisdom and not from jealousy as everyone had thought at the time.

The matter bore thinking about, but not now. The day had been very long, and there was no promise that tomorrow would be any shorter.

XX

The Double Hour of the Ox found Honey Dream one of a select group that included her father, Pearl Bright, Shen Kung, and Albert Yu assembled in Pearl's office for the purpose of attempting to contact the Exile Ox.

Although the Double Hour of the Ox was quite late—or quite early, depending on how one chose to view it—they had been present for at least another hour preceding the ceremony. Righteous Drum had insisted that even if modern Chinese-American custom did not insist on ritual purification, he thought such was wise, and since he was the only one of them with any but theoretical experience in such matters, no one had cared to argue.

Honey Dream smothered a yawn behind a hand that was permeated with the odor of incense. Although she had taken a long nap that afternoon, it had been a busy day.

That morning the physical training sessions had resumed. Once again, Nissa had declined to attend, but otherwise everyone was present. Deborah Van Bergenstein had assigned herself to teach Brenda and so Pearl Bright, with what Honey Dream was certain was malice glittering in her bright old eyes, had offered herself as Honey Dream's partner.

As usual, Pearl's weapon had been the sword Treaty, while Honey Dream's was the snake-fang dagger that had come to her upon her ascension to the rank of Snake. Both weapons—and, more importantly, both combatants—were capable of casting spells as well as more usual cutting and stabbing. Moreover, unlike the three apprentices, Pearl was quite skilled in this, and had defeated Honey Dream once before.

Of course, I was distracted then, Honey Dream thought, the memory making her face hot. *And had already done a great deal of magic that night.*

But she would never articulate these thoughts. Righteous

Drum would tolerate a great deal from his much-beloved daughter, but excuses, never.

Following practice, Honey Dream had hoped to have some time alone with her associates from the Lands Born from Smoke and Sacrifice—especially with Flying Claw. Flying Claw, however, had opted for a quick shower and then to go to Pearl's house with Riprap. The big man was the only soldier—Honey Dream refused to think of him as a warrior—among the natives, and seemed to have an inexhaustible fund of questions about the creatures they might encounter both in the vicinity of the Nine Yellow Springs—their next destination—and elsewhere in the guardian domains.

Had Brenda Morris looked smug as she climbed into the van and took the seat behind Flying Claw? Honey Dream couldn't be sure, but she felt certain this was so.

Honey Dream pulled herself from thought, for the tide of motion in the room had stilled. Albert Yu, dressed in an absolutely gorgeous shenyi embroidered not only with cats, but with all twelve animals of the zodiac, was solemnly rising from where he had knelt in front of Righteous Drum and Shen Kung for the elaborate blessings and protective invocations that were the final part of the purification ceremony.

"We have five minutes," Pearl Bright said, glancing at the clock on her desk.

"I suggest we spend them in meditation," Shen Kung said. He was also clad in an elaborately embroidered shenyi, the fabric golden yellow, the ornamental dragons bearing in their five-fingered claws various items that invoked luck, wealth, and long life. Something about the fit of the shoulders and sleeves indicated that the robe had been made when Shen was a younger man and stood both taller and straighter.

Honey Dream felt a funny twinge in her gut, an ache of anticipated pain. She looked over at where her father stood, his own dragon robes hanging limp over his missing arm, wondering if someday he might seem as old and withered as Shen did. She thrust the thought from her as ill-omened.

*Think of good things. Think of seeing Mother and the rest
of the family. Think of seeing a true emperor elevated once
more to the Jade Petal Throne, and of standing on the most
honored dais, one of the Twelve.*

She sunk her mind into the deep ch'i flow of meditation,
and felt the five minutes pass both more slowly and more
quickly than they should. A chiming sound brought her back
into the present, focused and renewed.

Shen Kung set down the tiny mallet with which he had
rung the chime and looked over all of them.

"Pearl, as the most senior of our number, would you light
one of the red candles? Honey Dream, would you light the
other?"

An altar not much wider than Honey Dream's outspread
hands had been set up at one end of Pearl's office. It was
draped in deep red fabric, embellished with gold ribbon from
which depended silken tassels so long that they swept almost
to the floor. Freshly cut flowers were spread on the fabric that
covered the altar, and small plants in delicately painted china
vases were set at the corners.

The center of the altar was a large framed photograph of
an older woman. Surrounding this large photo was a collage
of other photos of this same woman. She was never depicted
as young, for the Exile Ox had been among the oldest of the
Exiles, but in most she was younger, in some, quite the ancient. In some pictures she was shown alone, but in a few she
was surrounded by people who Honey Dream had been told
were others of the Exiles, and, perhaps most importantly in
their current situation, the Exile Ox's adopted daughter, Hua.

Shen Kung was holding out lit matches to Pearl and Honey
Dream. In concert they lit the candles that flanked the photograph. Albert had told Honey Dream that their custom held
that two candles symbolized the joining of dualities—dead
and living, old and young, wise and innocent—that were
embodied at the heart of ancestor worship.

"Is it the same in the Lands?" he had asked.

"Not precisely, but close enough to be familiar."

So it was with the rest of the ceremony as it progressed. In the Lands, a family of good standing such as her own would have offered real gifts, not paper replicas to the deceased, but even in the Lands, the sacrifice of living things was no longer commonly done.

Shen Kung had been chanting various prayers, some in English, some in modern northern Chinese, but most in the Chinese of the Lands, for this was the language the Exile Ox herself would have spoken—her first language, and so the language of her heart.

". . . and you may wonder why, Honored Ancestor, friend of my grandfather who was as a father to me, and who spoke of you with both affection and respect, why we call upon you at this time, out of season, neither the New Year, nor the time of the spring festival of Clear Bright.

"We call upon you as the living have always called upon the Ancestors, to beg your counsel, to hope for your aid. We have never forgotten you though long years have passed. We hope some small seed of remembrance and reciprocal affection dwells within your heart."

Albert stepped forward at this point and lit a cluster of incense sticks waiting with their bases set in sand in a small round pot in the center of the altar, directly in front of the photograph.

"Here is smoke to make the road on which you may journey to us, Nine Ducks, Ox of the Twelve. I am Albert Yu, great-grandson of the emperor you swore to serve, grandson of the boy emperor you brought forth from the Lands into the Land of the Burning. I have kept faith throughout the generations, and although many years have passed, I request that you keep faith with me."

The smoke from the incense eddied up, hardly stirring in the still air of the office.

Hardly stirring, Honey Dream thought, astonished despite the detachment she had been so carefully cultivating. *Yet it should be stirring. The windows are closed, but Pearl has her artificial cooling system running, else this room would be stuffy. Yet the incense hangs before the picture, as if something holds it there.*

Albert knelt on the pillow that had been set in front of the altar, bowed his head, and clapped three times. The sound was somehow wrong—not muffled, but not as sharp as it should have been.

It's as if the sound is spreading into a bigger space than this room, into a bigger area, into . . .

The incense smoke began moving toward the picture of the Exile Ox. Honey Dream blinked and shook her head, forcing herself to focus. Part of her wanted to believe that the photographic image had changed, that the woman depicted within had pursed her lips and was breathing in the smoke. Her eyes told her this was not the case, that the photograph remained precisely as it had been, but Honey Dream knew that this was one case where the eyes lied. The image in her mind was the true one, for it was with the mind's eye that she was seeing the ghost of the Exile Ox take form.

Initially, the image was as white and insubstantial as the smoke, but within a few breaths it became more solid, taking on color, at first in light strokes—shadings from colored pencils, lightly applied—then darkening and gaining in vividness until the colors were as brilliant as spilled ink, and the seeming of a living woman stood before the altar.

Nine Ducks, the Exile Ox, was dressed in a formal shenyi cut from unfaded yellow silk. As was to be expected in a robe worn by one of the denizens of the House of Construction, symbols for luck, growth, and longevity were amply represented in the lush embroidery on the sleeves.

Given the density of the embroidery—the yellow fabric beneath was hardly visible in many places—Honey Dream was surprised how crude and awkward some of it was. Then insight flashed upon her.

Her daughter did the embroidery, this Hua we have heard so much about. Nine Ducks is armored in love and devotion.

The thought was humbling, and Honey Dream bowed her head in mute acknowledgment.

She raised her head when Nine Ducks spoke.

"Young emperor, grandson of the boy I knew, great-grandson of the emperor I served, you have called, and I have come. Although I have tasted the offerings you have never forgotten to give me, long years have passed since I felt truly remembered. Why have you called?"

Something isn't right, Honey Dream thought. *Her response is without the warmth I had expected.*

"Welcome," Albert said, rising to his feet, and bowing deeply. Honey Dream joined the others in echoing that bow, and Albert continued. "I am glad to know that the offerings we have sent to you have fortified you in the afterlife. You seem surprised that I have called upon you, but did you not think this would be so when the goal to which you devoted so much is about to be achieved?"

Nine Ducks looked interested, but also guarded. For the first time her gaze swept beyond Albert, assessing those present. When those wise old eyes within their well-earned lines examined her, Honey Dream felt a prickle of ch'i.

Nine Ducks's eyebrows rose slightly.

"I thought you spoke metaphorically, young emperor, but I see here two who are of the Lands Born from Smoke and Sacrifice, as well as those in whom I recognize scions of my old allies. Yet the Twelve are not all gathered here."

"Others are elsewhere," Albert said, not quite evading the implied question, "even within this house."

"I do not," Nine Ducks said, spacing the words deliberately, so that the challenge was evident, "see any of my line. Where is the Ox?"

Albert did not evade, nor did he look in the least shamed. "You must know of your own descendants, Nine Ducks, but if you need me to say it, I will. They have fallen away from the learnings of the Thirteen Orphans."

"And you did nothing to force them to remain within the fold," Nine Ducks said.

"I was a child of seven when your daughter Hua died, and your granddaughter, Hua's daughter, decided that she did not care to follow in the tradition. I suppose my father, who was then emperor, might have pressed her to remain within the tradition, but how could he have done so when her own mother had encouraged her otherwise?"

Honey Dream felt herself gasp in surprise, saw her father raise his head sharply.

They didn't tell us this, she thought, *but then it would be a matter of shame. Perhaps they hoped faithful Hua's infidelity would not arise.*

A new voice entered the dialogue at this point, Pearl Bright's sounding sharp as the edge of her sword.

"I was a young woman when you died, Nine Ducks. I had always admired Hua. Repeatedly, I wished that my father loved me as you so obviously loved her. I was shocked when in her quiet way Hua made clear that she intended to have nothing more to do with the Exiles' plans. Her daughter, although taught by both you and her mother, followed her mother's wishes."

"Yes," Shen added softly. "You might say that an excess of filial piety, rather than otherwise, drew your family from the way of the Orphans."

Nine Ducks had listened to this quietly, her expression unsurprised.

She knew, Honey Dream thought. *She knew, and rather than being angry at Hua, she is supportive. Why? Her daughter defied her and her wishes.*

"You wonder why I am not angry at Hua, Lady Snake?" Nine Ducks asked. "No. I cannot read your thoughts, but the question is there on your pretty face."

"I would like to know, Mother," Honey Dream answered politely, "if you would tell."

"My Hua was not pretty," Nine Ducks said, "not like you. She was a peasant girl, unloved and unwanted. If her parents had not been able to sell her, they would have thrown her out and left her to die. She had a broad face, and broad hands. Her figure was never slim, even in starvation she was merely skinny. But she was as loving a daughter as any mother could wish.

"Moreover, she was faithful to my associates. She helped to tend the boy emperor—that spoiled and insolent child. She helped care for the infant son of the Exile Horse when his father selfishly got himself killed because his beloved was pregnant by another man. She carried and fetched without complaint, and her relaxation in the evening was to strain her eyes with needle and thread, embroidering charms to protect me."

The Exile Ox's face twisted in such pure hatred that Honey Dream wondered if they had somehow erred and summoned a po ghost, but this could not be, for while the po ghost was unable to speak, this ghost was positively fluent.

"Have they told you the reward my wonderful, faithful Hua was given for her fidelity? She was told she was not good enough! She was forced to listen as my associates debated whether she might be a barrier to our return home. Eventually, she was forced to marry Shian 'George' Wu, a man younger than herself, all so that the bloodline of her children would be correct!"

Nine Ducks's expression softened for a moment. "At least that marriage was a good one. George recognized the gold in my homely Hua. He loved and honored her. While I lived, they both honored what they believed to be my wishes—that my granddaughter and the first heir of 'proper blood' be taught our lore. However, then I was gone, gone without commanding them to persist although as I lay fading into death Hua all but begged me to command her.

"But I did not, and so my family is one of those that has fallen away. Now I ask you, why should I honor the wishes of those who did not honor my Hua?"

Albert Yu clearly had no words left, and so Honey Dream took it upon herself to speak—for although Nine Ducks's outburst had been meant for all, ostensibly it had been addressed to her.

"Fear makes fools of us all, Grandmother," she said. "I will admit this, even if it means calling myself a fool, for I am very afraid. You see in me a daughter who—although blessed to have my father with me—fears I will never see my mother again, that I will never see my brothers and sisters, that I will never again burn incense on the altars of my ancestors."

"You are trapped here, then?"

"We are: myself, my father, and two others—our Tiger and our Monkey. Moreover, our exile is not one of voluntary nobility such as that you undertook, O infinitely stalwart Ox. Our exile is involuntary, and we have no way of knowing how those we left behind are—whether they live, or whether they are dead along with all who might remember their names."

Honey Dream had begun her speech merely as an attempt to buy Albert Yu and the others a moment to compose themselves, but somehow she found herself pouring out her heart to the ghost. Tears were flowing down her face, ruining her makeup, but she didn't try to stop them.

Perhaps pain speaks to pain, Honey Dream thought, and it seemed to her that Nine Ducks understood.

"So you are asking me for help in returning you home? I have no such power. I am an exile whose exile was never repealed."

"If I might explain, Grandmother," Righteous Drum said.

The ghost inclined her head, and Righteous Drum began the complex explanation as to how they hoped to circumvent the exile by means of the Nine Gates.

"It might work," the ghost admitted. "Legalistic, but then legalism has its place in the Lands, side by side with other traditions. What aid do you ask of me?"

Shen Kung, who had helped Righteous Drum with some points of his explanation, now spoke. "We were hoping for two things, Ancestress. First, we hoped that you would take the place of your great-granddaughter when the time comes for the Thirteen to return to the Lands. More immediately, we were hoping you would be guide and counselor to those of our number who must journey to the underworld and establish the link that will enable our Nine Gates to be joined with the Nine Yellow Springs."

"Thus empowering them to cross universes, as only life and death are capable of doing," Nine Ducks said.

"That is so, Grandmother," Shen said.

Albert Yu bowed before the ghost. "Will you aid us, Nine Ducks, the Exile Ox?"

The ghost considered. With a sinking heart, Honey Dream knew the answer before the words came.

"As to being your guide to the Nine Yellow Springs, no, I will not. To aid those who so insulted my beloved daughter—and they will be aided if you succeed, for their goal will be achieved—would be an insult to Hua. However, if you succeed in building the Nine Gates, and linking them to the Nine Yellow Springs, then I will not stand between you and your success."

The ghost of Nine Ducks turned and bowed to Honey Dream. "I will do this for a daughter who cried sincere tears out of fear she would never again see her mother. I will not stand in the way of such love, such fidelity."

Albert Yu was too good a ruler to argue. He bowed again deeply, and the others echoed his bow.

"Thank you, Nine Ducks. We will honor and respect your wishes."

Bending over had made Honey Dream sniffle. Surreptitiously, she drew a tissue from her sleeve and wiped fresh tears from her eyes. When she rose again, the ghost of Nine Ducks had vanished, taking with her both the light from the candles and the scent of the many sticks of incense that had been burned in her honor.

☆

The expectation that the Exile Ox would join them had been so strong that Brenda was shocked when she came down to breakfast the next morning to see the serious expressions on the faces of those already awake and assembled—and on the faces of those who had been unable to settle after the failed attempt.

Shen briefed Brenda on what had happened, and something of the despair the others must be feeling was evident in that the usual host of interruptions and clarifications were completely absent. Of course, this might have had to do with the fact that most of the others had come down before Brenda. Nissa and Lani were out in the backyard, and Riprap and Des were sitting at one end of the table, both looking gloomy. Only Deborah hadn't yet emerged.

Without asking, Brenda knew the matter had been discussed and rediscussed as each new arrival had filtered down, so she quietly set about making more coffee, putting on water for tea, getting herself something to eat, and, most importantly, listening.

"We must try again," Des said. "We've settled that. The only question is who: Horse, Ram, or Monkey?"

"There are objections to all of them," Pearl said. She looked very tired, more tired, even, Brenda thought, than after the battle with the Three-Legged Toad. Then Pearl had only been exhausted, now she had been beaten.

"So let's appeal to each in order," Albert said. "Horse next. The Horse is the most group-oriented of the remaining signs. Exile Horse may have personal resentments, but he may overcome them for the good of the group."

Or herd, Brenda thought. Aloud she said, "What House does the horse belong to?"

"The House of Gender," Righteous Drum said. "Perhaps not as auspicious as construction for our needs, but in its own way useful. Gender—like life and death—is one of the ruling dichotomies."

"Horse, then," Albert said, "and not today. All of us who participated in the ceremony spent a great deal of ch'i. We should rest and meet again at, say, ten-thirty tomorrow morning?"

"That will be fine," Righteous Drum agreed. "The altar is already set up. Purification of participants will not take long now that we all know the routines. Will someone drive myself and Honey Dream back to Colm Lodge?"

"I will," Brenda said. "Des, are we going to do fighting practice this morning?"

"Absolutely," Des agreed. "We have a quorum. Why don't you drive Honey Dream and Righteous Drum over now? The rest of us will follow in a few minutes."

"Great," she said. "I'll get my shoes and be right down."

There wasn't a great deal of discussion on the drive over, but once they arrived at Colm Lodge, Flying Claw and Waking Lizard must be told the entire series of events. This carried them until the arrival of Des with the others. Then Righteous Drum and Honey Dream retired and the rest gathered on the practice field.

Once again, Brenda was paired with Deborah, and once again she found that although the Pig might love to sleep in and would never refuse a second dessert, when it came to the fighting arts, she was far from slothful.

During their first practice, Deborah had discovered that Brenda's earlier injury had made her inclined to shy back when an attacker came at her, even if intellectually she knew perfectly well that most attacks could not get through the protective circle of the Dragon's Tail. Therefore, Deborah had decided to show Brenda a series of blocking maneuvers, designed to give her confidence that just because someone was coming at her with a weapon didn't mean the weapon was going to hit.

"Never forget," Deborah said as she put Brenda through a blocking exercise for the fourth or fifth time, "wild boars were more feared than lions or wolves in Europe. Indeed, the only creature that might have been more feared was an angry bear—and I like to think that even bears came up second, because I don't recall anyone ever inventing a 'bear spear.'"

"What about in China?" Brenda panted, moving her stick

rapidly to avoid getting rapped on the knuckles. "Aren't Chinese pigs lazy, home-loving creatures?"

"They may be," Deborah said, switching her grip, "but by now my genes are more European than Chinese, and I take my omens where I choose."

Brenda thought of this later, when practice was over, and she found herself sitting alone in her car with Flying Claw. Riprap had taken a nasty cut to his scalp during a much more lively exercise than the one Brenda had been given.

Deborah, in her capacity as former nurse, had ruled that stitches would be needed. A call had found Dr. Andersen with a nearly immediate gap in his schedule, so Deborah and Des had taken Riprap over.

Waking Lizard—who had delivered the cut—had asked if he might remain at Colm Lodge.

"I can see that I need both meditation and honing of my own skills. That blow should never have landed with such force. I will come over to Pearl's house later, perhaps."

Flying Claw, however, had promised to babysit Lani so that Nissa could focus on her magical studies, and so Brenda found herself really alone with him for the first time since that acutely memorable day when she had driven him off to the rendezvous with Honey Dream—the rendezvous that would remove Foster forever from Brenda's life.

Take your omens where you wish, Brenda thought. *I just wish I could decide if this is a good or bad one.*

Flying Claw tossed a small daypack into the backseat and got into the passenger seat.

"Buckle up," Brenda reminded him.

"Right," he said in English, reaching up over his shoulder for the top of the buckle with the muscular grace that made Brenda's heart beat faster.

The buckle clicked home and she realized that she'd been sitting there staring. She felt her face grow hot as she turned the key in the ignition, and pulled the car through the circular drive and back out onto the surface roads.

"Brenda, do you have any money with you?"

She blinked in surprise. "A little. Twenty bucks or so. I have my credit card, too. Is there something you need?"

"I was thinking that we should stop and get Riprap something—maybe a pastry. He's going to need cheering up."

Brenda tried to remember whether or not people with head injuries were supposed to fast, then decided it didn't matter. The gesture was what would count, and with so many people in the house, no food ever went to waste.

"Sure," she said. "How about that German place?"

"Strudel," Flying Claw answered in a tone of voice that made clear he approved. "Cherry or apple."

"Or both," Brenda said.

They laughed. At moments like this, Brenda could almost forget he wasn't the Foster with whom she'd shared so many long walks.

So, get to know this guy, idiot!

"I'll call Pearl," she said, "so they know we'll be a little behind schedule."

"Give me the phone," he said. "You shouldn't use the cell phone and drive."

After the call was made and they were congratulated on their idea, Brenda said, "You know, I realized the other day that even though we talked so much, back—back when you still lived with us—I still don't know much about you. You mentioned having siblings. How many? Are you really close?"

"Five." Flying Claw considered for a moment. "We are—and we aren't. I went into training so young that in some ways we didn't have a lot in common. On the other hand, when I came home, they always made me welcome. I enjoyed my visits, and felt very proud when my older sister began to earn fame for the family through her gifts."

"What did you do when you went home?" Brenda asked. "Feasts, I guess, but what else?"

"Kite flying," Flying Claw said. "If the winds were with us, and—later, when I had some training—even when the winds were not. Through the grace and sacrifice of Thundering Heaven, my family had retained a good deal of land, but not all of it was suited for planting or even for grazing. No one minded a wind out of season there."

He went on, talking happily about a marvelous kite he and his brothers had labored over for most of one long holiday, refining and rebalancing it so that it seemed to fly almost of itself. Brenda liked the happiness in his voice, and was definitely sorry when they arrived at the pastry shop.

The mood did not break there, however. Fresh strudel was just out of the ovens, and Brenda decided that her bank account—which was actually pretty solid because she had so few expenses and Pearl was paying her what she would have earned at a summer job—would stand to large strips of both cherry and apple.

She saw Flying Claw licking his lips, and grinned.

"We don't want to eat Riprap's present. Want to have a piece for the road?"

He had cherry. She did, too, although the apple, perfectly spiced with cinnamon, smelled great. They carried the pieces out to tables on a little sidewalk terrace in front of the store, him with a Styrofoam cup of tea, her with coffee.

The strudel was delicious. Brenda was sorry that the buttery pastry melted into nothing so quickly—sorrier still that they really should get over to Pearl's. She drank the last of her coffee, and dusted powdered sugar and flakes of pastry off her shirt.

"Ready?" she asked as Flying Claw looked up from dusting himself off.

"I am," he said, bending to pick up the white boxes holding the strudel.

They walked to where the car was parked around the corner, both suddenly quiet, but not in the least uncomfortable.

As Brenda unlocked the passenger-side door, then stepped back, she was aware that Flying Claw was watching her intently.

"What's wrong?"

He smiled. "You have a little sugar on your nose. It's very cute, but you probably don't want it there."

She reached to brush it off, but he caught her hand with his one free one, the move so quick she couldn't have dodged if she wanted to.

And she didn't.

"I'll get it," Flying Claw said. For a long moment, he stared into her eyes. Then he reached up and gently rubbed the tip of her nose. "There. Perfect."

Brenda held her breath, hoping, fearing he'd kiss her, but Flying Claw only smiled and slid into the car.

"Come on," he said. "The pastry is getting cold."

And I, Brenda thought, *suddenly feel very, very hot.*

XXI

"Are you sure that going to practice is a good idea?" Nissa asked Riprap the next morning. "I mean, so soon after you were hurt."

Pearl covered her mouth with her hand to hide a completely unexpected smile, but she didn't blame Nissa for her question. Riprap's head, neatly shaven in a long strip to expose the slice the edge of Waking Lizard's sword had put into his scalp, was rather ugly-looking. Yesterday, when Riprap had returned from Dr. Andersen's office, Lani had taken one look at him and burst into shocked sobs.

The little girl had adjusted by now, and even seemed to find the stitches fascinating. Nissa looked less certain.

"No sign of concussion," Riprap said. "No bleeding. Not even a leak. Deborah will be there. She's a trained nurse and has promised to sit on me if she thinks I'm overdoing it."

Nissa didn't argue, but Pearl noticed she kept looking very thoughtfully at the wound. When her gaze wandered over to Brenda's midsection, then to Lani, Pearl was certain of her train of thought.

Please don't back out now, Nissa. Please! We need every one of us.

But Nissa said nothing, and as Brenda, Des, and Deborah joined them around the table, Nissa joined in the conversation naturally enough that Pearl let her apprehensions fade away.

You're worried about how the Horse will react, Pearl thought. *Don't project those worries onto the others.*

"Where's Shen?" Brenda asked.

"He's out checking on our prisoners," Pearl said.

"Is it safe for him to go alone?" Riprap asked, half rising.

Pearl made a motion as if to push the big man down into his seat. "Relax. Shen is very careful—and our prisoners respect him as the Dragon."

"Okay," Riprap said, but Pearl thought he didn't look convinced. She decided to distract him. "We're going to try to summon the Horse in just a few hours."

"Are you certain you don't want us here?" Des said.

"Absolutely. Albert will bring Honey Dream and Righteous Drum over with him. Nissa will be in the house in case of emergency. Otherwise, the fewer distractions the better."

About an hour after Riprap, Des, Deborah, and Brenda left, Albert arrived with Honey Dream and Righteous Drum. Greetings were exchanged.

"The others were still going at it on the practice field when we left," Albert said with a grin.

"Did Riprap's head seem to be bothering him at all?" Nissa asked anxiously.

"Not if the way he was going after Flying Claw was any indication. They were both wearing some sort of helmets— riding or bicycle, I think, I didn't get close enough to look—so they're taking yesterday's accident seriously."

Righteous Drum, who had moved to carry a small bag into Pearl's office, now emerged again into the foyer.

"I believe they are. They have decided that purely physical protections are a good addition to spells, especially since although Riprap can work protective charms if he has time to concentrate, he is not swift enough to do so when the situation calls for quick response."

Pearl noticed Honey Dream's lovely upper lip curl in a slight sneer, but didn't comment. If Honey Dream hadn't yet learned that real courage involved doing something even when you weren't sure you were completely safe, then nothing Pearl could say would change the young Snake's mind.

Instead, Pearl offered refreshments. All declined politely, wishing to avoid the distraction that pressure from a nagging bladder would offer.

Those who would be participating in the summoning ritual retired into Pearl's office to begin the rituals of purification.

Pearl paused before following, sensing that Nissa wanted to speak with her.

"Lani's outside with Wong. I have a book, but is it okay if I use my phone or hook up a computer? I haven't checked in back home in a day or so."

"Absolutely," Pearl assured her. "I don't expect we will need to call on you. Just don't do any spells. We might as well avoid conflicting ch'i currents."

"That's not a problem," Nissa said. "Good luck."

As Righteous Drum had predicted, the purifications went smoothly now that everyone knew their parts. At the beginning of the Double Hour of the Horse, Shen struck the chime, motioning for Pearl and Honey Dream to come forward and light the red candles.

The introductory prayers were tailored to their subject, and Pearl made herself listen to every word, every note of Shen's voice rising and falling as he recited them, knowing her concentration would add to their persuasiveness.

When Albert came forward and lit the large bundle of

incense in front of the Exile Horse's portrait, she realized she was holding her breath and forced herself to breathe in and out, encouraging the ch'i within her body to circulate and gain strength.

Kneeling on the cushion in front of the altar, Albert invoked the ghost of the Horse in much the same words he had used for the Ox. Not a single word revealed the uncertainty he had confided in Pearl when he had called her that morning.

"What if we can't find a guide? What if the behavior of my father and grandfather has alienated the Ancestors from us?"

"We'll manage," Pearl had said with complete confidence. Not articulating the thought of what that failure might mean. *Even if we fail, we'll manage.*

The ghost of the Horse manifested swiftly, showing no trace of the eddying hesitation Exile Ox had shown. Pearl reflected how the Horse—like the Tiger—was a warrior sign. What was the Bible quote? "He saith among the trumpets. Ha! Ha!"? Eager for action was the Horse.

Pearl Bright had never known the Horse. Loyal Wind had died before the Orphans had left mainland China, first for Japan, later for the United States. Nor were there any photographs of him, for he had died when the Orphans were still very much wanderers. She watched as the smoke took shape, wondering how closely he would resemble the ink-brush portraits Des had found in his great grandmother's portfolio.

Her first reaction was surprise at how young Loyal Wind was—only in his early sixties. Influenced by her father's stories, in which the Horse was the wise war leader whose death had been a horrible shock, one which had forced Thundering Heaven into prominence, Pearl had forgotten that when Loyal Wind had died, he had been over a decade younger than she herself was now.

The Exile Horse was not precisely handsome, not in the way Flying Claw was or her father had been, but there was a strength of character to him, a firmness in the lines etched on his face that spoke of decisiveness. He wore a mustache and a small chin beard, not a goatee, but a slight ornamental tuft. His armor resembled Flying Claw's—although the cut was that for a calvary man, not a foot soldier.

"You have called me," the ghost said, "and I come both as duty bound and in thanks for the offerings that have made my afterlife bearable. Why do you call?"

"We seek your aid, Honored Ancestor," Albert said, bowing deeply, then rising so he might address the ghost face-to-face—a choice that emphasized that although he was supplicant, he was also emperor.

"My aid? What aid can a dead man be?"

Albert explained, thoroughly and carefully, yet his earnestness creating of his words a type of poetry.

But the ghost of Loyal Wind did not seem to be swayed.

"So finally, after these many years," Loyal Wind said when Albert finished, "you are ready to fulfill the task your ancestors set for you—and not because you are dutiful, but because you dread a threat to this world—a world your father or your father's father should have forsaken long ago?"

The ghost was shaking with barely repressed fury.

"I gave up the one true love of my life because I believed in that goal. I accepted her belief that our—or at the very least our descendants'—return to the Lands Born from Smoke and Sacrifice was more important than our private happiness. And you tell me this is the end result—over a century later our descendants are still in exile, and some, my own included, were permitted to fall from adherence to our task because it began to seem unimportant?"

Loyal Wind clenched his fists at his side, and to her astonished horror, Pearl saw that he was transforming. No longer did the semblance of an entire man stand before them, but one horribly and mortally wounded. Loyal Wind no longer wore armor, but worn, baggy trousers and loose smock, such as a working man might wear. His left arm was missing from the elbow down. Blood streamed from a gash on his right thigh. More blood ran from a cut on his brow, flowing across his face, staining his teeth red as it flowed into his mouth.

When he spoke bloody spittle accompanied each word.

"And you wish me to help you? I gave my love. I gave my life. What more do you want of me?"

Pearl pushed herself to her feet, using Treaty—still sheathed—as a support, for she wasn't so young that she could kneel for long without some stiffness settling in her knees. She stood with her head held high, legs slightly spread, Treaty's point pressed into the carpet between her feet.

"What do we want?" she echoed. "Perhaps nothing, seeing what you have become. My father taught me to honor and respect you. You were the paragon against whom he balanced his every action. While your son was but an infant, my father had to be not only Tiger, but Horse—and he took on those responsibilities gladly."

Loyal Wind narrowed his eyes, as if he were seeing her for the first time. "What are you? A female Tiger? Abomination!"

"So my father thought," Pearl agreed, "and yet I have remained faithful despite that."

"Empty faith to a cause never pursued," Loyal Wind sneered.

"Perhaps. Perhaps you would have felt differently if you had lived, but looking upon you, I believe what I heard whispered is true."

"Whispered?"

"When I was a small child," Pearl said, "many of the Exiles were still alive. Everyone talks around children as if they are idiots, even more so when that child is despised and rejected by her own father. I was not an idiot, and I liked to listen. I heard the stories—speculation that your death had not been a tragedy, but an act of cowardice, a selfish suicide that destroyed others' hopes."

"I did not suicide! I died in honorable battle."

"Did you?" Pearl challenged.

"I did!"

"I heard you sought that fight out of jealousy. Look at yourself. Where is your armor? Where are your lance and sword?"

"I . . ."

"You sought your death," Pearl said. "We see the evidence before us."

She softened her tones, becoming conversational but no less relentless. "You may have thought your death did not matter, but you left the Exiles with an infant to coddle, rather than a warrior to lead.

"Your heir did well enough. The Rooster made sure he did not go either unloved or untaught. He lived a long life—long enough to watch his own son die of cancer—but without your guidance, he was always a follower, never a leader. Unlike the Exile Rooster's daughter and heir—who taught both son and then grandson—your heir had no one to instill in him belief in the cause."

"I didn't . . ." the ghost protested, but his wounds still bled and his protest was empty.

"My father didn't much like having me as his heir apparent," Pearl said, "but at least he didn't leave me untaught, at least he never left his responsibilities to others.

"You turned tail and ran. Now when we come to you, offering you a chance to redeem the honor you so besmirched, you have the gall to act as if we are the beggars. You should be kissing the young emperor's feet, weeping in thanks that he is willing to offer you a chance at redemption!"

Loyal Wind stared at her, and as he did, the wounds on his body began to close. He still wore the ragged peasant's costume in which he had died and the raw cuts were visible through the tears, but the bleeding had stopped.

Movements stately, he went onto his knees and bowed, first to Albert, and then—to Pearl's astonishment—to her. Still kneeling, he raised his head to look at them.

"Now I know," he said, "why we fear female tigers. They are indeed ruthless."

Pearl wanted to apologize for hurting him so deeply, but

then she remembered—her words had actually stopped the bleeding. There was no lying to oneself after death. Loyal Wind must have had a terrible afterlife, sustained by offerings from those he had betrayed.

Albert held out a hand, motioning for Loyal Wind to rise. "Will you join us, Loyal Wind? Or if you cannot bear to do so, will you at least consider retaking your bond with the Horse so that the Exiles may at last return home?"

"I will," Loyal Wind said, still kneeling, "be your guide, and I will help you to make your thirteen complete, so that the ninth gate can be opened, the unwilling exiles returned home, and perhaps your homes and families secured, as we once sought to secure our homes and families. This I swear, on the Horse I once was, on the warrior I will again be."

Pearl heard a muffled sob, and glancing over saw to her surprise that it came from Honey Dream. The young woman's eyes were not the only ones that shone with tears. Shen was frankly weeping, tears coursing down his face, but he made no move to wipe them away, nor to protect the costly embroidered satin of his shenyi.

Albert, however, had maintained a stern dignity worthy of an emperor. "I accept your service, and welcome you into our company. My son, I welcome you home."

☆

The triumph that burbled through their company as the news spread that the Exile Horse had agreed to assist them sustained everyone until evening when they all assembled on Pearl's back patio to finalize the next stage of their plans.

By then Honey Dream, at least, was feeling very apprehensive. She'd heard some of what her father and Shen had been discussing, and didn't like it at all.

As was right and proper in a matter that so involved magic, the two Dragons assumed charge.

"We believe," Shen said, "that we have come up with the best possible means of connecting the Nine Yellow Springs to our Nine Gates—best because if done correctly, connecting each gate and each spring will not involve separate journeys into the underworld."

"That's a relief," Riprap said. "I'm not crazy about going to Hell once, much less nine separate times."

"But you will go if this is needed?" Righteous Drum asked.

"Absolutely," Riprap assured him. "What's the plan?"

Righteous Drum looked at Shen, who nodded for him to continue.

"By now, none of you need to be told that words have power," Righteous Drum began, "but those of you who were not reared within the culture to which we all share an ancestral link may not realize that this power extends into puns—especially puns based upon homonyms."

"Words that sound alike," Brenda muttered, as if reminding herself.

Honey Dream restrained a desire to roll her eyes. She didn't like certain elements of this plan in the least, and only by acting as reasonable as possible could she hope to amend them.

"Words that sound alike," Righteous Drum agreed. "I will leave Desperate Lee the task of explaining the finer aspects of the various Chinese languages, and ask you to simply accept that in tonal languages, the opportunities for such puns are nearly infinite.

" 'Men'—meaning 'gate' or 'door'—actually has fewer associated sounds than many other words, but there is one that is particular significant for our needs, for 'men' can also mean 'family.' "

Des nodded. "Probably because those within your gate or door would be considered your family."

"Quite possibly," Righteous Drum agreed. "This is a very good relationship for our needs, because what we will do when we have arrived at the Nine Yellow Springs is request that they make a 'men' or 'family' with the 'men' that are the Nine Gates. The fact that this 'men'-to-'men' relationship is needed to enable the gates to function as a 'men' or family-group of gates makes the association particularly potent."

Honey Dream glanced around, hoping someone would protest, but no one—not even Riprap—had a question.

Shen took over. "We've worked through who should go on the expedition to the Nine Yellow Springs. With the Exile Horse's assistance, this may not be as dangerous a journey as some of you are imagining."

"You mean it's easy to get to Hell?" Riprap said with a somewhat forced grin.

"Put that word from your head," Shen advised. "The old commentators may have translated the Chinese terms for the afterlife as 'Hell' or 'Hades,' but they were usually expressing their own cultural bias. Christians do not have the concept of an afterlife that is not a paradise or a punishment."

"Okay, afterlife," Riprap repeated dutifully. "But it's easy to get there? How about getting out?"

Des answered, "In Chinese folktales, the afterlife was often easy to reach—sometimes in dreams, others by means of spells. Getting out often was as easy as waking up or reversing the spell."

Riprap nodded and looked a bit abashed. "Okay. I'll stop worrying. Who's on the team to seek the Nine Yellow Springs?"

Shen began ticking off on his fingers. "Since this spell will involve family, and since fortuitously we have both Orphans who represent the House of Family, we would like you and Deborah—as Dog and Pig—to go."

"Right," Riprap said.

"Count me in," Deborah agreed.

"Since we are constructing a link," Shen went on, "we wanted at least one representative of the House of Construction. The Ox is out, and Gaheris Morris cannot be here by tomorrow—which is when the auguries say we should set out. Therefore, we're going to ask Brenda Morris to stand in."

Honey Dream thought Brenda looked a little pale, but her

nod was decisive enough as she said, "If you think I can do it, I'll be happy to go."

Shen nodded. "We would like a representative of the House of Expansion as well, since we are seeking to expand our connection between the Lands and this world. A Tiger would be best, since we will be linking our first gate, which is into the realm of the White Tiger of the West. I've discussed this at length with Pearl, and since it is essential the Lands be well represented in this project, she has nominated Flying Claw."

Flying Claw inclined his head in a gesture that was half a nod, half a bow of respect to the senior Tiger, but otherwise he did not speak.

"Finally," Shen said, "a representative of the House of Mystery would be best, because the House of Mystery rules magical lore. Righteous Drum and I discussed this, and I have agreed that he would be best, since in this way the Lands will have two representatives and in any . . ."

Honey Dream could not restrain herself any longer.

"This cannot be!" she said. "Father, have you forgotten that you are missing an arm? You cannot craft spells as you once did. Let me go in your place! The Snake also represents the House of Mystery."

Immediately, Honey Dream knew her timing had been all wrong—as had her words. Not only had she interrupted an elder, she had reminded her father that he was weak. His eyes flared and his frown was as lowering thunderclouds.

"I am perfectly capable," Righteous Drum said very coldly, "of doing all that will be expected of me. If you had permitted Shen Kung to finish his explanation, you would also have heard that since the Nine Springs are water, and water has been associated since time immemorial with Dragons, a Dragon would add to our chances of success."

Honey Dream swallowed hard, and Righteous Drum continued, his voice hard.

"Additionally, the Snake is a yin sign. This is a yang undertaking. Kindly note that other than in the House of

Family, where we are blessed with both elements, our choices have all been made to emphasize yang."

Honey Dream did not let her gaze flicker to Brenda—that female associated with a yang sign. The Orphans violated all that was right. If she mentioned this, she would risk incurring Pearl Bright's anger, and after the old woman's performance last night, no one could doubt her suitability for her affiliation.

Besides, Honey Dream must not let anyone realize how much she did not wish Brenda to go, or if Brenda must be included, that someone be there to make certain she did not have her way with Flying Claw.

"Father," Honey Dream pleaded, hoping that some of the Snake's legendary diplomacy would stir her father to compromise, "I stand corrected. May I most humbly request to accompany you, to balance you as yin does yang throughout the cosmos?"

Righteous Drum shook his head, but he looked less angry. "No. I must refuse you. Shen Kung and I have spent many hours today working calculations. The chances for success in this expedition are greater if the count of both the living and the dead are odd numbers."

In response to the confused expression on the three apprentices' faces, Des said, "Odd numbers are yang. Even numbers are yin. Yang is associated with expansion, aggression. Yin with sustaining and maintaining."

Righteous Drum smiled at Honey Dream, and she saw he wished to comfort her. "When we have our gates established and linked, my daughter, then yin will be needed to supply the balance. This time you shall remain here and assist with researching what might be threatening Pai Hu. You can also keep watch on the prisoners."

Honey Dream could see that arguing would be useless, so she bowed her head in what she hoped would seem appropriate submission. "Hoped" because inwardly she was seething.

* * *

Honey Dream was still seething when some hours later she returned to Colm Lodge with her father, Waking Lizard, and Flying Claw.

Watching Flying Claw get his gear ready in the living room, or listening to Waking Lizard shower the Tiger with advice about what to do if he ran into this demon or that evil spirit, did not make Honey Dream feel any calmer.

But what made Honey Dream feel worst was what she found when she went by her father's room. She had hoped to convince him to reconsider, to argue that aggression was amply represented, that as the ghost of Exile Horse would be solitary—and therefore yang—it would be better if the living group was yin. In short, all the arguments she thought of after the meeting had broken up.

Righteous Drum's door had swung open when she knocked, and Honey Dream had stepped in. The room was empty, but she could hear water running behind the closed bathroom door, and knew where her father was.

On the table in front of the window rested ink, brush, and a sheet of paper partially written upon. Seeing the characters for her own name at the top, naturally, Honey Dream read further.

"My daughter, Waking Lizard will give this to you if I do not return . . ."

Embarrassed, hearing the flow of water cease, horrified at the possibility of being discovered snooping, Honey Dream fled. Down the stairs and out the front door she went, out into the heat of the summer night.

She thought she heard Waking Lizard calling after her, and yelled back, "I'm fine, just stretching my legs."

She ran down the long graveled driveway, wanting to flee this place, wishing she could outrun the roiling emotions that conflicted in her liver.

Fear for her father, anger that if he doubted he would return, how could he go at all.

Love for Flying Claw, misery at her suspicion that he had never loved her as she did him.

Resentment at not being sufficiently respected, insecurity that she had not done enough to earn that respect.

These carried her through the darkness, making her feet light, giving her ears to hear the voice that called to her from just outside of the wards that surrounded Colm Lodge and its grounds.

"Hello, Honey Dream," a man's voice said, speaking her name in Chinese flavored with the accent of a local speaker. "The omens told me this meeting might occur this evening, and here you are."

The speaker sounded very pleased with himself, but Honey Dream was very tired of men who were confident and pleased with themselves.

"What of it?" she hissed. "So you say, but also you could have been standing here since we returned. Spying . . ."

"My omens told me you would be irritable," the voice said.

Honey Dream followed the voice and saw the shadowy figure of a tall man dressed in the ugly tailored suits that were formal wear for men in this horrible land. He stood among the trees that bordered the road, and she suspected he was visible neither from the road, nor from Colm Lodge.

"Franklin Deng," she said. "What do you want?"

"Irritable," Deng chuckled, "but also very clever. I had, however, expected more subtlety from the Snake."

"Perhaps I wish you to underestimate me," Honey Dream said, amused despite herself.

She was interested, too. Up until this point, she had relied on the reports of the others as to the nature of their adversaries—"competitors" might be a better term. She had not doubted the truth of what had been said—Snakes were very good at hearing outright falsehoods—but she had suspected bias.

"You have gone to great trouble to make yourself available

for this meeting," she said politely. "While I will not invite you within our wards, I can extend you the courtesy of listening to what you have to say."

"Thank you, Gracious Lady," Deng said, and she saw him bow. "It is useless to hide that I have desires, goals of my own. What, however, may not have been accurately represented to you and your associates from the Lands Born from Smoke and Sacrifice is how those goals are associated with your own."

"Oh?" Honey Dream put an inviting lilt into her voice.

"Yes. You desire to return to your homeland, and to defeat those who have upset you from your rightfully earned places there. I seek to redress the imbalance to my world that came into it with the advent of the Thirteen Orphans."

"I," Honey Dream replied, "was told that what you desired was to learn how to work the Orphans' peculiar form of magic."

"That is Tracy Frye's goal," Deng said dismissively. "She collects magic as magpies collect bright trinkets—and cares not whether what she finds are diamonds or broken glass as long as they sparkle."

Honey Dream heard both truth and lie in this—Franklin Deng was not as indifferent to the Orphans' magic as he would have her believe, but he also was honest when he spoke of concern regarding an imbalance.

"What do you wish of me?" she said. "Of me and my associates from the Lands?"

"Make me your ally," he replied promptly. "To this point, you and your associates have been forced to cooperate with the Orphans because you need them to return home. This has meant that you must accept them as equals, let them dictate your policy, when actually they should serve you, and return to you the power their ancestors stole from the Lands."

"And you would change this how?"

"By putting the greater weight on your side of the balance."

"We are already allied to the Orphans, our alliance sealed by treaties so complex that breaking them would likely be fatal."

"I am not asking for you to break those treaties, only to make new ones—ones that would make you the more powerful."

Honey Dream thought of her earlier dreams—especially that of severing the ties between the ghost Orphans and their heirs. Having met the Ox and the Horse, she could now see that managing this severance might not be as simple as she had thought. Franklin Deng offered an alternative, a very attractive alternative. When Waking Lizard had initially brought the news that they had been ousted from the Lands, their party defeated, it had seemed that an alliance with the Orphans was their only option if they hoped to return home.

Now Honey Dream could see that in their shock they had acted rashly, had let Pearl Bright, then Tigerishly confident in the flush of her victory over Righteous Drum, carry her aggression onto a new battlefield.

Even so, this was not the time to act hastily, not now. Honey Dream had learned that much at least.

"I will consider," she said loftily, and turned away.

"Consider," Deng said, not raising his voice, but the words penetrating seemingly to her soul. "But not for too long. Time is running short, and you don't want to be on the losing side, do you?"

Honey Dream did not deign reply, but moved without lingering—but also without haste—up the driveway.

Behind her, she heard a faint laugh, followed by the slamming of a car's door, the rumble as the engine caught, and its purr as it pulled onto the blacktop and eased away.

XXII

As before, their point of departure was Pearl's warehouse. The Men Shen permitted them passage, apparently with Pai Hu's approval, for this time the transition was as simple as stepping over the raw pine lintel from concrete onto grass.

The White Tiger of the West was not there to greet them, but Loyal Wind, the Exile Horse, was. A large, lightly armored chestnut horse stood to one side of the pine door, cropping grass. For a startled moment, Brenda thought this was their guide, then Loyal Wind rose from where he had been sitting, leaning back against the trunk of a tree. Although he was a ghost, here he seemed as solid as any of them.

Like his horse, Loyal Wind was armored. His mustache and light chin beard did not conceal a certain sternness to his features. His eyes narrowed in assessment—and perhaps criticism—as he surveyed their small group. Brenda wondered what he thought of them.

Flying Claw and Righteous Drum were both dressed as appropriate for those of their calling in the Lands—Flying Claw in armor, Righteous Drum in pale yellow long tunic and baggy trousers, heavily embroidered with propitious signs and sigils.

In contrast, Brenda, Deborah, and Riprap were dressed for hiking. Riprap wore cargo pants, Brenda and Deborah jeans. On top, all wore layers, because Righteous Drum had admitted he had no idea what sort of weather they might encounter on their way to Hell. The two women carried light packs, Riprap one slightly heavier, but they'd left behind most of the camping gear they'd carried during their earlier "field trip," since the plan was not to linger longer than would be necessary to carry out their task.

However, if Loyal Wind found their choice of clothing at

all strange, he did not comment. Righteous Drum made introductions, concluding by bowing to the ghost.

"And now, honored Horse, where shall we begin?"

"Since the Yellow Springs give rise to the river that carries the suns west to east beneath the Earth, there are two places from which those in the upper world may access the Suns' River—the farthest east and the farthest west. Since we are in the West, we shall seek out the western opening. From there, we will journey alongside the river eastward, to where the Nine Yellow Springs are to be found."

Righteous Drum was frowning, the expression thoughtful rather than angry.

"The farthest west is a great distance away, Loyal Wind. Time is not to be wasted."

"I had thought of that," Loyal Wind said. He gave a low whistle and the turf beneath Brenda's hiking boots shook with the rhythm of galloping hooves. The chestnut raised his head from grazing, and Brenda noticed that although the horse wore a saddle, it wore neither bit nor bridle, the sole purpose of its halter being to support the armor that protected its head.

"I have recruited," Loyal Wind said, "horses to carry us swiftly to our destination."

Brenda thought she heard an odd inflection in how Loyal Wind pronounced "horses," but decided it was some fluke of the translation spell that enabled her to understand the Chinese of the Lands. Flying Claw apparently also heard that odd note, for he looked between the approaching horses and Loyal Wind, his brow knit in consternation.

"You say horses," he said. "Then these are not merely the spirits of some noble steeds, drawn from the pastures of the afterlife?"

"No," Loyal Wind said. "For this task, we will need more than even the great courage embodied in the spirits of once-mortal warhorses. I have called along the lines to those who once served the same Earthly Branch with which I had the honor of being affiliated. They will summon the winds beneath their hooves to give us speed. Nor will they shy or be afraid as even the bravest mortal horse must be in the places we must go."

Brenda didn't know whether this encouraged her or not.

Deborah looked up at the pale grey with charcoal-black mane and tail who had come to stand before her.

"Loyal Wind, I'm no great rider. In fact, I think the last time I was on a horse was at my granddaughter's birthday party, and let me tell you, the horse was in charge, then, not me."

Loyal Wind's stern face twitched in the slightest of smiles, as his gaze rested on Deborah's rounded, fireplug figure.

"Do not worry, Grandmother Pig. These horses are prepared to take charge in this case as well. They understand your goal and wholly approve."

The horse that walked over to Brenda and blew gentle inquiry into her face had a coat of pale, shimmering gold. Its flowing mane and tail were silvery white. Brenda had never been as horse-crazy as some girls, but as she reached out to tentatively stroke the horse along the wide white blaze that ran from its forelock to above its muzzle, she thought this horse might convert her.

"Do we just mount?" she asked, looking at the horse's very intelligent brown eyes, and feeling distinctly weird at the idea of climbing on the back of what had once been a man. "Aren't we doing introductions or something?"

Loyal Wind's mouth twitched in what was definitely a smile. "Certainly. He says to call him 'Leaf.'"

"Was that his name?"

"A nickname. Now, mount up. As Righteous Drum has reminded us, we have no time to waste."

Flying Claw walked over to Brenda, his own mount, a bright blood bay without a trace of white, trailing him with evident curiosity.

"I'll help you up," he said. "Since there are saddlebags, you might as well split the stuff from your pack between them. Both you and the horse will be more comfortable. You can put your water bottle here, where you can easily reach it."

He showed her, moving efficiently, but without the least condescension.

Why should he condescend? Brenda thought to distract herself as he helped her get into the saddle. *We've shown him everything from how to flush a toilet to how to open a bottle of liquid soap.*

Riprap had declined offered assistance, saying that he regularly led trail rides back in Colorado.

"The saddle's different," he said, "but the horse is a whole lot more cooperative."

He clapped the bulky liver chestnut that was his assigned mount on one shoulder as he said this, then looked embarrassed.

"Sorry. I guess that's not exactly polite."

Loyal Wind smiled, more easily this time. "Regard is never impolite, especially when coming from a giant who might be out of legend. Forgive me if I stare, but I have never seen skin so dark, nor hair that curls tightly as yours does."

Riprap shrugged. "I guess I'd better get used to stares if we are going to the Lands one of these days, but then I guess all of us had better do so. Nissa's turquoise eyes and blond hair aren't going to be any more common than my particular oddities."

"No," Righteous Drum agreed. He had managed to get into the saddle of his own mount, a handsome dapple grey, although with some awkwardness due to his missing arm. "I have considered whether or not we might use your varied physical appearances to our advantage someday, but that is not a consideration for now."

"No," Loyal Wind said, mounting his own horse. As soon as he was in the saddle, the horse started walking, presumably west. "Not for now. We will travel for a short while at a normal pace, but as there is not a moment to be lost, my associates and I will ask you to trust us."

Brenda thought she heard Deborah mutter, "Do we have a

choice?" but when she glanced over, the Pig's expression was tranquil, even interested as she glanced around at their surroundings.

"Have you ever been in the guardian domains before, Deborah?" she asked.

"I haven't," Deborah said. "The Pig is the most home-loving of all the signs of the zodiac, and I guess I'm a good Pig. I've never felt the urge to venture far. I should have tried sooner. This is incredibly beautiful."

"And it hasn't even gotten strange yet," Brenda said. "Just wait until you see a fish with a dog's head or a unicorn. Then you'll really know you're somewhere else."

Gradually, their pace increased. Brenda felt the breeze tugging loose little tendrils from where she'd pulled her hair back into a twist. Her horse's gait was smooth, especially once they increased their pace beyond a trot, then, without warning, it became smoother still. The sound of her horse's hooves hitting the turf vanished between one stride and the next. When Brenda looked down, she saw the pale golden horse was running a good foot above the ground.

She stifled an "eep" of surprise, but saw Flying Claw grinning at her sideways. She grinned back.

"This is cool," she said, "and a whole lot more comfortable, but Mr. Loyal Wind, are we really going fast enough that we'll get to this farthest west without having to ride for weeks?"

"We are," Loyal Wind said. "Not only are we going as fast as these tireless horses can carry us, but the winds are also carrying us. Because we are upon the winds, you will only be aware of the speed of the horse, but we will be moving faster by far."

They were also moving higher. Her horse's hooves were brushing the tops of trees, their dark green jungle foliage tossing as the winds passed over them.

Conversation was possible because there was no engine noise, nor did the rushing winds that carried them roar in their ears. Righteous Drum took the opportunity to lecture them about some of what they might encounter once they entered the afterlife. Although Brenda did her best to concentrate, she found her attention wandering.

It's just that even though I'm riding a horse above the treetops, this is all so unreal. I feel like I'm going to wake up any minute now.

Her sense of unreality was not helped in the least when Leaf turned his head to one side, fixed her with a warm, brown gaze that was somehow familiar, and started talking to her.

"You must succeed," the horse said. "The situation is far worse than you imagine."

"What?" Brenda said. Only tremendous effort on her part kept her from saying something stupid like, "Were you talking to me?"

She glanced around, but although they were riding in a loose diamond formation, with her between Flying Claw and Riprap, Righteous Drum ahead and Deborah behind, no one seemed to have noticed either her or the pale golden horse's words. Indeed, Righteous Drum had not paused in his tale of Yu the Great and his apparently endless battles against a water demon called Gong-Gong.

Then Brenda remembered she'd heard this voice once before, only that time it had spoken to her from a pool.

The speaker had been a woman then, but Brenda supposed that if she could handle a species shift, why should a little thing like gender bother her?

She'd always hated stories where the characters spent a lot of time refusing to believe what they were in the middle of—and anyhow, if she was going crazy, not believing it wasn't going to change anything.

"Far worse?" she said, hoping she sounded conversational. "Would you like to tell me about it? Oh, and shouldn't you watch where you're going?"

"Only if it makes you more comfortable," Leaf said, and politely turned his head forward. "I will explain, but I am going to ask you not to tell the others—not yet."

"I'm not sure I'm comfortable with that," Brenda said. "Why can't I tell them?"

"Because then time will be wasted," Leaf replied. "Right now, the course you are following seems the best one by far. Establishing the Nine Gates and assisting Pai Hu to find the reason for his disturbing nightmare are both very necessary."

Brenda remembered how Pearl and the others could talk and talk, sometimes to no end, and reluctantly nodded.

"Okay. That's reassuring in a way, I mean, since you say we're doing the right things. But who are you and why should I trust what you're saying to me?"

"I am one who has a long association with your family—your maternal family, not your paternal family."

"And so I should trust you?"

The pale golden horse shuddered his skin, and Brenda felt reprimanded. She decided to back off, but she also promised herself that she'd reserve judgment.

"Tell me about why things are worse than we imagine," she suggested.

Leaf seemed mollified. "Righteous Drum and his associates believed that their overthrow was simply one among the many coups that have occurred in the history of the Jade Petal Throne. It is, and it is not. Those who overthrew their emperor had allies, dangerous allies. Already, they are regretting the alliance."

"Why are you telling me this?" Brenda asked, "especially since you don't want me to tell anyone?"

"Because someone should know," Leaf said. "Someone should be warned. Our people are aware of this danger, because in times past these dangerous allies have been our enemies. We have kept a watch on them, and are fearful of what will happen if they succeed in their current efforts. They will not forget our old wars, especially when they become more powerful."

"Why not tell . . ." Brenda began, heard the whine of protest in her voice, and stopped. She breathed deeply a few times, organizing her thoughts. "And I'm a good someone to tell, because you can get in touch with me. And because I'm also tied to the Thirteen Orphans, and the Thirteen Orphans are the only ones who—as far we know, at least—can get into the Lands, and the Lands are where these nasty allies of our enemies are currently invested."

"Very good. You have a Rat's keen mind."

"But you didn't tell my dad. You told me."

"Your father does not have the dual heritage. He is not of our blood—your mother is."

"My mom? She never . . . I mean, I didn't . . ."

"Your mother is a mortal woman, nothing more, but her heritage is interesting."

Brenda, remembering her great-aunt, a creepy old lady who smoked a pipe and really did seem to have the second sight, nodded. When Aunt Meara had been hit by a car, as she was crossing the street after church, they'd gone back to her house and found she'd left a copy of her will and notes as to her funeral arrangements neatly arrayed on the kitchen table.

Brenda rubbed her forehead and temples with her hands, smelling horse sweat and something that might have been her own fear.

"But you," she said. "You're one of the horses from the Lands, at least that's what Loyal Wind said. How can you be something else—your voice sounds sort of Irish? I mean, what's going on?"

"The afterlife is one of the few places where all worlds cross," Leaf said. "That's why you're using the Nine Yellow Springs to give ch'i to your gates, is it not?"

"That's what they said," Brenda admitted. "So did you just sort of sneak in?"

"I made an agreement. Horses are very important where I come from, far more than they ever were in China. There is a link I have exploited."

Something in the tone of voice—although Brenda was far from certain that either of them was actually speaking in the fashion she had accepted as "normal" until a few months ago—discouraged further inquiry.

"So you won't always be here. Sometimes this . . ." Brenda slapped the pale golden horse's shoulder, "is just a horse."

"A very interesting and unusual horse, but, yes . . ."

"Will you be back?"

"I might. I might not. You are warned, but do not look for help other than that warning. I a . . ."

Leaf's voice stopped in midword. There was a change in the quality of the rushing wind that told Brenda that no good would come from calling after.

What have I gotten into?

There was no answer, but then Brenda did not expect one.

They arrived at the opening to the western end of the Suns' River after long journeying through lands that grew increasingly strange the farther west they went.

From time to time, mists would rise, and the lands beneath them would vanish entirely. Brenda, recalling Pai Hu's nightmare, found herself imagining that there really was no solid ground there at all, only mist and beneath that mist, void.

But the wind-running horses always carried them beyond the mists, and there would be solid land—usually rich green, sometimes jungles, sometimes mountains, sometimes marsh planted with what Flying Claw told her was rice.

They camped several times, and each night Brenda's dreams were stranger. She never could remember them, but sometimes a word or gesture from one of her companions brought back a face or a few bars of music or a fragment of a scene, and she would find herself struggling to remember the rest.

The journey might have become tedious—even with the unusually fascinating experience of having Flying Claw as a companion—but that Righteous Drum took it upon himself to continue Brenda and Riprap's education. Deborah encouraged him, saying she could use a refresher. She had not dwelled on matters of the art of magic and the lore of the

Lands since the days when she had been teaching her own daughter.

Flying Claw also listened intently, and Brenda was reminded that the Tiger is a warrior. She suspected that he might appreciate some of the more exotic theories Righteous Drum—often with contributions from Loyal Wind—expounded.

But there might have been another reason entirely for the general attentiveness. Righteous Drum, pedantic in conference, proved to be an eloquent and fascinating teacher. Enthusiasm gave his tales of gods and monsters a vividness that listening to them from the back of a horse that ran upon the wind did nothing to diminish.

But none of his tales had prepared Brenda for the entrance to the underworld, to the place where the suns went when they set.

Righteous Drum had explained that the common belief was that there were many suns—sometimes nine, sometimes ten. They lived in a tree at the eastern edge of the world, and one at a time were chosen to rise.

Another story said that they rose in sequence, because the world was so vast that they grew tired from their long journey, that one was traveling under the earth while another was in the sky, and still others were resting.

A famous tale told how one day a mistake had been made, and all nine—or ten—of the suns had risen at once and had refused to set until Yi the Archer had shot them down. This action had gained him both the gratitude of the parched land and the peoples upon it, and the enmity of the suns' mother—or father—or the suns themselves.

"And which of these stories is true?" Brenda had asked.

"All of them, none of them," Righteous Drum had answered with a smile. "Reality—which is what you mean by 'truth' in this case—in the Lands Born from Smoke and Sacrifice is a very fluid concept. That fluidity carries over into the guardian domains, which take their shape from our version of reality, not the one of your world."

And Brenda had thought she was satisfied with this, even comfortable. After all, wasn't she having visions? Wasn't she riding on a horse that had talked to her? Wasn't that horse also a human hero whose achievements Righteous Drum had told them about all one long afternoon?

But she wasn't ready for the entrance into the Suns' River.

It began with a wide lake, an unnaturally round lake, the edges of which were bordered in fine-grained black sand, sand that suddenly changed to white about a foot from the shore. Despite the quantities of clear water—Brenda could see the sandy bottom as the golden horse carried her over—no plants grew around the edges, nor did any fish swim in the clear depths.

Although nothing appeared to feed the lake—not a river nor a stream marred the perfect black and white rings that surrounded its waters—the lakeshore did have one break. Its westernmost edge fell over the side of the world, down, cascading into infinity.

"The suns set here," Righteous Drum said conversationally, following the direction of her gaze. His tone was matter-of-fact, but his eyes were shining with wonder and delight. "That is why the sands are black around the edges. Even with the quenching of the water, the heat is so great that the sands are burned."

Loyal Wind glanced back to the east. "We have many hours before tonight's sun sets. I suggest we do not delay."

"We're going . . ." Brenda pointed to the edge. "There?"

"That is so," Loyal Wind said. "Did you expect the way into the underworld to be easy?"

"I . . . I guess not," Brenda managed, and she saw Flying Claw nod in approval. She took some comfort that Riprap and Deborah both looked at least as appalled as she felt.

"We're going over the edge," Deborah said. "I hope the horses are going with us."

"Oh, yes," Loyal Wind assured her. "They will remain."

"Good," Deborah said, and Brenda saw her twining her hands in the grey's dark mane. "Right. Shall we be at it then?

I don't think I can let myself think much more about this without screaming."

"Do we need to work any spells?" Riprap asked. "A Dragon's Tail or something to cushion us?"

"If we fall," Righteous Drum said, "no dragon's tail, nor host of dragon's tails would be cushion enough. We must trust to Loyal Wind and the guidance of his associates."

"Right," Riprap said, reaching behind him and making certain his saddlebags were laced tightly shut. "Right."

"Trust us," Loyal Wind said. "We will not let you fall."

And with those words he said something to the horses and all of them broke into a gentle canter. Looking down, Brenda saw the winds upon which they ran ruffling the placid waters of the clear lake. The horses broke into a gallop, tossing their manes and stretching out their necks as they ran.

The ruffles blended into ripples, and then one by one, the horses were turning, bending, going over the edge, falling, surrounded as they fell by air damp with warm spray, air that misted them entirely but never became heavy or sodden.

A scream tore from Brenda's throat, a scream part fear, part pure exhilaration, like she was riding the wildest, best roller coaster in all the universe. Brenda hung on, going with Leaf as he leapt over the edge of the world.

The horses were running, falling, down, down, ever, endlessly down, falling into infinity.

Or maybe not quite infinity. Shading her eyes and peering ahead, Brenda thought she saw another lake—smaller than the first, possibly, although that might only be distance. Mist billowed up from one edge of the lake's surface, and she realized that was where the waters from the first lake hit.

This second lake was also ringed in black, then white, but the black ring was smaller. Brenda guessed that the suns lost some of their heat from the first quenching and this long fall.

I wonder that the rushing air doesn't make them ignite, like when you blow on a coal. Or maybe I should be won-

dering why the force of the air doesn't blow the suns out?
The air is wet enough. Or maybe I should stop wondering
and just hold on. . . .

As they drew closer to the surface of the second lake, the
horses carried them away from the waterfall, circling lower
and lower, bearing them on a course that ran parallel to the
lake's surface, rather than taking them crashing into the
waters.

Now Brenda saw that on its eastern edge the lake over-
spilled, falling and rippling into cascades, cascades that in
turn became a river, a river that disappeared into the mouth
of a dark chasm, the rocky sides of which were melted from
the passage of ten thousand thousand suns.

"That's where we're going," she said, pointing ahead.

"That is," Loyal Wind said, "the headwaters of the Suns'
River."

"Looks pretty dark in there," Riprap said. "Anyone know if
a flashlight will work? I brought a couple, but I'm remembering how our watches stopped working when we went camping with Des."

Brenda could hear Riprap forcing himself to be calm and
matter-of-fact, though she knew he had to be at least as
freaked out as she was. She felt proud of him—of all of them.
Even Righteous Drum had never been through anything like
this before.

"Flashlights will be unnecessary," Righteous Drum said.
"I have prepared the means of lighting our way."

He glanced over at Loyal Wind, and the ghost inclined his
head. "This would be a good time," he said. "The sun does
not hold its passage for our convenience."

Righteous Drum nodded, and turned to the other four living members of their group. "If you don't mind? This spell
will not harm or restrict you in any way, but it will enable you
to see as if the sun was about an hour from setting."

"Enough light, then, that we shouldn't stumble or whack
our heads against the wall," Riprap said.

"That is so."

Deborah looked thoughtful, "And that is all the spell will do. Will you swear it on the Dragon?"

"I will, and do." Righteous Drum placed his hand on his midsection. Brenda had learned enough of the Chinese's odd association of certain emotions with certain organs to wonder if he was covering his heart, or maybe his liver. "By the Dragon, I swear that this spell will enable you to see in the dark, nothing more, and that your permitting me to use it in no way obligates you to me in any other way than we are already mutually obligated."

"Pretty," Deborah said, "especially for something you came up with on the spur of the moment."

"Actually," Flying Claw said, as Righteous Drum began tracing an elaborate series of gestures with his one remaining hand, "such oaths are common in the Lands."

"I guess they would be," Riprap mused. "A different world entirely."

Brenda watched carefully as Righteous Drum worked his spell, trying to understand the gestures. She thought she recognized something of the "All Green" that the Orphans used to see magical workings, but the recognition was on an instinctual, rather than certain, level. She might just be fooling herself.

However, Righteous Drum wasn't fooling them. When the horses carried them over the surface of the second lake, and into the chasm where the Suns' River began running underground, Brenda found that she could see clearly. Indeed, the diminishing of the intense brilliance of the sunlight reflected off the lake came as something of a relief.

She took off her sunglasses and, leaning back, tucked them under the flap of the right-hand saddlebag. When she turned forward again, she saw Flying Claw smiling at her with approval.

"The tunnel the river has cut with its course is comfortably high," Loyal Wind said. "But it is not quite wide enough for us to continue riding as we have. I suggest pairs. Righteous Drum could come forward with me, and Flying Claw should drop to the back. Deborah, I had thought to have you ride in the rear because your magic is stronger than either of the apprentices', but that would rob us of the Dog's admitted martial abilities should we be attacked. Do you have a preference?"

"Put me in the middle with Brenda," Deborah said without hesitation. "I'm not in practice either magically or with what weapons arts I know. And in the middle I will be better able to use my magic to help if trouble comes from either side."

"Very well," Loyal Wind said.

"Do we expect trouble?" Riprap asked.

"No," Loyal Wind said, "but you have been a soldier. You know that trouble comes when you least expect it."

They readjusted their marching order, Brenda feeling decidedly like the last person picked for the team. Then she straightened, patting the golden horse—who at this moment was merely a transformed sorcerer—on the side of the neck.

No one is leaving me for last. Like Deborah, from here I can help if trouble comes from either side.

"I'm ready," she said, and hoped she really was.

XXIII

"Some serious questions have arisen regarding how the Orphans are handling this situation," said Dr. Broderick Pike.

He and Pearl were sitting in his office, a pleasant although not overly large space in the private areas of the Rosicrucian Museum. The room's larger window was behind his desk, and through it, Pearl could see the top of a lotus column portico, the elegant sculptures enhanced—but not obscured—by white climbing roses.

Pearl crossed her hands in her lap. She met Broderick's gaze with an illusion of mild interest—illusion because beneath her exterior calm she was fuming at being asked to this meeting, furious that the Orphans should need to answer to anyone at all.

"Yes?" she said, raising her eyebrows in gentle inquiry.

Dr. Pike looked uncomfortable, and Pearl reminded herself that he was a friend—if not a certain ally.

"Tell me," she added, allowing herself a smile, one that she hoped held rue, not anger.

"Tracy Frye claims that two valuable mah-jong sets she bought, legally and legitimately, were stolen from the house where she was staying."

"Really?" Pearl had expected this, and discussed how to best answer with the others. "Stolen? Why, then, has she not gone to the police?"

Broderick tilted his lips in a smile that did not reach his eyes. "You know perfectly well why not. She has no proof the police would accept, but plenty that many of us do accept."

"Such as?"

"Pearl! I asked to be the one to speak with you because of our long association—friendship, I had hoped. I know perfectly well that what Tracy Frye and Franklin Deng did was at the very least in bad taste."

"Blackmail always is," Pearl said. "And my saying that doesn't mean I am admitting to anything."

"Blackmail," Broderick said with a slight nod. "Very well. The other matter is more serious—and possibly one where you might find yourself dealing with the police."

"Oh?"

"Yes. The accusation has been made that you are keeping prisoners on your property."

"Ah . . ."

There was a long silence while Pearl considered how to handle this. When she and Shen had spoken to the Rock Dove Society in New York, they had deliberately not mentioned the prisoners. Now, however, she wished she had done so, but perhaps it was not too late?

She remembered the three figures they had seen skulking on the side street near the garage. Someone had suspected for several days that something was out of the ordinary at Pearl's house.

Pearl made her decision. Briefly, as if filling out a police report, she told Broderick Pike about the attack at the practice field at Colm Lodge. She did not enumerate the number who had died, but she did not hide that there had been deaths. Nor did she hide that her own people had been injured—severely in the case of Righteous Drum and Brenda Morris.

"Now," Pearl said, "you're a smart man and a wise one in the bargain. I don't need to tell you why Shen and I didn't mention this to the Rock Dove Society."

Broderick inclined his head slightly in agreement.

"You can also understand why the matter of my guests—or prisoners, if you prefer—should not become a police matter."

"No identification," Broderick said. "Unknown people raise uncomfortable questions."

"Worse," Pearl said. "Strangers who will speak a form of Chinese any translator will find very peculiar. Men who will bear on their bodies the scars of archaic weapons. Given the current climate regarding immigration, do any of us really want questions asked? And one of them—Twentyseven-Ten—is a talented adept. At least one other can work minor magics. We have hobbled their abilities, but if they are taken from our care . . ."

She trailed off, knowing she didn't need to say any more. Broderick was nodding his head in avid agreement.

"Do you wish me to keep this to myself?" he asked. "I can. I can swear under oath that I have questioned you, and as to this matter, I agree with your course of action."

"If I had wished to swear you to silence," Pearl said, "I

would have done so before I began. I trusted your common sense. I still do. The Orphans have adversaries among the members of the Finch and Rock Dove Societies, and probably within affiliated societies as well. Do you think all of them would put the greater good before their own vendettas?"

Broderick smiled, and this time it was a real smile that touched his eyes.

"No. I don't. I choose to interpret your cryptic comment about blackmail to mean that whatever went on with those mah-jong sets was meant to pressure you into a course of action contrary to what you and Shen promised the Rock Dove Society you would undertake. In such instances, not everyone needs to know all the details."

He unfolded his hands, tapped his nose with his forefinger, as he considered, then sighed.

"But I think it would be wisest if I confided in a few chapter heads. I will bind them to silence, however, and so the information will go no further. One final question."

"Yes?"

"Have you made any progress in establishing these Nine Gates you mentioned at the Rock Dove Society meeting?"

"Yes. And more progress is being made even as we speak."

I hope, Pearl thought, as they went through the various formalities of departure, *that I am telling the truth. The others have been gone for several days, and the auguries as to their success are far from certain.*

☆

The walls were what made it all real. Although the rock was cool to the touch, it showed signs of having been exposed to tremendous heat. There was smoothness where the rock had run molten, bumps that were tiny bubbles, and pocks where those bubbles had burst. The molten rock showed ripples, as if terrific wind had accompanied that heat.

The sun—suns—had repeatedly raced down this river, so

hot that their passage melted stone, and Brenda Morris *believed*.

She kept looking at those walls, extending her hand to touch the rough-smooth stone, imagining she could feel heat still lingering, that the walls were warmer than they should be.

They *were* warmer than they should be. Brenda patted Leaf's neck and he cooperatively moved over so she could rest her hand against the stone. It was warm. Warmer than it had been a few minutes ago. About the exterior temperature of a mug that held freshly poured coffee or tea.

She swiveled in her saddle, looking back. For once she had no eyes for Flying Claw, though she did notice that, whether by chance or design, he rode directly behind her.

Is that light back there or am I imagining the glow? Is it some relic of Righteous Drum's spell?

She faced forward, closed her eyes to clear them of any image but the memory of the tunnel behind them. Swiveling once more, she opened her eyes and studied the tunnel again.

Brighter. Yes. And that means . . .

"I think we're in trouble, folks," Brenda said, keeping her voice as level as possible. "The wall is getting warmer. Feel it. It's almost hot. And there's light behind us. It's dim, but growing brighter."

A moment of motion as the other five checked her comments, then Loyal Wind said, "I feared this. The sun is catching up to us. I had hoped that we could outpace it but . . ."

He nudged his mount, but the chestnut had already increased its pace, stretching out from its wind-riding canter into a full gallop. The other horses did the same, and Brenda felt her hair and clothing whip straight back.

"Can we outrun it?" Deborah asked, her voice tight.

"No." Loyal Wind replied. "We can only hope to reach a wider spot in the tunnels before the sun reaches us. If we do not, then we must dive into the river and hope the water provides a sufficient shield."

"Breathing optional?" Riprap, his deep voice booming off the walls. "I mean, you may not need to breathe, but the rest of us . . ."

"There are spells," Righteous Drum called back, "shields. We may need to trust to them."

"Against the sun?" Deborah said, but Brenda could see that she was already reaching up under the cuff of her shirt, moving a cluster of amulet bracelets into play.

Loyal Wind gave a wintry smile, his eyes narrowing as he looked back over his shoulder to judge the approach of the sunlight. Brenda followed his gaze. No need to guess, anymore. The light was definitely brighter, not headlight-bright, but about the brightness of a handheld flashlight.

"I revealed my concern to Righteous Drum," Loyal Wind said, "but we did not wish to alarm you over something that might not arise. This is the best course of action he and I could come up with. Your spells need not last long, for the sun's passage should be swift."

"Easy for you to say," Riprap said. "I'd have liked to have a chance to contribute to the game plan."

"There was not time for endless debate," Righteous Drum said.

Loyal Wind seemed to hear personal criticism in Riprap's words.

"If we remain, the horses and I are no safer than you, for in this world the dead are as prone to damage as the living— perhaps more so."

"If?" Riprap said.

Definite criticism colored his words, and Brenda didn't blame him. The Dragon's Tail she'd selected seemed fragile protection against heat that could melt stone. Hadn't Des told them that Dragon's Tail worked less well against nonspecific threats. Maybe some combination of winds? But winds fed fire, didn't they?

"We can disperse," Loyal Wind said, ashamed, "and that would be our best course, to disperse and to rejoin you later."

Brenda leaned forward, bringing her head next to Leaf's neck so that she could see his head clearly. For the first time, the golden horse showed physical signs of its tremendous exertion. Its eye was wild. Foam flecked his lips. Brenda didn't know if a ghost horse who was really a transformed sorcerer could founder, but she had a feeling it could.

"Loyal Wind, you're right," she said. "You've got to get out of here, you and the horses. The tunnel seems to be widening ahead, but there's not much space, really not much— and if we end up having to go underwater, it's going to get crowded with six people *and* six horses."

Flying Claw's voice came from behind her. "I agree. The area ahead is definitely becoming wider. Take us to the widest possible place, let us off, then go to what safety you can find. If the worst happens, someone must survive to bring word to the others."

"I agree," Riprap said, and Brenda saw Deborah beside her, and Righteous Drum in the first rank, nod.

The horses tore over the water, and from behind Brenda could now feel the heat on her back. It wasn't bad, yet, no more than the pleasant glow of a summer day. Glancing back she saw that the light was now too much to look at directly. It filled the tunnel and she turned her head away, remembering that one should never look directly into the sun.

The horses pressed themselves, faster, ever faster. Brenda saw pink coloring the foam around the mouth of Deborah's grey. She gripped the golden horse's silvery mane, and leaned forward, trying to take her weight onto herself rather than asking the horse to bear it.

She saw their destination ahead, a place where the tunnel widened enough that there was a shoulder, not much wider than that of a country road, but wide enough that they could stand to either side of the now steaming waters.

But the rock is melted, Brenda thought. *Even at the farthest edge, it's melted. We're gonna get cooked.*

As the tunnel widened, so did the river. The horses, which

had been running in ragged pairs, now separated. The right-hand set—those carrying Righteous Drum, Deborah, and Riprap—veered toward the right bank, those carrying her and Flying Claw veered to the left. Only Loyal Wind remained in midstream, but he had turned to face directly behind. Brenda saw he held his bow in his hand, strung, an arrow nocked to the string.

She remembered the tale of Yi the Archer who had shot down the suns and knew that Loyal Wind wasn't abandoning them, that he'd wait there while they dismounted, while they got their spells up, while the horses got away.

Knowing this, Brenda practically flung herself from Leaf's back as soon as they reached the shore, splashing one foot into the shallows. The water was hot, not just warm, but hot—like uncomfortable bathwater.

She stumbled on stiff legs, slapping Leaf on his rump and yelling, "Get out of here! Get out while you can!" In her next move, she slammed a Dragon's Tail to the ground, and felt the Tail wrap her in what protection it could offer.

Brenda's feet and legs didn't feel like they were part of her, but they reluctantly obeyed as she turned and moved toward the wall. There was no tidy alcove, no convenient cleft into which she could thrust herself, but there was a dip, slightly deeper than the rest of the surface.

She pressed herself into this, and grabbed Flying Claw by the wrist when he started to take a place slightly more exposed.

"This isn't a time for manners," Brenda snapped. "Get in here. I don't think our spells will conflict."

"No," he said, his eyes wide and slightly startled. "Your Dragon's Tail has meshed with my own."

Brenda felt this, but didn't bother to think about it. Leaf and Flying Claw's blood bay had vanished, but Loyal Wind still stood midstream. Steam was rising from the waters, wreathing the lower part of his horse, and shrouding the other bank.

"If you have any great ideas for fireproofing or heat resistance," Brenda said, "I'd go for it now. Loyal Wind has given me an idea."

She fumbled along her wrist until she came across the bracelet containing the most powerful spell she'd brought with her: the Twins of the Sky.

She smashed it to the stone floor. When the Twins in their archaic Chinese armor and cloud-embroidered robes of blue and white rose in response, Brenda motioned toward the onrushing wall of heat—a visible, tangible thing.

"If you can do anything to keep that back," she said, "I'd be very grateful."

The Twins produced long-handled weapons, something like spears, and with a slight nod that included her as well as each other began spinning them in front of each other. Brenda felt the heat diminish slightly, but she feared it would not be enough.

So, it seemed, did Flying Claw. He was etching patterns in the air in front of him, patterns Brenda could tell were in the shape of Chinese ideograms, but not ones she could read. The result, however, was that of rain falling on them both, rain that turned to steam as soon at it hit the increasingly hot stone underfoot, but rain that cooled the rock around them.

No longer did Brenda find it necessary to look upstream to see how close the sun was. The light was overwhelming, so overpowering that it seemed the most natural thing in the world that she bury her head in Flying Claw's shoulder and that he bury his face in her hair.

The heat grew intense, then overwhelming. The air became almost too hot to breathe.

Brenda could smell her hair starting to singe, felt one of the metal studs on Flying Claw's armor burn straight through her shirt and against her wrist. She adjusted her grip, and felt the arms she only then realized were holding her tightening, tightening as if by the sheer force of his embrace Flying Claw could protect them both from the overwhelming heat and light that surrounded them.

The heat grew more intense. The light burned through no matter how tightly Brenda screwed her eyes shut.

Brenda felt the Dragon's Tails untwine, then fall apart, heard the cries of despair as her Twins of the Sky evaporated beneath the force of the sun's touch, but by then the worst was over, the waters of the river still steamed, the rock upon which they stood creaked and hissed as it began to cool, but the rain from Flying Claw's spell continued to fall around them.

Sighing in relief, Brenda rested her head against his chest for a moment longer.

"We made it through," she murmured, holding her parched lips up to the rain. "I can't believe it. We stood on the edge of the sun, but we made it through."

Flying Claw looked down at her, and although his face was streaked with sweat and the glossy black of his hair was dulled, his eyes shone with happiness.

"We made it through," he repeated, and brushed her forehead with his lips.

☆

Honey Dream was growing deeply worried. Her father and Flying Claw—and the others—had been gone now for several days. She and Waking Lizard had worked various auguries, and the Orphans had done several of the complicated rituals involving those irritating mah-jong tiles of theirs, and the answer was always indecisive.

They were fairly certain that at least some of the expedition was still alive, but since one member of the expedition, at least—the readings got really strange when they tried to clarify that point—was a ghost, that complicated matters. Readings for a specific person were no less comforting than those for the group as a whole.

Shen Kung speculated that this was because the expedition had been successful, at least as far as achieving their goal to enter the underworld or afterlife. In a sense, they belonged now to that realm. Therefore, readings as to whether they were living were confused because in Chinese cosmology one of the things that differentiated the living from the dead was in which of many varied realms they dwelt, not the state of the body.

Or, as Des Lee put it with one of his annoying smiles, "Magic 8-Ball read: 'Answer cloudy. Try again.'"

In the privacy of her room, Honey Dream had tried rituals of her own, focusing on only her father or only Flying Claw, but the results she garnered were vague at best. The pity she glimpsed on Waking Lizard's face after one particularly exhausting private session made her squirm. She'd forgotten that he was likely to have sensed the terrific amount of ch'i she was channeling in her efforts, and guessed what she was about.

Embarrassment—and powerful dislike for seeming a child who could not wait in patience and calm—kept Honey Dream from trying again.

Daytimes were busy enough to keep her from worrying— at least too much. Physical practice sessions had continued, and now Nissa Nita had joined them. Nissa said that seeing how even Riprap could get hurt made her realize she'd better know something at least about defending herself.

Practice pairs shifted, but more often than she liked, Honey Dream found herself facing off against Pearl Bright. The old Tiger seemed to have it in for her, and pushed Honey Dream to the limits of her abilities. Or at least those abilities that could be used in practice, Honey Dream kept telling herself. She was forced to refrain from using the variety of poisons that were part of any Snake's arsenal. Although Shen Kung knew the spell that enabled damaging physical effects to be magically synthesized, so that those who had been "poisoned" or otherwise harmed felt the effects, although they were not really hurt, Honey Dream didn't think this was at all the same. A person who knew their every exertion made their own heart carry death more rapidly through their system reacted differently than those who knew in their gut that the damage was synthetic.

At least, she had. . . .

Physical practice was followed by preparation for the battles that must come even if those who were creating the Nine Gates were successful, and that must come if they failed.

For the Orphans, this meant the making of those annoying mah-jong tile amulets. For Honey Dream and Waking Lizard, spells were inscribed on paper, color of both paper and ink coordinated to give the spell its best effect.

And there were domestic chores as well. Honey Dream tried not to be humiliated that she was the least adept at cooking, that Lani would rather play by herself than look at Honey Dream.

Honey Dream didn't forget her father's injunction to keep an eye on the prisoners, but there was little she could do other than assist Shen when he carried over their meals, so the task didn't help build her sense of importance. She reminded herself that in her own land she was a lady of quality, and didn't do servants' work, but she was humiliated nonetheless.

But all of this activity still left Honey Dream too much time to worry—about her father, about what Brenda Morris might be doing to corrupt Flying Claw, about whether she would ever see her mother again, and about how those who had overthrown their emperor might be treating the families and friends of their enemies.

Honey Dream found herself going for frequent walks, both on the Rosicrucian Museum grounds and on those of Colm Lodge. One night, she wandered down the driveway, and again, as she suspected she had known it would, a voice spoke to her from the darkness on the other side of the wards.

"Franklin Deng," she said, speaking in the Chinese of the Lands, a sort of relief warring with the hopelessness that had been her companion with increasing frequency over the last several days. "You've come back."

"I am still seeking an ally," he said, replying in his own Chinese, "but you sound as if you need a friend."

The kindness in his voice brought tears, sudden and uninvited, to her eyes. If she let herself, she could almost believe that strong, deep voice speaking from the night was her father, home again and safe.

Honey Dream had been trained in the ways of court intrigue, but her father's faction, the faction to which she had been a latecomer, a substitute, had not lasted long in court—not through any fault of their own, but due to betrayal. Part of her knew she was being "gotten at" as Riprap might have put it, but that part of her was drowned out by the far larger part that did not care.

"I suppose," she said, "I am a bit lonely. My father has been gone for some days, Flying Claw with him. Snakes and Monkeys, while not strictly opposed, are not compatible."

"So it's just you and Waking Lizard?" Deng asked. "You must rattle around in there."

"We're at Pearl's residence most of the time," Honey Dream said. "As you must know . . ."

"Ouch! Touché!" came the reply. The second word did not sound like English, but nonetheless it was translated via the spell that let Honey Dream understand English as meaning something like "A hit. A touch." She thought she understood.

"Well," she said, laughing softly. "You do watch us, you or your minions."

"Associates," Deng said, laughter in his own voice. "Please. 'Minions' makes it sound as if they are my servants, and I assure you, they are not. They are allies who share related, if not common, goals. Indeed, my dear, I believe my goals have more in common with your own than they do with those of—say—Tracy Frye."

"So you assured me," Honey Dream replied, "the last time we spoke."

She expected him to press her, to ask her if she had considered his offer of an alliance. He did not.

"Your father is away, then? One of my associates reported that a van full of people went to that warehouse owned by Pearl Bright. The van is still there. The people have not been seen."

"You've kept a watch on that building all this time?"

"I have my ways," he answered with an air of mystery, and Honey Dream, remembering what she'd learned about surveillance cameras and the like—the mechanical servants that were as common here as those of flesh and blood were in the Lands—thought that she knew how Deng and his associates could be so omnipresent, and yet never be seen.

"We thought they were involved in some sort of training," Deng said. "We detected a surge of ch'i at one point, several days ago, but nothing since. However, even ch'i use can be shielded, and Righteous Drum certainly knows spells that could keep us ignorant if he so wished."

Honey Dream warmed at the praise to her father. She had never felt the Orphans appreciated him for his full abilities.

"He could," she agreed complacently.

"My auguries," Deng said, "suggest that Righteous Drum is dead, as are Flying Claw, Brenda Morris, Deborah Van Bergenstein, and Charles Adolphus. Have you checked inside the warehouse?"

Panic seized Honey Dream, panic so strong that she felt herself rising to her toes, as if she would run, as if she would scream.

Then she remembered. Franklin Deng was probably getting similar readings to those she herself had. However, not knowing where Righteous Drum had gone, he would, of course, read them incorrectly.

But what if she was wrong? What if his magic was more powerful? After all, he was of the indigenous magical tradition, not an interloper like the Orphans—or herself. And she knew that her own magics were attenuated by the fragmentation of the sixth Earthly Branch—the branch associated with the Snake.

What if Deng knew the truth that they had all been striving to learn? How could she learn?

Deng was speaking again. He had come closer to the stone fence that bordered the front edge of Colm Lodge's grounds, the line along which they had run their wards. He did not cross it, nor did he touch it, but she could see him more clearly.

He looked nothing like her father, being tall and thin where her father was almost—almost—dumpy. But there was something fatherly about his aura, and Honey Dream longed to cross that invisible line and beg him for guidance.

She would not though. She contented herself with resting her hands on the stone wall, pressing her fingers into the rough blocks, grounding herself with the slight pain of that contact.

"My father is well," she said. "My own auguries assure me this is so."

"Liar," he said, but gently, even playfully. "Pretty little liar. I can see the tears bright in your eyes, but I can see how you have recovered yourself. Admirable, and indicating, perhaps, that you have some reason to hope."

"I do," she said. "I know where my father has gone. I also have faith in his powers."

"O ye of little faith," he said in English, and Honey Dream had the sense that this was a proverbial expression of some sort.

"I don't need faith," she said. "I know. Father and the others have gone into the afterlife. That is why your reading is muddled."

"Afterlife? Well, that's impressive. And they can do so from that warehouse . . ."

Honey Dream had the feeling she had said too much, but she didn't know how what she had said could hurt. The Men Shen would not let anyone through the door who was not approved already.

Still, she noticed uneasily that Franklin Deng was smiling,

the glow from the streetlights glinting off his straight white teeth.

"Contact with the afterlife sounds like necromancy," he said. "My culture frowns on that. Doesn't your own?"

"That just shows your ignorance," she snapped, angered out of prudence. "In the Lands, we recognize many realities, interlaced and interdependent. Are you so one-sided here?"

"Perhaps we hold different views," Deng said, his friendly mildness making her ashamed of her outburst. "Tell me, do the mah-jong sets have anything to do with this? I did not have the sets in my hands long, but long enough to notice that the tiles were not plastic, but bamboo combined with something else—bone, I thought. I have some experience differentiating ivory from bone."

Honey Dream tried to school her expression to neutrality, but she feared she had given something away nonetheless. She looked down and found those betraying hands were twisting against each other.

"Bone," Deng said softly, "and I think not cattle bone as is usual, but perhaps . . . Think about being my ally, Honey Dream. Necromancy is very frowned upon in our modern culture. Those who have tools made from human bone will quickly lose the sympathy of those who would otherwise have been their friends—and not only within the magical community. The reaction is stronger from those outside our little realm."

Honey Dream knew her expression was now perfectly neutral, but she also knew it was too late. Deng had suspected, and she had confirmed his suspicions. She remembered how Des Lee had reacted when Pearl and the others had suggested contacting the ghosts. She remembered how Riprap had spoken of the "road to Hell." His tone had been light, but his dark eyes had been filled with fear. They belonged to this world, and their reaction must be what Deng spoke of—and perhaps less forceful than many would be.

Franklin Deng gave her a very proper bow, one of equal to equal. Then he straightened, and smiled.

"Remember," he said. "I have offered to be your ally. Remember, you can have me as a friend, and you may well need a friend."

He stepped back, and vanished. Honey Dream did not wait to hear him depart, but turned and ran back up to the house, her soul twisting with dread.

XXIV

Loyal Wind and the horses returned after the sun had passed, and the company was reunited. Once the waters of the Suns' River had cooled, they paused long enough for everyone to bathe off sweat and soot, Deborah and Brenda's privacy assured by a convenient bend in the river.

The river's waters were still warm, prompting Brenda to ask once they had all remounted, "Loyal Wind, how far is it to the Yellow Springs? Will we reach there before the next sun passes?"

"I hope so," he said, "but distances here are deceptive, and much depends on the speed of the winds. With all of your permission, I will scout ahead periodically, not only to seek the springs, but to look for places where you might take refuge if the next sun's passage comes before we reach our destination."

Everyone agreed that this precaution was wise, but Brenda allowed herself to hope that it would be unnecessary. It wasn't that she hadn't liked being pressed into Flying Claw's arms, but if nearly burning to death was the price of that contact, she wasn't interested in a repeat.

After the sun's passage, Flying Claw had returned to his

usual friendly politeness, but Brenda was very aware of him riding there behind her. She wondered if he was equally aware of her, and tried not to slump in her saddle, even when their progress extended hour after bone-wearying hour.

And she tried to tell herself that when she looked back over her shoulder, she was looking for hints that the sun might be rising, not for the smile that flashed across Flying Claw's face when their gazes met.

Loyal Wind returned from his fifth or sixth scouting trip at a gallop.

"I've found the Yellow Springs!" he announced. His smile had been broad with satisfaction, but then he frowned. "However, the springs are not unguarded, and the guardian is unlike anything I have seen. It has the appearance of a snake, but there is something wrong about it. It looks like a snake, but it does not move quite like a snake."

"Tell us about it," Righteous Drum said, but Loyal Wind shook his head.

"No. We are almost to where you can see the springs for yourself, and I may have said too much already. I would prefer you make your own decisions."

Brenda had noticed that Leaf had increased his speed as soon as Loyal Wind returned, but he slowed a few moments later, when Loyal Wind made a motion with his right hand.

"The river goes underground here, and . . ."

He stopped speaking, for they could see for themselves. The Suns' River vanished underground, thundering down into a wide, deep declivity. The rock surrounding the chasm was smooth, melted so slick that there were not even bubbles, but dramatic as the thundering fall of water was, Brenda hardly had eyes for it. Her attention was demanded by the room beyond the chasm.

"Room" wasn't the right word; neither was "chamber" or "cave" or anything else that implied contained space. As far as Brenda could tell, they had emerged once again into an open area that was "outdoors."

The air was fresh—more than fresh, perfumed with some

familiar flower. The sky overhead was brilliant blue, and held a few wispy clouds. She could hear birds twittering. A few yards off a rabbit was nibbling what looked like a perfectly normal dandelion.

Brenda looked beyond the rabbit, and across a vast meadow where lush green grass starred with wildflowers grew over gently rolling hills.

The only odd thing about the area—other than that it existed at all—was the angle of the light, but she couldn't figure out why.

"Have we come out into the guardian domains again?" asked Deborah in a hushed voice.

"No," Loyal Wind assured her. "This is simply another part of the underworld. All of you, dismount and follow me. I will lead you to the place from where you can see the springs and their guardian."

He pointed, indicating a narrow path cut from the living rock of a rock wall that Brenda guessed must be the last remnant of the caverns from which they had emerged. The path led to a ledge that projected over the edge of the meadow like some sort of strange balcony. It looked sculpted, but Brenda was getting used to environments that violated just about everything she had been taught to believe.

She dismounted from Leaf's saddle, surreptitiously rubbing the tops of her thighs, and hoping she wouldn't stagger when she started climbing. Deborah grinned at her.

"Just imagine how it feels when you're my age, with a whole lot less leg," Deborah said. "I'm going to remember how it feels to be this out of shape when I'm home again, and want to skip a trip to the gym."

The path was narrow enough that they had to ascend in single file. Loyal Wind took point, and Flying Claw brought up the rear. Brenda was tempted to drop back to be closer to the young Tiger, but remembering the strange creatures they'd seen, she didn't. She was getting better at responding to a crisis, but it was going to be a while before she was the equal of either Flying Claw or Riprap.

The path was steep, not in the least kind to muscles that had been bent close to the barrel of a horse for days, but Brenda made it to the top without complaining.

Cross-training, she thought. *That's what I need*.

Then she arrived at the top, looked out over the meadow, and forgot about anything as mundane as aching muscles.

From here, Brenda could see that the meadow rose and fell in undulating hills. Nine hills, she realized after a moment. The hills bore few plants other than the covering grass and an artful scattering of wildflowers. However, the one plant there made up for the lack.

It was a tall tree, so tall that "towering" seemed an understatement, a poor attempt to compare its vastness to something human hands might make. Its boughs were wide and spreading, like those of an oak or maple. Its leaves were boat-shaped, like those of a magnolia. Its flowers were enormous and white.

Brenda sniffed tentatively, and realized that the pervasive perfume she had been smelling since they had entered this area was very like that of a magnolia tree: light and sweet, floral with a hint of melon.

The tree, she now realized, was the source of the light, and the reason that light was somewhat peculiar, for it emanated from the blossoms high on the tree, some brighter, some dimmer. Brenda did not need Righteous Drum to tell her that the glowing flowers each held a sun, recovering from its long journey through the skies and under the earth.

Brenda felt shaken, awed with a comprehension of reality that, while it did not fit anything she knew, still seemed perfectly right. She let her gaze drop, studying the much less overwhelming rise and fall of the grassy hills. That was when she realized that between the hills curved something scaly and serpentine.

"Is that the snake, Loyal Wind?" she asked softly.

"It is . . . something," Righteous Drum replied, puzzlement replacing the usual pedantic confidence in his voice. "It is like a snake or dragon but . . ."

"Hush!" Deborah cut him off, her voice firm, sharp, alarmed. "It's moving! Has it seen us?"

Almost as one, they flattened themselves against the stone wall that backed their vantage point. Brenda felt her right hand moving toward the bracelets on her left wrist.

"No! No, it hasn't see us," Flying Claw said. Alone of them all—even the ghost—he had held his place. He stood in front of them, straight-backed and alert. "I am certain that whatever is down there has not seen us, but Deborah is correct. It is moving. It? They? No. It. Righteous Drum, come here. Look more closely. What do you see?"

Righteous Drum moved away from the wall, but Brenda noticed he kept a little behind Flying Claw, even as he leaned to take a closer look.

"Nine heads!" Righteous Drum said in consternation. "Nine heads issuing forth from one body. Yes. I am sure of it."

Brenda forced herself to move forward where she could see. Separating the creature from its surroundings took a moment, for its scales were shaded a dirty brass hue that blended surprisingly well with the shadowed greensward.

Righteous Drum was right. The thing had nine heads, each one at the end of a neck so long that it could have qualified as a separate body, if length was all that mattered. The body— thick and sluglike—was half buried in the turf. Or did it emerge from there? She couldn't tell.

"Parasite," Riprap said. He had possessed the forethought to take with him the small set of binoculars from his saddlebags. Now he was viewing the ground below through them. "Leech. That's what it reminds me of, not a snake, a leech. There's something reptilian about it, but . . ."

"Whatever it is," Righteous Drum said, "Loyal Wind was correct. This is not any of the many types of snakes I have studied. In the creature below, it is as if the snake has been subsumed by some horror—still there, but merged with something else."

The creature had continued to move, each head gliding

sluggishly from some central point among the declivities. There was an ugly caress to the movement, but Brenda noticed that none of the heads went near the trunk of the tree, and although their necks were long, they kept well below the overshadowing branches.

Reassured by the monster's lack of interest in them, they had all crept forward to watch. Brenda regretted that she hadn't had the presence of mind to bring her own binoculars. They each had a pair, but now she could see that only Riprap and Flying Claw—the trained soldiers among them—had thought to bring them.

"Look!" Brenda said, embarrassed to hear her voice squeak. "What's it doing? Is it drinking? All those heads at once?"

"Sucking," Riprap clarified, his upper lip curled in revulsion. "Sucking the water from each of the Yellow Springs."

"Those spring's don't look yellow," Brenda said. "Are you certain we're in the right place?"

"The waters are named from the brilliance of their color when they lift the rising suns," Loyal Wind said. "This is the right place. I could not be easily mistaken."

Brenda nodded. There was a long silence while each of them studied the meadow and its grotesque occupant.

"That thing isn't," Brenda said, "a usual guardian, is it? I mean, I'd sort of expect a place like this to have a guardian—magical springs, roosting place of the suns—but this is something else."

Righteous Drum nodded, round, wide face unhappy. "This creature is not a guardian such as I have heard of in any legend from any time or place. It is something else, but what?" He turned to Loyal Wind. "Great Horse, have you ever heard of such a thing? Perhaps during the years you have run in the afterlife?"

"No," came the reply almost before the question could be articulated. "No idea. I . . ."

Brenda looked at Flying Claw, who was watching the creature through his own binoculars.

"Flying Claw, could this be what Pai Hu, the White Tiger of the West, was talking about?"

Flying Claw lowered his binoculars and looked at her, considering. "You mean the source of that sense he had of being drained away? Perhaps. I am no scholar, nor do I think this is a scholar's problem. A monster that sucks dry the wellsprings of the waters that raise suns—and in so doing interferes with our making 'men,' family, with those springs is a bane. That is enough reason for me to desire it gone."

Flying Claw had dropped the binoculars to hang by their strap around his neck, the modern piece of equipment contrasting oddly with the snarling tiger's face worked into his breastplate. He reached for the bow at his back.

"Wait!" said Righteous Drum. "Flying Claw, are you forgetting the Sage King Yu and his battle with the serpent with nine heads?"

Flying Claw let his hand drop from his bow, consternation on his face. He bent his head and recited, as if from a lesson often repeated.

"In days long ago, there was a terrible serpent with nine heads. Each head oozed poison so potent that it shriveled and dried anything it touched. The serpent with nine heads lay wrapped around nine hills, even as this monster does, and any who sought to attack it found it impossible even to approach, for with nine heads it could watch in every direction, so it slew those who came after it before they could raise sword or spear or bow."

Righteous Drum nodded. "And the Sage King Yu took pity on his people, and went after the serpent himself. For a long while, he studied it. Yu realized that although the serpent kept watch on all sides, it never looked up. Then Yu enlisted the help of the Winged Dragon. He rode astride it, and they approached from above, in this way managing to cut off the serpent's heads almost before it realized it was under attack. But although Yu was successful, killing the serpent only created more problems."

"Yes," Flying Claw said. "I remember. Poison spread from

each of the heads, and leaked from the body, so that the surrounding lands were destroyed. Eventually, Yu came up with a solution, but not before much had been ruined."

"And we are not Yu," Righteous Drum said, "and we cannot make an artificial island in an artificial lake to contain the corpse as a solution to the problem."

"And," Deborah said, frowning, "with the Nine Springs here, who knows where the poison would be carried? On the other hand, do we know that this monster is poisonous?"

"Heads look as if they might be," Riprap said, handing her his binoculars. "I wouldn't take a gamble."

"Nor I," agreed Flying Claw, "but what do we do?"

Brenda had borrowed Flying Claw's binoculars. By modern standards, they were primitive: no autofocus or electronic enhancements, because Des had figured these would probably malfunction. Nonetheless, they did a good job of bringing the creature below into focus.

"The monster is dug in there," she said, "off to one side. The body goes in who knows how deep. See? There's even grass growing around where the body is rooted in. That thing hasn't moved for a while, and doesn't look as if it plans to do so."

"I guess," Riprap said, taking back his binoculars from Deborah and grinning at Brenda, "that rules out my brilliant plan. I was going to have you go down there and start screaming to lure it off. Then we could have our talk with the springs and get out of here."

Brenda stuck her tongue out at him.

"Seriously," she said, "if we can't kill it in case it floods the area with poison, and we can't lure it off, what can we do? I'm just guessing, but that thing doesn't look friendly, or like something that will ignore us if we wander down there. It's got a positively proprietary attitude toward the springs."

"You're right," Riprap agreed. He turned to face Flying Claw, Righteous Drum, and Loyal Wind, all of whom were studying the layout below, their faces showing almost matching expressions of fascinated horror. "You folks have any idea? Me and Brenda and Deborah, we're not exactly experienced with fighting monsters."

"I do not have any insights as to how we can attack it safely," Righteous Drum said. "Flying Claw? Loyal Wind?"

Tiger and Horse shook their heads. Brenda moved to where she could kneel at the edge of the balcony and study the monster, while resting her increasingly achy legs. She watched as it sucked at the hills, almost as if nursing on enormous, grassy breasts. The notion was revolting, and embarrassing, too, because once it got into her head, she couldn't get rid of it, and she felt like a pervert.

Every so often, one of the heads would lift and look around, but like its mythical counterpart, the Nine-Headed Leech, as she dubbed it in her mind, never seemed to look up.

"The sun rises because it's lifted up by those springs?" she said. "They don't look very powerful. Even when the Leech isn't sucking, they just sort of trickle."

Righteous Drum shrugged. "In some tales, the suns are birds in a tree, and a divine figure, usually their mother, picks one to fly up into the outer world each day."

"Perhaps," Flying Claw offered, "the springs gain force when the sun heats the water."

"Or maybe each spring just goes off at the right time, like Old Faithful," Riprap said. He explained when the three from the Lands looked confused. "That's a geyser that always shoots off at the same time every day."

"Or maybe," Deborah said, "the Leech doesn't like drinking boiling water. Maybe the springs heat up like the river did when the sun is ready to rise. Then the Leech pulls back and the sun can get a lift."

An idea had been niggling at the back of Brenda's mind for a while now, and she'd been trying not to let it take form because she guessed she wouldn't like it much. Now, though, she turned around and gave it a look.

"We can't shoot the Leech with arrows," she began, "and we can't cut it up because we don't want to risk spreading poison. We don't think it will run, and even if it could, it would just come back. Pretty lousy 'men' we'd be to the Nine Yellow Springs if we left them being sucked up by that monster."

"I hear," Flying Claw said, "something other than defeat in your voice."

"The Suns' River," Brenda said. "I keep thinking about the Suns' River. It goes underground here. I bet anything it feeds the Nine Yellow Springs."

"That makes a sort of sense," Deborah agreed, "but what of it?"

"I keep thinking," Brenda said, feeling her way into her idea, "that if we could do something to the water from the springs, that would affect the Leech, because it's drinking the water."

"Do something?" Righteous Drum asked. "Such as?"

Brenda looked sharply at him, but he wasn't mocking her. His expression was thoughtful and serious.

"I don't know," she said with a certain degree of frustration. "Poison them? Fill them with sleeping potion? Run red ants up their noses so they'll be so distracted that Riprap could tie the necks into knots? I'm open to suggestions."

Brenda expected to be laughed at, to be reminded of her basic ignorance, but she was surprised. She'd forgotten that the Landers originated in a place where the rules of myth and legend were as valid as those of physics and chemistry were in her own.

"That's a thought," Righteous Drum said. "A good thought. We'd need to take care only to taint the water going into the springs. I suspect the Suns' Tree also gets its water from where the river runs underground. We would not wish to harm it. We might harm the suns."

Everyone agreed. Before possible courses of action could be suggested, Loyal Wind suggested that he scout down into the chasm where the Suns' River had disappeared.

"After all, a general cannot plan a campaign of action until he knows the battlefield. Although in many ways I am as vulnerable to damage as any of you, I do have the advantage that if I find myself unable to get back, I can disembody as I did to escape the passage of the sun."

Brenda realized with a certain amount of surprise that Loyal Wind felt guilty about leaving them. She'd thought what he'd done had only made sense, but she guessed that was the difference between a Rat's practical nature and a Horse's heroic one.

Riprap and Flying Claw lowered Loyal Wind down on the longest rope they had, and hauled him up, dripping wet, not long after. His initial report was not encouraging.

"The waters spill into a vast lake that, as best as I could see, touches the surface above it—like a full wine bottle turned on its side, rather than a bowl. I swam and felt a strong tugging. I swam further, and could feel where the waters were being drawn up by the Nine Yellow Springs."

Helped, Brenda thought, *by the Leech*.

"So there are distinct entry points for each spring," Riprap said, "but each of them is under water. Not good. If we're to make certain whatever we put into the springs doesn't backwash into the lake, we're going to have to hand place it where the pull of the springs will make sure it gets into the Leech."

"It's a shame," Deborah said, "that none of the twelve animals of the zodiac is aquatic."

Brenda ran through the twelve in her mind—rat, ox, tiger, rabbit, dragon, snake, horse, ram, monkey, rooster, dog, and pig.

"Wait!" she said. "What about the dragon? Des told us that in Chinese myth, the dragon has its origin as a sort of water spirit. Later, the dragon's role expanded: into the sky first— since water falls from the sky—and then as the imperial emblem and a directional spirit and a bunch of other things. What about it, Righteous Drum. Can you breathe water?"

Righteous Drum looked startled and a little annoyed at himself. "Actually, when I am a dragon, I can."

"When you are a dragon?" Brenda repeated. "You mean

you can actually change your shape? This isn't something symbolic?"

"Why are you so surprised?" Righteous Drum asked. "Haven't you been traveling on a horse that was the ghost of a Horse?"

"I thought . . . I mean I guess if I thought at all, I figured it had something to do with them being, well, I mean, dead."

Brenda heard her voice drop off to nearly a whisper and felt very embarrassed.

Righteous Drum reached out and patted her on the arm. "My apologies, Brenda. I keep forgetting that not only haven't you had the education one of our own would have had, you belong to another culture entirely. To answer your question: Yes, I can turn into a dragon. A real dragon, as solid as the Horse."

"Not symbolic or a sort of astral projection?" Brenda asked, wanting to be perfectly certain.

"I can use those aspects as well," Righteous Drum said, "but, yes, with the proper preparation, I can turn into an actual water-breathing dragon. I can even—as is told in our folktales—extend the ability to breathe water to one who accompanies me."

Righteous Drum moved his right shoulder and his empty sleeve shifted. "However, I cannot do anything about this. Even if I were to turn into a dragon, I would be a maimed dragon. That would limit considerably what I was capable of doing. For example, I do not think I could both swim and maneuver to insert spells or amulets into the access points of the springs."

Riprap took a deep breath, and Brenda was pleased to see he was trying to cover his own astonishment.

And he's probably pretty excited, too, she thought. *After all, as the Dog, he can learn to change shape.*

"How large a dragon," Riprap asked, "do you become?"

Righteous Drum considered. "About the size of a horse—although longer and thinner in body, with shorter legs."

"So you could carry a passenger."

"A small one," Righteous Drum qualified, "the smaller and lighter the better, given my lack of a forelimb. I'll be struggling to propel myself, and a great weight would be a disadvantage."

"That rules me out," Riprap said, obviously disappointed. "Although if someone showed me how, maybe I could turn into a small dog."

Flying Claw laughed. "Forgive me, Riprap, but I cannot see you doing that. The shapes we take match our images of ourselves to some extent. You might try to turn into a Pekingese, for example, but you would likely end up a Pekingese the size of a chow chow or larger—more like a Fu dog."

"Oh," Riprap said. "No choice then?"

"No choice for novices," Flying Claw agreed, his tone making quite clear he considered himself one of those novices, and that therefore this was not intended as an insult.

"So that rules you out as well," Riprap said, "either as you are, or as a Tiger."

"That is so," Flying Claw agreed. "I believe either Deborah or Brenda will need to accompany Righteous Drum."

Brenda didn't know whether to be thrilled that her suggestion had been so quickly adopted or horrified at the direction this talk was taking.

Deborah was looking her up and down. "I've shaped a pig only once—as a sort of graduation exercise after my mother died. And I was a hefty sort of pig even then."

Brenda could see where this was going, and decided she'd better say something fast. It would be better to volunteer than to get volunteered.

"Look, Deborah, I don't know how much you weigh, but I think that even though I'm taller, I'm probably lighter."

Deborah laughed, the warm laugh of someone who is stout and has long grown comfortable with the fact.

"That's true enough."

Righteous Drum looked interested. "Brenda, as I recall,

you have had some experience already with shape-shifting, have you not?"

When Brenda simply looked astonished, he went on, "The night the Three-Legged Toad was accidentally drawn down to Pearl's house. I thought I was told you manifested a Rat then."

Brenda shook her head. "Not really. I mean, it was sort of a dream-state thing, astral projection or something, when Nissa and I were resetting the wards. It wasn't real."

Righteous Drum shook his head, but his face was amused. "Brenda, Brenda, we must teach you to accept that 'real' has many more dimensions than you were taught. What you did that night was 'real,' as real as the shape of your soul."

Deborah cut in. "But Righteous Drum, Brenda wouldn't need to shape a Rat, would she? Certainly, she's light enough for you to carry. You see, from what Albert told me, that occasion was a fluke, a direct result of Gaheris's—let's call it his 'incapacity.' "

"Brenda would not need to shape a rat," Righteous Drum said, "but if she could, I would find carrying her much easier. Because of how a dragon is shaped, whoever is my passenger will need to ride along the front end of my body, so that I can lift her—or him—toward the top of the chamber, where each of the springs draws up the waters. It would be much easier for me to repeatedly lift a rat than even the most slightly built human."

"Small would be better for another reason as well," Loyal Wind said. "When I took my swim, I felt where the waters rose to feed the spring, and the openings were not large. A human hand could get into them, but not an entire person."

"Well, all of that does make sense," Deborah admitted. She turned to Brenda. "Are you willing to try it? I can take you aside and teach you what you'll need to know. Otherwise, I'll see if I can manage a little pig. Ever since my kids started growing taller than me, I've felt smaller and smaller. Maybe I can channel that feeling."

Brenda felt tempted to refuse, to start making excuses, but

she wasn't going to let herself—and not just because Flying Claw was watching her, his face showing clearly his confident expectation that she would agree. She couldn't forget the warning Leaf had given her. Moreover, deep down inside, Brenda needed to prove to herself that she wasn't just a tagalong.

"I'll try," Brenda said, "but I have a question. Can I do it? I mean, I'm not really the Rat. Dad is."

"Shape-shifting is not limited to those who are affiliated with the Earthly Branches," Flying Claw assured her. "There are many who can take another shape—or many other shapes. However, for those of us with this affiliation, certain shapes are easier."

"Another thing that may encourage you," Righteous Drum added. "You said you hadn't questioned the horses' ability to change their shape because we are in the afterlife. There is actually a nugget of wisdom in your supposition. The afterlife is an environment in which malleability is more acceptable. You may find less resistance to the process."

"Thanks," Brenda nodded to them both. "I'll try it."

"Good," Deborah said. "Now, I suggest that we all go back into the Suns' River tunnel while we prepare. It isn't as pleasant as this area, but it is infinitely more private. Also, I think the walls will shield our ch'i manipulation. We shouldn't alert the Leech that anything is out of the ordinary. I'll work with Brenda, and the rest of you come up with some sort of charm she and Righteous Drum can carry to the sources of the springs."

"We'll set up wards as well," Righteous Drum said.

"And I will keep watch," Loyal Wind added, already turning back, "so that the next sunset will not catch us unawares."

XXV

"Pearl, I want to know where my daughter is." Gaheris Morris stood in the entryway of Pearl's house, his expression tight with worry and anger. "Her mother has been trying to call, and keeps getting no answer, and Brenda's mailbox is full."

"Keely is going to have trouble reaching Brenda on any phone," Pearl said, her head thrown back so that she could meet Gaheris's eyes. "Brenda has gone to the afterlife."

Gaheris blanched reflexively. Then he nodded slowly, understanding not seeming to mitigate his anger in the least.

"I suppose this is my penalty for not dropping everything and rushing to do Emperor Albert's bidding. I didn't follow him to Hell, so now he's dragged my daughter and heir apparent there?"

Albert stepped from Pearl's office, where, until the ringing of the doorbell had interrupted them, he and Pearl had been going over some old scrolls Shen's grandfather had left. Albert's smile when he met Gaheris's shocked and embarrassed gaze was not kind.

"Actually, I'm here. Brenda went on her own initiative—or rather when she was asked. That's more than I can say for her father."

"Why didn't you go if this is so damn important?" Gaheris retorted. "I suppose your business interests couldn't spare you. Or was it because the emperor must be kept safe at all costs?"

"My business," Albert said, his words very clipped, but his tone no less angry, "has been functioning fine without me—as any well-run enterprise will do, if the CEO isn't a complete control freak. As for my safety, that has never been an issue."

Pearl cut in. "Gaheris, the auguries made very clear that our chances for success in this venture were raised if we had either a Rat or an Ox—a representative of the House of Expansion—as part of the group. An Ox was out of the question, so Brenda became our best—our only—choice when you weren't available. She's in good care. Righteous Drum is an experienced father. He's not going to let anyone harm a young girl—and neither is Deborah or Riprap—neither is any of them. Brenda is just along for her symbolic value. That's it."

Gaheris had dropped his gaze to the carpet as Pearl spoke. Now he set down his sample case—clasped in his clenched fist since he had crossed the threshold—and bent his head. After a moment, he looked up and forced something like his usual grin.

"Yeah. You told me when you called all that about the House of Expansion. I guess I didn't think you'd ask Brenda to step in when I couldn't go."

He drew a deep breath, and when he let it out, his shoulders had relaxed and his smile looked almost natural. "Brenda is probably fine, probably just a little frustrated by her 'uselessness,' even."

"Or," Pearl offered, "she is pleased because we have let her be part of something important. Either way, I'm certain she's fine, just fine."

Pearl glanced at Albert, hoping that her words sounded convincing to Gaheris. When she thought about the days that had passed, and the ambiguous results of the auguries they had cast since the expedition's departure, she was less than certain that everything was "just fine."

But I can't swear, she thought as she listened to Albert make stilted attempts at conversation with Gaheris as she ushered them to the kitchen and a snack she hoped would smooth over some of the awkwardness. *And I hope to heaven that Gaheris doesn't ask me to do so.*

☆

Brenda wasn't certain what finally made the transformation possible. Maybe it hadn't been any one thing. Maybe it had been the meditation Deborah had guided her through. Maybe it had been her memories of the little rat that had sat on her head and guided her from disaster.

Maybe—and she suspected this rather strongly—Deborah had used a little magic to push the tranformation along.

Whatever the case, after a timeless interlude, Brenda found herself looking at the face of a rat in the small mirror Deborah produced from a powder compact she took from her saddlebags.

As rats went, it wasn't a bad-looking rat. The fur was silvery grey, and not in the least coarse. The—her—dark brown eyes were rimmed with a darker pigment, making them seem luminous, like she was wearing eyeliner. Her ears were pale pink. So was her long, naked tail.

Brenda had the most difficulty getting used to that tail. All the other parts of her Rat self more or less matched limbs she'd had before, but the tail was something else entirely. She could move it and curl it. It came in very useful for balancing when—under Deborah's urging—she practiced standing on her hind legs.

"That's good," Deborah said. "Very good. You're probably going to need to do that when you push up into the springs whatever our friends have concocted for the Leech. How are your paws for manipulation?"

Brenda tried and found them remarkably agile. They weren't hands, but they weren't as clumsy as she had worried they would be.

"That's nice," Deborah said with a slight sigh. "Pigs have trotters. It's like having your hands in mittens knitted from steel wool. On the other hand—if you'll pardon a humano-centric phrase—the snout is amazing."

Brenda nodded. She'd already discovered that although she could squeak, she couldn't talk. Deborah had told her that there were spells that permitted mental communication, but that they'd better check with Righteous Drum before trying one.

It turned out that this would not be necessary.

"Dragons," Righteous Drum said, "are highly magical. When I am in that form, I will be able to understand Brenda if she wishes to talk to me."

Can he read my mind? Brenda thought dismayed.

Righteous Drum was not a father for nothing. He anticipated her question.

"No. I cannot read your mind, but if you 'talk' to me in whatever fashion seems most natural to a rat, then I will understand."

Relieved, Brenda sat up on her haunches on Deborah's shoulder. Her rat's vision was different from her human vision—the focus narrower, the colors in some spectra more muted—but the difference didn't bother Brenda. Her sense of smell was marvelously acute, as was her hearing. Her skin seemed more sensitive as well, fur and whiskers both transmitting a wealth of information.

Brenda glanced over at Riprap and Flying Claw and found them both looking at her: Riprap with a certain degree of doubt and admiration, Flying Claw with what she took for pleased speculation.

"What have you come up with while Brenda and I have been gone?" Deborah asked, looking at a makeshift table that had been constructed from the heaped saddlebags.

"Amulets of banishment," Righteous Drum said. "Nine of them. I wrote three and Flying Claw—with Riprap using a spell of Knitting to enhance the available ch'i—wrote the other six."

Deborah looked at the folded packets of paper. "Won't the ink run off as soon as you go under water?"

"No. Proof against that has been written into the spell. When Brenda inserts each amulet into the appropriate intake tube, she will say 'release.' This will both give the spell a nudge in the right direction, and remove the waterproofing."

Riprap met Brenda's eyes, and Brenda thought he must have seen some aspect of her personality, because a tension went from his posture.

"Squeak 'release' actually," Riprap clarified with a grin.

"We made sure the spell would be sensitive to intent, not actual sound. The 'nudge' Righteous Drum spoke of is similar to the spell they use when they're throwing the spells—that stiffening that makes them fly like darts rather than blow around."

Brenda squeaked understanding and felt her whiskers curl forward in what she realized was a rat's equivalent of a smile. It felt simultaneously natural and very, very odd.

"The sun," said Loyal Wind, "will not be here for a while yet. I have sent my associates back along the river so that we will have news of the sun's arrival relayed almost as soon as it descends. Still, since none of your timekeeping devices are working, perhaps we should begin."

Riprap glanced at his wrist from which he'd removed a useless watch soon after their arrival in the guardian domains.

"Who would have thought simple mechanical timepieces would be so hard to find on short notice? Everything at the stores Des and I hit used a battery."

"Or that we would need watches," Deborah agreed. "Des has promised to check while we're away. We'll have plenty next time we come this way. Now, Righteous Drum, are you ready?"

"I will be," he said. "I will step away and meditate to focus my ch'i. Thanks to Riprap's ability to assist Flying Claw, I needed to spend very little to make the amulets. I shall return shortly."

And then, Brenda thought, eyeing the dark chasm into which the Suns' River made its thundering fall, *we'll go*.

Why Righteous Drum had chosen to go away from the larger group to change his shape became readily apparent when he returned. Brenda had wondered, having read that, like the Rooster, the Dragon enjoyed showing off.

True, he'd probably have to strip unless he wanted to ruin his clothing. Deborah had told Brenda that clothing could be a real problem if the creature you were shaping was larger than you or very differently shaped. Brenda hadn't had this problem. She'd just crawled out of the tangle of her shirt, leaving the clothing behind like a shed skin.

This meant, of course, that she left her amulet bracelets as well, and leaving them left Brenda feeling more naked in some ways than did her lack of clothing.

Righteous Drum did not return by land. Instead, he swam down the shallows at the edges of the Suns' River, sliding the length of his body between the larger rocks with sinuous grace. With the current to carry him, his missing foreleg did not appear to be much of a disadvantage.

"Flying Claw," Righteous Drum said, revealing yet another advantage the Dragon had over the other members of the zodiac, "tie the amulets to my antlers if you would. Brenda, I believe you will find a somewhat wider, flatter area on my neck, directly behind my head. If you seat yourself there, you will be able to reach the amulets with ease."

He had been treading water while he spoke, his long tail coiled around a rock to hold him steady. Now he came further into the shallows, resting a segment of his body against the stone of the riverbed, and raising his head.

Brenda very closely examined the dragon Righteous Drum had become as Deborah carried her down to the river.

Unsurprisingly, given his fondness for the color yellow in all its hues and shades, as a dragon, Righteous Drum had scales of a deep rich gold so pure that it was almost metallic. The scales that banded his belly were a lighter gold. His contrasting dorsal fin was a pearlescent white, as were his claws and antlers. The long whiskers that trailed from his lower jaw mingled white and gold in about equal parts, with the pair of long—almost tentacle-like—whiskers above each nostril being white.

His eyes, however, were brown, startling in their very human expression.

Brenda was squeaking at Deborah to let her down when Flying Claw turned from where he had been tying the amulets—each strung on a length of fine cord, this in turn tied to a slightly thicker cord that was suspended between the two antlers. He reached up and took Brenda from Deborah's shoulder, cupping her very securely in his warm hands.

Brenda felt very glad that rats couldn't blush, because she was pretty sure she was blushing all over at the thought of her naked body cupped in those strong hands. Flying Claw carried her over to Righteous Drum and set her on the promised wider space.

"Riprap and I made you a seatbelt," he said, showing her an extra strap tied to the one that connected to the amulets. "I will loop it so, and tie it snugly. It has sufficient play to permit you to move into the intake tubes, but it should keep you from getting carried off by a strong current."

Brenda felt very grateful, and wished she could tell Flying Claw and Riprap how much she appreciated this, but when she tried, all she did was squeak.

She heard Righteous Drum chuckle. "Brenda asks me to tell you that she is very grateful for your forethought. She was so worried about everything else, that she didn't think about something as mundane as currents."

"Thank you, Righteous Drum," Brenda thought at him, shaping the words as if she were talking.

"No inconvenience at all," he said. "Now, are you ready?"

"As ready as I'll ever be, I guess."

"Then we will go. Give us some time before you reenter the cavern where the Leech is," he reminded the others. "Loyal Wind will have the best idea how long this may take us."

"We'll watch," Deborah promised, walking swiftly along the bank of the river as Righteous Drum moved out into the current. "I've cast an All Green in the hope that we'll see when your spell starts taking effect."

Brenda had thought her fur would be plastered flat by the water, but apparently the dragon's affinity for water included providing a protection from getting soaked, as well as the promised ability to breathe water. She felt the spray, but as one would feel the touch of the wind: there, but not in the least cold or uncomfortable.

"Righteous Drum," she thought at the Dragon, *"just what is this spell we're going to give the Leech? Someone called it a banishment spell—where are we banishing it to? Will banishing it kill it?"*

"I don't know," Righteous Drum replied. "While you and Deborah were away, I did some calculations. One of these confirmed what we all felt—that the Leech is not, or is at least not wholly, a natural part of this place. We considered trying to poison it, but could not decide what poison to choose—after all, it might be immune. We considered trying to put it to sleep, but Riprap pointed out quite sensibly that since it was obviously meant to be a guardian, it might not need to sleep."

"So you decided to banish it," Brenda said, *"to make it go back where it came from—and that's why you don't know if this will kill it. Okay, but why do we need to give the spell to each head? Wouldn't one do?"*

"It might," Righteous Drum admitted, "but we decided to be careful. There are snakes that when cut into piece become a nest of snakes. We did not wish to risk creating more difficulties for ourselves. Now, we are approaching the lip of the chasm. Hold tightly. This will be where we go under."

Brenda held on as tightly as her little rat claws would let her. She considered biting down on something, but decided against it. Righteous Drum might slap her like a fly, without realizing what he was doing. Or she might cut through her "seatbelt."

The noise of falling water was deafening now, echoing up from the rocks, amplified by the rounded hole in the rock as a shout is amplified by cupped hands. She felt her ears fold down closer to her head and her whiskers flatten back against the length of her nose. Then they were going over the edge and as once before there was a sensation of falling.

This time, however, Brenda was not securely in a saddle

with knees to grip and hands to hold. Without the length of ribbon tied around her midsection, she might have been dragged away. As it was, she could feel her tail trailing behind her, snapping alarmingly as the competing forces of air and water pushed her about. Then there was a splash, more felt than heard, and they were in darkness, the thunder of falling water muffled, and only the fizz of air bubbles to remind her that they were under water.

"Are you with me, Brenda?" Righteous Drum asked. There was urgency to his voice, and his swimming was rather lopsided, but he was managing. Brenda noticed that he was speaking—really speaking—even here completely surrounded by water. She was beginning to get serious Dragon-envy.

"I am," she reassured him. "I was just trying not to distract you while you got used to this. Doing okay?"

"I am fine. I am pushing upwards, trying to find the roof of this cavern. Then we will seek the first intake. How is your vision?"

"Your spell is holding up. I can see about as well as I would in a light fog."

"Good. Then while I concentrate on swimming, you see if you can locate an intake."

Brenda wasn't quite sure how to do this, but she thought that the disturbance might be visible. She peered about, sometimes catching a glimpse of the tip of her own nose and feeling distinctly startled. Water surrounded her, but breathing was so automatic that she quickly forgot it, just as you forget air unless the wind is blowing really hard.

It was her tail, that odd appendage that because of its very oddity she had trouble forgetting, that helped her find the first intake. She felt a drag there, as if something was pulling lightly on the bare skin.

"I think I've got one," she said. "Go right and back. No, this direction."

She leaned back and tapped with one paw, pressing hard against the yielding surface of a scale.

"That's it. Good."

"I believe I see it," Righteous Drum said. "You must have excellent vision. I commend you."

I've got a smart tail, Brenda thought, but she didn't vocalize that one.

They found the intake, and Righteous Drum pushed them up, so close to the ceiling that parts of his dorsal fin squashed against the stone. Brenda bit through the string that tied one of the amulets—they were identical, so she didn't have to choose—and reared up on her haunches, feeling for the opening.

"Make certain it's well in there," Righteous Drum reminded her. "There are other currents, including the ones I am creating by swimming."

I know. I know, Brenda thought, but she could tell he was nervous, and didn't say anything. Instead she concentrated on finding the opening, reaching up with the amulet held firmly by the string, making sure neither to let go, nor to bite through. She let her head and shoulders enter the opening and immediately felt the tug of the water.

Mingled with the swirling that was the water's own current was a rhythmic pulse that made her heart beat faster. She knew without explanation that the pulse was the Leech, sucking then swallowing, then sucking again.

She opened her jaws and let the amulet go. As she did, she squeaked, "Release!" as she had been told. The folded paper opened, flowering above her, and a trail of green ink tinted the water before diluting into the upward flow.

Grabbing the line of her "seatbelt"—Brenda was thinking of it as a lifeline by now—Brenda kicked her back legs and worked her way down onto Righteous Drum's back.

"One down," she said. *"Let's find the next opening."*

Finding the second opening proved much easier. Righteous Drum had remembered that the Nine Yellow Springs were arrayed in an elongated circle around the gigantic magnolia tree. A few roots of the tree had penetrated even this deep, giving them a center point. He now calculated the approximate arc, and swam where the second opening should be. Brenda felt the pull of the water before Righteous Drum labored them into position.

He's going to get really tired, Brenda thought. *I wonder if he'll be able to get us out of here?*

But she didn't have attention to spare for even such a worrisome thought. Each intake tube was unique. The second had a nasty curve around which water flowed smoothly, but where the paper holding the spell caught. Brenda was pretty certain the spell would work even without the paper, but she wriggled up to push it free, just to make sure.

The third and fourth tubes went well, but by then Brenda was feeling very tired. Rats swam, but what she was doing here wasn't quite swimming, but rather combined pushing and climbing with swimming. Then, too, Brenda wasn't used to this shape, and although Deborah had told her she could tap something she referred to as "body memory," that went only so far when asking a body to do unusual acts.

Brenda struggled with getting the fifth spell into the tube, and as she readied herself for the sixth, she was aware that Righteous Drum was also losing strength. Extra effort was needed to bring her close enough to the ceiling that she could insert the paper into the tube. Moreover, he sank down almost as soon as she pushed off.

"Please come back up here," she thought at him. *"There was a bit of water in my last breath."*

Righteous Drum didn't say anything, but her breathing cleared.

After inserting the sixth spell, Brenda grabbed on to the lifeline to guide herself back. She'd worked out a hauling motion with both paws pressed together around the line. It didn't quite make up for the lack of a thumb, but it helped. She was tugging hard, trying to get back to Righteous Drum so she could suggest he take a rest before they finished inserting the last three spells, when with a quickening of her heart she felt the line sag, then tighten.

"The line's breaking . . ." she managed to think, and then it broke.

The force of the water drew her upwards, into the smoothly polished interior of the intake tube. Brenda lashed out, trying to grab a hold on the wall.

Sun-polished, she thought. *Of course it would be, with the sun setting in this pool once a day. I wonder if the waters boil?*

But the thought was fleeting, gone before it was really shaped as she scrabbled and kicked. The pull of the stream dragged her up, and she had the sense to hold her breath, not trusting Righteous Drum's magic to penetrate this far.

Her head pounded. Reddish lights thudded behind eyes she didn't know she'd squeezed shut. Panic played a drum in her head: drowned rat, drowned rat, drowned rat . . .

Then almost simultaneously, two things happened. The current slowed, almost stopped, and something twined around her middle. It wrapped around her, squeezing hard, squishing her last hoarded breath from her lungs. She gasped, expected to breathe water, but met with air.

"Righteous Drum?"

"I have you," he said, "and will pull you forth."

He sounded exhausted, so she didn't ask more. Instead she looked down at herself, wondering how the dragon had managed to grab her. To her astonishment, wrapped around her was one of the long tentacle-like whiskers that adorned the dragon's nose. It looked bruised, and Brenda thought it probably wasn't intended for such a task.

Righteous Drum drew her forth, more by sinking down and letting Brenda guide herself (and the whisker) out of the intake tube, than by any systematic planning. He reached a point in the waters where he could drift, and he did this for a time, regaining his strength.

"Thanks," Brenda thought shyly.

"What happened? You were there, then not."

Brenda inspected the lifeline. *"I think the line may have*

been nicked when I pulled myself out one of those times. I had to use my teeth a couple times—not having hands—and they're pretty sharp."

"Yes. That might do it." There was no blame in the words, only assessment and fatigue. "Can you continue?"

Brenda was inspecting the line. *"Not with this. Can you hold me with your—uh—nose tentacle like you did before?"*

"I can, but it might be better if I held on to your tail. Getting the tentacle into that intake tube was difficult. This way my protections will extend to you, and I can draw you out when you are finished."

Hearing determination, but certainly no confidence in the words, Brenda asked hesitantly, *"Are you sure you're up to it? Do we really need to finish? We've gotten six of the nine in. Surely that's enough."*

"I believe I can. I have rested a little here, and feel much stronger."

Brenda didn't believe he felt all that much stronger, but she wasn't about to argue. Maybe it was her imagination, maybe it was all this exertion, but she thought the water was getting a little warmer.

Their new technique worked rather well, although Brenda didn't much like the feeling of the tentacle wrapped around her tail. She didn't have the same freedom of movement, either, but at least she didn't need to pull herself back.

The seventh amulet went into the tube, the eighth, then the ninth. Brenda watched the ink—golden yellow this time, so one of the spells Righteous Drum himself had written—vanish up the intake tube. She hadn't felt the pulsing of the Leech's sucking this last couple of times, and hoped that meant it was out of action.

Of course, it might simply have been taking a break, as it apparently had been doing shortly before their arrival.

Righteous Drum congratulated her, then sank down to that midpoint where he could rest with the water holding him in place. Brenda realized she was panting.

"Righteous Drum! The water's getting warmer. I think the sun must be coming."

No answer. Brenda realized that he must have fallen asleep. She stretched forward and bit him on one ear. He started.

"The water's getting warmer," Brenda repeated. *"You've got to get us out of here!"*

Righteous Drum moved his whiskered head from side to side. "Can't. Too tired. No ch'i. Honey . . . I'm sorry, Honey . . ."

Incoherent as the speech was, Brenda suddenly understood several things she had not before. She'd envied the dragon's varied abilities, but she hadn't realized that all of them had used stored ch'i. Now that ch'i was depleted, and if they didn't get out of this underwater prison soon, they were likely to drown.

Drown or be boiled. What a choice. I can't count on him to get us out of here.

For a moment, Brenda considered abandoning Righteous Drum. If she let go her hold on his back, she could probably swim to the surface. There she might find air pockets, useless for something the size of a dragon, but adequate to sustain a rat.

I could do that, she thought. *Then when I'm out of here, I could bring help. My leaving might even help him, because he's probably using ch'i to make it possible for me to breathe.*

But Brenda couldn't fool herself. Who could get in here and retrieve the nearly comatose dragon?

If I had a rope, I could tie it around him and try and pull him out, but I don't have a rope and I'm too small. A thought teased at the edges of her mind, a thought she didn't want to consider for some reason. Brenda made herself pin it down. *I don't need to stay small. I can go back to being human. Then I can tow Righteous Drum out of here. As long as I'm holding on to him, the ability to breathe water should extend to me. If not, well, I'll just have to hope to find an air pocket at the top.*

Turning back into a human was easy—in many ways staying a rat had been harder. Brenda let herself slide off Righteous Drum's back, and moved around to his front end. To her relief, ordinary swimming motions worked, although the surrounding water still felt a lot more like a breeze against her skin.

Brenda felt immense relief when she saw Righteous Drum's eyes were heavily lidded, almost closed. She knew Righteous Drum currently was a dragon and that even when he was human he was older than her dad, but still she was already blushing all over at the thought of pulling this man behind her naked butt.

She didn't see how she had many choices though. Even at its narrowest point, the dragon's tail was fairly wide, and getting a grip on it would be complicated by the wide, flaring fin that fanned out from the tip. That left tugging Righteous Drum by his remaining arm or by his head.

Long ago, Brenda had learned a variety of lifesaving carries, and one—used for either an unconscious or unresisting victim—involved cupping one hand under the rescue's chin and then swimming either sidestroke or in a modified backstroke. She tried this, and after adjusting her grip several times, she found one that worked.

Her legs were sore from days in the saddle, but she managed a fairly powerful scissor kick, reserving her arm to steer. There was no doubt as to the direction she should go—a distinctly warmer current showed where the Suns' River dropped into this underground pool.

Brenda kicked harder. The dragon—its eyes completely shut now—came along smoothly, seeming impossibly light.

Maybe the dragon's affinity with water is working with us, Brenda thought. *Maybe he's just aerodynamic, or whatever the word is for things that glide well underwater.*

Brenda knew she was thinking nonsense, but anything was better than the panic that was rising despite her best efforts to keep it back. She resisted the temptation to count each stroke, to try and calculate how far each one carried them. Instead she let song lyrics with a strong beat flow through her head, both last year's hits and the classic rock her folks liked.

Anything but thinking about water so hot that it made stone melt smooth. Anything but thinking about how much she wanted to leave behind the inert form she was dragging behind her. Anything but thinking about what would happen if she failed.

About the time the water started growing painfully hot, Brenda became aware of a new sensation. It took her a moment to place, then her heart lifted as she recognized the vibrations of the waterfall. The current fizzed with air bubbles.

"We're almost there!" she cheered, but if Righteous Drum could hear her, there was no sign.

How am I going to get him up? she thought. *What if everyone left? What if they think we've both drowned? What if the sun is too close and they've already retreated to someplace safer?*

Brenda kicked harder, letting panic give force to muscles gone limp and rubbery. She swam, angling upward, upward, and finally her head broke the surface of the water.

"Somebody! Anybody!" she yelled. "Get us out of here!"

XXVI

A scream ripped through the scholarly peace of Pearl's house. Pearl, who had been nodding over a scroll of notes, flung her head back so suddenly she rapped it on the back of her chair.

Shen stopped copying out an elaborate design, dropped his ink brush—ruining hours of patient labor—and bolted to his feet.

Upstairs, where Des and Nissa were making amulets, the

study door flung open, striking against one of the book-shelves in the hallway. Almost immediately thereafter, two pairs of footsteps thudded down the stairs.

But Pearl had not waited for them, or for Shen. She was running toward the back of the house, toward the kitchen, in the direction from where the scream had come.

If Pearl had any thought other than to act, it was that Waking Lizard or Honey Dream had been cut or burned, but something in how her legs moved with a fluidity that Pearl had thought lost to her showed that her body knew otherwise, knew this was urgent.

Pearl found Honey Dream on her knees, head thrown forward, dark hair caught in a loose ponytail falling to curtain her face. Waking Lizard knelt next to her, one hand on the young woman's shoulder, his face anxious.

"What's wrong?"

"I don't know. We were both meditating. Her scream brought me out. I found her like this."

Pearl knelt next to Honey Dream, bending her head so she could see the girl's face.

Honey Dream's expression was one of blank horror, and her lips moved, repeating the same word: "*Ba Ba*." "Daddy."

"Honey Dream! Honey Dream! Snap out of it! What's wrong?"

Pearl was vaguely aware that Des, Nissa, and Shen had joined them.

"Des," Pearl said without looking away from Honey Dream, "check out the windows. This could be meant to distract us."

Honey Dream was still muttering, "*Ba Ba! Ba Ba!*" and now tears were streaming down her cheeks. Still she did not seem completely aware of her surroundings.

Pearl glanced up at Waking Lizard. "She seems caught between states. Do you have any special way to break her out of it?"

"My teacher always threw cold water at us," Waking Lizard admitted, tugging at one side of his mustache, "to shock us, but Honey Dream seems shocked enough."

Nissa had pushed her way in, and now she wrapped an arm around Honey Dream's shoulders. Waking Lizard and Pearl moved back to give her room.

Nissa was murmuring something soft and soothing. Pearl felt a touch of ch'i woven into the words, and wondered if Nissa realized she was weaving a spell of comfort, of mother love.

Slowly, Honey Dream seemed to hear. Her breathing, which had been both irregular and ragged, eased, fell into more normal rhythms. She made as if to pull herself upward, and Nissa helped her, easing her to a seat on the carpet. Honey Dream's eyes were no longer blank, but the horror remained.

"*Ba Ba*," she muttered, then shook herself and looked around. As soon she registered where she was, she began pushing herself to her feet.

Nissa pressed her down. "Easy. You've had a shock. What's wrong?"

Honey Dream continued to move onto her feet, and Nissa let her, rising in cadence.

"What's wrong?" Nissa repeated.

"My father," Honey Dream said. "I heard him talking to me. He was in terrible trouble. Dying. He was apologizing to me for not coming back."

As she spoke, she had tried to move for the front door. Waking Lizard grabbed her by the arm, a courageous gesture, for the young woman's eyes were becoming quite wild, and in their days of combat practice Pearl had come to respect her abilities.

"Where are you going?" Waking Lizard demanded.

"My father," Honey Dream said simply. "I've got to go find him. I've got to save him, or if I can't I must bring him out."

"He's days' travel from here," Des protested, coming into the room and indicating with a crisp shake of his head that he hadn't seen anything wrong outside the house. "One way or another, you couldn't reach him before whatever you sensed was over."

"If you sensed anything," Waking Lizard said. "How do you know this isn't a trap of some sort?"

Honey Dream stared at him. "I know. And who would wish to trap me?"

"How about those very interesting people you have been talking to in the darkness?" he said.

Pearl and Shen exchanged confused glances, but Honey Dream clearly knew what Waking Lizard was talking about.

The anguish did not leave her, but now surprise was there as well. "You knew?"

"Of course I know," Waking Lizard said. "You've already proven yourself unpredictable—and unreliable. Do you think we haven't been watching you?"

"But you let me?"

"Why interfere? We might learn something, although I think they probably learned more."

Honey Dream shook free of his grasp, and stood considering.

"Waking Lizard, I know. That was my father I heard. He was in agony, wrung out, dreading something so horrible that he knew he was going to die. I know his voice . . ."

The last words were a plea, but there was not a trace of doubt in them.

"And what are you going to do?" Waking Lizard said. He didn't move, but Des had inserted himself in the door that led to the front of the house. His posture was casual, but Pearl knew how quickly Des could move and was certain Honey Dream would not get by him. The backyard was a dead end. Ever since the night of the prowlers, the locks and wards had been intensified so that even if anyone got in, they would never get out.

Honey Dream seemed to realize she was trapped, and her shoulders slumped. "Please. I have to go. I have to help him. You didn't hear him. He needs me."

"What were you going to do?" Waking Lizard persisted.

Pearl wanted to ask other things. Were the others in equal danger? Were all of them dead? She bit down on the questions and schooled her expression to calm interest. Whatever the nature of Honey Dream's vision—true or false—it had clearly been intensely personal.

"I was . . ." Honey Dream looked as if she was considering the details of her plan for the first time, and realizing how tenuous they were. "I was going to go outside. Find a cab. Get it to take me to the gate. Beg Pai Hu to take me to where I could find my father."

"Not bad," Waking Lizard said. "And now?"

"Please!" Honey Dream said. "I have to know. Auguries won't tell us anything. Let me at least go and beg Pai Hu if he knows anything."

She stopped. Swallowed hard. Then with incredible ease and grace she fell to her knees in front of Pearl and began beating her head against the floor in a humiliatingly groveling kowtow.

"Please, Tiger. Come with me. Help me ask the White Tiger of the West about my father's fate. He might not care about Righteous Drum, but surely he has some sense of the other Tiger. I beg you!"

"Child!" Pearl grabbed those slender shoulders and forced Honey Dream to her feet, surprising herself with her own strength. "Stop that! You could have just asked."

"I am unworthy. I am an unworthy ally. I have consorted with our enemies. I am lower than the dust beneath a snake's belly. I have been jealous, envious, and lazy, but in one thing I have been true. I have been a good daughter to my father. I beg you, you who should be upheld with Miao Shan as an exemplar of filial piety in adversity, please, help me."

It was quite a speech, and Pearl found herself wondering if it had been rehearsed, but there was a red mark on Honey Dream's forehead where she had struck it against the floor. The tears in her eyes were genuine, as was the anguish on her face.

Pearl looked around at the others. "Well," she said slowly, "I don't see what harm could come from asking. What do the rest of you think?"

"Two of us should stay," Nissa said promptly, "in case Honey Dream is being manipulated. We know we have adversaries in the Rock Dove Society, and the prisoners might have pulled something off. Lani will be back from a playdate with some of Joanne's other prospects in an hour, so I'll stay."

"I had better, too," Shen said. "My spells will work better in defense than in the field. I fear I have let myself become too much of a scholar."

"Then the rest of us will go," Pearl said. "Des, can you bring the town car around?"

"Done," he said. "I'm going to run upstairs for a few things, then I'll be off."

"Don't forget we must be careful not to create an incident," she said.

"I remember," Des agreed. "In fact, I've prepared a kit precisely for this sort of thing."

"Waking Lizard? Do you agree that we need to let Honey Dream reassure herself? And do you understand that if this is a trap, we must take special care not to create an incident that can be used against us by Franklin Deng and his allies?"

"I do." He reached into an umbrella stand and pulled out his hard whip, a stiff rod that to an untrained eye could be mistaken for a walking stick. "See? I won't even carry a sword."

Pearl, who had seen him do amazing things with nothing but a length of bamboo, only smiled. She turned to Honey Dream.

"Wash your face and pull yourself together. I'm going to phone Albert and Gaheris. This may be nothing—I hope it is—but we're not going to leave without taking precautions."

Honey Dream looked calmer, but there was still a wildness to her eyes. "We won't take long?"

"We'll take less time," Pearl promised, "than you would have to find a taxi in this neighborhood at this time of day."

☆

Pearl was still on the phone talking to Albert when Des brought the car around. She got in the front, and motioned Honey Dream and Waking Lizard to the backseat.

Nissa had come out with them, and now she handed in Pearl's sword case, and a handful of amulet bracelets.

"Good luck," she said, and closed the car door firmly behind them. Honey Dream watched as if she were still in a trance as Nissa ran up the porch steps and closed the door of the house. She imagined she could hear the Rabbit snapping closed the locks and resetting the wards.

Des pulled away from the curb, muttering as he navigated the sudden congestion of traffic as some event let out at the museum. Waking Lizard sat very still and quiet on his side of the seat, but Honey Dream did not mind. She needed to think.

Part of me feels half asleep, as if I still haven't broken out of my meditation. Another part of me—it's as if I'm awake for the first time in a long time. What has happened?

Honey Dream looked deep into her own soul, and tried not to flinch away from what she saw. She saw how for many months now she had been wrapped up in herself, so deeply involved with herself and her own desires that every event was distorted by the broken prism of self-interest.

Even before they had left the Lands, she had felt this way, even before she had been anointed the Snake. She had so wanted to prove herself, so wanted to stand out, to be remarkable, to be unique that she had not cared what happened as long as she could turn the opportunities to her benefit.

And why? A face rose into her mind. Flying Claw. It was his fault. If he had only looked at her, not scorned the love she had thrown at his feet . . .

At his feet. Honey Dream had a sudden image of herself just a few minutes ago, down on the floor, beating her head against the floor. She touched her forehead with one finger and found it slightly swollen. It would bruise.

And she realized she didn't care. And she realized that Flying Claw was not to blame for not accepting her love. Love wasn't something that could be forced, but she had tried to force it. He had even been noble. There had been times . . .

She blushed and was glad that no one was looking at her. Yes. There had been times. Not only over these last several months, not even since they became Tiger and Snake, but before: when they met at court events, when they had "chanced" on each other.

How little "chance" had there been in some of those encounters, but Flying Claw had not taken advantage even when she had given him ample excuse. Honey Dream wanted to hate him for being noble when she had been debased, but in her current rawness of soul she could not. The rawness hurt, and she dug a mental finger into it, probing for the root of this new honesty.

What has broken me so? Where have my illusions gone?

And she knew. No matter what the others thought, she had heard Righteous Drum's voice, full of pain, but unmistakable nonetheless.

"Honey . . . Honey . . . I am sorry."

Sorry. Sorry because he wasn't going to come back. Sorry because he had tried and failed. Sorry because now she was going to have to push on alone, and even if she succeeded, her reward would be telling her mother that Righteous Drum was dead, that he had gone into the underworld, and was not going to return.

Honey Dream knew she loved her father, knew that love to be as sweet and pure as a drop of honey from the comb. For him she had studied and striven, for him she had sought the Snake's lore, because if she could not be a Dragon as he was, then she would be the Dragon's match—the Snake.

How angry she had been when they came to this world and she had seen how everything was distorted, how there were female Tigers and male Roosters. It had been an anger to feed other angers that had been brooding since before they had left the Lands—anger at those who had not thought her worthy of being the Snake, anger at those who did not believe Righteous Drum's theory explaining why their powers were attenuated, anger at the enemies who pressed their emperor—and even anger at the Snake she had succeeded for not having given Honey Dream enough time to prove herself.

Anger. All her life for days and weeks and months had been colored by anger, but hearing Righteous Drum's voice, hearing it fading had washed that anger away with something far more powerful—grief, grief and terrible, horrible, overwhelming fear.

Des's voice, sharp and imperative, broke Honey Dream's reverie.

"Don't anyone turn around, but I think we're being followed. There's been a car behind us since we got out of the crush at the museum. Tan sedan. Pretty average. Driver's wearing shades and a hat, but I think it's Downhill Ski."

Waking Lizard glanced over at Honey Dream. She shook her head and even smiled. "I didn't do anything. I didn't send any messages. If they're back there, it's because they've been watching us for days."

"I agree," Pearl said, surprising Honey Dream somewhat. She'd never thought the old Tiger would give her the benefit of the doubt.

And no wonder, Honey Dream thought. *Since you broke into her house, and attacked one of her guests.*

"My wards," Pearl said, "would be difficult to breach without my knowing. If our adversaries somehow sent a vision to panic Honey Dream, that's not her fault. It could have been whichever one of us was deep enough in meditation to stray into vulnerable territory."

Pearl swung around in the seat and looked directly at Honey Dream. "And I'm not saying that's what happened. I accept you believe your father is in danger. We're going to find out what has happened—whatever it takes."

Waking Lizard patted the seat by his leg. For the first time, Honey Dream noticed he held his hard whip, the short staff that was one of his favorite weapons—especially when subduing an enemy, not killing him was the goal.

"If they do come after us," he said, "what does the Tiger direct?"

Pearl chuckled, an unfriendly sound, like a Tiger's cough.

"Des is going to drive us directly through the gate into the warehouse. If they attempt to follow us there, I call both the business park's security and the police. If somehow they block that, then we do our best to behave in a fashion that will get us the favorable ruling when the matter comes up before judgment."

"In other words," Des said, turning in to the industrial park, "we improvise."

"Within limits," Pearl agreed.

Honey Dream nodded and fingered the handful of bracelets Nissa had thrust in along with Pearl's sword. For the first time, she considered the tremendous expenditure of both time and ch'i they represented. It had been a generous gesture— especially since her own broken mediation had left her own ch'i at a lower ebb than would be usual.

I will live up to your generosity, she thought. *The time has come for me to live up to someone other than myself.*

☆

Brenda listened but the water thundering down from above made that an exercise in futility. She glanced over at the waterfall. Was that steam? No. Just spray.

She swam to where she could position her feet on Righteous Drum's back. The Dragon was positioned in what she'd been taught to call a "deadman's float," head hanging, arms and legs limp. She knew it was supposed to be a very energy-efficient posture, and she knew he wasn't going to drown, even if his nose and mouth were under water, but she didn't like how it looked.

Was he even breathing? She put a hand to one scaled side, but she couldn't tell.

Feeling like a louse, Brenda climbed up onto the Dragon's back and worked herself into a standing position. That put her head a good five and a half feet above water level.

She yelled again.

"Get us out of here! Riprap! Deborah! Help!"

She kept yelling as long as she had breath, deliberately varying the cadence and pitch, hoping to find the sound that would carry over the roar of falling water.

She was taking another breath when a horse's head leaned over the edge. A grey with a dark mane. Deborah's mount.

It turned its head, made some sound she couldn't hear, but a moment later, Loyal Wind and two other horses joined it. Loyal Wind's eyes widened slightly, and Brenda remembered that she was stark naked. She fought the impulse to cover herself, realizing she'd look much more vulnerable if she did so.

Try and look like running around bare-assed naked is something you do every day, Brenda, she coached herself.

Loyal Wind had swung up into his saddle. Now he was running over the edge. From how his mount moved, Brenda guessed that the footing—even for ghosts—was rather chancy.

Brenda dropped back into the water. Loyal Wind was uncoiling a rope, and she didn't need to guess what they'd need to do. When he dropped an end, she seized it and dove under, looping it under the Dragon's torso behind his front set of legs. She came up again and tied it off. The knot wasn't very tidy, but she thought it would hold.

Loyal Wind had urged his mount upward almost before the knot was tied. Slowly, still hanging limp, Righteous Drum rose free of the water. As he did so, Brenda became instantly aware of two things.

One, she was now soaking wet, and two she was breathing in as much water as air. The water also felt hotter than it had, and she realized that Righteous Drum had been protecting her from some of the variations in temperature as well.

Maybe that means he's alive, she thought, treading water hard, and angling to where Leaf was now making his way down. *But don't unicorns' horns keep their virtue even when they're cut off? Maybe it's the same for Chinese dragons.*

The chasm was rather tight, at least when two horses, a grown man, and a Dragon were all trying to maneuver using the wind for footing. However, they managed, and Brenda wasn't quite drowned when the golden horse got down to her. She reached up with alarmingly fading strength for one of the dangling stirrups, and grabbed hold.

Leaf didn't wait any longer. He dug in and Brenda could feel the tremendous straining of his muscles as he sought a foothold on nothing. His upward progress was irregular and jerky, but Brenda held on to the stirrup although her fingers screamed protest. She swung back and forth, hitting the heat-polished rock walls several times, but at last the golden horse had cleared the edge. He rose further, hauling her up so that he could set her on her feet on the edge.

Brenda wanted to do nothing more than crumple, but one glance down the tunnel through which the Suns' River had its course told her this would be fatal. When she and Righteous Drum had descended, the tunnel had been dark—would have been inky black except for the spell Righteous Drum had worked on her eyes. Now it was well lit, not quite the retina-searing brilliance she had experienced once before, but bright enough that she didn't need Leaf's urging to keep her feet.

She staggered forward a few paces, found her balance, and kept moving in the direction of the meadow that held the Nine Yellow Springs. It seemed terribly unfair that no one but the Horses had come to their rescue. Now even Loyal Wind was gone, presumably getting Righteous Drum to safety. She forced herself to move step by labored step.

Leaf landed next to Brenda, nudged her with his nose,

obviously offering to carry her, but Brenda didn't think she could get her foot up into the stirrup. She leaned against the horse, her arms and legs both punishingly weary from the unaccustomed exertions. The leaning helped, and she moved more rapidly.

Brenda guessed when she was safe by a combination of the reduction of sound from the river and the fact that Leaf would let her move more slowly. There was grass beneath her feet now, and she fell forward, almost without volition.

Something caught her before she hit, but she passed out before she could decide what or who.

Brenda came around to the heavy scent of magnolia blossoms and the gentle sound of tinkling fountains. She was lying on something soft, with something softer pulled over her. She ached everywhere, but the crippling exhaustion that had come upon her as a result of her final exertions was mostly gone.

She remembered everything, including the horrible limpness of Righteous Drum as Loyal Wind pulled him up out of the water. Her eyes came open of their own accord, and she discovered that at least part of the softness she was lying on was Deborah's lap.

"You're awake this time?" Deborah said softly.

Brenda wondered about the "this time," and tried to speak. She discovered her throat was raw, and the effort made her cough. She rolled slightly, and Deborah held a cloth to her mouth.

"You've been coughing up water for hours," she said. "Loyal Wind says that the air down there where the waterfall hit was more water than air—especially with the steam rising. We're very lucky you didn't drown."

"Ri . . ." Brenda started coughing again, and Deborah bent her knees to help her get air. There was something practiced about the motion that told Brenda she'd probably been doing that repeatedly.

"Righteous Drum is alive," Deborah said, "and in some

ways in better shape than you are, because the Dragon's form protected him even after he passed out. He's over talking to the springs."

Brenda didn't feel any urge to ask how one could talk to water. She could almost hear a voice in those light, tinkling notes.

Deborah went on, "You must be wondering why we weren't waiting to pull you out."

Brenda nodded, and felt a vague triumph that the action didn't start her choking.

"Quite simply, we didn't realize you'd need help. Loyal Wind assured us that the Dragon could swim upstream as easily as down—even with a missing forelimb. We had no idea that you were in such difficulties."

Brenda managed a weak, "Ah!"

"Then we were having troubles of our own."

"Oh?"

This last was followed by another fit of coughing. The manner in which Deborah efficiently dealt with the slime Brenda coughed up reminded Brenda that she'd been a nurse.

"Yes. Almost from the start, we realized that you and Righteous Drum were succeeding. Our first sign was when the Leech heads began dropping off of the springs. Then, somewhere around the fifth or sixth head, the Leech began thrashing around. It wasn't until the seventh head that we realized that the thrashing was not the purposeless motion of a dying or wounded creature, but some sort of battle."

I'm glad we didn't quit after my lifeline broke, Brenda thought, but she didn't try to say anything. She made a sound she hoped indicated interest, and Deborah continued.

"The Leech was being attacked by the Nine-Headed Snake—the guardian of the springs. From what we could tell, the Leech had actually possessed the Nine-Headed Snake. Even though the banishment was working, apparently the Nine-Headed Snake wasn't going to let the Leech go without exacting revenge."

Brenda grinned, and Deborah laughed. "I can't blame it either."

Her expression grew serious. "When the Nine-Headed Snake won, our troubles started. You see, the Nine-Headed Snake wasn't completely sane—or maybe it wasn't too bright. It saw us and came to the conclusion that we were the source of its difficulties. Unlike the Leech, it wasn't anchored to the ground, and it came after us."

Brenda gasped, swallowed a cough, and motioned for Deborah to keep talking.

"We had a real problem then," Deborah said, "because we didn't want to hurt the Nine-Headed Snake, but we couldn't retreat down the tunnel, because the relay of horses had already informed us that the sun was setting. I refuse to give you a play-by-play. Ask Riprap if you want one. I'm certain he'll remember the details. What I remember is a flurry of defense spells on our part, and Loyal Wind and the horses—carrying us—swooping around those nine heads while we did our best to loop rope around them. We finally managed, and got the creature hog-tied."

Deborah grinned. "If that's the right word for bundling a bunch of necks together so the thing couldn't move. We went over to try and talk to it. Flying Claw felt certain it must be at least somewhat intelligent. He also reminded us that the springs, once they recovered from being abused, would possess intelligence of a sort. Then there was the tree . . ."

She shook her head in wonder. "Loyal Wind hadn't forgotten the approaching sun, though, and he was worried you would be in difficulty if you remained below much longer. He went back to check. Do you remember the rest?"

Brenda nodded.

"Good. Then all that's left is to get you tidied up a bit and for us all to go over and speak with the springs. As soon as they came to themselves," she gestured at the nine elegant fountains that now spurted where the Leech's sucking heads had been, "they were eager to express their thanks. Making 'men' between them and our gates will not prove the least difficult. However, they insisted that you be present, since you risked so much for their freedom."

Deborah helped Brenda get cleaned up and dressed. Standing actually helped with the coughing, and Brenda decided to resist asking who other than Loyal Wind had seen her naked.

"I'm one big bruise," she said, looking over herself as she pulled on her jeans, and reached for her shirt.

"You're lucky to be alive, without broken bones," Deborah said, "but, yeah, you do look rather like a banana a couple days past sale date. And you'll look worse before you're better. Unless . . ."

She left that, because Riprap was coming over to them. He had a bandage wrapped around his right forearm, and another around one thigh. Apparently, Deborah had downplayed just a little the dangers involved in "hog-tying" the Nine-Headed Snake.

Looking around for the first time, Brenda realized that she and Deborah were in a hollow between two of the hills. The gigantic magnolia tree overhung them, accounting for the delicious perfume in the air.

"The springs told us Brenda was on her feet again," Riprap said. "Congratulations, kid. You had us all worried."

"Thanks," Brenda said, fumbling to finish buttoning her shirt. "I'm doing a lot better, but I don't think I'll be singing anytime soon. My throat's shot."

"Righteous Drum says you towed him out of there," Riprap said, "after nearly getting drowned putting those amulets in place. You've been a champ."

"No more than anyone," Brenda said.

Deborah nodded, and Brenda saw that she had a bandage wrapped around one ankle.

"Think if we lean on each other we can make it over there?" Deborah asked. "Righteous Drum is doing well for someone who should be dead, but actually, he isn't very mobile."

Brenda thought with no pleasure about the days of riding necessary to take them back to their gate.

But what choice do we have? she asked herself. *Maybe we can rest here a few days. Maybe. But time's running out, and every sunset we wait may be one too many.*

"You lean on Riprap," Brenda said, testing her own footing and finding it steady enough. "I'm certain I can walk."

XXVII

Pearl tucked her phone away after finishing filling Albert in on the changed situation. She hadn't been able to reach Gaheris, but that wasn't surprising. She wasn't certain he was even in state. He'd apologized before leaving her house that last time, asked them to make sure Brenda called when she "gets back from her adventure," and had promised to make himself available the minute the Nine Gates were established.

"That's why I'm working so hard, now," he'd explained as he was heading down the steps. "So I can take a leave of indefinite duration—with no cell phone or computer contact to the office—at short notice."

Pearl didn't comment that Albert had already taken leave from his business—and Des, Riprap, and Nissa from their jobs. Gaheris was prickly enough as it was.

But Pearl didn't want to think about Gaheris Morris, or even what might await them at the warehouse. Honey Dream's comparison of her to Miao Shan had left her startled—and deeply flattered.

Every child raised within the Chinese culture knew the story of Miao Shan. The versions varied, but one thing remained constant. Despite the opposition of her father, Miao Shan had managed to follow her own desire to pursue a religious life rather than marry, and yet had still been a loyal daughter. Miao Shan's treatment by her father had made Thundering Heaven's scornful rejection seem mild, but in the end Miao Shan's piety and determination had won out. To this day she was held up both as a model of filial piety (by the Confucians) and divine compassion (by the Buddhists).

And Honey Dream sees me as an exemplar equal to Miao Shan? Pearl thought. *If only she knew how black and hateful my thoughts have been—have always been. If only she knew how much I'd give for one word of approval from the old Tiger.*

"Uh-oh," Des said as they turned the corner onto the street that fronted Pearl's warehouse. "We've got company—ahead of us, as well as behind."

Pearl saw that a long, black limo had drawn up in front of the gate that protected the warehouse. She reached for her phone. Static.

"My phone's jammed," she said. Des reached with one hand and handed her his. "Yours too."

"Do I park?"

"Why not?" she said, glancing to see if Waking Lizard or Honey Dream had anything to add.

Both looked quietly watchful, but offered no protest. Honey Dream in particular looked like she might go right through anyone who got in her way. She was fingering a handful of amulet bracelets, and Pearl saw they were already arrayed with a defensive spell first, followed by a variety of attacks.

"Let's talk first, all right?"

Honey Dream nodded. Des pulled the car up alongside the limo, and turned off the engine. Pearl got out first.

"Why hello, Franklin," she said, as brightly and lightly as if they were meeting at some charitable function. "Would you mind moving your car? I need to get into my warehouse."

Franklin Deng blinked. Obviously, he'd been prepared for a good number of reactions to his presence, but not this.

But then you were always a bit unimaginative, Pearl thought, *at least regarding anything other than frozen food.*

"I believe this is a public road," he said, glancing over her.

Pearl heard another car pulling up, and knew the sedan had arrived. She didn't react, even though now they were surely outnumbered by a minimum of two. She could see at least a driver and two others in the limo, and Des had noted there were at least two in the sedan.

"Actually," she said, continuing conversational, "I believe this is all private property, owned and maintained by the business park."

From behind her, Tracy Frye's voice came mocking and brittle. "So why don't you call the cops? Why don't you call the police? Hoping Security will make a patrol by here soon? I wouldn't hold my breath."

"Tracy!" Franklin said, but his reprimand held a note of weariness. Pearl didn't doubt that the urbane restaurateur was very tired of this abrasive woman. She also didn't doubt that Franklin and his associates had worked something to keep Security away. There were spells of aversion and misdirection, as well as wards. There was also the simple incentive of a bribe.

Pearl glanced over and saw that Downhill Ski and Tracy Frye had gotten out of the sedan. Her own group were out of the town car. Waking Lizard was ambling loose-limbed over to Pearl's side, while Honey Dream had moved to where she could see if the gate was completely blocked by the limo. Pearl didn't doubt that it was.

Des was leaning against the driver's side of a town car, but Pearl didn't doubt that he was ready to act or react as needed.

"Kindly move your vehicle," Pearl said, putting steel in the words this time. "My young friend," she angled her head in Honey Dream's direction, "feels a very strong need to get in there."

"We will let her in most gladly," Franklin replied, "but we would request an invitation to join you. We have been told that you have installed a very interesting device there, and we wish to inspect it."

"Yeah," said Tracy Frye. "Look it over so we can tell all the other bird fanciers that whatever you are doing is being kept all safe and sound."

Pearl knew Tracy was trying to annoy her, and knowing that didn't mean the woman was any less annoying—just as a sword doesn't become less sharp for having seen it in the process of being honed.

What did interest her was Franklin's reaction. Clearly they were not playing a scripted game of "good cop/bad cop" or "reasonable versus unreasonable."

"This is all private property," Pearl repeated, "building and road both. Please give me access to them."

"Or?"

The word hung in the air between them.

"Please, Franklin," Pearl said. "Be reasonable. It is broad daylight. There are rules—rules set by your organization, but by which mine abides."

"We are not violating them," Franklin replied. "My car can be moved, but only when you agree to let us come with you—wherever you are going."

"And if we do not?"

"The fence is high," Franklin said, his pedantic tone that of someone reciting bad poetry, "and topped with barbed wire."

"Snakes slither," Pearl recited mockingly, "monkeys climb. Doors are needed only some of the time."

She had been holding the keys to the gate in her hand. Now she palmed them to Waking Lizard. At the same moment, Honey Dream smashed down a Dragon's Tail amulet. Even as the protection wreathed her, she ran forward, graceful as a gazelle, agile as the snake she was.

During their practice sessions, Pearl had pressed Honey Dream to become creative in her combat. The young woman was not the fencer or archer that Flying Claw was, but her training had not been exclusively scholarly. She showed that now as she gripped the wire fence, and scrambled up, springing up and over the barbed wire, trusting the Dragon's Tail to protect her from becoming snagged.

Her action temporarily distracted Franklin and his allies. In that moment, Waking Lizard showed that he might be an old man, but he was still a Monkey. Murmuring some few words in his own language, he released a small explosion of ch'i that carried him in a single bound from Pearl's side to the roof of the limousine.

Waking Lizard laughed, long hair and beard flying in a perfect, even elegant halo of shining white about his head and shoulders as he bounced off the roof of the limo, into the air, turned a perfectly unnecessary flip, and landed lightly on the ground on the other side.

He flipped a finger at Franklin Deng and Tracy Frye, handed Honey Dream the keys with a courtly bow, and turned to Pearl.

"Shall I let you in?"

"We're fine here," she said, swallowing laughter at the expressions of astonishment and anger on their opponents' faces. "Let us know what Pai Hu says."

"I can do that, too," Tracy Frye growled. She ran at the fence, murmuring a string of words that sounded like Russian and fingering one of the many small bundles that hung suspended from the belt at her waist.

She came ready for action, Pearl thought. *Not like our meeting at the museum.*

Des, silent to this point, called, "Please, Ms. Frye. I really wouldn't if I were you."

"You're not me," she snarled, and ripped the bundle from her waist. She threw it at the fence and launched herself forward all in one motion.

Pearl stood perfectly still, not certain if this was a test of her forbearance, if Franklin had watchers stationed elsewhere—perhaps that still unseen pair in the limousine—who were present to witness her breaking the regulations by which the Orphans had been suffered to live with their own magic in this world.

Franklin's face gave nothing away. Tracy's bundle hit the ground a few feet in front of the fence. She leaped, much as Waking Lizard had leaped. The bundle emitted a force of ch'i—mana, psychic energy, ki—one energy, as many names as there were traditions, that lofted her upward like a super-charged springboard. Lofted her up, but when she moved to go over, she hit solidly against the wards Pearl and Shen had installed the night before the gate into the West was installed.

They were very good wards, barriers, not merely alarms, and meant to keep both intruders out and anything that might find passage through the Men Shen in. They were el-egantly designed, able to sense intent and to react with ap-propriate force. Tracy hit them like she was hitting a brick wall, and fell back, unconscious.

Franklin did not move, but Downhill trotted over and knelt to check.

"She's breathing." Long pause as he manipulated limbs with a care that said his battles had not only been fought in boardrooms, and he knew more than a little field medicine. "No sign of a broken back or neck, but I won't vouch for her right arm. She came down on that hard."

"We have been very careful," Pearl said, "to assure that no harm will come to anyone. Now, will you leave or must we do so? Albert Yu has been told that if he does not hear from me within the hour, he is to bring representatives of the Finch Society here to investigate."

Franklin looked at her. His gaze was flat and expression-less, but anger bubbled through. He turned to his chauffeur, who had been sitting with feigned unconcern in the front seat of the limo through all of this.

"Zhang, help Mr. Ski move Ms. Frye onto the backseat of the sedan." Then he turned and looked at Pearl. "This is not over."

Des laughed. "Actually, Frankie, I think it is."

He held up the compact video recorder he had kept shielded from direct notice by the bulk of the town car.

"We anticipated you might try something, and we're getting really tired of being threatened. Some friends of Pearl and mine in Hollywood turned us on to these a while back. We've got a record. Maybe we'll show it around, and maybe we won't, but you can bet if you get in our way anymore, we're going to make sure everyone who needs to sees what happened here today."

Franklin Deng's lips ripped back from his teeth in a snarl of purest rage. It took every ounce of Pearl's composure not to step away, but she held her ground, refusing to say a word that might dilute the moment.

Franklin turned stiffly. He stalked around to the passenger side of the limo and got in the front seat. A few minutes later, the driver returned and got in.

The limo, followed by the tan sedan, pulled away. Only when they were completely out of sight, and a few checks told Pearl that they were indeed gone and had left no snoopers behind, did she permit herself to sag back against the side of the car.

Des was chuckling, punching buttons on the camera.

"There. I've connected to the Internet and sent back copies, both to your computer at home, and to Albert's account. We're covered."

Pearl smiled and patted his hand. "You did well. Now, with that little interruption out of the way, shall we go handle the business we came for?"

Des nodded, his face suddenly somber. He went to the trunk of the town car, put in the video camera, and extracted a small pack that held his Rooster's Talon and other gear.

Pearl drew Treaty out of the backseat, and checked to make sure nothing had been forgotten.

"Ready," she said.

"Just as soon as I've locked the car," Des replied.

☆

Every step Brenda hobbled toward where Righteous Drum sat on a knoll beneath the outspread branches of the magnolia tree, the voices of the Nine Springs became clearer. Their sounds did not resolve into words, rather her mind re-formed, gaining the ability to understand sounds that were not words.

The sensation was not in the least strange, rather the opposite, as if understanding the voice of falling water, of the winds through the branches of the towering magnolia, even of the grass rejoicing as it regrew where the Leech's intrusion had stripped the rich soil bare, was more natural than not.

Welcome! Welcome! Thanks! Joyful Thanks! said the falling waters in plinking and splashing notes. *We were parched. Weary. Worn to nothing.*

Brenda found herself smiling. The springs shared an exuberance with Lani, but rather than being the exuberance of innocence, this was the burbling joy born of deepest wisdom, the wisdom that has learned how to value the being of now, because change is inevitable.

Flying Claw was standing to one side of Righteous Drum, and if the sunshine of his smile at seeing her up and moving belonged to Brenda's memories of Foster, the alertness of his stance belonged wholly to Flying Claw.

For the first time, Brenda did not see these two elements as in contradiction, but as the wholeness they were. Foster could not have possessed the warm personality that had touched her heart had those qualities not been his—had not been Flying Claw's—before his memory had been stolen.

This did not make Flying Claw the least bit less dangerous—a killer who could play with small children as one of their own combined a terrifying mixture of untouched innocence and lethal experience—but with this revelation Brenda felt she was one step closer to understanding Flying Claw, and to regaining her beloved Foster.

As Brenda exchanged greetings with Flying Claw and Righteous Drum—accepting the one's pleasure and the other's thanks—Riprap gently lowered Deborah to the turf a few feet from Righteous Drum.

Then Riprap settled himself into a cross-legged seat a few paces away. His dark brown eyes were unfocused, and

Brenda knew without asking that his heart and soul were full to overflowing with the wonder of hearing water and wind given voice.

Riprap and I are luckier, Brenda thought, *than the Landers. They grew up knowing what is to us miraculous was possible, even if not commonplace. For us the wonder has the freshness not only of discovery, but of revelation.*

And the waters said, *"Family! Family! Gladful family! Your gates. Our waters. Connecting. Spreading. We shall. You will. When you would cross, speak to us. We will come."*

A new voice, sighing, breathing, tickling with an undercurrent of solemnity that was not devoid of joy, interjected itself into the springs' continued affirmations. *"Pai Hu wishes to speak with you. Quickly. Faster even than ghost horses upon the winds may carry you. Upward the waters will lift you, lift you high even as the suns rise into an eternally daylit sky."*

Brenda recognized this new speaker as the magnolia tree. Through the tree's joy at having the monster who had cut through its roots banished, the springs that fed it saved, she felt a touch of fear vibrating beneath the otherwise matter-of-fact announcement.

No wonder, Brenda thought. *If the White Tiger of the West has news urgent enough to demand our rapid return, then I'd be afraid—even if I was a tree who reincarnates the suns.*

Loyal Wind had stood to one side, listening to this interchange, his expression thoughtful.

"The time has come for us to part," he said, "for you return to the lands of the living, whereas my place is among the dead. However, when I am needed—and I know my duty to my descendants is not yet ended—then do not hesitate to call upon me. Like the Nine Yellow Springs, I will answer."

Righteous Drum bowed where he sat, but that he did not attempt to rise said volumes as to how exhausted he remained.

"If we may beg a further favor of you, Loyal Wind . . ."

The Horse bowed in return. "I would be pleased to be of aid, brave Dragon."

"Please then, seek out the ghosts of the Exile Ox, Ram, and Monkey. Tell them we will need their help if we are to open a way back into the Lands Born from Smoke and Sacrifice. I realize that as one who is not among their descendants, I am perhaps speaking out of turn, but as one who is an exile myself—very eager to return home—I beg this favor."

Loyal Wind's serious mouth sketched a thin-lipped smile. "I wholly understand. I will seek my old associates and endeavor to sway them to your—our—cause."

The thin-lipped smile broke into a wide grin that crinkled around Loyal Wind's usually serious eyes as he laughed with unexpected gusto. "Indeed, you ask what I intended to do myself. After years of considering myself a failure, I find myself offered the opportunity to be part of a winning campaign."

"We appreciate your help," Righteous Drum said, and the others murmured their thanks in a rippling echo that, to Brenda, didn't seem all that different from the voice of the Nine Yellow Springs.

When Loyal Wind and the horses had departed, Deborah asked no one in particular, "Just how do we go about getting back to Pai Hu? Do we go sit on the springs?"

"As the suns rise," promised the Nine Yellow Springs, *"so you will rise. We have strength now. Strength and to spare."*

Deborah made as if to rise, but the voice of the magnolia tree patted her back into place. "Wait. You are wounded, and nothing to lift compared to the sun."

Afterward, no matter how she struggled to articulate the experience, Brenda could not put what happened into something as restrictive as words.

There were rainbows and mist, but there was also an enormous yet delicate flower with the creamy petals of the largest magnolia blossoms in the tree that dominated their garden back home in South Carolina.

Was she a little grey rat who rode up through the sky in the boat that was the flower? Did she dissolve into the rainbow and become water beads and light? Did she stand over a geyser and laugh as it carried her through the layers of the universe, straddling the force of the cosmic pulse?

Brenda never could explain. Later, after several attempts, she realized that she didn't really want to try. To do so would be to force what had been her first taste of a broader understanding of that cosmic pulse into the limitations of the human mind.

She arrived outside the raw pine door that was the first of the Nine Gates. Despite a sensation of having been surrounded by water, she was completely dry. She remained tired, and her strained muscles still ached, but her soul exalted from the joy and delight of that wild journey. This was very good indeed, for as she looked around the jungle glade, seeking Pai Hu, Brenda immediately realized that something was terribly wrong.

The greensward on which the five of them now stood felt brittle beneath her feet. The color of the grass was similar to winter lawns spray-painted a uniform, artificial green. The leafy, viny jungle spread about on all sides, but the foliage was stiff and unmoving.

Like a painted backdrop on a stage, Brenda thought, *not like living vegetation.*

The flowers were still lush and of impossibly brilliant colors, but they seemed fake—and not even good imitations: plastic molds rather than painted silk.

Worst of all, the Pai Hu who spoke to them from the edges of the jungle was a ghost of his majesty at their first meeting, a translucent projection, still holding color, but lacking substance.

"Pai Hu!" Flying Claw cried out, and something in his voice reminded Brenda of a child seeing his father reduced by sudden illness. "What has happened to you?"

"The dream has taken hold, each moment, each breath, I am being unmade," the White Tiger of the West replied.

"Who? What? How is this happening?" Flying Claw protested. "It is impossible."

Pai Hu coughed, reprimand and laughter in one hoarse breath.

"Nothing is impossible, fierce little kitten. Your denial—no matter how heartfelt—cannot change that. The force of which I dreamt is taking hold, gaining strength far more rapidly than I had ever imagined—even when I imagined it could be and did not think it all some taste of insanity."

"How long do you have?" Riprap asked. "I mean, until it has you entirely."

"I have strength yet," the White Tiger said. "My realm is vast, and my power is great. I am resisting. However, I can feel myself slipping. Without help this is a battle I will lose. I warn you. If I lose my battle, the one that will come to you will be far closer to being impossible."

"Nothing is impossible," Flying Claw retorted. "Hold fast, Grandfather. We will find what is eating away at your vitals."

Righteous Drum nodded agreement, but his expression, though thoughtful, was also a little afraid.

Brenda felt a flash of understanding. She knew without need of explanation that the Leech that had preyed on the Yellow Springs, the danger of which the golden horse had reminded her, and this last disaster were all connected.

"We're with you," she said. "All of us, both here and those at home. We've made a bunch of promises, and we're not going to break a single one."

At Brenda's affirmation—an affirmation that was not hers alone, but belonged to them all—the White Tiger seemed to grow more solid. The ground beneath their feet regained some of its verdant resilience, and the flowers some of their perfume.

"Remember the nature of the universe," Pai Hu said, and then he was gone.

But the renewed greenness remained, and Brenda took this as a reason for hope. Deborah turned to face the pine door, walking toward it as quickly as she could on her damaged ankle.

"We'd better hurry," she said. "I can't see how we're going to keep our promises without the others' help. In any case, this place may not stay solid for long. I, for one, have no desire to be set adrift to join Loyal Wind and his herd ghosts."

"If there even will be ghosts," Righteous Drum said. "What threatens the guardian domains threatens all the realities they touch—those of the living and those of the dead."

☆

Honey Dream and Waking Lizard ran through the warehouse toward the pine door that marked the way into the western-most guardian domain. There was no reason for them to run, but Honey Dream's blood fizzed with a heady mixture of anticipation and dread, so that walking sedately was all but impossible.

Clearly the reason behind Waking Lizard's matching her stride for hurried stride was not the same. He was still bouncing, almost skipping, and little snorts of laughter as he recalled the trick they'd played on Franklin Deng and his obnoxious allies showed that in him the Monkey was ascendant.

Never mind, better a lively monkey than a tired old man. Honey Dream would do the thinking for both of them.

She was lowering herself into a bow in front of the pine door, an invocation to the Men Shen who guarded the portal rising to her lips, when she felt a surge of ch'i from the door.

"It's active!" she said. "Someone is returning . . ."

"Or," Waking Lizard cut in, suddenly serious, the hard whip he'd carried with him over the fence spinning in his hands as he ran it through a complex defensive maneuver, "someone has overcome not only our allies, but the Men Shen as well."

Yanking the door open from this side would not only have been unnecessary, but potentially dangerous as well, so Honey Dream stepped back a few paces, and tried to calm her wildly racing heart. What would she see when those rough pine panels swung back? Nothing good, surely. Her father's voice had been so loud within her thoughts.

The door swung open and Deborah Van Bergenstein limped over the lintel. She looked surprised, but relieved to see them. Honey Dream tried not to feel hopeful when she saw no pity touch the Pig's expression.

"I should have guessed," she said, and now Honey Dream noticed that her ankle was tightly wrapped, and her trouser leg smeared with blood, "someone would come searching for us by now. Or did Pai Hu call you, too?"

Her words made no sense, but that hardly mattered. Another figure was taking shape within the door, the image indistinct, as if seen from a great distance, then becoming more and more solid with every breath.

Riprap came through so close behind Deborah that he nearly trod on the woman's heels.

"Sorry," he said, giving Deborah his arm to lean on and hurrying them both clear of the door. "I didn't want you alone here in case . . ."

Riprap seemed to see Honey Dream and Waking Lizard for the first time. A tired grin lit his dark face. Honey Dream noticed that he, too, was bandaged. Fear for her father lit a cold fire in her soul.

"Good to see you," Riprap said. "Did we get folk worried by being gone so long?"

Honey Dream was vaguely aware that Waking Lizard was speaking, but her attention was wholly fastened on the door where another figure was taking shape. This one seemed about the right height, and there was something painfully familiar about that stocky round build.

"Ba Ba!"

She nearly flung herself into Righteous Drum's arms as he stepped over the threshold onto the warehouse floor.

Nearly, for she immediately saw the pallor on Righteous Drum's cheek, saw the beads of sweat on his forehead. The Snake had trained with the Dragon, and she immediately recognized the symptoms of nearly fatal ch'i depletion. Instead of throwing herself at him, she shoved herself under his remaining arm and bore him clear of the door.

"What happened, Father?" she asked, frantic with worry. "I thought . . . I thought you were dead. I heard you calling me."

"I was nearly dead," he said. "I thought I was. You were right, my daughter. The loss of my arm weakened me more than I imagined, but we will tell you all—all of you—the details when we have gathered."

His voice grew very soft and for a moment Honey Dream thought he was speaking for her ears only, then she realized that exhaustion had struck him anew.

"Details," he said, "and terrible developments."

Righteous Drum let Honey Dream lower him to a seat on one of the crates that still littered the interior of the warehouse.

"Thank you. Are the other two through?"

Honey Dream turned to check, surprised to realize that in her joy and relief at seeing her father still alive, she hadn't even thought about the fact that the last two to return were Flying Claw and Brenda Morris.

Brenda had apparently been next through the gate, and she looked almost as bad as Righteous Drum. Worse in some ways, for ch'i depletion does not batter and bruise the body, and from how Brenda moved, there wasn't a part of her that didn't ache.

Flying Claw tucked his arm around Brenda, withdrawing it quickly when Brenda winced.

"Sorry. I feel like I hit a wall," she said, laughing around a sudden intake of breath.

"You did," Flying Claw said. "From what Loyal Wind says, repeatedly. Here, try leaning on my arm."

"I'm okay," Brenda protested. "I mean, I can walk."

They shared grins, companionable and easy. Honey Dream was reminded of when she'd spied on "Foster," and saw a return of that ease he had felt with his captors. She felt a twinge of the familiar jealousy, but tamped it firmly down.

"They are both here," Honey Dream said to Righteous Drum, and jealousy was washed away in the unexpected joy of seeing her father alive when she'd truly believed him dead. "You all look as if you had a rough time of it."

"We'll tell you all about it," Righteous Drum promised, "or rather the others will. I may not be dead, but I must sleep."

XXVIII

Pearl listened as the tale unfolded. With its monsters and close brushes with the sun, with long miles traveled on the back of ghost horses, it seemed more like one of those epics her mother would tell her at bedtime than the dryly factual report Riprap and Flying Claw gave between them.

She guessed that was why Nissa had let Lani be present—the toddler had returned from her outing and was now drowsily content to sit between her mother's feet and play with paper and crayons spread on the floor. Lani's contentment was a relief, because at this moment their resources were stretched rather thin.

Deborah was upstairs tending to the truly astonishing amount of battering Brenda's slender body had sustained during her rescue of Righteous Drum. Nissa had offered to help, but Deborah had waved her way.

"I know what happened to us," she said, "and you're going to need to hear this in as much detail as possible."

Honey Dream was also present, convinced that Righteous Drum needed nothing so much as uninterrupted sleep. With a sense of attentiveness she had not shown to this point, the Snake had taken her place in the group now gathered around the long table in the family room. At first, Pearl had cynically attributed Honey Dream's attentiveness to a desire to be near Flying Claw, but Honey Dream watched him calmly.

No. Not calmly. Not detached. She's still very aware of him, but that hunger. That look as if she'd eat him alive if he'd just hold still long enough. That's what's missing.

Pearl wondered at the change, then decided there were too many variables to account for to be certain. Was Honey Dream feeling guilty for having been caught in her trysts with Franklin? Was she simply relieved that Righteous Drum was alive? Was she overwhelmed by the enormity of this new task that had been put before them? Before Des had insisted they recount important events in order "or else we'll constantly be asking questions, and you'll end up taking longer," Flying Claw had blurted out that Pai Hu was in terrible danger, and that they must save him.

Too many variables, Ming-Ming, Pearl thought, *and our carefully planned campaign smashed almost before we set it in place. I'm beginning to think we should be grateful we got one gate in place.*

Riprap was finishing up. "So we're back, and we have the promise of the Nine Yellow Springs that they'll facilitate our gates—but I'm wondering if that's going to matter."

"I believe it will," Shen said, "possibly more than ever. If something is attacking the West, then it is quite likely that it is attacking the other guardian domains as well. Once we figure out what that is, we're going to need to get to it."

"And since the Nine Yellow Springs run through all places," Flying Claw said, "or so it was explained to us, they may be able to take us to our enemies."

"Can we just ask them to do that?" Riprap asked.

"I think not," Shen said, shaking his head slowly. "I would like to consult with Righteous Drum—he is far more knowledgeable than I am on such things—but I don't think the Nine Yellow Springs have intellect and intent as we do. I don't think they necessarily know what an enemy is."

"Which would explain," Flying Claw said, "how something as monstrous as the Leech got close to them."

"Do you think the Leech is connected to whatever is after Pai Hu?" Nissa asked.

"I think so," Flying Claw replied. "There are similarities—the draining away rather than the actual destruction."

"I wonder," Waking Lizard said, "if their enemies are somehow related to our enemies. You weren't there in those final days before our emperor fell, but there was something wrong about the armies we faced. I wish we could learn more."

Nissa brightened. "We could. We still have our prisoners. That Twentyseven-Ten seemed smart, and he's had time to think about what that 'captain' of his got him into. Maybe he'll be more willing to talk—and if he's not, maybe one of the others might know something useful."

"It can't hurt," Riprap said, surging to his feet with an eagerness Pearl admired. She'd helped Nissa change the field dressing on Riprap's wounds. They'd both agreed that although the slice on his forearm was long, it wasn't wide enough to merit a trip to Dr. Andersen. Even so, Riprap had to have bled a lot, but an hour or so of steady eating—when he wasn't talking—seemed to have renewed his resources.

Youth, Pearl thought, and decided she was glad to have it on her side.

"Wait," Shen said. "Do we wish to begin with Twentyseven-Ten? He has had his say, and nearly three weeks have passed since then. I wonder if one of his associates might be more eager to talk."

"You mean, after being bottled up in there, just the four of them?" Riprap said. "You know, I think that's likely. At first the other three were probably pretty grateful not to be killed, but now they've had time to consider how differently they would have handled matters."

"I have," Shen said almost apologetically, "visited them occasionally. I've been very careful," he added in response to the horrified looks this confession garnered him from

Nissa and Riprap. "Pearl has always known what I was doing."

"Of course," Des said with a grin. "Wards."

"And common sense," she responded.

"My visits have been short," Shen went on, "and by necessity restricted, but I have gathered a sense of their personalities. Flying Claw was correct in assessing Twentyseven-Ten as the ranking member. He is the only one with sophisticated magical training. One other—Thorn—also has some abilities, but I do not think he had the same training. I have detected some rivalry between him and Twentyseven-Ten, kept in check because we present a much larger threat, but there. He might be the most likely to talk."

"Why don't I go with you and bring Thorn out?" Riprap suggested. "I can be the muscle, but if you've established a relationship with them, let's use that."

Pearl nodded. "But Riprap, if you're going to act as muscle, change those grubby clothes and make sure they don't see those fresh bandages."

"Right."

Thorn was a short, stocky, powerfully built man. A broad white line of scar bisected one eyebrow, making it curiously hard to focus on his eyes. He was clad in a tee shirt with a sporting-goods logo and loose jeans. His feet were bare, and Pearl noticed that his toenails needed trimming.

Tea was offered and accepted, as were refreshments. These matters of politeness taken care of, Albert set down his cup and addressed the prisoner.

"What can you tell us about the man who commanded the expedition into this world?"

"The Captain?" Thorn's voice had a rough edge that Pearl recognized as fear concealing itself beneath aggression.

"That's right. Is that the only name you have for him?"

"Yes." Thorn paused. "I think even that is a lie. I think his rank was more than captain or less."

"How can that be?"

"I am not certain he even had a rank." Thorn paused

again. No one offered to help him along. "What I mean is that he came to us with soldiers of his own—just a few— and told us to call him 'Captain.' He wore a uniform, too, but he didn't seem—I've had time to think . . ."

Bitter, Pearl thought.

"He did not seem like a military man. He seemed accustomed to command, but not military command—or if military, then not military that I know."

Albert caught this last. "This Captain, then—we'll call him that for convenience—he was a stranger to you?"

"Yes. A stranger to me, and to all the others who the Horse assigned to this mission. I do not think he was a stranger to the Horse, but I do not think he was well known to him either."

"They did not act as if they were friends?"

"Not as enemies," Thorn hastened to clarify, "just as associates."

"Where do you think the Captain was from?"

"I don't know. He looked like a person." Thorn's eyes widened as he realized the magnitude of his error in this room where one man's skin was dark brown, where a woman had fair hair and blue eyes, where unlike was more like than like. "I mean, like a person from my homeland. Your friends saw him—or at least they saw his body. They know what I mean."

"They do," Albert said soothingly. "As do I. Leave physical appearance aside. How did he speak? Did he have an accent?"

Thorn's gaze flickered to Riprap, and Pearl wondered at this.

"Sometimes he spoke quite well, but with a slight accent. There were other times, though, that he spoke as I have heard this man . . ." Now Thorn's gaze rested squarely on Riprap. ". . . and some others of your company speak. I believe in their case a spell is involved?"

Albert nodded. "Very perceptive of you, Thorn. More tea?"

"Please." Thorn held out his cup.

"Yes. A spell is involved that eases communication between members of our company. So you think the Captain used something similar."

"I think so. I think he spoke our language fairly well—very well—but sometimes he seemed to pause and I would sense that the word I heard and the one he spoke were not the same. Often these were military terms."

"Thus your deduction that for all his giving himself a military title," Albert said, nudging a bowl of toasted, sugar-dusted almonds that Thorn had already shown a preference for closer to their prisoner, "that he was not a military man."

"Yes. I think this was so. I am sure of it."

"How long did you work with him before coming to this world?"

"Not long. A few days, enough for us to learn the basics of what was expected of us, to coordinate some maneuvers."

"Did you have a sense that this matter was considered urgent?"

Thorn considered, reaching for a nut and rocking it gently between the tips of his fingers. Pearl noticed with some amusement that Flying Claw was watching this action, ready for Thorn to try something—perhaps use the little nut as a projectile. But the almond was popped into Thorn's mouth, and he answered as he crunched it between his teeth.

"Not urgent. Not so much that. More that the means were there and with the means the opportunity. I do not think they thought this would be a difficult task, especially with sixteen against four. We thought we were coming after only four," he clarified.

" 'They,' " Albert said. "You say 'they.' Was the Captain then not the only one of his type you met?"

Thorn's expression became uneasy. "Well, as I said, the Captain brought a few of his own with him. Three. They're dead, too."

Albert made a slight noise in his throat, a prompt that

acknowledged this information but hinted that he thought this was only a partial answer. Thorn buckled.

"Yes. There were others. Especially toward the end, when our victory seemed assured. Rumors came from odd quarters: scouting units or those who worked the siege equipment. They spoke of 'advisors' who used peculiar spells or adjusted equipment. Most of us simply concluded," Thorn lowered his voice, looked a little ashamed, "that they were barbarians."

"And who is to say they are not," Albert agreed. "There is no reason to think otherwise. Did you gather any information about where they were from?"

Thorn hadn't, and neither had the other two when they were brought in and given a chance for tea and chat. Twentyseven-Ten was last, the idea being that he might be more talkative if he thought he was being slighted, but, although he did talk more freely than he had before, none of the details he offered seemed useful.

"Yet," Riprap said, after he returned from helping Shen escort Twentyseven-Ten to the apartment over the garage. "Yet. Something we heard today may make more sense when we've learned more."

" 'Remember the nature of the universe,' " Nissa mused aloud, paraphrasing Pai Hu's final utterance. "I wonder what he meant by that?"

"Something philosophical?" Des offered. Then he shook his head. "No. I can't believe that of the White Tiger. There's something practical about him."

Waking Lizard said, "What if he means the nature of *our* universe in particular? The more closely we look, the more whatever this enemy is we face seems to have first shown himself in the Lands."

☆

Honey Dream thought Waking Lizard might be jumping to conclusions, but she knew why he was doing so. The connection felt "right" in a way she could not intellectually justify. She leaned forward, ready to pursue the matter.

"All right, so what's the shape of the world?" Des asked.

Lani, who was coloring on sheets of paper spread out around her mother's feet, said, "Round!"

"Our world is round," Des agreed, "but . . ."

Nissa smiled, and leaned down to stroke her daughter's silky hair. "I'm guessing that the answer you want is either 'square' or 'a cube' because that's how the ancient Chinese cosmographers envisioned the universe."

"And that's why," Riprap added, "the original Twelve adopted mah-jong, especially as played with tiles, to encode their magical system. The 'great wall' that is built at the beginning of each hand evoked the universe for them."

"Good," Des said. Clearly he'd resumed his schoolmaster role. "Riprap, what's at the center of the square that is the universe?"

"China," Riprap said promptly. "The old name for China—Chung Kuo—meant 'center' and is why texts often translate it as 'Middle Kingdom.' "

Nissa looked thoughtful. "I guess that's a common enough idea, isn't it? I mean, the old Norse envisioned our world as Midgard, which means something like 'middle world.' "

"If you study comparative mythology," Des agreed, "you're going to find that idea over and over again. It's not as odd as you'd think. Those ancient cultures envisioned the universe much as they experienced it. Your midpoint is your starting point, and from there you go out and find out what is elsewhere."

"All roads lead to Rome," Pearl murmured. "There's no place like home."

"Okay," Des said, "now that you've got that, let's try drawing this version of the universe. Lani, can I have a piece of your paper?"

"Sure," the little girl said, and generously extended a half-dozen sheets, their corners crumpled in her pudgy hand. "And crayons. Anything b'pink, an' yellow. I'm usin' dose."

"Thank you," Des said. "I'll just take these."

He gathered up a small handful of crayons and set them

alongside the stack of paper. "You folks from the Lands, make sure I don't screw this up. I only know it in theory."

Taking up an orange crayon, Des drew a rough square in the center of his piece of paper. Spiky triangles representing mountains were drawn in near the edges of the square in green. Next, with a light blue crayon, he drew squiggly lines representing the four great seas, each separated from the others by comparatively narrow land bridges. Then Des took up the orange crayon again and drew vague land shapes beyond each of the seas.

The drawing was crude, but not unlike those Honey Dream recalled from her earliest geography lessons.

Des slid his drawing to where everyone could see it. "This represents the Lands Born from Smoke and Sacrifice. I know this will seem odd to most of you, but the center area really is square—some maps show it as a cube—because that was one of the dominant images of the world when the first Ch'in emperor ordered all those books to be burnt."

"And the universe took its shape from theory," Riprap said, "rather than theory from the universe. Cool. Seems like they'd be a bit crowded though."

"No more so than on this world," Des insisted. "Theoretically, the residents could see the edge of their world if they went far enough, whereas we have the illusion that the horizon continuously moves more distant as we move toward it. That's the only difference. In fact, from some of the things my grandmother said, I had the impression that the surface area of the Lands might be far larger than that of this world."

"What's that beyond the waters?" Nissa asked. "It looks as if you've drawn land that isn't square."

"Various sources give those lands different names," Shen said when Des glanced over at him. "I rather favor the 'great wilds.' They are usually designated by the directions, just as the seas are."

Nissa was studying the drawing, puzzlement on her face. "So what's at the edge? I mean, if you crossed the seas and then those wild lands, what would you find?"

Flying Claw answered. "There is a wall, but before you ever reach the wall, you must cross even more oceans. And before you reach those oceans you must traverse regions that become wilder and wilder, the creatures that populate them more and more fierce, so that not one warrior out of a hundred, not one sorcerer out of ten, can penetrate safely to the shadow of that wall. When you reach the wall, the area at its base is lapped by water, for all the waters of the universe come there to be refreshed before draining into the underworld, from whence, via the power of the Nine Yellow Springs, they come again to the upper world."

"Have any of you been to this wall?" Riprap asked.

Honey Dream shook her head. Waking Lizard and Flying Claw did the same.

"My father hasn't either," Honey Dream said, just to confirm. "Even with magical aid, even flying on dragonback, it would take years."

While they had been talking, Des had pulled his picture back to him, and added to the sketch using different-colored crayons. Now his square was surrounded by four other squares, each with its base set beyond the great wilds, but aligned with the sides of the central square. He quickly wrote the four compass points inside the appropriate squares. Honey Dream noted with approval that he'd drawn his squares with the colors most commonly associated with the directions.

"This is really oversimplified," Des said, "but it's how my grandmother described the way the guardian domains touch the Lands. I'm not at all certain if they're squares as well, but that's how she drew them."

Flying Claw shrugged. "The theories as to the shape of the guardian domains differ with the theorists."

Honey Dream added. "The description your grandmother gave you, Des, is as good as any. The guardian domains are not places one lingers. They belong to the Land, and yet they do not. They are borders that are yet their own places. The one thing all the theorists seem to agree upon is that there are landmarks within them that remain more or less constant."

Des looked pleased. "That's about what my grandmother said. She felt that the guardian domains belonged to the Lands in a sense, were an outpouring of all the contradictions the Lands could not contain. That's why from them—through them—one can touch things that are also integral to the Lands themselves."

Des moved his map toward the center of the table. "We've been talking about universes as if they are all distinct, but some places—like the guardian domains, which exist by virtue of the need to create a buffer between two areas—are more permeable than others."

" 'Need to create a buffer'?" Nissa repeated. "Whose need? What's need?"

Honey Dream was surprised to hear herself laughing. "That's one of the great philosophical questions, Nissa. Really. It's simply that reality is more complex than those of us who live in relatively solid areas can grasp."

"Solid?" Nissa echoed, but she was smiling back, and Honey Dream was amazed how good that made her feel.

"Various types of existence," Honey Dream went on, glancing over at Shen and seeing that, Dragon though he was, he was perfectly happy to have her explain, "are often classified by how easily manipulated they are. Manipulated by other than physical force, I should add. Some, like the afterlife, can be very easily adapted by the expectations of those who are there."

"One man's heaven is another man's hell," Riprap muttered. "I mean, what I'm trying to say is that what's wonderful and what's horrible depends quite a bit on the person. So if you have an afterlife, and that afterlife includes the ideas of reward or punishment or even renewal, then that reality is going to have to be flexible. Otherwise it won't work."

Honey Dream nodded. "We could spend days on this, and we don't have days, so since I see you're following me, I'm going to jump ahead. Magic involves shaping reality. In this world, magic works only with great effort. In the Lands, it works with less effort, probably because the underlying myth of creation is different. In the guardian domains, reality is so flexible, that you can hold a discussion with a creature like Pai Hu and find it completely reasonable."

Everyone was nodding encouragingly, so Honey Dream looked at Des. "May I add to your drawing?"

"By all means."

Honey Dream slid the drawing toward her, and put a finger on the red square Des had labeled "South." Then she slid her fingertip until it passed out of the red square and into the vacant area to the right of South, below the green "East" square.

"Des hasn't colored this in on his map because what is there is impossible to map. Remember how the Lands can be considered not only a square but a cube?"

Heads nodded all around. Even Lani had stopped scribbling and was listening seriously, a pink crayon in one hand.

"Very well, extend this drawing in your mind until the center square is a cube and the others are matching cubes. Above and below are the Void, but in these 'empty' areas to the sides are compressed layers upon layers of realities. Even more than what we have called the guardian domains, these layers are the infinity of places where realities touch realities. They may even extend into what we think of as Void. They probably do, actually—at least according to my teachers, and they were great theorists."

"So if we were traveling in the guardian domains, we wouldn't just walk out of 'South' and into 'West' or 'East,'" Riprap said. "We're blocked on both sides."

"That's why Nine Gates are necessary," Des said, giving Honey Dream a courteous nod. She was startled by how the small gesture warmed her. "Our initial plan was to establish two each in the four guardian domains. The ninth would be our entry point into the Lands. One of the things those of us who haven't been jaunting off on field trips have been doing is calculating where best those gates should be built."

Nissa was looking at the drawing with alarm. "I don't understand. I really don't understand. I thought Pearl or Shen or someone said something about the Nine Gates being tied to the Nine Yellow Springs because everyone everywhere had an underworld or hell or something. Now we're talking about square-cube worlds surrounded by layer cakes of alternate realities. I don't get it! I really don't."

Pearl reached out and patted her hand. Lani, who had been alarmed by the edge in her mother's voice, climbed up into Nissa's lap.

"Nissa, remember what Honey Dream said. These are vast philosophical points. We don't need to understand them any more than you need to understand how an internal-combustion engine works to drive a car."

Nissa nodded. "Right, but I think I have about as much of this as I can handle. Can we focus in on what's next?"

Albert had been studying the elaborate crayon drawing, and now he ran his finger along one of the roughly triangular areas that represented the "layer cake" realities.

"Into the Void. Nature abhors a vacuum. Draining away." He shook his head violently, as if to clear away conflicting impulses. "Something is attacking Pai Hu—and probably the entirety of the guardian domains. Let's start there. If we save him, we save the lands he protects. If we do that, I have a feeling that Nine Gates or no Nine Gates, we're going to find our way to the borders of the Lands made a lot easier."

Waking Lizard, uncharacteristically silent to this point, nodded somberly. "And if we do not, then I have a feeling it won't matter. I think the Lands themselves will then be under attack and our return won't make the least difference."

XXIX

Brenda could have sworn she was sound asleep, but there was a woman sitting cross-legged on the end of her bed, a woman she didn't think she'd ever seen before, but who nonetheless seemed familiar.

The visitor's age was hard to peg. At first glance, Brenda had thought she was young—younger even than Brenda herself. Her eyes, though, leaf-green and brilliant, held a depth of living experience that made Pearl's knowing gaze look like that of a child. The visitor's body was slim and graceful, with none of the stiffness of age in her posture. Her reddish-gold hair, worn long and unrestricted, was untouched with either silver or grey, but Brenda was certain those rich hues had not come out of any bottle—not even from the careful chemistry of a salon.

The woman's attire was what made Brenda wonder if she might be dreaming. At first glance, Brenda had taken it for a loose tee shirt worn over shorts—not in the least inappropriate for a summer afternoon in San Jose. Now, propping herself up on her pillows to get a better look at this all-too-comfortable stranger, Brenda saw the woman wore a tunic. It wasn't quite Greek, more like the illustrations Brenda had seen in books of fairy tales.

And then the woman moved slightly, pushing her hair back from her face with one graceful hand, revealing for a moment an ear that was slightly, but most distinctly, pointed.

"You're an elf!" Brenda demanded, and the words were as much question as exclamation.

"These days," the woman said, and her voice was melodious and familiar, "we really prefer the term 'sidhe folk.' It retains a certain amount of dignity that the other lost in Queen Victoria's reign—despite the efforts of good Tolkien and others to restore it."

Brenda remembered then. Remembered the face in the pool during her first visit to the guardian domains, remembered the golden horse, and knew why this creature, no matter that this was the first time she'd actually seen her, seemed so familiar.

"You!" she gasped.

The sidhe woman looked pleased. "You recognize me, then? That's very nice."

"I've met you twice before," Brenda said. "As a face in a pool—I'd forgotten that until just now—and a golden horse named Leaf."

"Three times, actually," the woman said. "Your grandmother Elaine introduced us when you were just a little thing."

"Grandma Elaine?" Brenda felt shocked. Grandma Elaine was eccentric, yes, but did this mean her claims of consorting with the fairy folk were true?

"Close," the sidhe woman said. "Your grandmother was very receptive, but she lacked the gifts that let you sit and talk with me this way."

"You mean the Rat thing?" Brenda asked.

"The Rat thing, yes, and . . ." The sidhe woman paused, considered for a long moment, so long that indeed Brenda didn't think she'd add anything, and then went on. "And a little manipulation on the part of Gaheris Morris. He was in over his head, you see, and decided that you might as well come into a bit of your inheritance ahead of time, rather than it all being lost. When he tapped into your—shall we call it 'psyche'? Such a pretty word. Your psyche, he wasn't as neat as he thought. He left a little tear, and that's still there."

"Is that why you can talk with me only like this?" Brenda said. "I mean. I'm asleep, aren't I?"

"Oh, I could talk with you in other ways," the sidhe woman said, "but those would cause difficulties. In any case, for a creature such as myself, in between spaces are easier. More natural, really."

Brenda wanted to ask a million questions, but she remembered how the golden horse had cut off so suddenly.

"Are you here to warn me about something? Tell me something I need to do?"

"Clever. You really are a good Rat. Better than your father, if only you would accept it, but that's neither here nor there."

Brenda was beginning to feel the aches in her body, and she suspected this meant she was dangerously close to waking.

"Would you, please, kind lady, beautiful lady," she said, struggling to remember the courtesies that had been used in the stories Grandma Elaine had read her. She didn't think she'd gotten them right, but she didn't think they hurt either. "Please, tell me what it is you've come so far and under such great inconvenience, to tell me."

The sidhe woman smiled. "Prettily spoken. Very well. I wanted you to know that the others are right. If you don't save Pai Hu and his fellow guardians, the rest really won't matter."

"Is that all?"

"Isn't it enough?"

"Not really. What's in it for you?" Brenda threw tact out the metaphorical window. "Sidhe folk are Irish or Celtic, if you prefer. Pai Hu is distinctly Chinese. Are you friends? Maybe. But I think it's something else."

"The Rat smells a rat," the sidhe woman said. "Shall I tell her? Why not? It will be amusing."

Brenda wondered if she was reading the sidhe woman's thoughts, as the sidhe woman had clearly been able to read hers, or if the creature was scatty—or talking to someone else. To this she got no answer, unless the sidhe woman's expression turning serious was an answer.

"You speak of human nationalities—or racial and cultural designations—as if we were bound by them. I'd like to state with imperious dignity that this was not so—but I'd be lying and lying would not serve either you or me at this time."

She paused, and Brenda kept her mouth shut and her mind focused on the pattern of sunlight spilling through the window. Nothing that could distract. The aches from her body faded, and she guessed she was falling more deeply to sleep.

Odd to sleep with one's eyes open, and ears listening.

"Essentially," the sidhe woman said, "what preys on Pai Hu will turn its attention to my place sooner or later. Our 'Lands Beneath the Hills' are much like the guardian domains: shapable, permeable, vulnerable to the right sort of attack. The attackers have gone for us in the past, but we have been able to rebuff them—your stories do not show us as a warlike people without reason. We will not be able to rebuff them if they come after us armed with what they will have drawn from the guardian domains, from the Lands . . ."

"But who is the enemy?" Brenda said. "How can we succeed where someone like Pai Hu cannot?"

"You can succeed because you are realer than Pai Hu. Trust me on this. And you can succeed because—at this moment—you are of secondary, even tertiary importance. But that will not last, and if you do not act, the enemy will grow stronger."

"But how can we attack something we've never heard of, that we don't know how to find?"

The sidhe woman met Brenda's gaze. "Go where Pai Hu has gone—is going. They are not destroying him. They are devouring him. Go to the belly that is swallowing the beast."

☆

The morning following the expedition's return from the Yellow Springs, Pearl looked around at the group gathered in her family room. The two invalids were up, although Righteous Drum had been settled on the sofa, rather than in one of the chairs around the long table. Honey Dream sat on a chair pulled next to that sofa, anxious to tend to her father's least wish.

Repentance? A desire for redemption? Pearl wondered. *Or simply an all-too-acute awareness of how easily she might have lost him?*

Pearl didn't expect they'd ever know exactly, but she did know that Righteous Drum had been told just how close Honey Dream had come to betraying them—and that the girl had insisted on doing the telling herself.

Waking Lizard had reported that soon after the four from the Lands had returned to Colm Lodge, Honey Dream had gone to her father's room, first making clear to Flying Claw and Waking Lizard that "No one needs to tell my father what I've done, because if he has strength enough to listen, I will tell him myself."

So that matter was wholly settled. A copy of Des's video showing the events outside the warehouse had been sent in a sealed package to Broderick Pike of the Rosicrucians. An identical package—including a copy of the letter requesting Pike keep the recording, as it contained evidence for a possible action Pearl and Albert were contemplating against Franklin Deng, Tracy Frye, and several of their associates—had been sent to them. Pearl thought the threat would be enough to keep that cabal in check, at least for now.

So now, Pearl said, *we can focus on the matter at hand.*

Among the last to join them were Brenda and Deborah—and not because either had slept in. Deborah had insisted that Brenda take a long shower, and then had rubbed ointment into the numerous bruises and grazes that marred the young woman's skin. Over twelve hours of sleep had done a great deal to restore Brenda's strength, but she settled into the recliner that had been reserved for her without protesting that she'd be "fine, just fine," as Pearl had expected her to do.

The remainder wore fresh bandages. Deborah's limp was markedly less.

But still, Pearl thought, *we're a sorry lot to take on something that's eating a universe, for the distinction between the guardians and their domains is a fine one indeed.*

Nissa came in last, finishing a call from one of her sisters on her cell phone. It was clear to Pearl that Nissa missed her sisters, but the dread Pearl had felt that the young mother would gather up her daughter and head for the familiarity of the Virginia mountains had not materialized. Joanne was very happy to help settle Lani into a routine of playdates, like the one she'd left for shortly after breakfast. Pearl had overheard Nissa talking with one of her sisters—Nancy, she thought—about schools.

Our Rabbit may be wiser than the rest of us. We're still thinking in the short term, from crisis to crisis, but she's digging in.

Pearl glanced at Albert as Nissa pocketed her phone and settled into one of the chairs around the long table. He took a last swallow of coffee, and began.

"Last night, we agreed that if we don't do something about whatever is going after Pai Hu—and presumably the other guardians and their domains—any effort on our part to set up the Nine Gates will be useless. Does anyone have any thoughts about how we should begin?"

Albert glanced between Shen and Righteous Drum as he concluded, obviously expecting the Dragons to be the most likely to have a practical answer. Pearl was certain she was not the only one to be surprised when Brenda spoke up.

"We need to follow Pai Hu," she said. "He can still talk to us—even if it's hard for him—so he's still alive."

"Follow him?" Albert repeated, clarifying, not mocking.

Brenda nodded and bit her upper lip. "Look. It doesn't make sense, and I know it, but most of this doesn't make any sense. I had a dream, and in that dream Pai Hu was, well, sort of there in the West, but he was also being pulled elsewhere. I mean, if he was a usual sort of person, this wouldn't make sense, because we can only be one place at once."

This time she was the one who glanced at the Dragons. Shen made a seesaw motion with one hand.

"That's not quite accurate. You yourself have had some experience with projection, that time you helped Pearl repair her wards. However, I don't think that's what you're talking about—you mean that the White Tiger is physically in more than one place at once."

"That's it," Brenda agreed. "He's being stretched or dragged or something. That's going to leave a trail. We can follow that trail and find out who is pulling on the other end, then stop them, like we stopped the Leech."

Albert rubbed his short beard. "Interesting . . . I had some such thought yesterday, but couldn't make it clear to myself. Yes. I agree. This might be the way to do it."

"I agree," said Righteous Drum, his voice rusty. "We are fortunate in that we have two Tigers, and that Pai Hu has befriended us, given us the freedom of his domain."

He glanced over at Shen, and Shen continued, "Just as we have two Tigers, we also have two Dragons. Some time ago, when Des took you young people off on that first field trip, Righteous Drum and I made some preliminary overtures toward the Azure Dragon of the East."

"How do you do that?" Riprap asked.

Shen shook his head. "Ask me when this is over. We have no time for theory. What we did was nothing fancy—a feeling-out. Rather like sending a note to someone you've heard of, but don't know personally, saying that you might be in the area, and could a visit be arranged if you do come.

"What disturbed us was how minimal the response we received was. At the time, we thought the Azure Dragon was probably waiting to see how Pai Hu responded. Now, though, we wonder if as Pai Hu suspected, all the guardians were under assault."

Nissa leaned forward, elbows on the table. "Shen, are you saying we have one chance and that's it?"

"I'm saying," Shen said, "that what Brenda suggests may be our best chance, and if so, we had better make it good."

Of course, this didn't settle matters. They needed strength, yet their company was far from strong. Even the relatively short initial meeting drained Righteous Drum enough that he went off to rest and meditate on the parlor sofa. Clearly, he couldn't go charging off into the West and beyond for some days yet. Shen, while a powerful enough Dragon, was the first to admit that he was not Righteous Drum's equal in matters of practical application.

"I'm like a writing instructor who's never sold a novel," he said to Pearl privately when they'd broken into smaller groups to brainstorm. "Or an archaeology professor who last did fieldwork in graduate school. I'm sound on theory. I don't know how I'd do in practice. I mean, look at the shape Righteous Drum is in."

"He overestimated how well he was healed from losing his arm," Pearl reminded Shen, patting her old friend on his own sound right arm. "Remember that."

"I will, I will. Still, I'd be happier if we could arrange matters so that Righteous Drum could go along."

"I'd be happier," Pearl agreed, "if all of us could. Brenda is talking to Gaheris right now, explaining that we're going to need him and finding out when he can come."

"If he did," Shen said, counting off people on his fingertips, "that would give us twelve—thirteen with Brenda. Not a large army, but still, enough to allow for various approaches and tactics."

"As I see it," Pearl said, "one of our problems is going to be whether or not whoever is attacking Pai Hu will know we're coming after him. From everything we've heard, the Leech was difficult enough to defeat, and it was relatively mindless. Whoever is behind this is far from mindless."

"I agree," Shen said. "And probably very powerful as well. I've been thinking about that a lot—ever since we first heard about Pai Hu's 'nightmare.' What can attack a universe?"

"We'll know," Pearl said, "when we get there. Let's not worry about it for now. I have an idea how we might get Righteous Drum up to snuff faster. What do you think about a variation on Triple Knitting?"

"That might work," Shen agreed. "Let's see . . . Who would be the most effective donors?"

They began working through the intricacies of the spell,

and Pearl found herself thinking about Shen's question. She might have dismissed it aloud, but in fact she was very, very worried. What could attack a universe—and how could they, even at their best, hope to stop it?

☆

Honey Dream carefully reviewed the spell Shen and Pearl had designed to restore Righteous Drum's ch'i, but although she tried to find errors, tried to find some indication of a hidden agenda, she could not.

There were spells similar to this "Triple Knitting" in the Lands, so it was not the spell itself that both impressed Honey Dream and awakened her innate sense of caution. What impressed Honey Dream was that the Orphans were willing, at a time of such great risk to themselves, to donate ch'i to one who had been—such a short time ago—an enemy. True, they needed Righteous Drum for the coming venture, but still . . .

The Triple Knitting called for three donors: Shen, as another Dragon; Riprap, as the Dog, the sign that sits in direct balance to the Dragon on the zodiac wheel; and Honey Dream herself, as the Snake, the Dragon's yin counterpart.

As with any spell that linked ch'i, this Triple Knitting called for an element of trust, belief that Righteous Drum would take what was offered, and nothing more. But so the trust was given, and so it was deserved. That evening found Righteous Drum nearly restored to himself. A good night's sleep, in which the various ch'i streams would be encouraged to mingle and blend, would finish the preparation.

Earlier that same day, the same Dr. Andersen who had treated Brenda's belly cut on the day the assassins had made their failed attempt came to call. He had been told that Pearl's friends and students had gotten a bit carried away in some martial arts practice. Although Honey Dream saw his eyebrows rise when he saw the extent of some of those injuries, he treated bruises, cuts, and batterings without asking any questions.

Honey Dream knew enough to guess that the thick envelope Pearl handed the doctor was meant to buy his silence, in addition to his medical skills.

Before he left, Dr. Andersen took a look at Righteous Drum's arm. Honey Dream had some experience detecting lies, and she knew the doctor was sincere when he said there was nothing he could do—and that he could have done nothing, even if he had been on the spot when the injury was dealt.

"You've been practicing a bit too roughly," Dr. Andersen said to Pearl as he was taking his leave. "Please take care. There are injuries that cannot be treated without recourse to a hospital."

After the various patients had gone to their beds, Nissa went to settle Lani to sleep. Des was about to fetch the van so he could drive the four from the Lands back to Colm Lodge, when Flying Claw rose from the chair where he had seemed half asleep and spoke.

"Des, wait. There is something . . ." Flying Claw looked at Pearl, Shen, and Albert. "If you can tolerate our company a short while longer, I have a suggestion as to how we can increase our forces significantly."

Albert cocked his head to one side. "Without involving anyone new? We don't have time for detailed explanations. We're hoping to depart tomorrow, as soon as Gaheris has arrived. Are you thinking of a summons, perhaps?"

Flying Claw shook his head. His eyes were no longer drowsy, but snapped bright and alert.

"Not a summons—using a resource we already have. We can include our four prisoners: Twentyseven-Ten, Thorn, and the other two."

"Chain and Shackles," Shen said. "Do you think we could trust them?"

"There are bindings," Flying Claw said, "and perhaps more importantly, oaths. They have been prisoners for many days now. We can't leave them forever imprisoned. Here they are a danger to you—people whose very existence will cause questions to be asked if they are ever discovered."

"Do you think they would agree to these oaths and bindings?" Albert asked. "Especially, since what we are asking them to do is risk their necks in our cause?"

Flying Claw nodded crisply. "I would not present the matter to them in that fashion. I would tell them we are offering them an opportunity to return to the Lands alive. Then I would tell them the nature of the danger we face—and that if it is permitted to spread, it will be a danger not only to the guardian domains, but to the Lands, and even to this place."

"Remind them," Albert said thoughtfully, "that their safety is only relative."

"Yes. I believe I will also share with them our belief that the attacks on the guardian domains may somehow be connected to their mysterious captain."

"Do we really know that?" Pearl asked.

"We do not," Flying Claw admitted, "but I do wonder. So many new things all at once . . . Our enemies having an ally with strange spells, then strange monsters attacking both the Yellow Springs and the four guardians. No. I cannot swear they are connected, but I can certainly argue the possibility."

"Four trained warriors," Albert said thoughtfully. "We even have appropriate armor and weapons. It is tempting, but . . . What do you think?"

He addressed his question generally, and Honey Dream was pleased to realize she and her father were included. Again, the acceptance of the Orphans for their allies astonished her.

But then, she thought, *perhaps I am only astonished because I was such an unworthy ally. They have done nothing but live not only to the word, but to the faith of our treaties.*

"I like it," Shen said. "I've talked to all four of these men. They've had time to think—and I'll admit, I've encouraged some of that thinking myself. I know they wonder why no rescue attempt has been mounted. Chain, who I think is the least acute thinker of the group, even said as much in my hearing."

"Would we be safe?" Albert asked.

"Safe," Pearl said bluntly, "doesn't enter into what we're about to do. This wouldn't be the first time in military history where prisoners have been given a chance to risk their lives to gain their eventual freedom. I know some of the bindings Flying Claw mentioned. The one I'd favor would render a traitor paralyzed—unable to defend himself—if he broke his word."

Righteous Drum spoke from his seat on the sofa. "I agree with Pearl. We are only thirteen. Four more adds a significant percentage to our force—and, realistically, we lack trained soldiers. Flying Claw and Riprap are the only two who have trained in that profession. Several of the rest of us are battle trained, and even blooded, but it is not the same."

"It's worth the risk," Honey Dream said, "if we use appropriate bindings, and don't trust them at our backs. If some of you would like to speak with them, I can sit and write out the bindings. They would be best presented as treaties, rather than inflicted as nonmaterial chains."

"I agree," Pearl said. "Good thinking. Anything that permits a modicum of dignity makes a stronger tie."

After a short amount of further discussion, it was decided that Flying Claw, Shen, and Albert would go speak with the four prisoners. Honey Dream settled at the long table sketching out Pearl's binding in pencil on a sheet of scrap paper. Then, after her father and Des had reviewed it, she began writing each out in careful calligraphy, trickling a small amount of ch'i into each character.

There was only one interruption, Albert returning for a copy of the binding/treaty. They gave him the scrap paper—by then Honey Dream had one copy done—and Honey Dream immersed herself in her labors. In the background, she was aware of her father's gentle breathing as he meditated, of Pearl explaining matters to Nissa when the other came downstairs, but she did not listen, shaping every character and the power it contained as if it might save her life.

Honey Dream was finishing the fourth and final copy of the agreement when Albert came back in through the patio door.

"They've agreed," he said shortly. "Flying Claw is to be their commander, and they will answer to him personally. Twentyseven-Ten thought this better than having them feel afraid of the consequences if they received conflicting orders."

Honey Dream noticed that Albert looked directly at Pearl as he said this, and knew he was waiting to see if his old teacher would object. She did not.

"Good. Flying Claw knows their ways and tactics far better than I ever could. I will bring Treaty. Shall we swear them in tonight?"

"We had better," Albert said. "They still need to be armed and armored. Probably in hopes of escaping, they've taken advantage of the size of that apartment to keep in some sort of condition, but they'd probably benefit from a chance to stretch."

Des had been reviewing Honey Dream's calligraphy, and now he set down the final copy of the binding.

"Nice work," he said. "Not only is the writing perfect, I can feel the power in the paper. Have you drained yourself too far?"

Once Honey Dream would have taken this as an implied insult—as if she could not do four such written spells without incommoding herself. Now she recognized it as the offer for assistance it was.

"I should regain what I lost through meditation and sleep," she said. "These take much of their ch'i from the one who swears to abide by the conditions."

"Good."

The prisoners were escorted in one at a time, each standing between the two Tigers—the one with her sword, the other their new commander—and swearing to the conditions agreed upon. Honey Dream watched carefully, but she saw no indication that they intended ill faith.

Twentyseven-Ten was the most distinctive of the four. He would have been handsome, except for a certain hardness around his eyes. Thorn, the other adept, was almost his opposite: short, thickset, scarred. He'd shown a fondness for sweets, and it showed along the line of his jaw—this despite the exercise routines the prisoners had maintained in the capitivity.

Chain and Shackles—Honey Dream guessed some cruel barracks humor in those nicknames—were the common soldier type. Chain was the taller, his arms heavily muscled, one hand curled as if he habitually carried a spear or banner.

Shackles was taller than Thorn, but no one would ever call him tall. He walked with a shuffling step, but his gaze was clear and alert. Honey Dream reminded herself that although neither of these men had magic, each must have had some skill or quality to recommend him, or he would not have been chosen for this elite mission. She let the thought encourage her.

Probably they want to get home as much as we do, she thought. *Probably they will all fight very hard toward that goal. Still, oath or no oath, that Twentyseven-Ten bears watching. I don't like how he looks at Flying Claw when he thinks no one is aware.*

Honey Dream was reminded how she had glowered at Brenda Morris, and felt uncomfortable. Had her hatred and resentment been so obvious? She suspected so.

Well, I don't exactly love Brenda now, she thought wryly. *And I doubt she loves me. Nor have I resigned Flying Claw to her—only my illusion that he was ever mine.*

Now Des brought around the van, and their augmented company went back to Colm Lodge. Des came inside with them, staying to assist with outfitting the new recruits from the items stored in the attic.

He left within an hour or so, reminding them that getting

a sound night's sleep was probably the most important thing any of them could do to prepare.

"Gaheris's flight is due in around nine tomorrow morning," he said. "I'll be here around ten, and we'll go from here directly to the warehouse."

And from there, Honey Dream thought as she locked the door behind him and mounted the stairs to her room. *Where will we go from there? And how many of us will return?*

XXX

Brenda actually felt good as she got out of her dad's rental car. They'd parked around the corner from Pearl's warehouse. Around front, both the town car and the van were unloading a rather odd assortment of even more oddly dressed passengers, but none of the vehicles that went by on the main road through the industrial park even so much as slowed.

Well, I guess this is California, Brenda thought, rummaging in the backseat of the car for her own pack, *and the last people to rent this warehouse were a traveling circus. Maybe we look perfectly normal by contrast.*

But Brenda doubted it. Their augmented company now included five men dressed in archaic-style Chinese armor. Almost everyone else was wearing elaborate Chinese-style ceremonial robes. Only Riprap, Nissa, Gaheris, and Brenda herself were dressed "normally." Judging from the rather large bag he was extracting from the trunk of the car, Dad had plans to change, too.

Brenda let her hand touch the little black stone frog carving Des had brought her, realizing as she did so how she had grown into her own peculiar role as the in-between. No longer did she feel a need for a title. She'd proven herself on that journey to the afterlife, and she'd be a perfect idiot not to accept that.

So she shouldered her bag and turned to Dad.

"Need a hand with any of that?" she asked.

"Nope, the old man's still up to carrying a few suitcases," Gaheris said. "Come on. We don't want to fall behind."

Brenda nodded. Flying Claw had directed his little army in ahead of the rest, and now the others were filing in, each bearing some pack or bundle.

Brenda hadn't quite decided how she felt about the new recruits. On the one hand, she was glad that their rather dubious army was so enlarged. On the other, despite the binding agreements each had signed, Brenda did worry that one of them would try something. Twentyseven-Ten in particular bothered her. She didn't need to have two brothers to recognize the jostling for authority going on between him and Flying Claw.

Oh, Flying Claw's technically in charge, Brenda thought, holding the door open for Dad, *but Twentyseven-Ten would like that to be only "technically" and Flying Claw is determined it be for real. Idiots!*

When they were all inside, Gaheris vanished into the big closet. When he emerged, he was clad in shining black robes. Brenda noticed that the embroidered charms leaned rather heavily in the direction of prosperity, with fewer for luck. She guessed that was in keeping with the Rat's focus, but somehow it made her uneasy—like the Rat was supposed to be too smart to need luck or something.

When I have my robes made, Brenda thought, feeling very strange at the thought, for when she donned those robes Gaheris would be dead, *I'll not forget luck. It's been with me so far, and I'd not want to forget to show I'm grateful.*

In one hand, Gaheris held a flat case. Brenda's first thought was that he had brought a small notebook computer. Then she realized the case was embroidered with various signs of protection.

She wanted to ask Dad what was in there, but Albert and

Righteous Drum were already conversing with the Men Shen. The pine door was swinging open, showing that curiously flattened, distorted version of the West spread before them.

"We're moving out," Nissa said. Her turquoise-blue eyes were rimmed with red. She'd managed to hold back her tears when she'd left Lani in Joanne's care, but Brenda knew how hard that had been. When she'd awakened during the night, and stumbled into the bathroom, a faint light had peeked under the door connecting Nissa's room. Through the old-fashioned keyhole, Brenda had seen Nissa asleep, sprawled on the bed with her clothes still on, Lani clasped in her arms.

The little girl had been awake. Brenda had shied back as if the child might see her, for those open eyes had been preternaturally thoughtful, as if Lani was aware of everything her mother had not told her, and was bravely maintaining a conspiracy of ignorance.

Certainly that morning Lani had gone off with Joanne easily enough, not even whining that she wanted to wait and say good morning to Foster.

Brenda shouldered her daypack. It was light enough, packed with a first-aid kit, high-calorie ration bars, binoculars, and similar survival gear. Most importantly, inside one of the zippered compartments were extra amulet bracelets to augment those currently hung around her wrists.

She hadn't made all of these—not even most of them. The Orphans who had remained behind during the trip to the Yellow Springs had not been idle. The more experienced members had contributed some very powerful spells, and samples of these hung on both of Brenda's wrists, ready for an emergency.

I hope I can get to them if I need them, Brenda thought, mentally practicing the slightly more awkward left-hand throw. *I hope I don't need them at all.*

Without really noticing, Brenda—Nissa still close at hand—had come up to the pine door. Albert, very serious and looking horribly inscrutable and Chinese in his formal robes, was standing to one side. He surveyed those remaining.

"Gaheris, come through next, would you? Shen and Righteous Drum have gone ahead, but I think we're going to need your particular talents in tracking Pai Hu's trail."

Gaheris hefted the mysterious case. "This. Yeah. Shen and I talked about that a bit over the phone. I'm set."

He turned and winked at Brenda. "See you on the other side, Breni."

Nissa looked at her. "What was he talking about?"

"No idea," Brenda admitted. "But I think we're going to find out."

She looked around. Of their company of seventeen, only five remained: Albert, Nissa, Waking Lizard, Deborah, and herself.

"Who's next?" she said, trying to sound bright.

"Waking Lizard, then Deborah, Nissa, you, and I'll come last and close the door," Albert said. "Gaheris's insisting on changing into his robes means we're going to be a little delayed, but hopefully that won't be vital."

He doesn't like Dad much more than Dad does him, Brenda thought. *But I'm not sure I blame him given how Dad has been the one perpetually not available. Maybe Dad doesn't realize how important—and dangerous—this is. If so, I'd better keep an eye on him.*

Brenda gave Nissa a reassuring pat on the shoulder, accepting one from Waking Lizard as he left. Then it was her turn, and thinking back to the first time, Brenda realized she would have given a lot to be walking through the gaping tiger's jaws because then that would mean Pai Hu was all right.

But the passage was as simple as she could wish. The grass her foot touched, although green and apparently lush, was as dry as drought beneath the sole of her sneaker.

Flying Claw had taken his four soldiers over to one side and was running them through elaborate drills. Waking Lizard had joined them and was apparently standing in for the enemy.

Shen, Righteous Drum, and Gaheris were seated on the ground over on the side of the grove, right about where Brenda remembered Pai Hu being when they'd had that first talk with him. Dad was pulling whatever it was out of his case, and Brenda had a strong desire to go over and snoop. She was a little hurt, though, that Dad hadn't confided in her, and so she went over to Pearl instead.

Pearl was wearing her Tiger robes, and Brenda noted that these, unlike the shenyi style worn by most of the others, were more a long tunic over pants. The hem of the tunic was well clear of the ground. A practical arrangement, suitable for a warrior, if not as impressive as Flying Claw's armor.

"Any sign of the White Tiger of the West?" Brenda asked.

"Flying Claw—who was the first through—received a faint greeting. I received one even fainter. Since then, nothing." Pearl nodded in the direction of the clustered Rat and Dragons. "Since that's where we 'saw' Pai Hu, that's where they're starting their search."

"I thought you and Flying Claw would be more involved," Brenda said.

"We are. We will be," Pearl said somewhat equivocally. "But for now I'm leaving this to the experts."

Brenda had her opening.

"What's Dad's part of this?"

Pearl smiled at her, and Brenda knew the older woman wasn't fooled by Brenda's apparent nonchalance.

"Each of the original Exiles," she said, "created a specialized magical item—a means of focusing some aspect of their Branch's specific powers. Many were weapons, like my sword or Des's Talons, but the Rat was rather more creative. He wanted something that would help him assess probability and so he created an abacus."

"An abacus," Brenda said. "You mean one of those things

that looks like a kid's toy? Wires in a frame, each strung with beads?"

"Precisely," Pearl said. "Many historians speak of the abacus as the first practical computer. The Rat's abacus makes possible—among other things—a more rapid calculation of auguries."

"Auguries, like those you do with the mah-jong tiles."

"Auguries were considered a very serious science in ancient China," Pearl corrected. "In fact, writings on augury were one of the sciences preserved in the original burning of the books—but of course they made their way into the Lands nonetheless."

Brenda glanced over. Her father had settled down into a very comfortable-looking crouch, and now bent over—she moved slightly to get a clearer angle—what did indeed look like an abacus that had been placed on a rock.

As Brenda watched, Righteous Drum did something with a compass and recited the reading. Gaheris Morris's fingers flew, the beads moving back and forth on their wires so vigorously that Brenda could hear the rattle over where she stood.

"There seem to be lots of beads," Brenda said after a moment. "And am I right that some of the wires run vertically as well as horizontally?"

"You are," Pearl said. "Exile Rat designed a very elaborate machine—but one that could also function as a perfectly normal abacus. The extra beads and wires are stored in a drawer at the bottom, where they look like nothing so much as replacement parts."

"I don't ever remember seeing it," Brenda said, "not around the house, I mean."

"You father kept it in a safe," Pearl said. "It is, after all, not something small children should be permitted to play with and possibly break. It can only be repaired with great effort."

Brenda caught the whisper of a story there, but she didn't get a chance to ask. Gaheris had surged to his feet, triumph in every line of his body.

"Flying Claw! Auntie Pearl! We think we've found our trail. Will you come and sniff it out?"

The two Tigers immediately hurried over. Brenda trailed after, and listened to the nearly incomprehensible discussion of ch'i flows, personal auras, and the difficulty of distinguishing Pai Hu from his own "background noise." One thing was clear, however. Pearl and Flying Claw both agreed they now could trace Pai Hu.

"Then we're going?" Nissa said, a trace nervously. "Where?"

"Beneath and toward the center," Flying Claw replied. "Along a way that appears to lead into the Void."

☆

To Pearl, Pai Hu's trail appeared as a long streak, fuzzy, opaque white adorned with irregular lines in less blurred black. She concentrated, seeking to resolve the blurring into something more solid. She felt her nostrils flare, and her ears seeking to cup and tilt as they would when she was a tiger, but she did not transform, for as useful as the tiger's augmented senses could be, she needed hands to use her sword and shape her spells.

After a long moment of such sensing, she realized that the path was not blurred through any lack of concentration on her part, but because the White Tiger himself was stretched out over space and time.

"He's all there," she said aloud, "but elongated by something that is pulling him over a vast area. Eventually, the strain will be too much, and he will lose his hold here. By then it may be too late for us to help."

"Pulled," Albert repeated thoughtfully. "Then we must stop whatever or whoever is doing the pulling. Can we get to the other end?"

Pearl glanced at Flying Claw. In his nod she saw agreement with her own conclusions.

"Yes," she said, speaking for them both. "We can."

"I suggest," Flying Claw added, "that everyone take precautions in advance, some form of protective spell at least."

"Also," Pearl said, "consider invoking the wind of your sign. I sense that maneuvering where we are going may not be easy. Having a wind at your back may help."

Shen cut in. "Pick a protection that does not rely too heavily on winds, then, because if our enemies take steps to banish winds, you could find yourself both motionless and unprotected."

Righteous Drum had been thoughtfully studying the place where, to Pearl, the trail clearly began.

"I believe," he said, "a spell to augment sight would be useful. In this place, the eyes of the soul are what will guide us, not those of the body."

Preparations were concluded quickly, the apprentices taking care of themselves, and the more senior members supplying protections for the soldiers who had no magical skills of their own. Twentyseven-Ten insisted on working his own spells, and other than inspecting to make certain they were suitable, no one interfered.

Nor was there much argument regarding the order of their descent. Flying Claw and his soldiers were to go first, followed by the masters, then by the apprentices.

"We can't plan further," Pearl said, when Riprap protested his placement, "because we don't know what we're up against. Consider yourself rear guard if that makes you more comfortable."

Riprap nodded crisply, and shifted to the very end of the loose line, herding Brenda and Nissa in front of him.

And so the descent began. As soon as Flying Claw and his front line stepped onto the trail, it became evident that just as it did not seem to have precise length, it did not have precise breadth. Still, the footing seemed best in a central band of about ten feet in width.

Flying Claw arranged his men in a sort of wedge: himself in the center, flanked by Twentyseven-Ten and Thorn. Chain and Shackles took their positions slightly out from Twentyseven-Ten and Thorn. This left a gap in the center of the second line. Waking Lizard stepped forward to fill it.

In answer to Pearl's glare—she'd been moving into the space herself—he said, "We need to spread out our Tigers. I am not as sensitive to arcane forces as either of the Dragons—and I understand the tactics Flying Claw will use."

And you called yourself a coward for your behavior not so long ago, Pearl thought, looking at the gangling figure with real affection. *Do you seek to redeem yourself?*

Pearl stepped back. Everything Waking Lizard said made perfect sense. She took her position in a third rank, aligned behind Thorn. Des stepped up to partner her.

Righteous Drum formed the center of the fourth rank, with Honey Dream to his left and Gaheris to his right. Gaheris had armed himself with the Shang Gieh Kun, the three-sectional staff, that was among his favored weapons. Like many of the Orphans, he'd trained in weapons that were designed for subduing, rather than killing, for in the world where they lived, the penalties for murder were a factor for serious consideration.

And Gaheris has always considered . . . Pearl thought. *He'll rely on spells rather than weapons in any case, which gives us a very strong magical rank there.*

Albert and Shen made up the fifth rank. Nissa, Brenda, and Deborah the sixth. Riprap, taking very seriously his role as rear guard, made up the seventh by himself.

It was a good arrangement, one that backed fighting strength with magical strength, medical care and retrieval positioned where they would be able to see clearly how the initial phases of the battle progressed.

A very rational organization for a situation that ceased to be rational as soon as the descent began.

Pearl stepped forward onto that black and white course and felt her mind begin to hum and throb. No longer did she walk, but slide, and slide faster and faster, as if the way beneath her was as slick as wet ice. Summer child, California girl, she didn't have much experience with ice or snow, but in a long life, you learn more than you remember. Pearl leaned back and let the momentum carry her forward.

In her hand, Treaty sang a quiet song of blood on tiger's claws, of promises made, and promises kept. Pearl used that to give her balance as well, and found herself soon comfortable. She looked to her right and saw Des—Rooster's Talon adorning his right hand, a maniacal grin on his lips, shifting his weight like the surfer boy he'd been so long ago she'd forgotten that phase. His braid whipped out behind him, snapping like a whip in the wind.

Before her, Pearl saw Flying Claw had his recruits in hand. Twentyseven-Ten moved erratically, and Pearl noted that he kept his course to the more apparently solid black stripes. Thorn bunched down, keeping his center close and compact, his expression grim.

And so they flew down a trail that was also the back of Pai Hu, moving with all the speed of the White Tiger of the West's resistance of that which drew him into dissolution.

What is large enough to swallow a universe? Pearl thought, and wondered if the thought was her own. *Only another universe, and that one of hunger and emptiness. How the hunger calls. How I yearn to fill that emptiness, to be free of this pain for fullness.*

And Pearl knew that the thoughts she heard as her own were those of Pai Hu, and felt tears wet her face as she felt the tremendous agony inflicted by this battle against nothing.

Forever the sliding went on, so long that Pearl began to forget she had ever been other, done other than ride an eternity through eternity. She was broken into awareness by the gleam of silver and substance ahead, by an interruption of solidity and shape against what had been nothing but motion.

Ahead were blocks and boxes, stacked haphazardly on top of each other, sometimes on their sides, sometimes, improbably, on their points. These towers should have teetered, but held firm and intact. Each block shone metallic—silver dominating, but with shades of copper, gold, and bronze as well—the whole hard and impervious as metal or doctrine.

The White Tiger of the West was being drawn to this

place, drawn to smash against these shining, polished surfaces that seemed as if they should reflect, mirrorlike, but in a parody of true reflection, shattered and broke whatever light touched their surfaces.

For now, Pai Hu was managing to restore himself intact as he broke and split, looping himself back into himself, but Pearl could see that the battle was beginning to be lost. Tiny flakes of black and white flecked some of the polished surfaces, bits of Pai Hu that created sympathy with the rest, making himself his own worst enemy.

Three other trails met at this point: one red, one green, and one black. Each smashed and battered against these implacable cubes and rectangles, each gave up confetti glitter that was itself turned assailant.

Pearl knew these by their colors and their auras as the other three guardians: the Vermillion Bird of the South, the Azure Dragon of the East, and the Black Warrior of the North.

She saw, too, that they had given up less than had Pai Hu. The White Tiger was the hardest hit, the nearest to losing this weird battle. Pearl's soul rebelled against the idea that a White Tiger could be weaker than a Vermillion Bird, an Azure Dragon, a Black Warrior, rebelled and in rebellion found an answer.

Pai Hu was being attacked with the most intensity. Why? Because he had made himself their ally. Before, the drawing away had been of equal force, but when Pai Hu had given them his aid, sought theirs in return, he had brought greater danger to himself.

Treaty hummed in Pearl's hand, drawing greater power from fidelity betrayed, but thus far there was no enemy who could be fought with a cut or a slash. Indeed, other than these cubes and rectangles and the hunger of their undeniable need, there was nothing at all.

Nothing, Pearl thought, and the word rang like a gong in the confines of her thoughts. *Wait. What can swallow a universe. Another universe. An empty universe? Wait. Where is the sound?*

Her thoughts were a muddle and a jumble. Yet beneath the confusion was that grasping for understanding that is so frustrating because one knows the answer. Pearl *knew* she knew what she needed to know, but she could not make it come together.

So she concentrated on the smaller things, ignoring the larger as one ignores a cat stuck in a tree in the hope it will get frustrated with its predicament and climb down on its own.

Now she concentrated on something that had seemed natural until this moment: there was no sound. The Orphans—at least in their current incarnation—had proven to be a chatty group. Hardly any subject, from something as minor as what to have for dinner, to the planning of major expeditions did not get talked over—sometimes, she suspected, to the frustration of their allies from the Lands.

Yet here, at this key moment, when confronted with the most major challenge they had ever faced, no one had said a word.

She looked to her right. Des stood, tapping his chin with one forefinger, his expression thoughtful. She swung to look behind her.

Honey Dream looked frightened and kept glancing to her father, her body language indicating both a desire for guidance and a ferocious promise to protect.

Righteous Drum was studying the prospect below, his expression one of calm calculation. To his right, Gaheris looked frustrated and a bit angry.

Pearl inspected the rest of their company, and on all their faces she saw variations of the same emotions: fear, calculation, watchful alertness, but not a one showed a willingness to act. Nor, she noted, did any of them seem to notice her own motion.

We are caught within the nothing that can swallow a universe, she thought. *So this is how it got a hold on the guardians. They might have felt some small unease, but until the hold was set and locked and their very essence drawn from them, they felt no impulse to act.*

Pearl wondered if tiny colored flecks would be visible in time as their own lives were drawn from them to feed the hungriness beneath. She found herself wondering what color her own thread would be. Would it be the Tiger's green or perhaps a multicolored rainbow representing the various other ruling passions of her life. What color was acting? What hue philanthropy? Were resentment and anger as black as they felt, or might they be the muddy purple-black of brooding storm clouds?

Treaty twitched in Pearl's hand, swinging back, biting her on the exposed skin of her neck.

No one reacted to Pearl's cry of shock and surprise. Neither Deborah nor Nissa, entrusted with the bulk of the company's medical supplies, raced forward to bind the wound.

"Ah," Pearl said, forcing herself to speak the words aloud, although she wondered if even her own ears would hear them. "I am in danger of violating my trust. Thank you, Treaty."

No one moved. No one reacted, but Pearl continued to force herself to think aloud as she wiped the blade clean. The nick on her neck was not deep or dangerous, and Pearl continued to let it ooze forth blood, for the hot dampness saturating the collar of her robe was a good reminder.

"I must find myself a partner. Who among these others would be most likely to hear me?"

Three immediate prospects came to her newly focused mind. Chinese magic works strongly on correspondences. Here in this group there were three who had such with herself: Nissa, as the Rabbit, was her partner—the yin to her sign's yang. Waking Lizard, as the Monkey, was her direct opposite on the wheel of signs.

And Flying Claw was himself a Tiger—in a sense, herself.

Pearl felt immediate revulsion for the idea of connecting with Flying Claw, but she had come to distrust those immediate reactions. She knew her mind was not wholly her own.

Therefore, before the reaction to the revulsion had done

more than take shape, Pearl forced herself into action. Flying Claw stood two ranks ahead of her, Waking Lizard only a few paces behind him. She forced herself into motion, and was shocked at how much effort this took. Her bones felt as if they had frozen at the joints; her flesh felt as brittle as glass.

But she willed herself to move, and slid into place between the two men. Treaty went into its sheath, and she swung one arm around Flying Claw, the other around Waking Lizard. They moved like pawns on a playing board, stiff and without any sign of awareness—but that lasted only for a moment.

Waking Lizard's eyes within their lines flashed alert and his wicked smile shone within his beard.

"Lady! You have finally noticed my admiration," he said, flippant and yet sincere. He bestowed a dry peck on one cheek.

Flying Claw—always less inclined to speech—looked at her. His hand rose and touched the still bleeding cut on her neck.

"What is this, Aunt?"

"I was reminded of my oath," she said, touching the hilt of her sword, then returning her hand to his arm. "How do you two feel?"

"As if I have been contemplating tactics for an exam," Flying Claw said. "How long have we stood here?"

"Long enough," Pearl said, "that the time for standing is ended."

Waking Lizard—the tallest of them—glanced from side to side. "The others still stare and sleep. Shall I rouse them?"

"Yes," Pearl said. "Start with Des, since the Rooster is the Monkey's counterpart. My nephew and I shall go below and take a clearer look at the situation."

Flying Claw looked surprised—but Pearl did not think it was her suggestion that they scout that had surprised him, rather that word "nephew."

The youth flashed a brilliant smile. Then he nodded, all

seriousness once more. "Yes. The danger here is giving in to the sense that there is nothing. But if something here can swallow a universe, then nothingness is an illusion."

Pearl drew Treaty from its sheath and let her hand drop from the young man's arm.

"What can swallow a universe?" she said.

"Only another universe," Flying Claw replied. "Did you sense it as well—that horrible hungriness?" She nodded. He began to pick his way toward the nearest of the cube towers as he spoke. "Yet I have the feeling that it is not the Void we feel, but rather something that seeks what it is lacking. There is too strong an identity in this 'nothing.'"

He shrugged, as if knowing his words inadequate, and Pearl answered with a half smile of comprehension.

"Another universe—other—separation of identity," she said. "There must be a point of connection."

"I agree."

"Why all these cubes and squares?" she mused when she stood at the base of one of the towers.

"In our teachings," Flying Claw said, "the universe is a square or cube or rectangle. I think that one of these holds what we seek. The others are blinds."

"How to tell which?" Pearl said.

"Ignore the blinds," said the young man simply. "Where is your heart drawn? Where are you being pulled?"

Pearl did not pause to think, but let the hand that held Treaty rise and point.

"There," she said, indicating one of the towers, no larger nor smaller than the others, topped with a cube balancing on one point.

At that single word, Nothing transformed into purest chaos.

XXXI

Brenda hadn't been thinking of much at all, just standing light and ready in the almost rearmost row of their battle formation. She knew without being told what her job was to be—pulling out those who needed pulling, being ready to step in where needed.

So Brenda stood, watchful and ready, when a terrible need took hold of her soul.

Flying Claw. Why had she let herself be stationed so far away from him? What would any of this matter if he didn't survive?

Brenda looked ahead, standing on her toes to see around those arrayed in front of her on the black and white striped road.

Panic flowered in her breast when she realized she couldn't find Flying Claw. Heart pounding, sweat beading along her hairline, she inserted the toe of one sneakered foot on the lowest band of the Dragon's Tail that encircled her. Using these coils as footholds, Brenda forced herself upward and at last caught a glimpse of Flying Claw's broad shoulders, his hair caught up in a knot at the back of his head.

He was down among those weird cubes and rhomboid shapes. (Brenda felt an odd flash of pride that she remembered the right word for a four-sided shape that was not a square.) He was looking up at the top of an otherwise unnotable stack. But what was he doing now? Why was he pulling out his sword?

Flying Claw wheeled, facing Brenda for the first time.

She blanched as she saw the horrible expression that distorted Flying Claw's handsome features into something monstrous. He was twisting around, his sword now free from its sheath, spinning and leaping with horrid feline grace. His target appeared to be the back of Pearl's neck.

But Pearl was also spinning, twisting with a contortionist's skill to bring Treaty up to parry that descending blade. The blades clanged off each other. In that metallic song of triumph, Brenda understood how the old lady, taken off guard, had managed that remarkable move.

Flying Claw was not fighting Pearl Bright—he was fighting the sword Treaty. And since, for some obscure reason he had chosen to violate the alliance that bound them, Flying Claw would lose.

"No!" The word ripped from Brenda's throat, ragged and multisyllabic.

Without thought, Brenda left her assigned place in their neat ranks. Without effort, she found the wind she had summoned. Grabbing hold and climbing aboard, she used the wind to carry her up and over the intervening ranks that barricaded her from her beloved and his doom.

As she passed over the others, Brenda was vaguely aware that numerous battles had broken out below her. Her dad was lunging toward Albert. Shen and Righteous Drum were screaming at each other. Golden yellow billowed around them in a visible aura.

Deborah had run forward and was trying to break up the various arguments, her round face livid red with anger.

Glancing back, Brenda saw that Nissa was trying to run up the road. Riprap was blocking her way.

But Brenda found none of this touched the raging desire and fear that was causing her to hurtle toward where Flying Claw battled Treaty. She urged the wind on which she rode to greater speed, and knew in a moment she would be there, that she must do something, if nothing more than die valiantly at his side.

She was so focused on her intention that she came up short, head rocking back against her shoulders, when something rose to bar her progress.

Honey Dream had risen into the air. The Snake rested lightly on a wind, her balance, even the flow of her inky hair, perfect and lovely. Acutely, Brenda felt her own awkwardness, her own lack of a true place within this assembly. More than ever she wanted to rescue Flying Claw from Treaty, save Pearl from committing an atrocity, and so prove both her love and her right to be in this company.

She'd show her dad that he shouldn't keep secrets from her, that he shouldn't treat her as a child when everyone else was treating her like somebody important. But first, she must rescue Flying Claw—and to get to him . . .

"Get out of my way," Brenda snarled at Honey Dream. "Flying Claw's in trouble."

"I want," Honey Dream said, her voice tight, the words a grating staccato flow, "to rip out your throat, to gouge out your eyes. . . . I hate you for rescuing my father, stealing my beloved, but . . ."

Honey Dream drew in her breath in a ragged gasp. Brenda, who had been trying to get around this unwelcome obstacle without success, stared in astonishment—for, despite the cruel words, Honey Dream was not making the least move to harm her. In fact, she seemed to be doing the opposite. The other woman had her fists balled into each other, clenching them so tightly that the knuckles were white.

"But," Honey Dream continued in a harsh whisper, "I will not. I remember thinking otherwise. I remember being grateful. I remember seeing my love for what it was. . . . These impulses are not me. Not me. Echoes of old desires, older hates . . ."

Brenda didn't want to listen. She wanted Flying Claw. Now. She could hear that clash of metal on metal, and knew that he was holding his own against Treaty—but for how long?

Honey Dream moved to one side, and Brenda raced forward marveling at the ease with which she found footholds in the air.

See, Dad? she thought with venom she hadn't known she felt. *See how fantastic I am? Why have you been holding out on me? Why have I been good enough to do your job when it wasn't convenient for you, but I'm not good enough to know your secrets?*

Honey Dream was beside Brenda, stumbling as she struggled to keep pace. "Look, Brenda. I'll help you rescue Flying Claw. Then will you listen to me? Something isn't right here!"

Brenda snarled. "I don't need your help. I don't need anyone's help. I can do anything I need to do, and I'm tired of being pushed around. I have nothing against you, but if you get in my way, I'm going to make those damn red robes of yours into applesauce."

Brenda didn't hear Honey Dream's reply—if there was a reply. Her head pounded. Her heart ached with desperate desires, desires only half admitted to until this moment. Her ears ached from the surrounding noise. It had been so quiet before, so peaceful. Why was everyone screaming? What was that horrible howling noise?

Brenda looked ahead. Flying Claw and Pearl were still fencing, blade striking blade so hard that blue sparks flecked the air. Twentyseven-Ten stood to one side, his own blade drawn, a look of supreme satisfaction on his features. Brenda didn't need to ask to know that the former prisoner was thinking that whatever the outcome of this duel, some desire of his own would be satisfied.

Thorn lay crumpled on the ground, blood trickling from his forehead, washing his face with red. Brenda thought that he must have tried to break up the fight, and met this poor thanks.

How am I going to pull it off? she thought. *There's got to be a way . . .*

Honey Dream had grabbed hold of Brenda's sleeve and was holding her back.

"Why is it that you can't see how insane this is? Would Flying Claw break a treaty? Never! Not without good reason, and there is no good reason."

Sure there is, Brenda thought. *Pearl must have said*

something, done something. She can be so annoying, such a know-it-all . . .

But the thoughts rang hollow in her head. Pearl had been very annoying lots of times, but neither as Foster nor as Flying Claw had the young man raised a hand to her. Brenda didn't want to admit it, but Honey Dream was correct. Something was wrong.

Brenda shook her head, trying to clear it, because even as she was thinking this, another part of her was shouting at her to get a move on, to get down there, to go after Flying Claw. Hit Pearl. Do something.

No treaty keeps you from hurting Pearl, that other voice said persuasively. *You're fine. In the clear. You might even gain her gratitude, for there's no way that Flying Claw— that noble youth—would strike an old woman when she was down.*

Brenda squinched her eyes shut tight and bent forward, teeth clenched, hands pressed to her ears. She shook herself, straightened, opened her eyes again, strove to see, really see, not to interpret.

And she saw. Pearl and Flying Claw were indeed fighting, but it was a weird and desperate duel. Treaty wanted the young man's blood, but Pearl was trying to regain control over the blade. Time and again a blow that would have severely injured, even killed the young warrior went astray because the old woman holding the hilt had kilted it aside.

For his part, Flying Claw was concentrating almost wholly on defense, parrying, parrying, refusing openings where he could have broken through Pearl's erratic guard.

"They don't want to fight," Brenda said aloud.

"And someone else has noticed," Honey Dream said. "We've got to stop him!"

For Twentyseven-Ten's face had lost its expression of bland complacency. He was drawing his sword, balancing lightly on the balls of his feet, looking for the opening that would let him strike without being struck in turn.

Did he realize that in doing this he would be opening himself to Treaty's vengeance? Did he care? Did he think that the sword would choose to finish with one target before settling on a second and that by then Pearl would be too exhausted to handle the sword to any effect?

Even as she wondered, Brenda was swooping down, running in the air, then on solid somehow springy ground, propelling herself with aching muscles as fast as she could, her target the back of Twentyseven-Ten's knees. She didn't know what Honey Dream was doing, but she knew the other woman would be in there somehow.

How odd, she thought, *to trust Honey Dream.*

But the thought was her own, no other's, and she knew the Snake worthy of trust.

Faster and faster, Brenda raced. Her focus was absolute, the world resolved to the few square inches that were her target. Faster she went, then she hit solidly, squarely, launching herself with the momentum of her wind into a tackle that took Twentyseven-Ten out behind the knees.

And Honey Dream was there as well, angling with far greater elegance and artistry, plucking Twentyseven-Ten's sword from his momentarily loosened grasp, bringing it around so that the flat caught him along the side of his helmeted head. He was unconscious before he hit the ground.

Brenda made sure of this. Then she struggled to her feet, inspecting her array of bracelets, looking for something, anything that would enable Flying Claw and Pearl to break from their battle.

Dragons, winds, twins, variations of them in different combinations. Winding Snakes, perhaps? But no, that would take too long. Wriggling Snakes—that had promise, but could it get past Pearl's defenses?

An insight, brilliant as such always is, came to Brenda. Fearing that thought would quell the impulse, make her realize just how dangerous what she intended was, Brenda dashed forward, letting her daypack fall from her shoulders as she moved so that it dropped first from her left shoulder, than fell down her right arm so that she could grasp it in her right hand.

She swung the pack underhand, letting the weight and momentum carry it so it smashed into Treaty's blade and Pearl's hand. Pearl's hand loosed its grip on the sword's hilt, and the pack knocked it free.

Flying Claw's blade, raised to parry and not finding the expected counterblow, hit the pack squarely, slicing through the nylon fabric so that first-aid kit, binoculars, a roll of hard candy, a package of chewing gum, a half-eaten high-protein bar, and assorted other detritus scattered on the ground.

Pearl was cradling her sword hand. A moan escaped her lips despite obvious efforts to hold it back.

"I think my hand is broken," she said in shock.

Brenda didn't stop to apologize. "Deborah! Nissa! Pearl's hurt!" she yelled, and was relieved to see Deborah part from the knot of shouting men up above.

Brenda didn't wait to see if anyone else was coming, or even what Flying Claw was doing. Waking Lizard was speaking, the urgency in his voice drawing Brenda in.

"We must break that," he was saying, pointing to the top of an unremarkable stack, "then not only should the madness cease, but so should the force that's drawing away at the guardians."

His audience consisted of Honey Dream, Des, Chain, and Shackles. Deborah was easing Pearl to the ground, talking comfortingly. Brenda turned to join Waking Lizard and the others. Later she'd let herself feel immensely guilty about what she'd done to Pearl. For now, the only way she could make her impulsive action good was to help.

Honey Dream made room for Brenda, giving her a stiff, approving smile, but the Snake's words were for Waking Lizard.

"Close it? Can we do so without trapping the guardians?"

"Good point." Waking Lizard frowned, twisting his beard around his right index finger.

"Amputation is kinder than death." The words were Flying Claw's. "And I believe the guardians may be able to regenerate what they have lost. We must move quickly. Whatever created this monstrosity has increased its pull."

No one asked how he knew, but Brenda suspected that Pai Hu was still able to communicate with the Tiger.

"It wants," Waking Lizard said, his eyes wild. "Can't you feel the desire? That's what has been driving us all crazy. It is empty and longs to be filled. It is incomplete and longs for completion. Let's give it a bellyful."

"No," Honey Dream said. "That's all wrong. This thing is trying to swallow a universe. How can we give it enough? Let's think . . ."

To Brenda's surprise, Honey Dream turned to her, dark brown eyes intense and focused. "Do you think this thing is live or un-live, made or broken?"

Brenda answered from her gut. She didn't much trust her intellect at this point.

"Un-live and made."

"What is a made break? What is a constructed hole?"

"A constructed hole?"

An momentary image of Dylan and Thomas when they were smaller, digging with their metal construction trucks and square-tipped sandbox shovels.

"Hey, Breni. We're digging a hole to China!"

Brenda herself, only a little older, wistfully remembering when she'd believed such things could be done.

Her voice shaped the answer. "A constructed hole? A made break. A tunnel. A gate."

"A gate," Honey Dream said. "That's it! This is a gate. Waking Lizard spoke truth when he said this thing is hungry—incomplete, but I do not think it is the gate that is incomplete, but rather whatever is on the other side."

Des said, his expression eager, "If whatever it is wants completion, and if it can find what will complete it here, then it cannot be alien to our understanding. In fact, I suspect it is very familiar. Whoever made the gate will have taken steps to protect it, to assure against unwanted intrusion."

"That's always the problem with gates," Waking Lizard said softly. "They work two ways."

Brenda remembered the seeming eternity ago when they had set up the pine door in Pearl's warehouse.

"Guardians? Men Shen?"

"Two points, weedhopper," Des said. "But these will not be our Men Shen. Men Shen are as infinite as the gates and doors they guard. Even so, I believe we can use this to our advantage."

Brenda looked back over her shoulder. Something was changing. Dad and Albert, Shen and Righteous Drum were no longer arguing. Dazed expressions on their faces, they were stumbling down to join the rest. Farther back, she could see Riprap standing tall, Nissa cradled limp in his arms as if she weighed no more than Lani.

Deborah had turned her attention to Twentyseven-Ten. His helmet was off, and she was doing something to the side of his face.

Pearl, arm now in a sling, was inspecting Thorn, her expression pinched with pain and worry.

It isn't trying to get at us now, Brenda thought. *That can't be good.*

"Why isn't there a guard here?" she asked, and heard the question come forth in a harsh, dry whisper. "This place is important to someone. Really important. Why isn't someone here?"

"But someone is . . ."

The words came as a rumble, hardly discernible as words. Brenda felt a vague urge to try and decide whether they were spoken in Chinese or English, but recognizing there the temptation to stumble again into madness, she jerked herself to wider awareness.

Immediately, she understood why her mind had found madness tempting, for the scene around her, the scene that she must accept as real, was in itself insane.

The piles of metallic rock were moving, inching like ponderous caterpillars, falling into heaps that reassembled into shapes that became cubist distortions of almost familiar things.

Was that a skyscraper? No. More a rocket ship or a limousine balanced on its trunk. Over there the rocks heaped up into an arch that started walking stiffly, thudding footsteps rattling the teeth in Brenda's head.

The assembled rocks moved without purpose that became purpose, assembling and unassembling, wall and bulwark, stocky legs like those of a brontosaurus. Sightless eyes made by dark gaps staring out. Gaping mouths leering. Nothing was in proportion, yet a face of sorts was emerging.

A voice like dripping lava shouted, "I am here!"

Brenda felt her hold on sanity trembling again. There was only so much she could take. She grasped out blindly, and found a hand—long-fingered, knobby-knuckled, slightly hairy across the back.

Waking Lizard gave her fingers a friendly squeeze and turned his grin on her. "You had to ask . . . Look. Whatever that is is not as purposeless as it seems. See? The formation that holds the gate is being moved steadily up. Whatever answered your question doesn't want us getting near the gate."

"If it's afraid of us," Des said, keeping his voice very soft, "then there must be something we can do to it, but for the life of me, I can't think what."

"Pai Hu," Flying Claw added, also speaking in almost a whisper, "says the pulling has ceased. He is still held, but no longer compelled."

"Tell him to pull back just a bit," Brenda suggested. "I mean, the more ways that thing is distracted, the better."

"I will try," Flying Claw said.

Honey Dream nodded. "Good thought. I'll speak with my father."

Brenda wondered what Righteous Drum had to do with Pai Hu, then remembered that one of the other guardians was the Azure Dragon of the East. Maybe Shen and Righteous Drum could do something in that quarter.

Rock, paper, scissors, she thought wildly. *What harms rock? Nothing. Rock breaks scissors, scissors cut paper, paper wraps rock. We'd need a hell of a lot of paper.*

Brenda heard herself giggle wildly, hysterically, felt Waking Lizard's comforting hand dragging her back to the present.

"What's so funny, Brenda?"

"Rock, paper, scissors. It's a game." She made the three signs with her free hand. "Everything has something that can defeat it, but we don't have enough paper."

Waking Lizard looked concerned, but Des—of her own world and culture—brightened.

"You've got something there, Brenda. The five elements. The cycle of creation and destruction." He muttered under his breath, "Water makes Wood, but quenches Fire. Fire makes Earth, but melts Metal. Metal makes Water, but cuts Wood. Wood produces Fire, but destroys Earth."

Brenda remembered this weird view of natural science from one of those endless lectures. There was a logic to how the Chinese had evolved their ideas, but right now she wasn't interested in logic—only in whether they could make it work for them here.

"How does Wood destroy Earth, Des?"

"Roots," Des said distractedly. "Plants feed on Earth. Even boulders can be split by tiny plants."

"Plants!" Brenda repeated, thinking of Pai Hu's desiccated jungle. Even if they made their way back up the trail, there wouldn't be anything they could use. "We're sunk."

But Shen, who had arrived in time to hear the discourse, shook his head. "Perhaps not. I think this is something we should discuss in private."

He broke an amulet bracelet, "Four Winds. I've told them to screen us. They won't last long—not here—but we should have a few moments."

Shen looked over at Righteous Drum, his expression

holding no anger, but rather an extreme awkwardness. Apparently, hot words had passed between them, but judging from the lack of evidence of physical injury, the argument had stayed on the intellectual plane.

That didn't mean it wasn't vicious though, Brenda thought.

"Righteous Drum," Shen began very formally, "our lore contains spells for creating or encouraging plants. Does yours?"

Righteous Drum pursed his lips, considering. "It does, but I fear . . ." He took a deep breath, and Brenda had a hint as to what the two scholars might have argued over, "I fear my training has focused on the practical, and in the Lands a sorcerer of my stature does not have time nor energy to concentrate on mere agriculture."

Shen nodded. "Whereas my life has been much calmer and more inclined to the esoteric. Moreover, my Umeko loves plants, and living in the city as we do, growing them is not always easy. I have two sequences I can draw upon from memory: Greta's Garden and Lily of the Valley. The one creates an instant garden of sorts, growing faster and larger the more ch'i one permits to feed it."

Des gave a crisp nod. "I used to do Greta's Garden before I started traveling so much that keeping a garden going in Santa Fe was hardly practical. I think I can pull it off."

"I know both spells," said Albert.

Brenda glanced his way, then looked back in astonishment. Albert's left eye was swelling, and a distinct shiner was forming. She looked at her dad. Gaheris Morris's left cheek bore four long, deep slices.

Oh, boy . . .

But Gaheris Morris spoke with remarkable calm. "My mother loves lilies of the valley. I used to suprise her with them out of season. I can do that one by heart."

Waking Lizard laughed. "I thought I had nothing to offer, but there was a spell I learned long ago, when training as Monkey—almost as a joke. Yes. It will serve here."

Flying Claw had not let his attention stray from the moving rocks, but clearly he had been listening.

"Good. You five prepare your spells—quickly." He glanced at Chain and Shackles. "Are you willing to provide cover and distraction?"

They nodded. Brenda wondered what torments the madness had visited upon the former prisoners, for both were pale and worn.

A voice spoke from behind, in a tone that did not brook disagreement.

"I'm going with you," Riprap said. He had come to join them, still carrying Nissa. Now he set her down gently beside Deborah. "Keep an eye on her. It was the staircase all over again, but worse, far worse."

Deborah blinked, but didn't ask for clarification.

Yeah, Brenda thought. *We're always our own worst enemies, aren't we? The spells on that staircase had been disabled before I got to it, but I remember . . .*

Flying Claw nodded at Riprap. "We will be glad to have you."

"Count me in," Brenda said.

"And me," Honey Dream echoed.

"I," Righteous Drum said, moving his shoulder so his empty sleeve flapped, "would perhaps do best to stay out of direct action. Perhaps Pearl should do the same?"

"I agree," Pearl said. "No need to give you someone else to pull out."

"Let's refine our plan before Shen's winds go down," Albert said, "over here."

Brenda didn't join the impromptu huddle, but instead looked shyly at Pearl. "Sorry."

Pearl nodded briskly. "These things happen."

"I guess," Brenda heard the doubt in her own voice. A hand came to rest on her shoulder. She looked over and saw her dad.

"Back me up, Breni?" Gaheris asked softly, his expression at once serious and a bit manic. She'd seen him like this on Halloween when he had a particular prank in mind.

"Doing what?" Brenda tried not to stare at the line of scratches on his face.

"Going after . . ." Gaheris was beginning, when the huddle broke up.

"Here's our strategy," Flying Claw said, speaking crisply. Brenda hurried over to listen, fighting the unhappy feeling that here her dad was finally paying attention to her and she was ditching him, combined with the sense that Dad had been about to get her into something dumb—something she was just as glad not to have to go along with.

Flying Claw's words continued with brisk efficiency, "Four of us—myself, Riprap, Chain, and Shackles—are going to go right up the middle, as if we're targeting the gate. Albert, Des, Shen, Waking Lizard, and Gaheris, you're to follow on our heels, but instead of charging to the top, your job will be to attack the stones themselves."

Shen took over. "If we set our plants to start growing on the bottom layer of rocks, we may succeed in unsettling the entire edifice. That should not only serve our direct purpose of getting that gate closed, but also provide some protection for our front line."

"Harder to throw rocks at us," Riprap said, shifting his grip on what Brenda couldn't help but think of as a Chinese baseball bat from hand to hand, "when they're worrying about keeping on their feet."

Flying Claw shifted his gaze to Brenda and Honey Dream. "You two back us up. We're going to be too busy looking ahead to notice what's coming from the side—or underneath. Improvise. You've both shown a gift for it."

"Right," Brenda said.

"Very well," Honey Dream agreed.

Righteous Drum nodded. "I can provide distractions from back here. I have a few prepared spells that will cover you while you close."

Flying Claw looked at Pearl and Deborah. "You two have the hardest job of all. Stay out of the fighting if you can. Keep the wounded protected. I don't know if that thing will throw rocks like Riprap said, but I don't think it's going to discriminate between combatants and noncombatants."

"The wounded's own protective spells have mostly faded," Pearl said, "and they're not in a position to set up others."

Brenda checked and noticed her own Dragon's Tail was a bit thin. She started to add another, then decided to switch to All Winds and Dragons. It was the most powerful protection she had, and she didn't think she should save it for a later that might not happen.

Honey Dream nodded curtly, but in clear approval. Around Brenda others were making last-minute preparations. Flying Claw glanced at his front rank.

"We can't know how much that thing overheard," he said. "It might not rely purely on whatever serves it for ears. Let's get moving before it has time to act."

XXXII

Honey Dream was not sure how she felt about being stationed in the back—her role no more prominent than that of Brenda Morris—but after consideration she decided that no insult was intended.

Although she had decent fighting skills, Honey Dream's recent practice bouts with Pearl had shown her that she was not a front-line fighter—and she certainly couldn't convince plants to grow from nothing and take root in what might or might not be rock.

Then she had no time left for wondering. Righteous Drum had lit the air above with a shower of shooting stars, a summons only slightly more beautiful than it was destructive.

The rocks ahead, which had settled into something like immobility, now reared and moved, shifting like blind worms to get away from the deadly lights.

Not wishing to have his spell harm his allies, Righteous Drum had aimed high, and most of the stars exploded relatively harmlessly in the air above the rocks, their streaks of red and green, blue and gold light turning the metallic hues of the rocks into an animate aurora borealis.

Running hard beneath the distraction offered by the shooting stars, Flying Claw was the first to reach the rocks. He bounded onto a lower tier, then up to the next. Honey Dream's heart clenched with a desire so powerful that she almost followed. A chance glimpse of Brenda Morris's face, caught between longing and determination, stayed her. Whatever else, Honey Dream the Snake would not be less faithful to her post than an apprentice Rat.

The rocks were reacting now, but most of the motion seemed to be on the upper levels. Honey Dream saw a solid arm shaped of small cubes punch out at Chain's shoulder. The man parried with his blade, and the metal clanged protest. Riprap was battering away at an ever-renewing wall that kept forming between him and the next step upward.

Flying Claw was a wraith of motion. One moment he was a man in armor, in the next Honey Dream could have sworn a tiger leapt from rock to rock. One thing was certain, wherever he passed, the rocks moved more slowly thereafter.

The sorcerers had reached the base of the formation, but it seemed that the mass of rock could split its attention in many directions. Waking Lizard had tossed something into the center of a tight cluster in front of him, but the others did not seem to be having much success. Gaheris Morris seemed to have vanished entirely, and for a moment Honey Dream wondered if he had fled or been knocked out. Then she saw a shadow flicker where Gaheris should be, and knew he was trained in the Rat's art of shadow motion.

Brenda called out, "Honey Dream, I think we've got to do something. What do you think about Twins?"

She held up an amulet bracelet, and Honey Dream, touched despite herself at having her advice asked, nodded.

"I'll summon a wind and direct us," she said. "That way you can use your amulets undistracted."

"Great!" Brenda said. "I've got a three-part set. We'll drop Heaven, Hell, and Earth where they'll provide cover for the gardeners."

Honey Dream had heard her father speak of these spells and highly approved. They were idealized warriors, and within limits had a certain amount of tactical volition.

She intensified her connection to the south-southeast wind, her own wind, and felt it respond. Spreading it as a carpet beneath her, Honey Dream swooped to pick up Brenda. They sped into the middle zone. As they closed the distance, Honey Dream noticed that Waking Lizard's spell had produced thick coils of vine. He now stood back, deep in concentration, feeding them ch'i so that they proliferated.

"I must learn that one," she said.

"It's cool," Brenda agreed. "Waking Lizard seems to have the middle in control. Let's set one of these to the left. They're not having as much luck."

Brenda cast down the amulet bracelet, releasing the blue and white of the Twins of Heaven. The Twins of Earth joined their fellows, and then Honey Dream skewed them off to the opposite side where the air now smelled strongly of lilies of the valley.

"Nice," Brenda said. "I always wondered what that perfume Grandma Elaine wears was. Funny how you don't think to ask."

Honey Dream managed a smile. The Ratling was nervous, and for good reason. The rocks were moving wildly now. Time and again, their protective winds were all that kept them from being battered. Yet, more troubling than the moving rocks, the pelting stones, the weird battle of Earth and Wood, was a tightness in the living ch'i of the place.

Scholars taught that all things are just variations in the

shape of the pervading living energy of the universe. Honey Dream accepted this, accepted that when she called upon a wind or worked some other trick, she was simply moving this energy from shape to shape.

However, never had she realized how superficial that understanding was, never had she felt the very tenuous nature of those forms that she perceived. But now something was manipulating those forces on a grand scale, and Honey Dream had the awful realization that she stood in great danger of being manipulated directly out of existence.

"The rocks!" Brenda shouted. "Oh, god. The rocks, they're falling! And Flying Claw, Riprap . . . They're all still up toward the top!"

Honey Dream struggled to hold her wind together, struggled against the fear her realization had engendered. Brenda, seeing the struggle, but not understanding its source, held out a hand cupped around another amulet bracelet.

"I'll Knit. You concentrate on getting to them. They're trusting us to pull them out."

Brenda's ch'i flowed into Honey Dream a moment later. It did not change the situation except in one way. Honey Dream was awed by the trust being shown to her—by the warriors who had climbed to the face of the gate, and by Brenda, who had no reason to love her.

She threw herself into action. They ripped through the air, grabbing Shackles as he stumbled and would have fallen.

Brenda somehow found the concentration to strip off a bracelet and hand it to the man.

"Smash this. Jump. It'll cushion you. We need the room."

Shackles, to his credit, did as he was told, choosing a moment when Honey Dream had circled out to avoid a hail of rocks thrown either at her or at Flying Claw, who now teetered on a rock that was pivoting itself around. In a moment it would fall, crushing him beneath its once-solid footing.

Brenda's ch'i continued to feed into Honey Dream.

Together, almost as one, they swept in, gathering Flying Claw just in time.

Riprap was nowhere to be seen, but Flying Claw read the question in her gaze.

"Riprap jumped. I think he made it down. Chain wasn't so lucky. The rock he jumped on split. He fell. I heard him scream."

Flying Claw's face was scored with dozens of tiny cuts and bruises, shrapnel that had gotten through when his protections had held the larger attacks at bay.

A yell from below—Des Lee—broke through. "It's coming down! It's coming down! Get clear! Get clear!"

Honey Dream obeyed. Fleeing was easy, for flight was the impulse she had been fighting, so easy that she might have continued had not Flying Claw squeezed her arm—hard.

"Hold. We must see what happens."

Honey Dream held, and only then remembered the debt she owed Brenda. The Ratling looked very pale and drawn, but when Honey Dream broke the contact between them, she still had strength enough to make a thumbs-up gesture.

But this was peripheral. Honey Dream was hardly aware of the other two who crowded so close.

Wood had conquered Earth. From the broken pile of no longer moving rocks emerged four terrible figures: the White Tiger of the West, the Azure Dragon of the East, the Vermillion Bird of the South, and the Black Warrior of the North.

Honey Dream's mind, sensitized as it was, saw the guardians both in the symbolic forms her ancestors had given them long ago and for a single, shattering moment as the entities they were. But the human mind cannot grasp infinity without breaking, and the four guardians were grateful.

The comforting, comfortable masks descended, freeing Honey Dream to see that miracles were not yet ended. The moving rocks had been reduced to tarnished rubble. This now was rapidly becoming overgrown with thick vines, domestic flowers, and incongrous patches of tiny white lilies of the valley. One rock, shifted on its tip so that it made a diamond shape, stood intact at the top of the heap.

This was the gate, and from it emerged the Men Shen, bristling with weapons, armored with fidelity, faces set in fierce defiance. But their defiance was not directed at the clustered humans (somehow without realizing it, Honey Dream had set the three of them down where Pearl and Deborah maintained their posts) but at the four guardians.

"You cannot pass!" they said as one.

"You were happy enough to let us through before," Pai Hu said, his ears pinned back, a snarl showing every bright fang. "We will go through and meet the one who called us."

"No!" the Men Shen said. Then one reached for the handle of a door that had not been there a moment before. "We shall lock the doors, and defend the gate against your passage."

Honey Dream thought she heard a faint wail of protest. It seemed to originate on the other side of the gate.

"Move swiftly," said the Vermillion Bird, flaring into flames, her eyes the yellow-white of heating coals. "For I fly!"

She flapped her wings, sending forth heat so intense that the heaps of rock began to melt and blacken.

The Men Shen needed no other prompting, but each seized a handle on the door and drew it shut with a clang. This was followed by the prosaic sound of a bar being dropped into place.

"Even so," said Des, "let's make certain it stays shut."

He was starting to strip an amulet bracelet from his arm when the Vermillion Bird said almost kindly, "This is our place. You have done your part."

She flew over the rubble heap and breathed not so much fire as light upon the door. The metal panels melted, becoming solid, becoming one. Then the Black Warrior thudded forward on sturdy tortoise legs. It reared forward, and came down hard upon the diamond-shaped rock, which split into dozens of tiny cubes.

Honey Dream felt the jangling sensation of distorted,

distorting ch'i ebb to almost nothing and knew the gate was not only closed, not only sealed, but completely destroyed.

The four guardians ranked themselves and looked over the gathered humans with expressions that despite their awful majesty held kindness.

"We are grateful," said the serpent that is the other end of the Black Warrior's tortoise form, "for the risks you have taken, to those of you who have lived and died and suffered. You will find no difficulty crossing the North when you seek the Lands."

"Nor the South," said the Vermillion Bird.

"Nor the East," said the Azure Dragon, and he tossed something small and round to Shen Kung and Righteous Drum.

"And your welcome in the West," said Pai Hu, "is more certain than ever. Come, I will take you home."

Pearl's voice broke the awed silence that followed these pronouncements. "Where is Waking Lizard?"

☆

They found Waking Lizard buried beneath one of the deepest mounds of rock, his hand resting on Chain's ankle.

"His protective spell held," Deborah said as she examined the nearly unmarred body. "His heart did not."

"Waking Lizard must have seen Chain fall," Flying Claw said, "and tried to rescue him. I feel horribly ashamed. I heard Chain scream, but did nothing."

Pearl put her unbroken hand on Flying Claw's shoulder. "That's not true, nephew. You were busy the entire time. If Honey Dream and Brenda hadn't come after you, likely you would have followed Chain. Don't blame yourself for things you could not have changed. I assure you when you've lived as long as I have, you'll have enough regrets."

Stiffly, Pearl knelt down next to a man who had been becoming a friend. Off to one side, she heard Brenda quietly weeping, Gaheris trying to find the right words to comfort her.

"Dad," Brenda said, her voice choked around sobs, "it's not that he's dead. I've been to the afterlife or something that passes for it. I believe like I never did before that we live on, somehow, some way. It's that . . . He was so kind to me. I was so scared, and I never got to thank him."

Brenda started crying harder then, and Gaheris gave up on reason, folding her in his arms and letting her sob. Standing where she was, Pearl was in a perfect position to notice Flying Claw's reaction to Brenda's tears, and guessed he'd be perfectly ready to take over when Gaheris got worn out.

Brenda wasn't the only one with tears in her eyes. Even Righteous Drum, whom Pearl had gotten accustomed to thinking of as rather stuffy—unless Honey Dream was involved, of course—was dabbing at his eyes.

Shackles, who was kneeling beside Chain's body, looked greatly comforted when Shen came over and put a hand on his shoulder.

"He died as he would have wanted," Shen said. "They both did. It's not much comfort now, but remember it for later."

"Thank you, Grandfather," Shackles said very softly. "I will. It just seems so wrong, so unfair. We were almost home, and now he'll never get there. He had a wife. I'll have to tell her."

"Tell her," came the voice of Pai Hu, "that although Chain died far from home, he died as a hero and his tomb will never lack for offerings."

The White Tiger had taken form among them as a tiger only slightly more overwhelming than the natural ones. Now he lashed his tail back and forth, and the rubble heap reassembled itself into a lovely burial temple. At each of the four roof corners, one of the four guardians was depicted.

"Lay them there," Pai Hu ordered. "This place is at the Center. My fellows and I will give them honor even when the memory of all humanity has faded."

No one argued. It was a tremendous honor.

So Waking Lizard and Chain were placed in the tomb,

and fifteen considerably battered humans followed Pai Hu to where the pine door maintained its vigil.

Nissa was walking under her own power again. Riprap wouldn't say what he had done, but Pearl suspected he'd knocked her out when she had tried to flee.

Did he do it for her own good, Pearl thought, *or because of his own desire to do something important? I'll never ask. I don't think any of us should ask what desires touched us when we were caught within the hunger of a universe struggling for completion. Not all of our desires were as innocent as a mother's yearning to return to her child.*

Pearl looked at Albert. His eye was swollen completely shut, and he had refused several offers of treatment. The long slices on Gaheris's face were less livid—probably he'd washed the worst of the blood from them at some point—but they'd take time to heal.

And which of them struck first? Pearl thought. *That's another question we shouldn't ask. After all, neither of them were completely themselves.*

Pearl remembered how she'd felt when Flying Claw's blade had made its hissing descent. Her reaction had not been fear or anger. No. It had been perfect understanding of his desire. There should not be two Tigers. Flying Claw's goal when he had left the Lands had been to reclaim, re-make his attenuated Branch. Under the influence of the terrible need on the other side of the gate, all the rationalizations for not taking what he wanted had vanished.

And she? Had her reaction been much better?

Not much, for all my years, for all my supposed wisdom, Pearl thought ruefully. *Only when we realized how we were being influenced, manipulated, did the nature of our conflict change. Before . . . It's a good thing we both had protective spells up, otherwise I'm not certain either of us would have survived.*

They were passing through the pine door now, one by one, each stopping to say a few words to Pai Hu.

Pearl held back until she was almost the last—she and Flying Claw.

"What was that on the other side of the gate?" she asked. "Do you know?"

"I do, but my answer will tell us little," the White Tiger said. "Someone created a mold, a form. A universe that was created without what we four guardians and our realm are, so that we would be drawn to fill the mold. We could not resist because there was nothing for us to resist against."

"But there was someone," Flying Claw said, "who created the mold."

"I cannot believe something so perfect was an accident," Pai Hu said. "But I never saw, nor smelled, nor otherwise sensed that person—or people."

"Not even when you crossed to the other side?" Pearl persisted.

"If you stuck your foot out a window," Pai Hu said, "would you see the colors of the flowers that grow in the bed planted beneath? Once I realized my danger, I did nothing that would help myself be drawn through."

"Not even peeking," Pearl nodded. "Yes. I can see that."

"But the gate is sealed," Flying Claw said; despite his confident tone, Pearl knew he was looking for reassurance. "And the guardian domains are safe—you are safe. We will be able to cross to the Lands."

"Yes. When you are ready, you will find the remaining eight of your nine gates established." Pai Hu looked as embarrassed as a gigantic tiger could—which was not much. "My associates and I have decided that using the gates—while somewhat cumbersome—will be a wise safeguard. They will remain closed until you and your associates need them, and so the integrity of our realms will remain intact."

"Wise, as well as generous," Pearl said. She turned to Flying Claw. "The others will be starting to worry. Shall we return?"

"After you, Aunt," he said.

"Very well." Pearl Bright stepped forward, knowing that she could trust him at her back.

☆

Honey Dream wondered that the Orphans were so surprised when they realized that something like thirty-four hours had passed during their sojourn into the West and beyond.

They could take so much, do so much, then be flabbergasted by something as ordinary as different time streams.

There was much talk about jet lag, and where various people should be dropped off. In the end, Deborah opted to come to Colm Lodge, so she could keep an eye on Thorn and Twentyseven-Ten. Thorn, in particular, would need skilled care.

Brenda volunteered to drive Pearl and Gaheris to Dr. Andersen's office. Apparently, Deborah and Nissa both agreed that something called an X-ray would be needed to discover just how to best treat Pearl's broken hand. A call had affirmed that the doctor would make himself available.

Brenda offered to take Albert, as well, but he refused.

"I think I can deal with this," he said, touching his swollen eye. "I believe I can see well enough to drive if I am careful. I will tell my associates I was injured in a martial arts exercise. It's true enough."

"Well," Gaheris said, laughing as he fingered his injured face. "I don't want to try and explain this to Keely. Maybe the doc can give me something to ease the redness."

"Perhaps that would be wise," Albert said.

Honey Dream wondered if she had imagined the emphasis on the first word. Looking at the expressions on Pearl and Brenda's faces, she thought not.

Gaheris Morris was a complicated person, but then most Rats were. . . . . A troubled and conflicted sign, as the tales of how the Rat came to be first among the twelve made very clear.

But it was evident that Albert Yu, among others, did not need to be told this.

At Colm Lodge, Flying Claw assisted Deborah. Honey Dream sat in Waking Lizard's room for a while and allowed herself to weep.

I'll have to watch out for myself, she thought. *I'm glad Waking Lizard was there to watch out for me when I needed watching.*

After drying her tears, Honey Dream drifted into her father's quarters. She found him sitting in a chair near an open window, wearing a pair of clean cotton trousers and a sleeveless shirt that did nothing to hide his amputated arm.

"The Nine Gates are in place," he said. "As soon as we assemble the Orphans, we will be able to go home. I wonder what your mother will think of this."

He shrugged the shoulder that held no arm.

"She will be glad to see you alive," Honey Dream said.

"I will be glad to see her," Righteous Drum said, "alive."

And Honey Dream, thinking of the defeat and chaos they had left behind them in the Lands, knew his words for a prayer.

☆

Brenda sat in the waiting room at Dr. Andersen's clinic, drowsing as thirty-four hours without sleep started taking their toll.

Or was it just everything that had gone on during those hours? All Brenda knew was that the large coffee she'd picked up from the café downstairs didn't seem to be touching the sudden tiredness that hit her.

But she'd manage. She knew she would.

A woman was sitting next to her. Brenda guessed she must have dozed off, since she hadn't seen the new arrival come in. Then Brenda recognized the red-gold hair, the leaf-green eyes.

"You!"

"Me. I came by to say you've done very well. Thank you. Those of us who dwell in the interstitial places are safer now."

"Safer? Don't you mean safe?"

"You closed a door. A nasty door, true. You destroyed a trap. A singular trap, but the trapper is still free."

"Is this supposed to make me feel good?"

"Since when," the sidhe woman laughed, "did you ever get the impression that making you feel good was anywhere on my agenda? I did come to thank you, though, and my thanks are not without meaning."

"You're welcome," Brenda said, and tried not to sound ungracious.

The sidhe woman leaned forward and pressed her lips to Brenda's forehead. Instantly, all the weariness vanished. Brenda blinked, and straightened in her chair.

The sidhe woman was, of course, nowhere to be seen.

Brenda smiled.

Not too bad. Really not too bad. Nine gates. Four guardians. One mysterious lady with an agenda all her own.

Brenda thought about when they'd all parted back at the warehouse. Flying Claw had turned before helping put Thorn into the van. He'd waved and smiled.

"See you tomorrow." Three words. Not "I love you," but pretty good words.

So Flying Claw is a friend. A scary friend, sometimes, but really a friend. I trust him. I trust Righteous Drum. I even trust Honey Dream—at least where most things are concerned.

I'm going to miss Waking Lizard, and I wish I'd gotten to know Chain, but that's backwards, and right now I'm ready for forwards.

One of the inner doors opened, and Dad came out. The red slashes on his face were faded, and probably would be nearly gone by the time he got back to South Carolina. She wouldn't be surprised if Dad found a bit of business to do to make sure he had time to heal before Mom saw him.

"You look perky, Breni."

"I'm feeling good," she said. "The coffee must have kicked in. How's Pearl?"

"Old bones break," Gaheris said, "but Auntie Pearl's are

going to heal—and without surgery. Healing will take time, and she'll need to rebuild the muscle, but the break should heal cleanly. If she's careful, she'll be swinging a sword with the best of them."

Pearl emerged a few minutes later, her head held as high as if she were walking down the red carpet at the Academy Awards. Her broken hand was neatly wrapped in a bright pink cast, suspended against her chest in a sling printed with tiny multicolored hearts.

Dr. Andersen came out with Pearl, insisted on taking a look at Brenda's formerly wounded stomach, and pronounced himself satisfied.

"No scars, just what I want for a pretty girl."

Brenda wondered. Not all scars showed, but she was willing to bear hers if that was the cost for all she'd learned.

"Are you up to driving us home, Brenda?" Pearl asked.

"I'm ready," Brenda said, jingling the car keys as she pulled them from her pocket, "for anything."

Read on for a preview of

JANE LINDSKOLD'S

FIVE ODD HONORS

Coming from Tor in May 2010

• • •

Brenda Morris was growing accustomed to having really odd dreams, but this one was about to get star billing.

She'd been half reclining on the grassy bank bordering a dancing, laughing stream. A handsome young man was seated next to her.

The young man's eyes were wide, round, and exactly the color of freshly opened spring leaves. His hair, the red-gold of dark honey, was curly, cut just long enough to look untamed without being in the least feminine. He had a wonderful mouth, full-lipped and sensuous. A moment before, he had been singing.

At least Brenda heard music: robust and rhythmic as any rock-and-roll piece, but flavored with harps and flutes rather than electric guitar and drums. She didn't know what you called this type of music, but she knew she liked it. She also couldn't remember the name of the young man who was sitting next to her, but she felt fairly certain he was about to kiss her, and she liked that, too.

Brenda felt a little odd about how much she hoped the young man with the green eyes and the red-gold hair would kiss her.

This was a dream. Certainly it was all right to let a man kiss you in a dream, even if . . . you loved another man? Something like that.

For a moment Brenda had a vision of that other young man, the memory of his face suspended between her and the youth with green eyes. This face had slanting, almond-shaped eyes, dark and serious. It was framed by silky black hair worn as long as her own, caught back with a leather tie.

This second man was as handsome as the green-eyed youth of her dream, but far less real. Brenda couldn't even remember his name.

The young man with the red-gold hair cupped Brenda's cheek in one of his musician's hands. There was an urgency in the brilliant green of his gaze, an urgency Brenda didn't think was entirely related to the kiss his lips still shaped.

Something was buzzing in her ear.

Brenda shook her head, moving out of reach of that cupping hand. She smelled horses. Sweaty horses. Hay and manure.

What had happened to the stream? Where was the grassy bank? Suddenly, Brenda was sitting upright on a straw bale, the freshly cut straw a brighter gold than the hair of the young man who sat next to her, bolt upright and looking distinctly uncomfortable. A moment ago he'd been wearing . . .

A cap-sleeved tunic? Yes! He'd been dressed like a page or young squire from that book of Arthurian tales her grandmother Elaine had loved to read aloud when Brenda had been too small to read for herself.

Now the young man wore denim coveralls and a short-sleeved, red-plaid cotton shirt. The music in the background blended temple bells and brass chimes incongruously with banjo and fiddle. The green-eyed youth no longer looked as if he were about to kiss Brenda. Now his expression was distinctly annoyed.

A chestnut horse had thrust its head in over the half-open door. Then a man stood there instead, a Chinese man with a full mustache and very short beard. He was wearing ornate armor and a helmet upon which a pair of the longest plumes from a pheasant's tail were set. These caught a faint breeze, giving the Chinese man an illusion of motion although he stood perfectly still.

Brenda recognized the new arrival at once.

"Loyal Wind! What are you doing here? For that matter, what am I doing here? I was sitting on a stream bank. There was a . . ."

She looked around. The young man with the green eyes had vanished like the dream he had been.

"Why am I in a barn?" Brenda concluded, not really wanting to explain that she'd been sitting on the riverbank with a young man who was not the dark-eyed, black-haired young man whose name she could now remember perfectly.

Flying Claw. His name was Flying Claw.

Loyal Wind chose to answer her last question. "Perhaps you are in a barn, Brenda Morris, because I am the Horse, and where else would you expect to find a horse?"

"In a parking lot," Brenda muttered.

Loyal Wind looked startled, and Brenda hastened to explain.

"A joke some little kids I knew told over and over. They had just discovered knock-knock jokes, but they didn't understand the logic behind them . . . Oh, never mind. What's going on? What are you doing in my dream?"

The barn was gone now. Brenda and Loyal Wind were standing, facing each other on a dry and barren steppe. Cliffs could be seen in the distance, burnt-orange, barren of all but greyish scrub growth in shadowed crevices.

"I am a bit surprised to find myself in your dream," Loyal Wind admitted. "I sought to bring a message to one of the Thirteen Orphans. I had thought my desire would connect me to Deborah or Riprap since they were among the Orphans who traveled to the Nine Yellow Springs under my guidance. Still, you took part in that journey as well. The Rat is the sign opposed to the Horse on the wheel. There is a strong attraction between opposites."

"But I am not the Rat," Brenda protested. "That's my dad."

She caught herself rationalizing aloud.

"I know, I know. Dad didn't go on that journey, and so maybe that's the reason you reached me and not him. Maybe the others are both awake. Is it easier for you to contact some-one who is asleep?"

"Infinitely," Loyal Wind said, and Brenda could tell that, for him at least, this explained the anomaly. She made a men-tal note to find out how late Deborah and Riprap had slept.

But Loyal Wind was speaking.

"I have come to bring the Orphans and their allies news of ill omen. You recall that when last we met, I agreed to jour-ney through the Hells until I found the ghosts of the Thirteen Orphans—especially of those four of whom we had need—then seek to win them to our cause?"

"Yes." Brenda nodded. "We've been wondering how you were doing. Quite a few days have gone by since we parted. We've all been recovering, but recently Righteous Drum has started hinting that perhaps we should try some more tradi-tional summons."

Quite a few days, Brenda thought. *Well, just five. And I, for one, have been glad for them. What happened at the end of Tiger's Road . . . I've needed time to think, to adjust.*

Loyal Wind, however, took Brenda's comment as a repri-mand. He answered with stiff, military exactitude.

"You do realize that the afterlife is vast, far vaster than the worlds of the living, and to locate five spirits—not all of whom recalled me fondly—"

"Yes. Yes," Brenda cut in. "I'm sorry if I seemed unap-preciative. Please, tell me what you learned."

Loyal Wind seemed appeased, but his words continued to hold the stiff tone of a report from scout to headquarters. "I located Nine Ducks, the Ox, first. I related to her the heroic tales of the dangers undergone in order to link the Nine Gates to the Nine Yellow Springs. This proved sufficient to win her to our cause."

Brenda remembered that Nine Ducks had been halfway won over already, but nodded understanding and approval.

"Next in order on the wheel is the Snake," Loyal Wind went on, "but as the Snake is not as greatly needed as the other two, I decided to leave Gentle Smoke for later. Equally, the Ram, my yin counterpart, was likely to be easy to convince—or so I judged, given that in life Copper Gong was fierce in her desire to return to the Lands. Thus, next I went searching for the Monkey."

"And did he refuse?" Brenda prompted when Loyal Wind fell silent.

"Worse. I could not find Bent Bamboo at all—or rather, when I did, his trail blended with and then ended in that of another of the Exiles, one whom I had not sought."

"You're procrastinating," Brenda said. "Get on with it. I don't want this dream to end like dreams do in those stupid books where the dreamer gets woken up right before she learns something vital."

Loyal Wind's expression became vaguely disapproving, and Brenda remembered that in the strict hierarchy the Horse had been trained in, he would have expected more respect from a junior. Well, if he wanted abject respect, he shouldn't have come breaking up her dream—especially when she was about to get kissed.

"Where the signs showed me that I should find Bent Bamboo, the Monkey," Loyal Wind continued, "instead I found Thundering Heaven, who was once the Tiger. Fierce and defiant, Thundering Heaven awaited me before the dark mouth of a sheltered cave. I knew without asking that the Monkey was within, and that unless I fought Thundering Heaven, I could not pass into that place."

"So you came to report," Brenda said. "Smart."

Loyal Wind looked slightly embarrassed. "Actually, I was considering charging forth and challenging Thundering Heaven when I felt Nine Ducks seeking to contact me. Upon hearing her voice, I realized the wisdom in letting someone else know the situation before I confronted the Tiger, for Thundering Heaven manifested—even as did I—as a man in his prime."

"And Tigers," said Brenda, who had learned a bit in the almost three months since her world had turned so inside out and upside down that she took having conversations in dreams with ghosts of men who had died more than a hundred years before somewhat for granted, "are the best solo fighters of all the twelve signs, although Horses are the finest battle commanders."

"Precisely," Loyal Wind said, obviously mollified regarding her earlier impertinence by this recognition of his prowess. "I discussed what I had learned with Nine Ducks. We resolved that I would come and tell the living of this turn of events, while she would seek out and warn the others among the dead."

"And my job," Brenda said, "will be to pass on your news to the others. I wonder what time it is?"

As if in answer, an explosion of raucous rock-and-roll shattered the dream into fragments. Loyal Wind and the stable didn't so much vanish as never had been. Brenda sat bolt upright in bed.